"YOU'RE NO ONE'S PROPERTY, AMANDA!"

Sandy was angry now, and she wouldn't let Amanda give in. "You're not going anywhere. Not if it means you're running away."

"Didn't I say she had a fighter's heart?" Cass was on his feet and in full elfin battle regalia. "You have nothing to fear now, Amanda! With Sandy by my side, I will defend you to the death!"

"I'll do the defending here," Sandy said. "And not to anyone's death."

"Mrs. Walter, how can you defend the lady?" Davina asked. "It's the Fair Folk, the King of Elfhame you'll be facing! How can you stand against magic?"

Sandy smiled. "You forget," she said. "I'm a lawyer."

COMING IN MARCH

In the vast intergalactic world of the future
the soldiers battle

NOT FOR GLORY

JOEL ROSENBERG

author of the bestselling
Guardian of the Flame series

Only once in the history of the Metzadan merce-
nary corps has a man been branded traitor. That
man is Bar-El, the most cunning military mind in
the universe. Now his nephew, Inspector-General
Hanavi, must turn to him for help. What begins as
one final mission is transformed into a series of
campaigns that takes the Metzadans from world to
world, into intrigues, dangers, and treacherous dip-
lomatic games, where a strategist's highly irregu-
lar maneuvers and a master assassin's swift blade
may prove the salvation of the planet—or its ultimate ruin . . .

ELF DEFENSE

ESTHER M. FRIESNER

A SIGNET BOOK

NEW AMERICAN LIBRARY

To the memory of my dear cousin,
Margaret Raab

NAL BOOKS ARE AVAILABLE AT QUANTITY DISCOUNTS
WHEN USED TO PROMOTE PRODUCTS OR SERVICES.
FOR INFORMATION PLEASE WRITE TO PREMIUM MARKETING DIVISION.
NEW AMERICAN LIBRARY, 1633 BROADWAY, NEW YORK, NEW YORK 10019.

SIGNET TRADEMARK REG. U.S. PAT. OFF. AND FOREIGN COUNTRIES
REGISTERED TRADEMARK—MARCA REGISTRADA
HECHO EN CHICAGO, U.S.A.

Signet, Signet Classic, Mentor, Onyx, Plume, Meridian and NAL
Books are published by NAL PENGUIN INC., 1633 Broadway,
New York, New York 10019

First Printing, March, 1988

1 2 3 4 5 6 7 8 9

PRINTED IN THE UNITED STATES OF AMERICA

ACKNOWLEDGMENTS

Special thanks (always) to W. J., who gave me the title, and to Michael Jacob and Anne Elizabeth, who gave me the time to write the rest.

Prologue

The laboring woman groaned softly, as if fearing to make too much noise. The car sped through back-country fields of scrubgrass and scattered palmetto groves, a blur of headlights in the heart of the storm. Sometimes, when lightning flashed, the towering shape of a lone royal palm came into sharp relief against the hunter's sky, a mile-marker for the middle of nowhere. The rain poured down.

"Can't see a damned thing," Jeff grumbled, hunched over the steering wheel. He pushed a thick brown lock of hair out of his eyes. They had been on the run too long, and he wasn't used to a fugitive's life, not like Amanda and the boy. He couldn't remember the last time he'd had a real, barber-given haircut, though he had to laugh at how often he'd complained about getting regular trims, and how much he missed them now. His old life was a million dreams behind him, haircuts and all.

He tried not to think about it, tried to keep his mind on the road. He was doing his best to make time, drive safely, and reduce the roughness of the secondary road as much as possible, for her sake. He thought he was doing a pretty good job, but the woman moaned again, louder, and he heard his name in her cry. He pulled off onto the shoulder.

"What are we stopping for?" Over the woman's half-stifled gasps, a second voice came from the back: the voice of a very young man. Jeff flipped on the overhead and leaned over the back of the seat. By its light he stared into eyes blue as a razor's edge, huge and somewhat slanted. Matte-black hair looked as phony as it was, the amateur dimestore dye job already showing traces of ashy gold at the roots.

As if he'd trace us by sight! Jeff thought bitterly. *Poor Cass, why did you even bother changing your hair color? You can't hide what you are—not from him. You told me yourself that he hunts by scent! You look about as convincing as a fullback in drag.*

1

Aloud he said, "Come on, Cass, trade places and take a turn at the wheel. You heard Amanda: she wants me."

"She doesn't know what she wants. I have to stay back here with her! You don't know all that must be done if we're going to be safe. You might get careless. . . . "

"I might drive this stinking car into a ditch if the rain gets any worse! I can be just as careful as you, if you tell me what to watch," but I *can't* see to drive as well as you can in this storm." Another bolt of lightning flashed across the sky-bowl, thunder answered, and the rain gusted harder against the windows, as if to back up his words. "Please, Cass. You can get us there faster. And we've got a long way yet to go."

A loud snort of disgust came from the backseat. "All right, all right, I'll take the wheel. You've made your point." Two doors opened almost simultaneously, though only Cass slammed his shut once he was outside. He and Jeff circled the car, exchanging places, while the windshield wipers continued their hopeless task and Amanda pressed her knuckles against her teeth until Jeff was beside her. She welcomed him joyfully. Cass heard, and winced a little, in spite of all his good intentions to learn self-control.

Jeff shifted noisily, sitting down on the thick sheet of clear plastic covering the entire backseat and furled over most of the floor. It was a painter's dropcloth, the biggest and most durable they could find. Amanda grabbed his hand and squeezed it tight. Her grasp stemmed a stream of mild profanity as he struggled to get comfortable on the clinging stuff, made him forget all about his own minor discomfort.

"How are you, babe?" he asked. Nothing mattered but easing her pain.

Amanda smiled a little and bent her head to rest on his shoulder. His arm around her was all the shelter her soul needed. "A little hot—all this plastic—but what can we do? It's necessary. I'll be fine. We'll all be fine." She kissed him, then met Cass's extraordinary blue eyes fixed on her in the rearview mirror. "Please start the car, Cass. I'll tell Jeff what he's got to do."

"He's done enough already," Cass mumbled under his breath. They didn't hear him. He turned off the overhead light. The engine rumbled to life and the car rolled back onto the road. The storm continued unchecked. There was even more force behind the lashing wind now. The raindrops sounded like hail against the windshield, but the car roared on as fast and surely guided as if it had been full daylight and fair driving.

When they reached the small town of Jeff's memories, it

was bedded down and boarded up. It wasn't hurricane season yet, but the Gulf of Mexico was capable of spawning some mighty nasty surprises. Wise Floridians knew it. Here and there, Cass glimpsed slivers of light from the buildings, shining cracks beneath incompletely closed metal shutters. Mostly, though, he saw the street lamps' fuzzy balls of brightness, silly little fire-puffs hanging against the fearsome brilliance of the lightning.

"Now where?" he asked.

"Three more blocks—no, four—and hang a left. The clinic's the pink house at the end of the street."

"All the way at the end?"

"Pass it, and you're in the bay."

"Are you sure it's still there? How long has it been since you were in this town?"

"Five years; maybe six. Listen, I sent them a nice check every Christmas, and none of 'em came back. It'll still be there. The only thing that's changed might be the paint. Just drive, Cass."

"Please, dear," Amanda put in gently.

Cass followed directions. He took the left turn a little harder than necessary, but Amanda was making those strange, terrifying sounds again. This time there was a note of imminent panic in her voice. They were running out of time. The sharpness of the turn made everything in the car shift left. Amanda cried out as Jeff pitched up against her, sliding helplessly on the plastic seatcover. In the front, the small furry shape sharing space with Cass tumbled into his thigh. He felt claws sink in deeply, a reprimand.

"Ouch! Cesare . . ."

"Look!" Jeff thrust his arm over Cass's right shoulder, pointing. "They've got their lights on! Someone's still inside!"

"We won't have to call. Oh, thank God!" Amanda sighed.

They were there. Jeff leaped out onto the swamped gravel drive and ran around to open Amanda's door. He offered her a hand out, an arm to lean on.

"Be careful, you idiot! What do you think you're doing?" Cass was outside too, the rain plastering his long hair to the sides of his face. The cheap dye left black smears on his cheeks, stained the collar of his Hawaiian shirt past hope. He barred Amanda's way, refusing to let her out of the car. "Here, I'll take care of her."

Standing side by side in the storm, the two worked to-

gether. Next to Jeff's robust athlete's body, Cass looked thinner than he was, almost sickly, all bones and promise. His
youthful fragility made Jeff seem much older by comparison,
certainly much stronger. But then he reached into the backseat,
swaddled Amanda tightly in the clear plastic sheeting, and
passed her into Jeff's waiting arms as easily as if she weighed
no more than a kitten. Jeff carried her up the walk, struggling
to keep the plastic in place, while Cass checked out the interior
of the car.

"No blood," said a sleepy voice from the front seat.

Cass looked up sharply. A gray brindled tomcat perched
on the back of the seat and regarded him with a superior smirk,
whiskers quivering.

"Why waste your time looking? Trust me, Cass. Trust
my nose, if you'd prefer. There is no blood, not a whit, not a
sniff. Not yet. You did a perfect job of keeping it under wraps,
but you're not through yet. Hurry up and go inside. You'll
have to be twice as cautious in there."

"I will be," Cass said grimly.

The cat yawned. "Good luck." His mouth did not move
at all when he spoke, yet the sound of his words filled the car.
"Midwives may let husbands in the delivery room, but I'll bet
they draw the line at snotty teens."

"They'll have to let me in!" Cass spoke fiercely as he
yanked a fresh plastic dropcloth from under the front seat, un-
folded it, and spread it to cover every possible inch of space in
the back. "I can help Amanda more than any of them ever—"

"How?" The cat looked amused. "By pulling rank, or
just a rabbit out of a hat? Oh, go ahead and try. You'll see I'm
right."

"Cats," Cass grumbled, backing out of the car. "Think
you know it all."

"That's because we do," Cesare replied smugly, but his
words were lost in the sound of the back door slamming shut.
He spread his six-toed paws and begain to rip hell out of the
unprotected front-seat upholstery.

The clinic door was locked. Cass pounded on it, then
leaned on the bell. A small roof overhanging the doorway af-
forded little shelter from the sideways-driving rain, but he was
already soaked. Impatience and powerlessness made him frantic. He leaned on the bell again and didn't release it until the
lock clicked and the door opened.

"*Now* what is . . . ? Oh. You must be the son. Come
in." A plump young woman in nurse's whites, very harried,

turned her back on Cass as soon as she summed him up and asked him in.

He followed her into a square waiting room, the walls painted pale salmon pink. "Have a seat," she said, waving him to take his choice of two identical sofas, their waterlily print upholstery genteelly faded. She kept going, heading for the frosty glass-paneled door beyond.

"Wait!" He grabbed her arm. She glared, her expression so full of burning outrage that it startled him. He saw the tomcat's mocking face overlay her scowl like a ghostly mask.

Ah! Yes, Cesare, you were right after all, he thought. *A snotty teen, that's how she sees me. How do I dare to detain an adult like this? I forget myself. How do I even dare to touch her?* He dropped his hand, and the cat's face faded. The nurse was just another human being who wondered what was wrong with all these nervy kids.

"I'm sorry." He tried to put a quaver into his voice and bowed his head, doing his best to look awkward. It was easier to be submissive than to feign it. "I—I just want to be with my mother."

"Now?" The woman's look softened from anger to surprise to compassion. Cass had pushed the proper buttons. "Oh, dear, I wish I could let you, but it's out of the question."

"I won't faint, if that's what you're afraid of. I've seen tapes of births before, in—in my mother's La Maze classes. I'm sure she wants me with her. Hasn't she asked for me?"

The woman patted his arm. "Yes, she has honey." For some reason, she didn't imagine that he might resent unasked contact as much as she did. Given his apparent age, what he liked and disliked were trivial as far as she was concerned. "But we told her we don't have that big a space to work with, here. Just me and Dr. Pine can barely move ourselves around that table, and what with your daddy being in there too . . . Well, he's got a right to be there, I suppose, so long as we don't get any complications—"

She caught Cass's look and hastily added, "Not that we're going to have anything but a plain, easy birth here. Don't you fret, child. We're just a little-bitty town clinic, but all the same, we've helped birth more than a couple of infants when they couldn't wait for the county hospital. Your Mama's going to be okay. Now go sit and read a nice magazine. I've got to scrub."

Cass thought better of insisting. He could read people more easily than he could wade through the pile of old *Time* magazines in the waiting room, and he'd seen a stubborn streak running clear to the bone in the little woman. She'd made the decision to keep him out, and she'd defend it till dawn if he talked back. Amanda needed her helping in the delivery room, not arguing out here. He would just have to trust Jeff to oversee matters in there. Reluctantly he settled down.

He heard the rain slacken off, but it didn't stop. Time drifted over his skin like the breath of the sea. Then the woman was back, smiling. A plastic cap hid her short black hair, and a surgical mask dangled from her neck.

"You've got a little brother, honey; a fine, healthy little brother."

They let him see Amanda right away. She was lying in a long room whose three hospital beds were separated from each other by cheery aqua curtains. Jeff stood to one side of her at the head of the bed, a redheaded woman to the other. They were grinning at Cass like a pair of brain-scooped baboons.

"Come in, come in!" Cass wasn't coming as fast as the redhead would have liked. She strode across the room to drag him nearer. "You must be Cass. I'm Dr. Pine. Come on and say hello to your new brother."

Amanda smiled up at him. The baby was in her arms, wrapped in a blue-striped white blanket. She pulled back a corner of it so he could see the tiny face and hands, colored the deepest rose.

The sound of wonder in his own voice surprised him. "I . . . I thought they all looked like little red monkeys."

"Some do," Dr. Pine said. "Maybe you did, with that snow-white skin you've got. What about it, Mrs. Taylor? Did your big fella here look like that when he was born?"

Amanda made a noncommittal sound.

"We're naming him Paul Henry," Jeff said proudly. "After my father." He threw his arm around Cass's thin shoulders and hugged him close, beaming. "Truth be told, we'd name him after this fine young man right here, if we could. If not for him and his driving, little Paul'd be named Subaru."

"Well, you can't very well name one brother after the other," the doctor agreed.

Cass sidled forward unobtrusively and slipped his hand beneath Amanda's blankets. Something crinkled.

"Are you comfortable, Mother?"

Amanda knew what he was really asking. "Yes, love. I don't mind these pads at all. They're specially made water-proof to protect the real bed linens, and they can be thrown away so—"

"Where?"

The question was sharp, urgent. Jeff heard it, and suddenly he too heard more than the simple word.

"Oh my God! The delivery room!"

He ran from Amanda's bedside with Cass after him. Cass's keen ear just caught the doctor's confused questions, Amanda's soothing double-talk: *Well, you know how funny men get at a time like this, doctor. . . .*

The delivery room was clean. No one was there, though the lights still burned. There was no sign of the recent birth. Once more it was just another examination room where little kids came for shots and grown-ups came for bigger, more mysterious reasons.

Jeff jammed his foot down on the wastecan pedal. It was empty, smelling strongly of disinfectant. The plastic dropcloth that had wrapped Amanda was nowhere around.

He looked miserable. "I—got so excited when my son was born . . . Cass, where do you think they put . . . ?"

"How should I know?" Cass snapped. "Find the one who did this while you were supposed to be taking care of Amanda. Fine care!" He laughed, his face frozen.

They found the nurse in the office, toweling her hair with one hand while she typed hunt-and-peck with the other. She smiled when she saw the two of them. "Still putting it down out there, but not so bad as before."

Jeff grabbed her by the shoulders. Cass noted that she didn't glower at him for taking such liberties. All she could do was gape.

"Where is it?" Jeff demanded. He shook her once, just a little, but it was enough to freeze her tongue. *"Where is it?"*

"The plastic tarp," Cass said quietly, laying his hand atop Jeff's, making him let the nurse go.

"Well, I—well, what in . . . ? Well, I—I threw it out with the rest of the things when I tidied up the room. I—look, mister, are you fresh out of your *mind?* What the hell you want to keep that old plastic sheet for? A goddamn *souvenir?"*

"Where is it?" Cass repeated calmly. He wasn't angry anymore. Anger was useless now.

The nurse got some of her backbone back. She shook herself completely free of Jeff, pushed her wheeled desk chair away from them both, and retrieved the towel she'd dropped. "The dumpster." She attacked her damp hair briskly. "What do you think we do with trash? Can't leave a mess like that hanging 'round a clinic room. We've got patients coming in the morning, you know. Damn thing belled out like a sail, too, in that wind. Have to get Lonnie to police the back parking lot tomorrow, get all the bits and pieces blew free. Ugh.'' She tossed the towel onto her desk. ''Is that enough information for you? Or do you want to call in the police, have me arrested for stealing a mucked-up plastic sheet?''

Cass drew Jeff away. The burlier man looked stunned. He could only shake his head while Cass led him out of the clinic by the back way. The intermittent flashes of lightning from the departing storm showed the dumpster's massive outline against the rippling waters of the bay. White flutters of loose paper whirled in the wind, pitched up against the roots of azaleas.

''The sea,'' Jeff said. His voice was flat.

''Yes. Some may have blown into the sea. Some touch the earth, and earth and sea both house his messengers. He knows. He'll come.'' Cass sounded resigned. He tugged at Jeff's elbow. ''Come on. We have to get Amanda and the baby into the car and get out of here. He'll lose the trail if we're quick.''

Jeff's eyes remained fixed on the wavelets, the slowly growing motion of the sea. He would not budge.

''And what will he do if we're gone when he gets here? Go home?''

''You know better than that.''

Jeff nodded. ''He doesn't take defeat kindly.'' He jerked his arm out of Cass's grip. His voice lost all fear, became pure business. ''Go get Amanda. The doctor'll try to stop you, but do it anyway. Use anything you've got to do it.''

''Amanda said I wasn't to—''

''Forget your vow. This is one time you can be a prince again. No orders but your own.''

''What are you going to do?'' Jeff's abrupt transformation was disconcerting. Fear of the unknown enfolded Cass's heart in the petals of an icy rose. *I will never understand your kind, never!*

''What do you care what I do?'' Suddenly, Jeff was grinning. ''You'll have her all to yourself again; her and the boy.''

Cass tried not to looked too shocked. *Can they read minds as well as we?* He tried to sound cool as he replied, ''If you stay here, he'll kill you.''

''He'll try. He's tried before. I have a few tricks left— nothing like yours, of course, but maybe they'll do. And if we all leave, he'll kill whatever scapegoat's handiest—the nurse,

Dr. Pine . . . I call that a might poor way to weasel out of my medical bills.'' He chuckled. ''The Simpson house is down a couple from here, and they always keep a little motorboat tied to the dock. They won't mind if I . . . borrow it for a spin. Think he'll come from the sea?''

Cass shrugged. This little mayfly man spoke so easily, so casually about playing decoy in a hunt that would kill him, barring a miracle. And for what? To save the lives of those two women who'd just helped his son come into the world. Servants; he would save the lives of servants. Who ever heard of such a thing where Cass came from? By rights, he should laugh at the futility of Jeff's ploy—fools were made for laughter—but he had never felt less like laughing.

It was hard to know that you had come to love the one you once called enemy.

Jeff was speaking again. ''You take care of my son.'' He turned into the night.

Cass let him go ten paces before running after him and hugging him so tightly that it nearly drove all breath from the man's body. Jeff stiff-armed himself loose and stared at the silver tears streaking Cass's face.

''Don't go, Jeff! She needs you more than she needs me. You get her out of here. I'll''—his voice failed him for an instant—''I'll be the one to face my father.''

Jeff laughed in his face. ''Man, sometimes I think your whole race is nothing but the craziest sumbitches that ever were spawned. You know you wouldn't last a minute if you had to face off that old—ahhhhh, forget it. He's still your daddy.'' He gave Cass a friendly cuff. ''Go on, move it. Maybe if you snatch Amanda and Paul, you'll get the doctor and nurse to chase you. That way, when he comes, there won't be anyone in the building.'' Cass stayed where he was. ''I said *move!*''

Cass moved. Jeff's barked command snapped him into action. He raced into the clinic, back to Amanda's bedside. Dr. Pine tried to question him, but he shoved her aside. In one scoop of his arms he snatched up mother, baby, blankets, sheets and all, then turned to run again. Amanda screamed, more from reflex than fear. The baby burst into a fresh-waked wail.

Dr. Pine said a lot of medically inaccurate words. She tried to block the doorway and found herself flipping through the air, slicker than a hotcake, to bounce down on the nearest bed.

Arms full, Cass hadn't touched her. ''How the hell . . . ?'' Dr. Pine asked the ceiling. She hollered for the nurse.

Cass had to set Amanda down while he opened the car doors. Her sheets and blankets fell into a puddle. She stood shivering in the wind that gusted ever stronger and stronger from the west, from the sea. Holding the baby to her breast, she slipped into the seat, trying to control her trembling. She was barefoot and wore nothing but the yellow cotton hospital gown they'd given her at the clinic.

"Wrap yourself in the seatcover if you're cold," Cass directed, gunning the motor. He took off so fast that Cesare, still balanced on the top of the front seat, plopped over into the back.

"Cass, wait! Where's Jeff?" Amanda's hand was on his shoulder, a burning touch through his sodden shirt. "We can't leave without—"

"He *made* me leave without him!" The tears burst from Cass's eyes again, shaming him. "He said we had to get away."

"But what about *him*, Cass? What about *him?*"

"I'm telling you, he's the one who insisted. He's the one who told me to take you and go!"

"Oh God, oh my God, turn back, go get him, don't listen to him! For pity's sake, Cass, you can't let him stay behind! You can't have hated him that much!"

He ignored her words and drove. In the rearview mirror he saw the dwindling figures of Dr. Pine and the nurse. They were getting into another car. Jeff had called that one well. Would they give chase themselves, or realize how foolish it was after a block or two and drive on to notify the sheriff? He lost sight of them when he took the first turn.

Then he saw Amanda's face in the mirror: anguished, accusing. He could tell her the bare truth of it from now until the Unbraiding of Worlds, and she might never believe him. There was no hate in her eyes; only pity, and the eternal *Why? Why have you done this soulless thing?*

He drove on. They left the town, got back onto the superhighway not too far north. He pulled over once, before dawn, so that she might change her hospital gown for something more suitable. Cesare helped him dispose of it, and the few pads Amanda had accumulated. The firespell clamped over the plastic-swadled pile and devoured all, even its own smoke.

He was drained after that. The firespell's destructive power always took so much out of him that he wasn't able to use it frequently. He needed a rest, and a respite.

They stopped at a motel in Bushnell. Amanda went right

to sleep on one of the room's double beds, only waiting for him to cover it properly. The baby too seemed exhausted. He propped it on its side in the crib with a rolled-up blanket. He ached to stretch out too, but it was getting late, near closing time for most stores. They needed things, and if he wanted an early start next day, he had to do some shopping now. He went out, leaving Cesare on guard.

He bought more dropcloths at a local hardware shop, and some oilcloth table covers. In a big chainstore pharmacy, while getting things for the baby, he found packs of the same plastic-bottomed paper mattress pads the clinic used; he stocked up ten boxes' worth, and an equal number of trashbags.

Some game covers its trail. His mouth curved in self-mockery. *We seal ours in plastic. It won't be so easy to catch us again, my lord.*

He was on his way back to the room with the supplies when a quirky inner demon made him stop to buy a newspaper. While Amanda slept on one bed, he propped himself up against the headboard of the other, Cesare snoring at his feet. He opened the paper and scanned it until he found the story he dreaded finding, just a few column inches of filler: the puzzling tale from farther south of the freak wave that had reared itself out of the Gulf to crush a smalltown free clinic to fragments of stucco and tile. No one was hurt—not in the wreckage of the building—but the body of an unidentified man was found floating in the bay.

That part of the hunt was done.

Cass closed his eyes. The paper in his hands began to glow. The inky letters ran into a black whirlpool that spread itself into a vision of the night.

Jeff, alone in the little motorboat, cutting across the bay. He was smiling, so sure of his eventual escape, so proud of the wits he'd used to guarantee it. What was all the magic in the world against man's ingenuity. Pride . . . pride . . .

The wave came up beneath the boat's keel, the silvery curve of a horse's neck. It came out of nowhere, without warning, and pitched the craft over. Jeff tumbled into the water, his smile gone.

But the water turned to glass under him. He crouched on the surface and watched the wave ride on, ride in, mount to a hammer of foaming green to destroy one house alone out of all of those that lined the waterfront. Foam turned to dripping fingers, water formed a blue-green hand, tightened to a fist, sprouted into a fire-spiked mace that smashed the clinic to its foundations.

The vision trembled with the impact. Cass's fingers clenched, tautening the paper, willing back a clear seeing.

In helmless armor, with the gem of sea and star on his breast, a man-shaped figure grew out of the frozen sea, looming above the kneeling mortal. Sorcery robed his limbs in icy golden fire. Jeff lifted his head and looked into a blazing face that Cass remembered much too well. He had cringed before its scorn, shuddered away from its anger, but this powerless creature of flesh and blood met its gaze . . . and laughed.

A hand fell to grasp the hilt of a sword.

The seeing tore apart in a jagged chasm. Cass stared stupidly at Cesare over the two halves of the ripped paper. Shreds of newsprint still clung to the tomcat's paw. "No more, Cass," he said.

No more. That was true. There would be no further summons of that seeing. There could be none, for each portion of the past came only once to each summoner. Even a cat knew that basic law of conjury. Unless some other seer made Cass a gift of that segment of lost time, he would never know exactly how Jeff had died.

"You don't want to see it," Cesare said. His smoky yellow eyes held certainty. "You hate him enough as it is."

"Don't I have reason to hate him?"

The cat could not shrug, but he could give a good impression of it. "My kind don't bother with such things. We tolerate, or we kill, or we run away. I counsel the latter."

Cass crumpled the tattered halves of the newspaper together and rested his head on his updrawn knees. "We always run away."

"You could try killing him, for a change." The cat sounded hopeful.

"I can't."

"You can't, or you'd rather not?"

"Both."

Cesare's chuckle was disconcerting. Only the tips of his whiskers quivered while the human sounds issued from his tightly closed mouth. "Parricide *can* be hard to explain to the neighbors. You wouldn't have these inconvenient nips of conscience if you'd go back home. Contact with mortals has contaminated you atrociously, my Lord. Your people are so much more civilized when it comes to assassination."

Cass didn't answer, but his eyes strayed to the sleeping woman and child.

"Ah," the cat said, nodding. *"Capisco.* Well, if that's still your choice, shall we blow this pop stand?"

"Now who's been contaminated?" Cass skritched the tomcat's ears. "I wanted to spend the night, but maybe we need distance more than rest. I'll wake Amanda soon and we'll go."

"Where?"

"North, I suppose. Amanda told me she was from the north, originally; Connecticut. Some little town no one ever heard of called Godwin's Corners, all old Yankee farmers, horse country. . . ."

Cesare glanced at the baby. "Horse country. Good. Children like horses. Better the brat should yank their tails than mine. Shall we leave?"

"There's something I must do first."

Cass rose from his chair and went to the crib. He reached into his jeans pocket and pulled out a tatty chain of dimestore silverplate. A twisted strand of metal hung from it, the tangled design the twin of the silver symbol Cass wore around his neck, the iron one Amanda wore around hers. Carefully, lovingly he slipped the chain over the infant's head.

"His name is Jeffrey," he said. White fire seeped from his body, formed a halo of tender light that trickled down over his hands to lave the sleeping baby. The black dye in Cass's hair melted to ash, and the small vestiges of other disguise-spells changing ears and hands and mouth and more fell away from him. His borrowed mortal clothes also vanished in that burning. Tall and supple, white and blue and golden, sharp-featured and beautiful to the point of pain, he wore the mantle of his power and needed no other garment as he called his birthright magic home to bear witness at the naming of the child.

"I name you Jeffrey Paul Henry Taylor. I call you brother, friend, heir, knight-inheritor of your father's valiant heart, and captain in the ranks of my most trusted servitors. No harm in all the realms of air, fire, or water will touch you while you wear this sign of favor, no spell of harm or evil haunt you. To this I pledge my spirit and my name: Cassiodoron, prince and lord of Elfhame Ultramar."

The brightness died away. The baby still slept. Cass stepped away from the crib staring at his hands, the fingers too long to be human. "It has been so long. . . ." He shook his head, as if to clear away a lingering dream.

Cesare's nose twitched. "Very pretty." Only a corpse could have sounded more bored. "Nice gesture. Now if you're *quite* finished, I suggest you change the captain's diapers and we get out of here. And get some clothes on. Bushnell has a city ordinance against naked elves."

He had just managed to wriggle into a new shirt and pants from his suitcase when Amanda stirred and woke. "Cass?" she called, still drowsy. "Cass, what is it? Where are you going?"

He was beside her in an instant, holding her hand. "Connecticut, Amanda; we're going to find your old hometown. I remembered the name from all the stories you used to tell me: Godwin's Corners," he said.

"Godwin's—oh, Cass! How clever of you! He'd never know to look for me in Connecticut more than any other place. And Jeff—Jeff can find us there. I told him about it so many times, said I wanted to go home one day . . . He'll find us, won't he?"

Cass evaded the question. "What's more important is who *won't* find us; not ever. We'll be free."

"Free . . ." She spoke the word like a prayer and embraced him. Only Cesare saw the longing in Cass's eyes as his fingers stroked the dark blond richness of her hair.

"We must leave quickly, I'm afraid. My father's too close for comfort." His voice was husky. "Can you be ready to travel soon?"

Cesare curled himself into a ball of disdain as Amanda swore that she would be ready right away.

"Ready for Godwin's Corners?" the cat grumbled, nose under paw. *"Mavron'!* The question is whether Godwin's Corners will ever be ready for us."

Chapter One:

Nothing Ever Happens in Connecticut

"You were moaning in your sleep again," Lionel said. Sandy rolled over to stare at the alarm clock. The scarlet numbers said 5:36, which meant that homicide would be completely exonerated. She rolled back to glower at her husband.

"Times like this, Lionel," she said slowly, "I am very glad I kept my maiden name. It will make the divorce that much easier, and I won't have to spend a fortune getting all the monograms on my sweaters changed."

Lionel looked put out. "I thought you were having a nightmare. I only wanted to help."

Sandy ran a hand through her sleep-tangled red curls. "Did I *sound* as if I were scared of something?"

"Well . . . you were moaning." Lionel was a firm believer in self-justification by reiteration.

"People moan for a number of reasons. I have heard you moan when you ate one slice of anchovy pizza over the line, when they passed you over for tenure at Columbia, when I told you I was going into labor a month early, and when I put on that little number with the black lace, red feathers, and the panties without any—"

"All right! All right!" Lionel added a new moan to the catalog then and there. "I give up. Never start an argument with a lawyer."

"Some lawyer." Sandy dug both arms under her pillow and buried her face in it.

Lionel frowned. He'd screwed up, and he knew it. All he'd wanted to do was back out of a no-win situation with as much grace as possible, and he'd hit a sore spot.

Lately, though, it seemed as if Sandy was nothing but sore spots.

Lionel began to massage her neck. He leaned closer, his breath tickling her ear, his voice crooning consolation. "You finished law school, didn't you? Without any background in

15

prelaw worth mentioning. *And* you passed the bar exam the first time through.''

"Big deal," Sandy grumped. At least Lionel *thought* she'd said "Big deal." It was hard to tell with her talking into the pillow. He put more feeling into the neck massage. He felt her shoulders relax a little, then go totally limp. She turned her face out of the pillow, eyes shut.

She moaned.

"Aha!" Lionel bounced to his knees, finger pointing accusingly in Sandy's face. "Now *that's* just how you were moaning when I woke you up! In fact, you've been doing it off and on almost every night since you passed the bar. Sometimes you do it so loudly, you wake *me* out of a sound sleep. When you snore—well, hey, I'm used to that—but before I lose one more wink, I want to know what the hell you're dreaming about!''

Sandy propped her chin up on her hands. "Why? Afraid I'm having more fun without you than with you?'' She got out of bed and began to get dressed, paying no further attention to Lionel's complaints.

He was not to be ignored. As a teacher, he was used to lecturing to indifferent audiences. Lack of attention never deterred him, in or out of the classroom. "Recurrent dreams mean something, Sandy. *Loud* ones especially. I think you've got some unresolved frustrations that are coming out in your sleep. If you don't deal with them now, you might have problems digging them out of your subconscious later on.''

"I've yet to hear of anyone dying from ingrown dreams.''

Lionel persisted. "Maybe you'd like to talk to Dr. Kipling about it.''

"Dr. Kipling? Anything weirder than tennis elbow and he freaks. He's no psychiatrist.'' Sandy yanked open a bureau drawer and pondered her options. "More damn alligators than the whole blamed Okeefenokee,'' she muttered at her shirts.

"He could refer you to one.'' Lionel made the bed while continuing to fight the good fight. "Or a therapist, if you don't want a shrink.''

"I don't want *any* of this.'' Sandy slithered into one of a dozen skirt-and-shirt sets, identical in every detail save color, and slipped unstockinged feet into tasseled loafers. "You're the one who thinks there's something wrong with me just because I make a little bit of noise at night.''

"Look, what could it hurt to see a therapist? Maybe one who uses hypnosis? Then you could get to the bottom of what these dreams have been—''

"Yeeaaagh!" Sandy screamed at the ceiling, then bolted from the bedroom, leaving Lionel to babble on about the wonderful things hypnotherapy could do these days. In the kitchen, pearly gray light cast the slim shadows of maple saplings through the bow window and over the butcherblock table. Already the leaves were tinged with autumn colors, though September had barely begun.

Sandy started the coffee and sat down to wait out the longest minutes of the day, the time between hitting the BREW switch and the moment when the first caffeine fix hit the bloodstream running. She could still hear Lionel walking back and forth upstairs. If she got her first cup of coffee into her system before he came down, she might consider letting him live.

"Dreams . . ." She leaned an elbow on the kitchen table and stared out the window, chin in hand, "Can't he even leave me my dreams?"

"Mommy?" Her voice still muzzy with sleep, a little girl padded into the kitchen, rubbing her eyes. Sandy took her onto her lap and stroked her dark brown hair. The child's thumb popped into her mouth with an audible slurp.

"How's my baby?"

"I'm not a baby!" The angry assertion came around the thumb, still firmly anchored. Smiling, Sandy coaxed it out of her daughter's mouth.

"I'll make you a deal, Ellie. When you stop sucking your thumb, I'll stop calling you a baby."

Ellie's brows went up in a way that always reminded Sandy of her mother. Five years old was too young to be such a practiced skeptic. "I'll stop sucking my thumb if you stop making all that noise," Ellie said.

"What noise?"

"You know. At night. You sound like you've got a bellyache. Poor Mommy." Ellie shoved her thumb back in again and nuzzled deeper into Sandy's arms, content.

Sandy was considering asking the child whether she and her father were in cahoots when the guilty party himself bounded in. His gray Harris tweed jacket was slung over one arm as he made last-minute adjustments on his tie.

"No time for breakfast, we've got a faculty meeting this morning," he announced.

"No time? But it's barely after six!"

"It's a big meeting, not just departmental; all-school." He planted a kiss atop Sandy's curls, another on Ellie's head. "That means we have to use the refectory, and *that* means we

have to clear out of there before they start serving the boys'
breakfast. My own I gladly sacrifice for God, for country, and
for the Godwin Academy, long may she wave. Bye.'' He was
off and running for the door. Sandy heard it swing open, slam,
then swing open a second time. He was back.

"Oh yes, I nearly forgot. I'm bringing my advanced me-
dieval and Renaissance studies class home for tea today at four.
Don't worry, you won't have to do a thing. We'll pick up some
cake and stuff on our way over here. Bye again.'' This time
the door slam was final.

"Why is Daddy always in such a hurry?" Ellie asked.

"He was born in a hurry."

The morning trickled away in a stream of lists. There
were people to call, meals to plan, laundry to do, errands to
run. Ellie watched "Sesame Street" and "Mister Rogers,"
then went upstairs and staged a battle for the conquest of the
universe. Barbie beat He-Man two falls out of three.

"She's bigger," Ellie explained when her mother came
up to ask what the devil all that racket was about. "And she
ran Battle Cat over with her convertible, so she wins."

Sandy contemplated the wisp-waisted doll's indelibly
charming smile. "Hooray for our side. Come on, Ellie, time
to get ready for school."

The place where Ellie attended afternoon session kindergarten was close enough for them to walk, but Sandy felt too
wrung out to suggest it. Only Ellie's loud, strategic whine when
Mommy said they'd be taking the car forced Sandy into surrender.

"I don't *wanna* drive! Do we hafta? All we hafta do
is cross the street, go up the hill, go through the church parking lot, go down the hill, go through the green, cross the
street . . ."

Sandy knelt to straighten Ellie's hair ribbon. "But baby,
it'll only take us a minute if we drive."

"I DON'T *WANNA!*"

They walked. As they were cutting through the parking
lot of the Congregational church, Ellie asked, "Do you think
Jeffy will be going to school right now?"

Jeffy . . .?" Sandy squeezed her daughter's hand. "Oh,
so *that's* why you wanted to walk. Hoping to catch up with
your little friend?" Ellie allowed that this was so. "Is Jeffy
Taylor your best pal at school, then?"

"No. But he's real neat. He talks back to Miss Foster,
and he won't play in the playground at recess no matter what
she says, and he runs away and hides in his cubby every time

she reads us a book, unless it's Dr. Seuss, and when the other boys call him wimp he says that he's gonna get his big brother to burn them all up with a magic spell or else he's gonna get his cat to kill them, so they're scared and they leave him alone. When I grow up," she concluded triumphantly, "I'm gonna marry him."

"That's my girl," Sandy said quietly. "Always go for the heroes." Ellie didn't hear her. She was still chattering about all the neat things little Jeffy Taylor did to stir up Miss Foster's kindergarten.

They did not meet up with the notorious Jeffy enroute to class, but found him already there when they got to the kindergarten building, a yellow clapboard house of eighteenth-century vintage a stone's throw from the town green.

"I just *love* this old house, don't you?"

The question was squealed right in Sandy's ear a second after she released Ellie to join her classmates at free play time. She jumped, and came down facing one of Godwin's Corners' only moving landmarks, Cecilia Godwin Haines. Sandy was eternally amazed that this slim, bespectacled woman, mother of three, five years older than Sandy herself, had first introduced herself as "Yes, one of *those* Godwins, isn't it too delightful? Call me Cee-Cee."

Delightful wasn't the word Sandy would have used.

It did not matter that Cee-Cee clung to a name more apt for a Yorkshire terrier than a grown woman, Sandy thought. She was a force with which to reckon if your universe ended at the sign saying GODWIN'S CORNERS, EST. 1715. Veteran of a hundred PTA fairs and bake sales, chief instigator of the annual fall antiques show on the green, when Cee-Cee Haines talked, people who were too slow to pull an unobtrusive getaway listened.

"Sandra, dear, I've just been speaking to Miss Foster and she practically begged me to be room mother again this year after all I did when Bitsy was in her class—how could I say no?—and the first thing I think we should do is set up a bake sale for the same weekend as the antique show. We can sell just about anything halfway fit to eat to that crowd, so can I count on you for a plate of cookies or—"

A loud shriek, part indignation but mostly pain, cut Cee-Cee off the air. Every mother still in the vicinity of the classroom came to immediate attention, and three more who had been in the front yard came charging back inside.

"*Duncan!*" Cee-Cee forgot all about Sandy's halfway-edible cookies. The victim was her son. He was sitting on the

floor with a large lump of blue Play-Doh smooshed firmly onto
his head. Cee-Cee threw herself to her knees beside him, simultaneously trying to quiet the screaming child and work the
gunk out of his hair without snatching him bald-headed. Miss
Foster hurried over to lend assistance and serve justice.

"*Who* is not being a good neighbor?" she demanded,
wagging a finger at the assembled tots.

So this is the KGB, Sandy thought, trying not to snicker.
*Ve haff vays uf makink you talk, pipsqueaks. Confess, or ze
teddybear gets it!*

At the table nearest the victim, humming happily, Jeffy
Taylor was molding a winged horse out of what remained of
the blue Play-Doh.

Sandy saw him at his occupation and wondered how long
it would take Miss Foster to catch wise. *Circumstantial evidence, Your Honor, is inadmissible. Witnesses have already
testified that Mr. Taylor's usual MO when dealing with his
peers is to threaten death by cat or immolation by elder brother's sorcery. I move that the charges be dropped. Also the blue
Play-Doh. Preferably on Cee-Cee Godwin Haines's head.* A
titter escaped her lips, but she tamed it to an imitation sneeze.
She sidled out the door just as Miss Foster noticed what Jeffy
had in his hands.

The afternoon had grown cooler. As she strolled down
Main Street heading for the coffee shop, Sandy kicked aside
the first stray fallen leaves. The elms lining the road all seemed
to turn color and shed their leaves in perfectly orchestrated
unison, as if they were under contract to maintain Godwin's
Corners' reputation for being tastefully picturesque.

"This whole town looks like one big college campus,"
Sandy told the leaves. "God, I miss New York!"

*What do you miss? The crowds? The dirt? The crazies?
Why don't you get honest with yourself for once, Sandra Horowitz. It'd make a nice change. You're not homesick. You're
scared.*

"I am not scared," Sandy said aloud. It was an old habit,
arguing with herself, and one that passed unnoticed in New
York. In Godwin's Corners, however, she always checked the
environs for any potential witnesses. The gravest aberrant behavior the little town tolerated was voting Democratic.

Fortunately, she was still a couple of blocks from the
commercial center of town. She had the street to herself. The
only buildings here were architectural sisters of the kindergarten, and like it, they had almost all been converted from private

residences to more profitable properties. There was a dentist and opthalmologist sharing space in one, a real estate agent and interior decorator bunking down in another, Dr. Kipling's practice doing a three-way split with a hot new dermatologist and Cee-Cee's husband Dwight, allergist to all the right people. Gwendolyn Dixwell, the town's family therapist ("specializing in divorce counseling and parent-child communication, inquire about rolfing for juniors"), combined home and office in her Federalist nest.

Then there were the lawyers.

Their shingles swung in the cool September breeze, caught the dappled sunlight on their discreet gold lettering. Once, when Sandy's law school diploma was still hot off the sheep, she had tried to count the lawyers practicing in town. She did it twice, to be sure. The tally came out higher the second time, so she tried it a third. It was higher still. Every time she counted them, they multiplied worse than dust bunnies. New shingles appeared with the spring peepers, or new names added themselves to old signs.

Aha! Not afraid, are you? Bullshit, my sweet. Sandy's inner voice could be an obnoxious know-it-all with impunity. Lionel would never dare serve her the truth on a cold plate, but there was no way she could throttle herself for doing the same. *All these lawyers in town already, and where's poor Sandy going to fit in? You're afraid, all right. You're scared witless of the competition.*

"I am not." Head down, Sandy gave a small pile of elm leaves a particularly vicious punt. "There's always room for one more."

Is that what those replies to your job-hunt letters told you? Is that why all the local legals are at your door, begging you to get into their briefs? Face it, woman. If you want to practice law at all, you'll have to find a city job. Try New Haven.

"I don't want to commute that far. I'd have to put Ellie in daycare."

It's that or set yourself up in practice on your own. If you want to use your degree, that is. It's been a year since you got it, almost that long since you passed the bar. Don't you think three years' law school tuition is a bit much to pay for a wall hanging?

Sandy walked faster. She'd only escape herself if she got among other people. Already she was at the corner, and across the street she saw Peggy Seymour waving at her. "I'll use it, I'll use it," she muttered, hoping to get in the last word.

That's what you said about the twenty-dollar purple mascara from Bendel's, the voice concluded, and sank into smug silence.

"I'm *so* glad I caught you, Sandra!" Peggy grabbed Sandy by the elbow as soon as her feet met the curb. A clipboard clung to Peggy's concave bosom like a lamprey. Unkind friends claimed that she had been born with a petition in one hand and a Bic pen in the other, to make up for the absence of a silver spoon in the usual orifice. She shoved the clipboard at Sandy.

"What is it this time, Peg?" Sandy sighed. She scanned the top sheet, noting that it was already covered with signatures. There were three more pages beneath it. She assumed it was something to do with animal rights. No other topic could generate so much interest here.

"Come join me for a nice cup of coffee and I'll tell you." Peggy linked her arm through Sandy's and dragged her off. This too was part and parcel of Miss Seymour's mode of operation, the old latch-on-and-tow. It served her well, for there was something distinctly tanklike about the woman. She was seldom seen on the streets of Godwin's Corners without a victim being trawled after her. Privately Sandy thought of her as the Vampire Tugboat.

"Well, that's very nice, Peg, but I only have a—"

"Oh, this won't take but a minute, dear. And it's *terribly* urgent. Enormously vital." Peggy plowed into the coffee shop, nudged Sandy into a booth, leaned across the table, and whispered, "It's satanic."

"What is?"

"Two cups of coffee." This was directed to the waitress, and left Sandy nicely bewildered—was Juan Valdez in the pay of the Prince of Darkness?—until Peggy explained: "It's those boys at the academy. They're playing *that* game."

"Doctor?"

Peggy rolled her eyes. They were wintry blue and bulged slightly, so the spectacle was quite amazing. "*Don't* joke about a thing like this, Sandra. You know what game I mean. With those dice—"

"Oh, craps."

"—and those books, and pretending to be someone you're not—"

"Charades"

"—or even some*thing,* some *creature* that doesn't even exist in a sane mind. And the worst of it is, they're doing it with the help and consent of their teachers!"

"Oh," Sandy said. Her stomach wriggled into a granny knot, then plunged into her shoes. Now she knew exactly what had Peggy's ample bowels in an uproar, and her coffee took on an acidic tang in her mouth.

"I'm getting oodles of signatures from longtime residents, people who count for something," Peggy said, self-satisfied to the bursting point. "But I do think this petition will have added clout if there's lots of names from the academy staff too, to show the administration that the gown is right behind the town."

"True, very true," Sandy replied cautiously. *Especially since what goes on at the academy is none of this pissant quaint burg's business,* her inner voice added. *Of course a witchhunt would be too preciously colonial for words. We could combine the antiques show, the bake sale, and a public burning at the stake. That'll get us a spread in* Connecticut *magazine if anything will!*

Peg pushed the clipboard at Sandy. "Then you'll sign?" It was barely a question.

Sandy took a deep breath and let it out slowly. "No." She pushed the clipboard back.

"What?" the Vampire Tugboat blew her stack. "You won't? Why not? Don't tell me you *approve* of this—this—so-called game?"

"I don't approve or disapprove. I don't care either way. I'm not into role-playing myself, but if the boys at the academy find it fun—"

"I suppose if they started a drug ring up there and found it 'fun,' you wouldn't care either?" The words were excessively sweet, the tone reserved for dealing with village idiots. "Really, Sandra, do you even know what they *do* during these games?"

"Well, they don't do drugs. Not if they want to read those teensy little pips on the dice, anyhow."

"They pretend they're not themselves! They abandon reality! They behave as if they're in another world!"

Sandy had to laugh. "Peg, you've just described every teenager ever born."

"So you refuse to sign?"

"Since my husband happens to be one of the faculty

friends overseeing these imagination orgies, I think it'd be disloyal of me, don't you?''

Peggy rose from the table, huffing audibly. "*Well!* This puts quite another color on things, I see. You might have told me. We're just trying to do the right thing in Godwin's Corners, especially for the sake of the children. Lord knows we get no support from the people who should appreciate our efforts most. Just don't come running to me when your own child goes leaping off a cliff because she thinks she's a—a—an elf or something.''

Sandy's face froze. Slowly she stood up. "Elves don't fly, Peg,'' she said. "They walk, the same as you or I, only a damned sight more gracefully. Good-bye.'' She left Peg gawping after her.

Outside the coffee shop, Sandy leaned against the fake half-timbered facade while her inner voice did a wild war dance of victory. *Oh, you've done it now, lady! Miss New York, do you? You'll be back. What'll you bet Peg's next petition is to get you named visiting scholar at Bellevue? You almost made it there once, you know, and it's never too late. . . .*

"Oh, damn.'' Sandy's fists clenched, her teeth gritted. "Damn it all. Damn New York. Damn Godwin's Corners. Damn *him!*''

Damn him? The words were gentler now. *That's one curse you don't mean. I know your secret, Sandra Horowitz. Damn him, when your dreams are full of him? When you'd sell your soul to return to him? When you'd pay the passage between worlds with your heart's blood if only you could be with him again? Damn him?*

The lowering sun struck a spear of reflected light from the window of the dress shop across the street. It pierced the leafy branches of the elms and dazzled Sandy's eyes. She saw his face in the light, and the light melted time. She was young again, caught up in a span of magic when one day she had been an ordinary person—an art history major at Columbia University—and the next she had walked with legends. A dragon stalked a city, a knight followed, and she and Lionel and a boy playing squire all followed the knight into a world of wonders. Her fists uncurled slightly, holding a remembered sword.

But that was long ago, wasn't it? That was far away, and even the city has forgotten what happened there. And what would it matter if New York remembered? New York's the other end of the universe for the kind of people who live here. They see it as a clutch of fine stores, extortionate restaurants, thea-

ters, weirdos, celebrities, monuments. There's the stock exchange, of course, and some nasty sections that no one really nice even thinks about if they can help it. But what comes between all those markers . . . Ah! That's about as real as dragons to them. Dragons . . . and other things.

The voice within her was a fading echo. Memory claimed her. She stared into the glassy brilliance of the light, seeing the face that haunted her dreams: sharp as a silver arrow, wine-sweet, dawn-fair, beautiful as no mortal man could ever be. He walked through a vanished forest, his quiver and bow on his back, and not the slightest sound or movement of the woodland escaped the elfin archer Rimmon.

Elves? Peggy Seymour's high, nasal squeal burst into Sandy's thoughts. *Creatures that never existed in any sane mind! And certainly not in Connecticut! Don't think you can drag your schoolgirl daydreams into the flesh, Sandra. A woman wailing for her demon lover is all very well in New York—they're used to worse down there—but we have zoning laws in Godwin's Corners.*

Sandy's heart protested: But it *did* happen! He was no dream. He was real, my Rimmon, as real as—

Her fingers clutched the pendant of white rock whose chain she still wore around her neck. Its intricately incised pattern of alien flowers was never carved by clumsy human fingers, and its milky heart cradled a bloodstone.

And who remembers, except you . . . and your husband? Would he like to learn the real reason you wake him up nights? I do believe he'd rather have you be insane. Rimmon is dead, as dead as magic in this world. You're a woman now, with a husband, a child, a mortgage, a profession to follow, responsibilities. . . .Why, you're even supposed to be taking on an au pair girl this week, aren't you? Do you want her to think all Americans are crazy? Grow up. Let no one ever guess you had such silly dreams. Let your dreams go.

The coffee-shop door opened just then, and Peggy emerged, blinking in the sunlight. Dreams could wait. Escape was vital. Sandy made a break for the hills. Looking where she was going was secondary to speed, and so . . .

"Oh!"

"Ouch!"

"Excuse me, please, I was just—"

"My fault; I'm sorry."

The two women stopped and looked hard at each other.

"Aren't you Jeffy's mother?"

"Yes. And you're . . . Eleanora's?" Ellie's given name sounded strangely musical on Mrs. Taylor's tongue. Sandy noticed how strong the woman's accent was, the sort of old Yankee pronunciation more proper to dwindling backwoods towns than to suburban Connecticut.

"I plead guilty," Sandy said with a smile. "I'm glad we met, even if the introduction was a little rough." She indicated the battered paper bag Mrs. Taylor clutched so tightly. It had taken the brunt of the collision. "You know, our kids are thick as thieves. You're looking at your future in-laws here, if Ellie goes through with what she told me this morning. Said she's going to marry your Jeffy."

"I see." Mrs. Taylor gave Sandy a dubious look. She changed her grip on the little bag so that Sandy could see the logo of a local jeweler. "I'm—I'm sure that's nice. I'm happy Jeffy's made a friend. He hasn't much chance to play with other children, except at school."

"Well, he could come to my house mornings if he wants to play with Ellie. Or she could go to yours."

Mrs. Taylor's eyes went wide with alarm. "Oh no! That's impossible, I'm sorry, I—I have to be going." She fled like a frightened sparrow and ducked around the first corner to hide from Sandy's sight.

"It's been great running into you!" Sandy hollered.

"Hmph!" The steamy snort down Sandy's neck announced that the Vampire Tugboat had recaptured her incautious prey. "That Amanda Taylor; *there's* a queer bird. Keeps to herself in that big old house, her and those two sons of hers. Three years it's been since they came here, and no one sees the boys except when they're in school. Nobody even knew she had a second son until she showed up to register him for kindergarten!"

"Jeffy's her second child?" Sandy hated to play up to Peggy's gossipy nature, but Amanda Taylor intrigued her. "Who's her first?"

"Oh, *I* wouldn't know his name. Ask your husband, if he ever stops playing wizard. She put him into the academy the week they moved here—don't ask me from where. They have more money than God, and close with it? Not one soul in this town has ever been asked inside her house! Afraid we'll steal something, maybe." With a short, sarcastic laugh, clipboard to the wind, the *S.S. Seymour* sailed on.

Loitering in front of the coffee shop was not the done thing in Godwin's Corners. Sandy was on the point of wandering away herself when something sparkled at her feet. She knelt to pick up a slink of fine silver chain with a charm the size of a thumbnail hanging from it.

Hooves poised in midflight, wings drinking the wind, the silver double of Jeffy's blue Play-Doh horse spun lazily back and forth at the end of its tether.

The winged horse had to be a custom-made order, of the if-you-ask-you-can't-afford-it price range. Remembering the much-mauled condition of Amanda's death-gripped bag, Sandy guessed this treasure must have fallen when the two women had their unscheduled meeting. It wouldn't take a very noticeable tear to let something so delicate slip out. Fascinated by so much beauty in such small size, Sandy lowered the charm into the palm of her hand.

"Oh!"

The hooves moved. She felt them prick out a path across her skin. The wings flapped up, then back, as the tiny head lifted with rightful arrogance to meet her astonished eyes. Miniscule nostrils dilated and closed. The impossible creature shook himself briskly, so that the chain holding him slipped forward. The horse bit it once, and it snapped. Silver wings flashed, and in a starry blur it was gone.

All Sandy held in her palm was a severed chain.

Chapter Two:

Tea For Three

"**D**addy! Daddy! Daddy!"

At his desk in the small study just off the entry foyer, Lionel looked up from a sheaf of test papers. Ellie dropped her mother's hand at the front door and ran into her father's arms. He picked her up, grunting like a bear, and threatened to eat her belly, after a thick spreading of belly-jelly, of course. Ellie shrieked happily, pounded on the bear's head, and recounted the deliciously awful thing Jeffy Taylor had done to Duncan Haines that day.

"And even when Miss Foster made him sit in the think-

ing corner, the first thing he did when he came out was call
Duncan all kinds of names, like Duncan Donut, and Duncan
Haines Cake-Mix Face, and Infidel Dog, and—''

''You mean Devil Dog, don't you?'' Lionel asked,
smoothing back his daughter's wayward curls. ''Your friend
seems to like high-calorie name calling.''

''I dunno. But he ran away and hid in his cubby today
again too. Miss Foster read us 'Sleeping Beauty.' ''

''That bad fairy can be pretty scary.'' Lionel set the child
down.

Ellie shrugged. ''I'm gonna play with my Barbie some
more.'' She started upstairs, then paused midway. ''What's a
heretic geek, Daddy?''

Lionel blinked. ''A what?''

''Oh, never mind.'' Ellie took the rest of the steps by
two and was gone.

''Did she just say 'heretic'?'' Lionel asked Sandy.

Sandy didn't answer. She stood in the entryway, shoulders slack, and stared into the eagle-topped mirror opposite the
front door. She saw no difference—a pale, pointed face with a
sprinkling of freckles, the tormenting hint of incipient crows'
feet at the eyes, a thread or two of gray weaving through her
tightly curling red hair—but did your face have to change just
because your mind had kicked itself free of reality? She could
still feel the prick of tiny hooves pawing her palm.

''I've got to stop talking to myself so much,'' she told
the glass.

Lionel came up behind her and clasped her shoulders.
''Are you okay?''

It was a question Sandy didn't want to get into at the
moment. Instead she said, ''It's past four. I thought you were
having a class over for tea.''

''Something came up at school, so I asked them to come
by tonight after supper. You don't mind, do you, babe? We
can have the mad tea party for dessert. Will you join us?''

Sandy wished Lionel had chosen some other way to describe the planned get-together.

''Oh, have it without me. The boys won't want a woman
around, cramping their style.''

Lionel raised one eyebrow. ''Just how much do you know
about the style of seventeen-year-old boys?''

''You know what I mean. You told me yourself that you
like them to relax, to see that they can discuss academic stuff
outside the classroom too. How can they do that with me hang-

ing around? I'll just sit there, not knowing what's going on, and remind all of them of their mothers.''

"They should be so lucky.'' Lionel's hands glided down her arms, slipped around her waist, and pressed her close. His lips touched her neck, tingling.

"Besides''—she lodged her conclusive bit of evidence—"I'll be busy putting Ellie to bed.''

"No you won't.'' Lionel took her hand and led her toward the stairs. "That's the something that came up this afternoon.''

"Davina . . . what?''

"Goronwy,'' the raven-haired girl supplied. She had a charming smile and extremely fine features. The pity of it was, her dainty face looked as if it should be on another body. When Sandy was growing up, she'd had a girl cousin with Davina's build. The charitable way to describe it was "healthy,'' but charity always took a backseat to accuracy when Sandy's mother got her mouth on a topic.

"Low metabolism my eye. Your cousin Pamela eats like a horse, which is why she looks like one,'' Mrs. Horowitz remarked on more than one occasion. "The kind that pulls beer wagons,'' she specified.

Davina Goronwy didn't remind Sandy of a Percheron, but her short, sturdy body brought to mind Welsh ponies, Welsh corgies, and overindulgence in Welsh rarebit.

"So—ah—where are you from in Wales, Davina?''

"My folk are from Caer Mab, to begin,'' the girl said brightly, blue eyes dancing. Thick-set as she was, and seated on the edge of a prim ladderback chair, she still gave the impression of constant animation. "That's so small a town by the sea near Harlech that you won't have heard of it. Smaller and smaller it grew, and I doubt maps can find it these days. We moved to Bangor not three years ago, and then of course I went to London to study.''

"Davina was accepted at the Royal Academy of Dramatic Art. She was one of the youngest students they ever admitted.'' Lionel spoke of Davina's accomplishment as proudly as if he had some personal stake in the matter.

"The RADA? That's something. But . . . you can't have graduated already?''

"Oh, no, Mrs. Walters.'' The girl blushed true crimson, and the blood lingered in her cheeks. Sandy had never seen the like. Davina looked down at her hands, folded in her lap. "I left."

Lionel came in quickly. "Well, Davina, we hope you'll be just as happy in Godwin's Corners as you were in Lon—I mean, in Bangor. You go on with your unpacking, and call us if you need anything. See you at supper." He took Sandy's arm and steered her out before she could say another word to the girl.

Sandy didn't care for steerage. In the hall outside the small spare bedroom she dug her feet into the carpet and refused to take another step. "What do you think you're doing?" She twitched her arm away.

"Come in our room. I've got to talk to you."

"What about?" she brushed off her arm in the traditional New York manner that indicated she was ridding herself of his "cooties."

"About Davina."

Sandy cast an appealing glance to heaven and followed her husband into the bedroom. Once inside, Lionel shut and locked the door.

"That's a surefire way to bring Ellie running," Sandy said. "I swear, the sound of that latch clicking works on her like a bell on Pavlov's dogs."

"Maybe she's determined to stay an only child." Lionel grinned, but it shattered against Sandy's well-I'm-waiting stare. "So . . . Some surprise, huh? She came a week early and phoned me at the Academy from JFK this morning. I had to drive into New Haven to get her. How does it feel to have an *au pair* girl at last?"

"Delightful." Sandy crossed her arms. "What's wrong with her?"

"Wrong?"

"You hustled me out of her room and nearly dragged me in here by the hair because you've got to tell me some deep dark secret about Davina, so what is it? Is she into drugs? Is she pregnant? Does she belong to a cult?"

"Come on, Sandy, a Welsh Moonie?"

"Maybe she's a Druid. We'll have to lock ourselves in our rooms during the equinox, or whenever they sacrifice humans. *What* is wrong with Davina?"

"She's a dropout." Sandy's short burst of laughter made Lionel shake his head angrily. "I'm serious. She left the RADA. Quit. Dropped out. That's why she applied for an *au pair* job in the States. She wants to leave Britain far enough away so she can think about what to do with her life next.''

Don't I know the feeling! "Poor kid. Couldn't do the work?''

"Are you joking? We got to talking in the car on the way from New Haven. She told me all about it. She was doing as well as some and better than most, but she kept getting typed in . . . well . . . matronly parts: Juliet's nurse, Gertrude, Octavia—''

"Who?''

"Mark Anthony's wife; the one he leaves for Cleopatra. It wasn't the sort of career she had in mind. She wants to play Cleopatra and Juliet and Ophelia, not the also-rans.''

Sandy struck a pose reeking of righteous indignation. "I think it's terrible that some people are too prejudiced not to see past a person's appearance. If Davina can act the part, she shouldn't be denied it just because she's—athletic-looking.''

"When was the last time you saw a jowly Juliet?''

"Davina does *not* have—''

Lionel held up one hand. "Just a for-instance. I think we both know what appearances count for in some fields; especially weight. We might not like it, but that won't make it go away.'' He sighed. "Davina loved acting, and she was good.''

"It's not fair.''

"It isn't. But what can we do about it besides keep off the topic of theater, and London, and whether she's got any plans for the future?''

Plans for the future. Sandy's dormant law degree flickered across her mind's eye. She was fast becoming an expert on avoiding the topic of future plans.

"—and above all,'' Lionel was saying, "we won't make any comments about her weight.''

Jason Penfield nudged Cass Taylor in the ribs, jerked his head at Davina's retreating form, and snorted like a pig.

"What was that, Penfield?'' Lionel cut short his exoneration of Lucrezia Borgia and pounced.

"I—uh—I must've swallowed some tea the wrong way, Mr. Walters.''

"Through the nose is hardly the best way to savor a good Earl Grey. You are fortunate, gentlemen. You are the first of my students to taste tea brewed as it should be, by the hand of a young lady from Great Britain.''

"Young truck," Jason whispered to Cass.

Cass leaned forward to pour himself a fresh cup. As he settled back on the couch, he tipped the saucer. Hot brew streamed down Jason's leg.

Jason leaped up, yelling. The other four boys wearing the cadet-blue Godwin Academy blazer all jumped from their places, too, as if in sympathy. While Jason's classmates offered him their handkerchiefs and condolences, Lionel gave Cass a thoughtful look.

"I'm sorry, Mr. Walters." Cass was on his feet, the picture of flustered youth, eager to right what his clumsiness had upset. "I'll get some paper towels to blot the rug."

"Fine, Taylor, fine. The kitchen's through the dining room, back that way. If the towels aren't on the counter, look under the sink. Watch yourself. The light's off in the dining room and the switch is all the way across, next to the kitchen door."

"I'll be careful, Mr. Walters." Cass went where he was directed, doing his best to look more gangly than ever. He had a number of nicknames at the academy, most referring to his height, his thinness, and his way of never knowing where his feet were from one minute to the next. No one would ever imagine that what he'd just done with his tea had been on purpose. Scarecrow Taylor was disaster on wheels.

No one except Mr. Walters. Cass's classmates often said that there was something odd about that history teacher, and they didn't mean just his New York accent.

These were the same classmates who saw nothing at all bizarre in Twisted Sister, Ozzie Osborne, Weird Al, and Max Headroom.

What would his classmates think if they could see Scarecrow Taylor now, moving through the pitch-black dining room with the deft grace of a hunting cat? In front of the tightly drawn curtains, Cass danced with shadows. He danced with a freedom he didn't dare use at home. It brought Amanda too many painful memories. If anyone in the living room looked his way, their human eyes would see nothing. He shared blood with the night.

The shadow dance had to end at last. The class was waiting. He walked the thread of glow seeping from beneath the swinging kitchen door and balanced on the borderline between bright and darkness.

He heard voices beyond.

"—lovely gown."

"It's pretty, isn't it? Kind of silly to wear something so nice looking when no one's going to see it." Silky cloth swished.

"Someone will." Soft laughter, two pitches blending one high and tittering, one deep and comforting as the sea.

That voice took Cass by surprise. It had the sweet lilt of the lost lands, the dear heartspring countries that had borne his race. It was a sound he thought never to hear any more in this strange land, so rich with its ancient music. He could have listened to it for hours, remembering, and the Hounds take him if he cared what words it spoke. The other voice was more monotonous, a little nasal, commonplace. He imagined it must belong to the girl who had brought in the tea and cake. It would suit her. She hadn't said a word when Mr. Walters introduced her, only nodded and smiled. It would suit her. He tried to remember whether her dress had been as attractive as all that.

He called back clumsy Cass and pushed the door open.

" 'Scuse me, but could we have some, uh . . .' "

Both of the women at the wooden kitchen table turned from their teacups, but one of them melted into air. The other filled his eyes. He could not speak. He felt as maladroit as he had pretended to be.

Oh, she was lovely! She was taller than Amanda, and not so small-made. Under the shimmering royal blue of her gown he saw how her body curved, promising more than any of the willowy women of his own people could offer. Hate his father as he did, Cass still understood a part of the passion that drove him. Elfin women were air and darkness, the whisper of a shadow, the sisters of dreams. This mortal was deep-dreaming earth and silent flowing water and a fire in the soul that was time.

Cass saw how time had already changed her, read what she had been, knew how each second left its passing print on her. It didn't matter. Where he longed to take her, with all his heart, she would be shielded from the seasons and hidden from the gray hunter of all mortals. For that gift alone, she would love him. She would be a fool not to love him for that.

As Amanda loved your father? He pushed the question from his mind. He wanted her, not questions.

Then he saw what she wore around her neck.

"Yes? Can I help you, dear?"

The voice was wrong, but that was a detail now. Cass thought it a mighty poor way to run a world when this lovely woman had a voice unworthy of her, while the sweeter song

came from a girl who was . . . well . . . healthy-looking
enough for a whole lacrosse team. He had upended his teacup
into Jason's lap for the form of gallantry, to avenge an insult
against a lady, but in his heart he was just as guilty of the same
affront.

"I'm—looking for the paper towels."

Sandy glanced at the sink where a whole roll stood in
plain sight on the counter. She fetched it for him, yet still he
lingered, holding the towels and gazing at her. Then, waking,
he mumbled some thanks and excuse and left.

He heard them plainly, even through the closed door.

"—the nerve! It's not as if I'm Dolly Parton or anything,
but still . . ."

"You know how these young boys can be, Mrs. Walters.
It's the first he's seen a grown woman in her nightgown,
likely." The big girl had a merry laugh. Its sound had no further power to enchant him.

He mopped up the spill on the living room rug automatically. A bloodstone cupped in carved white stone twirled as a
trim star across his sight.

*She has known us! She has known one of our kind! The
carving on that white stone—I can't place its tribe, but still
. . . Oh my lady! Then when I tell you what I am, you will
believe. There'll be no need to convince you, to be afraid of
scaring you away, to go too slowly. You will know all I can
offer you, and you will welcome it quickly. That will be good.
Your breed don't have time enough for me to waste too much
in courtship.*

"Uh, Taylor, I think you've got it all." Lionel motioned
for Cass to resume his seat. "We were discussing some pretty
juicy gossip about the papal family. Cesare did most of the
killings, or commissioned them, but Lucrezia got most of the
blame. Why do you think that was?"

"It's always more convenient to blame the woman. She
couldn't defend herself. . . ."

Cass talked of Renaissance society and politics, but his
thoughts were elsewhere. It had just registered that the black-
haired girl had called the woman Mrs. Walters. Whoever had
been the giver of the lady's elfin token, he was gone. Why else
would she settle for a life shared with an ordinary man like
Lionel Walters?

Cass studied Lionel. As far as appearances went, he was
an acceptable comedown for a woman who had known an elfin
lover. The history teacher was one of those mortal men who

aged well. Years made his face look rugged, not saggy, and
the few shots of silver in his dark hair only added interest. He
was almost worthy of such a wife.

Almost.

Cass smiled. This would be easy. Lionel caught his eye
and innocently smiled back.

Sandy found a rose on her pillow the next morning. It
glowed silver, flower and stem, but when she picked it up she
knew that it wasn't made of any metal. It nodded between her
fingers, thrilling with its own life, each thorn a caress.

This was no time to fool with contact lenses. She groped
for her glasses on the bedside table and read the note tied to
the flower's stem. A flush of gold drenched the blossom of the
rose the moment she touched the silk-strung tag. Her face was
reflected in every petal.

You are of us, my lady, and my heart is yours.

"Lionel . . .?" Sandy's voice was a squeak. The place
beside her in bed was empty. She looked at the clock. It was
past nine. Ellie should have been on top of her hours ago,
demanding breakfast. "Ellie?" she called a litle louder. She
wanted witnesses to see the incredible flower. Without them,
she had no way to prove she hadn't gone insane in the night.

Her bedroom door opened. Davina sailed in carrying a
footed tray arrayed with coffee, hot muffins, strawberry jam,
butter, and orange juice. "I've given the little one her breakfast and dressed her for the day. So good and quiet she is,
letting you sleep late as I asked. Here's breakfast for you, now,
and I hope you like—"

"Davina, what do I have in my hand?" Sandy held out
the gold and silver rose. Her hand shook, but the flower swayed
back and forth to its own inner music.

"Holy angels above!" Davina set the tray rapidly down
on the bed, almost spilling the whole thing. Her blue eyes
showed white all around the iris. She reached for the rose.

When it passed from Sandy's hand to hers, the note vanished. Silver and gold turned to green and pink. It was a flower
like any other, and it stayed so even when Sandy took it back
from Davina.

The women looked at each other. *Did you see? I saw.
Did you? Yes.* The words didn't need to be spoken.

Sandy took a deep breath and let it out in a rush. "Either
we're both crazy or we're both sane," she said lightly, shifting
the breakfast tray onto her lap and helping herself to a cup of

coffee. She felt wonderfully relieved, knowing that the none-such flower really had existed. She would worry later about where if had sprung from. For now, she just wanted her morning fix.

"I'd not speak too carelessly of sane or mad." Davina suddenly took on the grave demeanor of a banker explaining poor credit risk. "Madness is spun from the moon, and they rule her with their dancings. They can play with a mortal's mind the way a tyke toys with an India rubber ball."

Sandy stirred in a spoonful of sugar. " 'They,' Davina?"

"The Fair Folk, Mrs. Walters. I've a touch of the 'sight' for knowing them, and this flower bears their mark as sure as I'm living. The Good People have a special way with the magic that governs flowers."

"*What* good people?" Sandy raised her cup to her lips.

"Elves."

Coffee stains being what they are, the blanket went to the dry cleaner's that morning.

Chapter Three:

A Green Thumb

"**N**o, honestly, I really couldn't. . . . "

Sandy's protests fell upon willfully deaf ears, or else were plowed under by the iron blade of Cee-Cee's hell-bent enthusiasm.

"Oh, now be truthful, Sandy dear. It's only a question of willingness to help with a worthy cause. If *I* can find time for this project, *anyone* can. And it's for our children's sake. I know that I simply couldn't live with myself if I let little Duncan down. I just could not look in the mirror."

"I have mornings like that," Sandy murmured, but she knew when she was beaten. She stretched out her hand limply to receive the list Cee-Cee had been trying to push on her for the better part of an hour, along with "just another sliver" of apricot torte. "I'll call them."

Cee-Cee was gracious in triumph. "You won't be sorry," she said, with absolutely nothing but pure faith to back up the statement. "It's for the children, after all. Only don't call them; go visit. It's much harder to turn someone down when she's looking you in the eye."

Sandy could testify to the truth of that. She said she had to be going. Mission accomplished, Cee-Cee made no move to detain her further.

"*Ciao-ciao,* Sandy dear. See you tonight at Peggy's?"

"I wouldn't miss it for the world." Somehow Sandy's tone of voice failed to lend credence to her words, but Cee-Cee didn't notice. Observing nuances wasn't her specialty, and in any case, the bubbly Mrs. Haines assumed that everyone shared her passion for spending a crisp fall evening in the inspection and purchase of self-seal plastic storage ware.

As Sandy left Cee-Cee's home—one of the authentic Federalist structures in Godwin's Corners and not a subcontractor's idea of generic Colonial—she gave herself a series of savage mental kicks. *Never* volunteer for anything. *Never* surrender. *Never* let the dog-faced bastards see you crumble, retreat, or even waver.

She asked herself how General George Patton would have fared in escaping a Parent Teachers' Association assignment.

"I guess I'm just not army enough to live," she said to the interior of her car. Before turning the ignition key, she gave the list a once-over. Cee-Cee's project was Alexandrian in its scope of new worlds to conquer. Not only was the little woman spearheading the usual PTA bake sale, to take place at the upcoming antiques show on the green, she sought to combine one fund-raiser with another by running a tag sale the week before.

"Not everyone can bake, or likes to bake, or can bake anything worth eating," she'd said, looking meaningly at Sandy. "But there's no one in this town without some junk they'd like to get rid of. That's why a tag sale is so perfect. We get the money from it for the PTA, yet we make it look as if *we're* doing the donors the favor of taking away their trash. God knows, some of it isn't fit for pigs to own, but there's no telling about taste."

Sandy wondered whether Cee-Cee's family castoffs did qualify as suitable for porkers to possess. She hoped so.

Her portion was not to waste time in speculating on the nature of the Haines's gar*bhage.* Hers was but to contact the ten women on the list and strong-arm them into promising to

bake a goody for the bake sale, no excuses accepted, as well
as pledging a mound of ancestral relics for the tag sale. They
were all mothers of children in Ellie's class, which association
made Cee-Cee assume that they'd either say yes to Sandy's
request or move out of Godwin's Corners by sundown.

You simply did not let the children down. It went against
the Code of the Suburbs.

"Farnsworth, McCall, Bascombe . . . Oh shit. Taylor."
Sandy smacked the steering wheel. "Christmas on crackers."

An Irish lace curtain in the Haines's front parlor window
twitched. Sandy caught a glimpse of reflected sunlight on Cee-
Cee's glasses. She felt like resting her head on her arms and
waiting for the falling leaves to cover her up, Toyota and all,
but she had the suspicion that Cee-Cee would call the constab-
ulary and have her towed a tasteful distance off the property to
have her angst attack.

She did not want to call on Mrs. Taylor. Not at all.

Sandy started up the car and backed down the driveway.
The Haineses owned a substantial lot at the back of the local
riding school. They did not own the school itself, *mirabile
dictu,* but their offspring boarded a pair of Morgans there. Or-
dinarily it was restful to watch the old stone fences slip past
and check the several paddocks for horses, but not this time.
Sandy didn't want to think about horses and Amanda Taylor
together. It made her palm tingle.

And then there were those sons of hers. . . . She no
longer found Ellie's tales of Jeffy's antics amusing. The child
gave her the creeps. Last week, when she'd come to pick up
Ellie at school he'd marched up to her, clasped his hands behind his back, and announced, "I lost my first baby tooth today."

Sandy had laughed and ruffled his hair in just the way
she'd found unbearable when she was small. "You take it home
and put it under your pillow and the tooth fairy will leave you
a quarter for it."

Jeffy made the face of one who did not bear fools gladly.
"My *mommy* would leave a quarter. The tooth fairy still does
dimes. Mommy *told* him and *told* him about how stuff costs
more now, but he's too old to change. Or too cheap, Cass says.
Anyhow, he already paid up for my whole mouth, in advance,
soon as I got my first tooth *in.* But that was just to keep the
trackers off us. If he came every time I lost a tooth, we'd be
in big trouble, Cass says. My brother sure knows a lot."

"Aha. I see your mother by the door. Run along, dear,"

Sandy said nervously. She no longer had the slightest wish to rumple Jeffy's hair.

She had about as much desire to seek out Amanda Taylor. She turned onto the main road, heading south for the center of town, firmly determined to tell Cee-Cee she had asked Amanda to help and had been politely refused. It would be only a small lie.

There is no such thing as a small lie. The Vassar-educated tones of Mrs. Horowitz sounded their stern admonition in her daughter's head. *Sandra Horowitz, you gave your word—foolishly, but we shall let that pass—and you can either keep it or live with the shame of a weak character.* Sandy's mother was never too far away whenever she found herself on the brink of an unpleasant situation. Her spirit was usually foursquare behind her daughter, ready and eager to shove her in up to the collarbone in the name of character-building experience.

You should not have promised to help out if you feel incapable, though why a healthy woman of your age should be incapable is beyond me. Of course I'm just your mother. You might have had the courtesy to tell me you've decided to go against all the values your poor father and I have sweated blood to instill in you. But that's all right. Don't call on Amanda Taylor. Tell lies. Let people down. Nice people who belong to the right portion of society. People who mean something. If it were some of those bummy New York types you used to hang out with, you'd be falling all over yourself to bend backward and jump the minute they said—

Sandy covered the distance between *chez* Haines and Amanda Taylor's house in record time. She didn't know why or how the still, small voice of her conscience had been ousted by the loud, implacable nattering of her mother—the phenomenon had happened shortly after the birth of her own daughter—but she wanted a word with the powers involved.

It was a beautiful day, September fading fast into the more glorious foliage weeks of October. In town the green was occasionally the site of a quick pumpkin sale. Most other flowers were gone, but asters and autumn crocus lingered, and pots of chrysanthemums—bronze and white, purple and yellow—flanked nearly every doorway. Indian corn was nailed up on the doors themselves in richly colored bunches.

Amanda's yard held June roses.

Sandy smelled them before she saw them, caught their unmistakable scent from the curbside where she parked her car.

The Taylor house had no garage, no driveway, and was strangely oriented in its lot, the front door not visible from the street. You could only see small sections of thickly curtained windows over the high hedges backing the white picket fence. Other houses on the same street were content with a similar wooden fence or a low privet, not both. When Sandy let herself in through the little wicket gate, she stepped on a cluster of violets, releasing their unique fragrance of April rain. The tulip beds were what she saw first, multicolored waves of them, backed by the tall spears of Dutch iris.

The fragrance of the roses still beckoned. The meandering flagstone path Sandy followed to the Taylor front door took her past plantings of hyacinths and daffodils and under a long archway of lilacs. Once through, she saw the front steps framed by a living wall of roses in bud and bloom.

In bud . . . in September. Sandy shook her head. She reached for the doorbell and pricked her finger on a thorny stem that had not been there before. "Ouch!" The finger went straight into her mouth, which was not a bad thing considering that it stopped her from screaming her head off as she watched the climbing flowers twine themselves into a protective knot that hid the doorbell from sight entirely.

"My mother's not home right now, Mrs. Walters."

Sandy turned sharply. Standing in the shade of the impossible lilac arbor, Cass Taylor smiled at her. He was out of his academy uniform, looking more substantial in a heavy Irish sweater and dark gray corduroy slacks.

Sandy could hear Lionel remarking. "That Taylor kid—Cass—he's one of my finest students, a day boy. A little clumsy, but that's to be expected at his age. They call him Scarecrow at school. He's all legs, like a new colt. A thoroughbred. Even if he does have a crush on Brooke Shields that the whole school knows about. Poor kid."

The lovely Miss Shields would be a fine match for this boy, Sandy thought. She'd be one of the few girls vaguely near his age who wouldn't need a step ladder to have an eye-to-eye chat with him. As he stepped out of the fragrant shadows, his hair blazed silver gold.

"Maybe I can help you?" He stood at the foot of the porch steps, offering her a hand down. The gesture was courtly, not what Sandy would expect from a boy whose nickname evoked Ichabod Crane more than Prince Charming.

"Oh! You've scratched yourself!" A white handkerchief

flicked out of Cass's pocket and was around Sandy's injured finger in a trice.

"It's nothing." When she tried to pull away, she found his grip too strong. Her hand came free when he allowed it.

He held her with more than his hand. Sandy's stomach contracted as if she'd walked into a table. His eyes were on hers, and a presence hovered at the edges of her mind. She could sense it even as she denied it entry.

She jerked her head aside, breaking eye contact. "Oh, what a pretty cat!" She knelt gratefully and reached out to pat the large, indifferent animal that had followed Cass out from under the lilacs. It wound its body around Cass's legs and regarded Sandy's kneeling adoration with disdain.

Cass knelt too, but he had lost the advantage. When Sandy looked into his eyes next, she saw only a noncommittal expression, the stonewall mask of a young man guarding his own thoughts.

You keep out of mine and I'll keep out of yours, Sandy thought, her mouth curving into a wry smile. She had to laugh at herself then. *Listen to me! I get the willies for no damned reason and right away I'm blaming it on this kid. I remember him. He was the one who came into the kitchen a couple of nights ago and gave me the glad-eye. And I'm wearing a knit dress today that's a recruitment poster for the Le Leche League. Serves me right if they haul me in for flashing my headlights at infants. Brooke Shields, huh? The Playmate of the Year's his speed, more likely. He wishes.*

The cat nudged her hand, demanding more attentive petting. "Cesare seems to like you," Cass said. His voice gave away no more than his eyes.

"Well, I like cats, but Lionel's allergic. Professor Walters, I mean." To Cesare she said, joking, "You come by our house anytime you want to be spoiled rotten, Kitty. There'll always be a slice of lox put by for you."

"Lox?"

"For Cesare?"

Sandy assumed Cass had asked both questions as one, though his voice . . . Well, even though he was near college age, a boy's recalcitrant hormones could still pull a nasty in matters of pitch and timbre.

"Sorry." She stood up, feeling more in control again. "I keep forgetting that not everyone speaks fluent New York. Lox is smoked salmon, and it's very good."

Cass rose, too, looked away from her. "You must think I'm pretty ignorant."

"Because you didn't know what lox is?" She patted his arm with all the condescension her advanced age allowed her to exercise over a mere teen. "Don't worry about it."

"Mrs. Walters, I—"

"Cass!" Amanda Taylor's shout was magnified by the tunnel of lilacs. Curling petals clung to her hair as she burst through, Jeffy trawled long in her wake. Her entrance spooked the cat, who bounded into the tulips. She didn't check her pace until she stood right between Cass and Sandy, forcing them both to make room.

"Why, hello, Mrs. Walters," she said brightly. "I didn't expect to see you. Can I help you?"

Cass had used almost the same words. They sounded as if they should be coming from a salesclerk eager to close a transaction and see the customer on his way. The lady leaned forward, making Sandy take another step back, away from Cass. Though Amanda smiled and smiled, Sandy had a hunch that there was more to her aggressive friendliness.

Don't worry, dear. I'm no Mrs. Robinson. Though you might dump a pail of cold water over your infant Romeo.

Briefly, Sandy explained her mission. Amanda's smile took on a frozen cast. She readily promised to bake three cakes, but as for the tag sale . . .

"We really don't have anything anyone else would want to buy. I'll bring the cakes to your house and save you the trouble of coming here."

"That would be very nice." *(Lock up your sons, ladies, Sandra Horowitz is back in town! Of all the—)* Two could play the game of synthetic smiles. "And why don't you have Jeffy come over to play with Ellie some time? They get along so well at school."

"That's a wonderful idea, Mother," Cass put in a little too quickly. "You're always saying how you'd like him to have more friends. He could play with Ellie in the afternoons and I could pick him up on my way home."

Amanda's smiling mask shattered. "No, Cass. I won't impose on Mrs. Walters. It's out of the question."

"It wouldn't be any imposition."

"No. Thank you."

Jeffy squirmed and began to whine. "But I *wanna* go to Ellie's house! I wanna play with her stuff. She's got some real neat toys. Mommy, I *wanna!*"

Without another word of discussion, Amanda hauled her younger son up the front steps and inside. She didn't even pause to fumble with a key. The door was unlocked, but the click of tumblers and the slide of a deadbolt from within told Sandy that it was more than securely fastened now.

"Well . . . I guess I'll be going." She was on her way even as she said it, and happy to be gone.

"Mrs. Walters, please wait." Cass caught up with her under the lilacs. He snapped off a branch of bloom and urged it into her hands. "For you."

Sandy could not resist taking the offering and pressing the nodding flowers to her nose. For her there was no greater temptation, no smell in all the world to match the lilac's springtime sweetness.

"How does she do it?" Sandy marveled.

"She?"

"Your mother. Does she use collapsible greenhouses or cold frames or what?" She made a sweeping gesture, necessarily confined by the in-crowding arbor flowers. "How does she manage to force so many out-of-season plants?"

She heard Cass's chuckle, very deep for one so young. "My mother acquired her talent over the years. It's a kind of . . . understanding she has."

Sandy shifted, ill at ease. She thought the perfumed bower was wider and higher than this when she'd first passed through it, but it seemed to have grown in on itself. Petals tickled her cheeks. She could hardly move without rustling the branches.

It would not do for one of Lionel's students to see his teacher's wife with the terminal heebie-jeebies. She pulled herself together and tried to keep up her end of the conversation. "With a garden like this, your mother must be the envy of the neighborhood. It's all I can do to grow marigolds in the summer."

"Do you like growing things?"

A warm breeze laced with a headier fragrance than lilac stirred her hair.

"Uh . . . yes."

"I could give you that. I could, as easily as I give you this." She heard another snap. More lilacs were in her hands, slender, strong fingers still around the stems.

It was dark in the flowering arbor. Sandy saw Cass's face backlit by the sun outside, the features indiscernible. Was it her imagination, or did two blue lights kindle there when she took the new lilacs from him? She didn't linger to make sure. She shot from the other end of the tunnel like an arrow.

"Mrs. Walters! Mrs. Walters!"

They both hit her car at the same time. "I have to go. It's later than I thought," Sandy babbled, rummaging for the key. "I've left Lionel home with Ellie all this time—Oh, and Davina's there, of course, but she said she'd be cooking dinner tonight, so if Lionel has some work he has to do, and Ellie wants to play—"

Cass stood, hands in pockets and shoulders crouched forward. Even the thick white knit of his sweater couldn't hid the fact that the boy was all knobs and gangles underneath. As Sandy watched, she saw a blush paint his face.

"Um, gee, I only thought that maybe you were going to the academy." Cass fidgeted and scuffed one foot against the other. "See, I've got this homework assignment, and I left my book back in Salem Hall, and it's getting kind of late, and Mom doesn't drive, and . . . Oh, never mind. You're going. I'll walk over."

Sandy fought down panic. *Am I really going crazy? Is this what I was running away from? This child? I can almost hear his knees knocking over the big deal of asking his teacher's wife for a lift! What's the matter with me?*

She forced a smile. "Don't do that. My husband can hold down the fort for ten more minutes." Unlocking the door, she tossed her bunch of lilacs into the backseat. "Come on, I'll drive you."

"Would you?" Cass looked pitifully thankful. Sandy's heart slowly stopped hammering her ribs. "Gosh, I really appreciate this, Mrs. Walters. I know right where the book is too. I'll just run in and run out."

He was as good as his word. While Sandy's car idled in front of the ivy-grown brick facade of Salem Hall, he came loping out with the wayward book held high. He must have removed his sweater inside the building, for he now carried it draped over one arm, and he nearly fell headlong into the side of the car when the white knit bulk slipped to the ground and snared his feet.

"Cass, be careful!"

He recovered, grinning sheepishly, and pitched the offending garment in on top of the lilacs. "Thanks. Thanks a lot, Mrs. Walters," he repeated for about the tenth time. He was still thanking her when they pulled up near his house and he got out, hugging the book to his concave chest.

As Sandy sped for home, a lithe gray shape eased itself through the hedge and the fence to butt Cass's leg.

"You forgot your sweater," Cesare said.

"I know what I did."

"Planting an excuse for her to come back? Clever. Amanda's not going to like this, you know."

"Believe it or not, Cesare, I don't care."

"Don't you? You used to."

"That was then."

"And this is now? Brilliant." Cesare purred. "Ah, the constant heart of youth!"

"Come *on*, Cesare. This is different."

The cat switched his tail. "They all are. It's spring when a young man's fancy's supposed to turn to thoughts of love. *Lightly* turn. Here it is fall, and your fancy's a whirling dervish. How long has it been since you. . . ?" Cesare raised one discreetly inquiring whiskery brow.

Cass mumbled something unintelligible.

"When, did you say?"

"1843."

Cesare marched through the garden gate. "Then you'll be wanting a cold shower before you reconsider bothering poor Mrs. Walters any further. And the *Sports Illustrated* bathing suit issue goes out in the trash tomorrow. You'd have the morals of a tomcat, if I'd let you. Trouble with you, Your Royal Hotness, is you mistake the call of the heart for the call of the—"

"Cesare!"

"*Andiam'.*"

Chapter Four:

Party Animal

There was nothing like a beautifully set table to make Sandy feel inadequate as a wife, mother, and woman. Just the realization that there were people capable of making cloth napkins into funny shapes was enough to depress her.

Davina was one such person. The menu for Wednesday night dinner was cold cuts and salad, yet the Welsh *au pair* had scorned paper plates, paper cups, even paper napkins for the real thing. Sandy felt like a paying guest in her own home. Her brain had even gone into tip-calculation mode.

"Wow," Lionel said when he beheld the splendor of the festive board. "I didn't know we had half this stuff." He picked up a paper-thin slip of lox with a two-pronged silver fork.

"Wedding loot," Sandy said, looking glum.

"Gee, this is pretty, Mommy." Ellie's mouth formed an *O* formerly reserved for the once-yearly New York City pilgrimage to see the Christmas tree at Rockefeller Center.

"Ah, my head'll be getting too big if you make so much of nothing." Davina dismissed all compliments airily. "It's no more than anyone else could do, given the time."

Ellie shook her head. "Oh no, Davina. My mommy never does anything like this, and she's got lots of time. Please pass the turkey, Mommy."

It would not have been nice to hurl the turkey at her only child, especially not when Sandy knew damned well Ellie was only telling the truth. Still, she might yet salvage a little face.

"This really is a pretty table, Davina. And I've brought home just the thing to make it perfect. You get a vase and I'll get the flowers from the car. Wait till you see them!" She pushed back her chair.

Though she outweighed Sandy by a fair number of stone, Davina had an actress's agility. She had the car keys from the back-door rack and was heading for the garage before Sandy was out of her seat. "Don't you bother, I'll see to it myself. Have your supper now, for didn't you say you had to be going to that party?"

When Davina popped out the door, Lionel asked his wife, "Aren't you taking her with you?"

"To a Preserv-a-Pak party?" Sandy took a large bite of her sandwich. "Don't you think the poor girl should learn about the Ugly American on her own?"

"It's just a bunch of women buying dishes and having coffee. She doesn't know anyone in town and she doesn't go out at all. She might like it. It's harmless fun."

Sandy rolled her eyes, too choked with emotion and cream cheese to speak. Lionel's innocence was touching. It should be cherished. She prayed he would never have to learn the truth about Preserv-a-Pak parties.

Davina returned looking bewildered. Sandy recognized

the thick white sweater draped over the Welsh girl's arm. She held a sheaf of brightly tinted autumn leaves in her hands.

"I looked all over the car for flowers, Mrs. W—Sandy, but it's only these I found under this jumper." She fanned the dead leaves.

"But—but couldn't you smell the lilacs?"

"Lilacs? In September?" Davina's musical laugh was guileless. "Wouldn't I give half my heart for a scent of lilacs now!"

Ellie was bouncing in her seat, clapping her hands. "Oh Mommy, those are *neat* leaves! They'll look great on the table. Put them down, Davina! Put them down!"

Davina obeyed, then shook a few flecks of dead leaf from the white sweater. "And where would you have me put this?"

The doorbell rang before Sandy could say where she'd like Davina to put the sweater, together with the entire Taylor family and their metamorphic garden. "I'll get that. I'm done with dinner anyhow." Though half her sandwich remained uneaten, it was no lie.

The fake coach lantern on the Walterses' porch shone on Cass's stiffly grinning face. "Uh . . . Hi, Mrs. Walters. I mean, good evening. I think I forgot something in your car. I hate to bother you. Am I interrupting your dinner or something?"

He was so *ordinary* looking. His hair was slicked back, fresh from the shower, a few droplets still clinging to the water-darkened strands. He had his hands jammed into the pockets of a ripstop windbreaker. Sandy could see the outlines of fingers fumbling nervously with whatever nameless horror of used Kleenex, furred candies, and free lint those pockets might contain.

"Come on in, Cass." If her mind had turned his boyish gift of autumn leaves to spring lilacs, he wasn't to blame. "You're not interrupting anything. It'll be Ellie's bedtime soon, and Davina and I were just about to go to a party."

"A party?" His eyes lit up, but only in the normally acceptable way. "On a Wednesday night? Sounds like fun. Gee, I wish I had your connections. I mean—" He turned red and mauled the contents of his pockets with renewed diligence to cover his embarrassment.

Sandy conducted him into the living room. In the dining room Ellie was leaning across the table to get a look at the visitor. Lionel pulled her back by the waistband of her overalls.

He spared the boy a friendly nod. Davina was out of sight, taking dishes into the kitchen in relays.

"Don't envy us, Cass. It's a Preserv-a-Pak party. You just ask your mother about it sometime. I'll bet she's too smart to go."

"I don't think she's ever been asked. But I doubt she'd go if she were. She doesn't go out at night at all. She doesn't want to leave Jeffy alone, not even with me."

"Why not? You seem like a competent young man."

Sandy didn't catch the flicker of irritation that momentarily changed Cass's blandly pleasant expression.

"Jeffy has bad nightmares. When he does, he just wants Mother. Once when he was little he had one at nap time while she was out shopping. He screamed nonstop for an hour until she came home. Now they just happen at night."

"I see."

Cass looked thoughtful. "I've heard about Preserv-a-Pak. It's these plastic dishes that're airtight and don't leak, right? They keep things sealed fresh?"

Sandy nodded. She'd been introduced to the wonders of Preserv-a-Pak technology in college when the smaller-sized containers were the status stash-keepers among her friends.

"You know, my mother could use some stuff like that, and I hear you can only order it at the parties. Mrs. Walters . . . do you think your friends would mind if I came along with you—you know, just tagged along—and ordered some pieces for Mother? As a surprise."

Lionel and Davina came into the living room as Sandy began her detailed explication of why it was unthinkable for Cass to attend a Preserv-a-Pak party.

"Now ladies . . . and gentleman," the Preserv-a-Pak rep said with an unbecomingly coy twinkle in her eye. "Please feel free to pass our new Leafresh lettuce bowl around. It comes in your choice of colors, so it'll match your other Preserv-a-Pak containers whether you're collecting our Bolds or our Shys."

Peggy Seymour was the first to hold the pink plastic globe with its cleverly embossed SealSup lid. She oohed and ahhed at length over it, demanding whether the other guests had ever seen anything half so wonderful this side of heaven. As the Preserv-a-Pak party hostess, it was incumbent upon her to stroke the fires of acquisitiveness in her guests. She might otherwise not receive her free set of SnakSnips—oversized plastic paper clips used for keeping opened potato chip bags fresh-freshfresh. This largess would be all Peggy's if the party's total orders topped a hundred dollars. She would make sure this happened or know the reason why.

When the sacred lettuce keeper reached Sandy, she passed it on to Cass so quickly that Peggy took note. It was always dangerous when Peggy noticed anything. It could mean another petition.

"Do you already have a lettuce keeper, Sandra?"

"Yes. I call it the refrigerator."

Peggy clucked. "You know that's not enough. Greens go bad before you can imagine. *I* like to care about the freshness of everything my family eats."

Sandy refrained from pointing out that Peggy Seymour's family consisted *in toto* of Kwai-Chang Caine, the most pissant Shih Tzu ever to curse Godwin's Corners. Even now she could hear the beast's dyspeptic yaps coming from the bathroom. Kwai-Chang Caine loved to bite ankles, but would take the fleshier, more satisfying taste of calf when he could get it. Peggy always accused the victim of provoking her precious pet, and Peggy was a vocal force with which to reckon. As the party continued and coffee was served there would be more than one lady torn between obtaining relief and facing down the midget Hound of the Baskervilles.

"Mrs. Walters, you ought to have another look at this." Cass passed the bowl back to Sandy. "It's something special. It really is."

Sandy gave Cass a quizzical look. Exceeding interest in plastic storage ware was not normal in a person of his age and sex. She wasn't sure it was normal for anyone, except those looking to make a buck off it. Bemused, she accepted the dish.

"Open it," Cass said. "Look inside."

She did.

Rubies redder than the blood of dragons threw back the light, made the bowl glow a deeper rose. Sandy's neck tingled. Carefully she reached into the lettuce keeper and poked one of the gems with the tip of her nail. It rolled over, making a solid enough click as it hit its neighbor.

Breath drifted over her cheek. Natalie Voorhees was peering over her shoulder into the bowl. "Oh, isn't that clever?"

"Clever?" That was hardly the word Sandy would apply to rubies.

"The way they've got those little spikes inside to keep

the lettuce from resting on the bottom and rotting. I always have that trouble with my greens, don't you?'' Natalie reached past Sandy's face to stick her own finger into the bowl and flick one of the rot-fighting spikes. The finger went right through the rubies. ''Mind if I have a second look at that?''

''Please.'' Sandy fairly thrust the bowl into Natalie's bosom. *I'm seeing things again. I'm nuts. I don't want to lose my mind,* she thought. *But if I must go insane, please Lord, don't let it be at a Preserv-a-Pak party!*

She glanced at Cass. He smiled at her. A blue spark glimmered briefly in his eyes and she smelled lilacs. Then the woman seated on Cass's other side handed him a Portamunch hors d'oeuvre tray. It distracted him only a moment. His hands touched Sandy's as he passed it on to her. The long fingers caressed her skin in a disturbingly familiar manner. They were smoother than they should have been, if he were nothing more than an ordinary seventeen-year-old boy.

He wasn't. Sandy knew he wasn't. The touch of such alien skin was too well known to her memory, too dear to be forgotten, though now it only came to her in dreams. She shook her head very slightly, a gesture of rejection almost too subtle to be seen. ''You can't be,'' she whispered.

''I am.''

''All right, girls, it's time to play a game!'' the Preserv-a-Pak rep shrieked. A cascade of multicolored plastic doohickeys poured into the center of the floor and instructions were given for how to obtain one or more. It was a contest of skill, talent, and rich reward. Some exchanging of seats was required, ditto the utterance of animal noises.

The Prince of Elfhame Ultramar won an olive-stabber and a pink swizzle stick topped with a teddy bear. He lost his seat next to Sandy. The shifts and place trades of the game put Davina there, and Sandy's wildly clutching hand held her to the spot.

''Don't leave me,'' she whispered between clenched teeth.

Davina gave her a searching look, but stayed put. ''Whatever's troubling you?''

''Do you see that young man over there? The one we came here with? Cass Taylor?''

Davina's brows raised slightly. The gentleman in question was now seated almost directly opposite them, waving his prizes proudly and accepting the compliments of his neighbors for a truly lifelike imitation of a tomcat's yowl.

"He's a fine-looking one, if you don't mind my being so forward. What of him?"

"He's—" Sandy's hand was cold and growing clammy. What good would it do to tell Davina the truth? Who would ever believe it but those whose lives had touched the elfinkind? Lionel would understand. He'd understand, but he wouldn't like it. What he didn't know of her past with Rimmon he had guessed. He wasn't stupid, but like many other husbands—and wives as well—he was happier remaining deliberately ignorant of his spouse's past.

"He's got a crush on me. I think." It was lame and sounded it, but what else could she say?

"A crush?" Davina's brows winged a bit higher. "Surely there's a greater feeling than that. I never knew the Fair Folk to have less than a grand passion for mortal women. Of what tribe does he come? I'd put him to the elfinkind, myself, but I've been wrong before this. The merkind sometimes walk dry land for a time and have that look. . . ."

Sandy gaped.

"Come with me," Davina said, helping her to her feet with a Nanny's no-nonsense grasp. "We must speak of this, for it may be grave danger touching you. I'd not have that for the world."

Sandy let herself be conducted out of the enchanted plastic circle and toward the bathroom. Behind the closed door, Kwai-Chang Caine yapped doom and death threats. Davina opened the door and in one smooth move scooped up the noxious creature, holding him at arm's length until she could flip wide the laundry hamper and pop him inside. She then shut and locked the door, seated herself on the hamper lid, and motioned for Sandy to take the throne.

"How do you know?" Sandy held her hand to her heart, feeling it flutter much too fast. The combined shocks of Cass's confession and Davina's casual familiarity with Faery were not doing her health any favors.

"I'm from Wales." Davina folded her arms across her substantial bosom. "And I'm Sighted besides. There were many such in my old village. My mother said it was due to all the remnants of the Old Blood lingering so thick in our region. There were precious many bastard children born with a fey look about them to our village girls, especially those as had a long and solitary way home to go of nights. Now the Old Blood's thin, though potent still in matters of the Sight. The years taught us to keep still about it. In other times they burned

us for witches or stoned us when our prophecies of evil came
true. These days they call us cranks. I can't say as I care much
for either. But you must be of the Sight as well.''

"Not me." Sandy shook her head. "I wish I was. Maybe
then I could see a way out of this mess.''

Davina leaned forward, her eyes searching Sandy's.
"You're afraid, but I see it's not ignorant fear. You know what
it means, the love of the elven—too sweet, too strong for mortals to bear long, that's what we used to sing. Oh, and far too
tempting to let us turn away. You've tasted it once, and much
as you love your husband, you fear the call will be too powerful.''

Miserable, Sandy confessed that this was so. She told
Davina of her dreams, and slowly began to recount her memories of Rimmon. By the time she was done, Kwai-Chang Caine
was howling fearsomely in the hamper, Peggy was pounding
on the door demanding to know what was going on, and Davina had made every known warding sign against evil in Western civilization.

"We must go home," the Welsh girl said, rising hur-
riedly from the hamper and removing the dog. He was half
smothered and wholly wilted, capable of only an indifferent
snap or two. "I've never heard the like!''

Sandy agreed. She opened the bathroom door. A solid
wave of women poured in, Peggy at the crest.

"*What* is the matter in here?" She gave Sandy a suspicious stare that bored deeper when she caught sight of her pet.
The former devourer of ankles now showed all the ginger of a
wrung mop. "And what have you done to my baby?''

"Oh, the darling dog!" Davina grabbed Kwai-Chang and
pressed him to her bosom. The Shih Tzu was too dispirited to
do more than roll his eyes and await a merciful death. "So
well behaved he was all the while we were in here. I wasn't
feeling quite myself, you see, and Mrs. Walters kindly took
me aside to look after me. We didn't wish to disturb the party."
She planted a wet kiss on Kwai-Chang's nose. "Isn't he the
dearest thing?''

The other ladies exchanged doubtful glances, but Peggy
took the dog from Davina, nuzzled him further into submission, and said, "Well, we were worried. It was time to fill out
the order blanks and we couldn't find either one of you. That
nice Taylor boy suggested the bathroom.''

Sandy glimpsed that nice Taylor boy over the heads of

the women. He smiled at her with something far more than Boy Scout cheerfulness. Her face burned and she looked away.

She placed her Preserv-a-Pak order without thinking. The sales rep was delighted. "I've never sold one of our Mammoth Melon-ball Keepers before. Would you like the five-gallon lid in matching or contrasting color?"

"Whatever. Come on, Davina. We're leaving now."

Cass was waiting for them at the door, his sweater over one arm. "I haven't finished giving in my order yet, Mrs. Walters." He leaned against the jamb, blocking their escape. Sandy saw blue fire in his eyes again, though banked and burning more gently than the blazes that had made her run scared under the lilac arbor. "I sure could use a lift home. It's late at night and—"

"Night was mother to all your brood, and air's the blood in your veins." Davina placed herself between Cass and Sandy and spoke low, lips curving. The elven blinked in surprise, took a step back, hesitated.

"By standing stone and fairy ring, I conjure and command you, let this mortal woman be." Davina's words came in a whisper so faint that Sandy had to strain to hear it. The other women, gathered around the Preserv-a-Pak rep, paid no mind to the scene going on in the doorway. "By iron edge and holy cross, I charge you—"

"Huh?" Cass' exclamation of disbelief was loud enough for everyone in the room to hear. He made a face at the Welsh girl. " 'Iron edge'? Who are you kidding with that old-style stuff? This is *America,* Taffy. Get real!" He laughed in Davina's startled face and swept regally out the door, letting his Preserv-a-Pak order form drop to the carpet.

Peggy was there and on it like a cat on cream gravy. "What was all that about, Sandra?" she inquired, running her eyes over Cass's discarded order.

"Lovers' quarrel."

"Really?" Peggy looked down her nose at the only two prospective candidates for the co-starring roles in such a tiff and discarded one as impossible, the other incredible. "Well, these teenagers . . . you never know. I'll just have Brenda total up his bill and you can tell him that the merchandise will arrive in ten days. He can pay me then." She whisked off.

Sandy leaned on Davina most of the way to the car. The Welsh girl offered to drive, but Sandy declined.

"I'll be all right." She fastened her safety belt with a firm snap. "Yes, it's much better now. Just knowing there's someone I can talk to about this . . . I can't tell you what a relief it is.''

"You must be calm, Mrs. Walters. Calm above all, when dealing with the elfinkind. They're a passionate race, all fire when roused. Even when they seem to contemplate us with the disdain immortals feel for death-bound beings, they burn with envy. Time stretches to infinity for them, unless death comes violently. They bore easily. They wish they had our talent for enriching every hour. We are as children in their eyes.''

"Good. Then we can drive them nuts.'' Sandy clasped the steering wheel.

Davina's full mouth quirked up. "A strange way of putting it, but a good one. Short-lived creatures must have long wit, or where did all the tales of mortals outfoxing elvens come from?''

"And how do you propose we outfox my young Romeo? He wasn't impressed by your conjurings, and I do want him to cool off.''

"Is that what you want truly?'' Davina sighed, and in an undertone added, "God gives bread to them who have no teeth.''

"Look, Davina, I told you what happened to me. That was in the past. If I've wished to have Rimmon back again . . . Well, I know it's impossible, and even if it weren't—''

"It's safer to yearn for a dream than to have it?'' Davina's brow rose in gentle question.

Sandy nodded, with some small regret. "I'm married now, a respectable wife and mother. I'm too old to go bouncing around a fairy ring with a kid young enough to be my—''

"Old enough, you mean; centuries old, centuries fair.''

Sandy flipped on the interior light and looked closely at Davina. "You want him.'' It was said with astonishment and understanding combined, and a trace of pity.

Davina heard it all. "My wants don't signify.'' She gazed down at her plump hands, folded in her lap. "It's you his eyes follow.''

"Well, they can damned well follow something else for a change.'' Sandy gunned the motor. "I'm going to do something about it.''

"And what's that, when all the ancient off-keeping spells only made him laugh at me?''

Sandy's teeth flashed. Her old spunk was back, now that she wasn't alone with her problem. "There's one spell that's never been known to fail for getting someone to back down.

More powerful than wolfbane! Stronger than iron! Twice the umph of holy water and the cross!''

Davina pursed her lips. "And what's that?''

"I'm going to tell his mother on him.''

As they drove to the Taylor house, Davina asked, "Are you sure that will work? The fey don't like to be told what to do by mortals.''

"It's only a theory, but I don't think Mrs. Taylor's any more fey than Arnold Schwarzenegger. Still, she's in the position of power in that whacked-out household, so she must have some sort of hold over Cass. Anyway, my motto's always been: It never hurts to ask. Here we are.''

The Taylor house was dark but for a tiny lick of light in one window of the upper story. Sandy got out of the car and strode purposefully toward the gate. She sniffed the air, thick with bitter woodsmoke from many a neighboring fireplace. Yet even so, she could still smell the rich perfume of impossible roses. She rested her hand on the gate just as a small gray shape slipped down the pathway from the house. The hinges whispered.

Legs stiff, neck-ruff bristling, the silver-white wolf curled back his upper lip and showed a row of sickle fangs. His growl raced up Sandy's legs and froze a knot around her heart. Her eyes locked with his, and behind her she was only marginally aware of Davina's voice whispering, "Oh, merciful powers . . .''

"Sorry. Mistake. Just going. Nice doggy.'' She skittered backward on her heels as the wolf stalked toward her, back arched bizarrely, menacing. With a garbled cry, she wheeled and ran for the car, slamming the door and flooring the gas as soon as she turned the key in the ignition. The roar of the departing car covered the scornful feline yowl that the great wolf loosed at the moon.

Several blocks' worth of peeled rubber later, Davina and Sandy crawled back home. They found Lionel studying a gaming manual while having herb tea and cookies at the kitchen table.

"Ellie's asleep. Have a nice party, ladies?''

"I want a drink.'' Sandy staggered over to the pantry where the liquor reposed. She poured herself what Lionel called a Suburban Sacrilege: two fingers of single-malt Scotch diluted with six ounces of Diet Coke.

"That good, hm?'' Lionel went back to his book.

"What is it that you're reading?" Davina asked, cocking her head to scan the manual's brightly colored cover.

"Oh, I'm thinking of running a new character in the role-playing game I've got going with the academy kids. I'm sort of fed up with being a wizard, but I can't decide what's next. What do you think, Sandy? Could I run a good elf?"

"You could run him all the way to Pittsburgh, with my blessings!" Sandy slammed out of the kitchen. They could hear her stomping all the way upstairs to bed.

Lionel looked at Davina. "It's only a game," he said.

Chapter Five:

A Word to the Wise
Is a Waste of Time

"If he doesn't want you calling on Mrs. Taylor, you'd not be wise to persist," Davina said as she buttoned Ellie's sweater.

Sandy drummed her fingers on the kitchen table. "I can live with that. Maybe the attempt was as good as actually having a word with the woman. Maybe now Cass will realize I don't want anything to do with him—anything beyond my role as his professor's wife, that is."

Davina shrugged and took Ellie's hand. "No law bars hope. Still, they can be a fearsome stubborn lot."

"Who can?" Ellie asked.

"Presbyterians," Sandy supplied. She gave her daughter a kiss. "You be a good girl at school now, and introduce Davina to your teacher."

"Yes, Mommy." Ellie took the *au pair*'s hand in proprietary fashion. As they walked out of the house, Sandy overheard her daughter telling Davina the latest Jeffy Taylor atrocity.

Maybe I should've told her not to play with him anymore, Sandy thought. Then: *No: what harm is there in the child? He looks normal enough . . . and so did Cass, until I took a closer look. Damn it, elves have got no business in Connecticut! Why can't they stay in—in—why can't they go back where they came from?*

She took another sip of coffee and tried to imagine where
elves did belong. Inevitably her mind kept skipping back to
Rimmon's land, the lost land of Khwarema, dead in dragon
fire, alive with ghosts. In pavilions of silk, in castles made of
stone, under the towering gray of monoliths, in the green shadows of ageless woodlands, between one plane of reality and
another, that was where elves and all the faery kind might
dwell and mortal minds accept them.

But must they lie so far away? The dreamwoods of
Khwarema faded into the last of the old-world forests. English
oaks ringed with moon-touched toadstools, French glades of
neolithic standing stones, the shadows of more than light and
darkness that played around the fallen pillars of old Roman
villas in Italy, the windswept peaks of German mountains where
more than birds sailed across the blue gulfs of air. . . . There,
too, the most rational person alive might encounter something
other and not have his mind flee from the hinted touch of magic.

But in America? All the standing stones were made of
steel and glass. Shadows only danced by night on television
screens. The forests not yet pulped were being steadily, re-
morselessly nibbled away. The only wizards lived on Wall
Street, or at computer terminals, and elves . . . ?

"California," Sandy said aloud. "If they're lucky. Definitely not in Connecticut."

Skeeeeee!

Sandy's skin caterpillared all over her body. Her shoulders shot up to shield her ears, but the piercing, nerve-fraying
sound penetrated like a laser.

Skeeeeee! Cat claws on the kitchen window just above
the sink. Sandy spied the Taylor's brindle tom with polydactyl
paw splayed, ready for a third scrape down the glass. She
rammed the breath out of her belly on the edge of the sink in
her hurry to get the sash up before the cat could do that again.

Cesare stepped prissily over the sill, skirted the sink,
leaped gracefully to the floor, and stared up at Sandy with the
nonchalant command of one born to terrify headwaiters.

"Well, what brings you here?" Sandy gave the beast a
condescending smile, hands on hips.

"Lox," said the cat. "You did promise."

Sandy folded her legs and sat down hard on the kitchen
floor.

Cesare strolled over to her and insinuated his head under
her limp palm. A few tentative buttings did not produce the
desired petting reflex, so he began to knead her thigh petu-

lantly. She felt it, even through the thick twill of her navy slacks.

"I don't see what you're taking on about," the cat muttered as he dug his claws in with increasing emphasis. "You're no virgin—figurative or otherwise—and not *too* thick, for a human. You know what Cass is. Why am I such a surprise? Did you expect one of his kind to keep a common cat?"

Sandy swallowed hard and wet her lips. "I—I never thought there was such a thing as a common cat."

Cesare abruptly stopped kneading and looked up at her. His whiskers curled forward. "Ah! *Bene.* You frighten easily, but you recover well. He might have done worse. Now, where is this lox?"

Sometime later, Sandy was finishing her fourth cup of coffee as she watched Cesare spear the last sliver of lox with two claws and daintily rasp it into his mouth.

"Excellent." The cat licked his chops widely and made a cursory toilette. "So. To business, *é vero?*"

"Business." Sandy polished off the dregs of her cup and felt a bit nauseated. "Listen, if your master's sent you as his ambassador, you're the cutest John Alden I've ever seen, but I'm sorry: I'm not buying."

"Buying?" Cesare's eyebrow whiskers quivered roguishly. "*Madonna mia,* you are mistaken. First, we will not speak of masters."

"True. You are a cat, after all. My apologies."

Cesare winked. "Second, my . . . master doesn't know I'm here. I am acting independently in this. As in all things, might I add. Third, and last, I haven't come to urge you to give in to my young friend's courtship. On the contrary, sweet lady, I am here to beg you to run as if a thousand devils were on your track, not to look back, but to keep running until you haven't breath, strength, or shoe leather to take you any further. Keep away from the one you call Cass Taylor, and farther from the lady under his roof. Roofs have a habit of caving in on occasion. It would distress me to see you caught in the rubble." His red tongue wrapped itself once around his muzzle. "Especially after having experienced your most succulent hospitality."

The cat jumped from the kitchen table across the yawning gap of air to the counter. He flicked his tail twice, and added, "You are the first mortal I have ever known to be elven-touched and still survive to lead a life that is—" he glanced about the tidy kitchen—"that *appears* to be normal, by your

standards. If that is what you want, then take my advice: Stay
clear.'' He bounded through the open window and was gone.

Sandy undid the chain holding Rimmon's bloodstone token to her throat. She let it trickle to the table where she sat
contemplating it for a time. In its milky nest of carved white
flowers, the stone glimmered with its own secrets. She raised
her eyes and took in all the bright, bland, everyday order of
the kitchen—the canisters of staples on the counter, the file of
coupons by the phone, the little notes held to the refrigerator
with plastic magnets shaped like butterflies and rainbows:

*Use up yellow stuff in pink Preserv-a-Pak bowl by Tues-
day, latest!*

Call rest of tag sale/bake sale list.

Pick up dry cleaning.

Get milk, lettuce, Spaghetti-Os, cake mix.

Call Mom or suffer the consequences.

Sandy picked the bloodstone up by its chain and let it
twirl in the light. She smiled.

''Who the hell listens to talking cats?''

Chapter Six:

Open House

''The cat speaks?''

''Would you expect an elf to own a common cat?''
Sandy replied archly.

Davina didn't know what to make of all this. ''In the old
country, the Fair Folk were a shy and secretive lot. They never
came out, except at certain seasons of the year, by moonlight.
Even then it took one of the Sighted to mark them and their
familiars. Here . . .''

''Americans don't stand on ceremony so much. We're
more outgoing.''

''Yes, but the elvenkind—''

''Naturalization's a funny thing. Only in this case, we're
dealing with supernaturalization. Whatever. All I can say is
I've had a *very* illuminating morning. The cat's visit, for one

thing, and for another—'' She reached into the buttondown
pocket of her man-tailored blouse and dropped a slip of metal
to the table. ''This came in the mail today. It was stuck inside
one of those 'You May Already Be A Winner' envelopes.''

It was cut square, no more than two inches on a side, a
piece of wafer-thin gilded copper. Davina carefully picked it
up between thumb and forefinger. The light flashed from it in
starry bursts, coruscating along the silver lines etched into the
surface.

''It's you. . . .''

''Not a bad likeness,'' Sandy allowed of the miniature.
''I may be buck naked, but at least he had the courtesy to
fantasize me without stretch marks or cellulite. Now see what's
on the flip side.''

Davina turned the square over and saw the image of a
winged horse. As she stared, her eyes widened. The creature's
wings trembled at the tips, then lowered, then rose only to
lower again in stroke after feathery stroke of flight. And from
the square's edge a twinkling hand crept around. The tiny,
naked, beautifully etched figure of Sandy Horowitz came
creeping around the corner to mount the winged horse and drink
the wind that blew as they flew across that metal sky.

The Welsh girl gasped and nearly dropped the square.
Sandy got it back and flipped it from one side to the other.
''Now Horsie and I are motionless and back where we started.
What do you make of that?'' she asked, tucking the glittering
square safely away again.

''A promise?'' Davina raised her palms, uncertain. ''A
pledge?''

''And maybe just the elfin way of saying, 'Hi, I'm Cass.
Fly me.' I ought to tell him that I'm scared of heights.'' She
toyed with the metal slip some more. ''Lionel was there when
I found this in the mail. He said he didn't see anything odd
about it. To him, it looks and feels like one of those cardboard
doodads you're supposed to stick in the YES! pocket if you want
umpty-nine issues of *House Meticulous* magazine. But you and
I can see it as it is.''

''I am Sighted, you are elven-touched.'' That explained
it all, to Davina. ''Will you return the token?''

Sandy's smile was crooked. ''Give an underage boy a
picture of a naked lady? A naked *me*? That would be corrupting
a minor, even if he is a gazillion years old. Take my word for
it, you can't be too careful when it comes to the law. Let him
magic up another feelthy peecture, if he insists. He's not get-

ting this one back, and I am definitely *not* sticking this one in his YES! pocket.''

The Welsh girl looked as if she felt an unexpected chill. ''It doesn't do to play high-handed with the Fair Folk. I'd feel more at ease if the old forbiddings worked, but this American breed . . . How can they be controlled?''

''Your guess is as good as mine. I can hardly control my daughter. Speaking of, it's almost dismissal time. Let's pick up Ellie. And maybe I can snatch a word with Mrs. Taylor too. Wolfless, if I'm lucky.''

''I never did have any luck,'' Sandy muttered as they neared the school. She gestured at a tall, skinny, pale-haired figure in the Godwin Academy blazer, out of place among the mothers waiting by the gate for their little ones.

Cass grinned when he saw her, a slow, sensuous smile that lingered in his eyes. Sandy noticed that he no longer bothered to cover up with his gawky teenager act, even when there were other people besides herself and Davina watching.

You're getting cocky, aren't you? she mused. *Good. That's one mistake. Let's use it.*

In a clear, far-reaching voice, Sandy belled, ''Why, Cass Taylor! Why aren't you in school?''

Heads turned. Cass squirmed under the massed inquisitorial eyes of Godwin's Corners' Concerned Mothers. These ladies believed in a place for everything and everything in its place, especially children. Truancy could lead to juvenile delinquency, as was well known by every mother worth her *Parents* magazine subscription; and juvenile delinquency could lead to drugs, liquor, sex, wild parties, and mailbox bashing, which was the horrid prelude to the ultimate degeneracy, a dip in property values. Suddenly Cass was not so alone with his prey as he might have wished.

Sandy pressed her lips together to keep from smiling as the elven quickly tossed on his so recently disdained role of adolescent goof. ''Uh—gosh, Mrs. Walters, it's okay. I've got a note and everything from school. My mom just—she just stopped by the academy and asked if maybe I could pick up my brother today. She has to be somewhere, see someone. . . .'' he fumbled in his pockets. ''I've got the note, honest!'' He was deliciously graceless, and mortified to the roots of his hair. When his eyes met hers, they glared.

Awwwww. Izzums angry? Sandy let her thoughts show on her face. In her best condescending manner she said,

"That's quite all right, dear. We'll trust you. My *husband* always tells me what a good boy you are." She turned her back on him. *That will teach you to come on strong to me.*

"Mrs. Walters." Davina's whisper in her ear was urgent. She let the Welsh girl draw her aside. "Mrs. Walters, you mustn't rile the Fair Folk at your pleasure. They've a terrible temper, every one. It's a woeful thing you'll do if once their favor turns to hate."

"So they carry grudges? Don't try scaring me with that, Davina," Sandy shot back. "My mother could teach Remedial Vendetta to the Mob. She's still toting a whopper she picked up at a family reunion back in 1968 when she found out Cousin Harriet went to a wedding in Taos and missed my graduation from Erasmus High. I don't know what brought Tinkerbell over there into my life, but I do know I want him out, and if I have to embarrass him cross-eyed to make him back off, I'll do it."

Davina was glum. "To banish the Fair Folk is never that easy."

"That was what everyone said about Cousin Harriet and buffet tables, but she hasn't shown up at a catered affair where she might meet my mom since 1969. Never mind him. Here come the children."

The door opened and they streamed down the steps, deaf to Miss Foster's ineffective exhortations of walk-don't-run. Mothers signaled and called to their young, like a scene out of a Disney nature film where, with much bellowing and thrashing of flippers, hundreds of mama seals picked their own pups out of the rookery rummage sale.

"Ellie! Ellie, over here!" Sandy was on tiptoe, wigwagging with the best of them. Only Cass and Davina remained quiet, sifting the crowd of children with eyes alone. "There she is! In the pink sweater! Ellie!"

But Ellie wasn't alone. She held Jeffy Taylor by the hand and ran only halfway down the path to the gate before stopping, whispering something in the boy's ear, and then taking off with him around the corner of the yellow house.

"*Ellie!* That child . . ." Sandy's fists were on her hips. "Now we'll have to wait until the bottleneck at the gate clears up before we can go in and get her." She looked at Cass. "And your brother."

"Why?" Cass was suddenly taut. "Won't they come out with the rest? Where did they go?"

"Now don't worry . . ." His fingers closed tightly on her wrist. The blue fires in his eyes were burning white. "Let go of me," Sandy said very low. "Let me go or I'll kick you, and I know that works on elves too." She felt his fingers unclench. There were faint marks on her arm. "Come on , follow us and don't get all upset. They've only gone to the play—"

Ellie's terrified scream leaped over the rooftree.

"—ground."

Miss Foster got there before anyone, which was a wonder, considering how Cass vaulted the picket fence and seemed to fly around the corner of the house. Sandy took the more conventional path, through the gate, followed by Davina and as many of the other mothers as were unable to dissuade their children from rubbernecking.

Sandy's first reaction was a wholehearted *Thank God!* when she saw Ellie kneeling in the dirt, frightened but uninjured. This was followed by a more leisurely backwash of guilt as she realized that there was an injury after all; a pretty spectacular one.

Jeffy Taylor lay on his back near the seesaw, blood streaming from his nose, while Ellie ineffectively tried to mop it up with her flimsy cotton hankie. The dainty rag was soaked scarlet and smeared with dirt. The little girl twisted it through her fingers over and over as she tried to make her friend stop his shrill, incessant bawling.

Cass froze in his tracks. Sandy had never imagined a man so fair could blanch further, but Cass did. It was as if he'd gone into a trance of some kind, or perhaps it was just the normal reaction of an inexperienced person when first confronted by a hurt child. The impulse to run away and let someone else take care of things was always a hair stronger than the urge to help the little one.

Miss Foster summed up the situation with a cold and practiced eye. "Just a bloody nose. I'll get the first-aid kit. Jeffy, Ellie, you know you're not supposed to go on the playground equipment without an adult to supervise. You will both have indoor recess for the rest of the week. Stop crying, Jeffy. My mind is made up." Jeffy's renewed howls followed her as she marched off to fetch medical supplies.

Sandy did what no one else seemed to think necessary. She got down in the dirt with the two children and gathered Jeffy into her arms. There was blood on her shirt and sweater, more on her own handkerchief when she pressed it to the little boy's nose, but it only made her cradle him more closely. "Don't cry, Jeffy. Hush, dear; don't worry, your brother's here. We'll take you home, won't we, Cass?"

She looked up. Cass was gone. Davina returned her startled gaze and shrugged, waving at the air as if to say that that was the route he had taken, witnesses be damned.

As soon as Miss Foster provided a coldpack and some fresh wadding, Sandy explained that she would be seeing Jeffy home. "His brother ran ahead to open the house for us and see about finding their mother," she explained glibly.

She didn't feel quite so glib when they got to the Taylors' gate and found Jeffy's mother standing in the front yard, waiting for them. The look on her face was chilling. Sandy had seen people wear such expressions many times, but always in newsreel footage of natural disasters. That face belonged on a woman who'd returned to find her home burned to the foundations, or inundated by a mud slide, or torn to flinders by a whirlwind.

It seemed a bit much for welcoming home a small child with a bloody nose.

"He's all right now," Sandy tried to tell her. The dead-eyed look remained. "Really. It stopped bleeding halfway here."

"I was only trying to show Ellie something, Mama," Jeffy quavered. "I told her about Bantrobel, how she flies when she spreads her cloak on the winds, and the only way I could do that was to have Ellie hold down one end of the seesaw while I climbed up to the other end, only her hands slipped, and the seesaw came down, and I fell, and—" He was blubbering again.

His mother made no move to take him into her arms.

"Will you come into my home, Mrs. Walters," she said. It wasn't a question, or even an invitation, but a concession to the inevitable. For form's sake, she added, "Please."

Sandy held Ellie and Jeffy both by the hand. She felt her daughter's fingers twine more tightly through hers. Jeffy was still sniveling; his little paw was ice. She gave them each a warm, reassuring squeeze, and boldly said, "Why, thank you very much, Mrs. Taylor. But please call me Sandy. And this is our *au pair*, Davina Goronwy. I think that you ought to know that she's Sighted."

The strange word had no obvious effect on Amanda Taylor. "I know. Cass said he suspected that much. It won't matter. Inside, the wards are down." She held the gate open for them and led the way through the garden.

Sandy heard Davina gasp behind her as they ducked beneath the lilac arbor. A brindle gray cat bounded into the mid-

dle of their path before they mounted the steps to the front
door. He was holding a small white drawstring bag in his teeth.
His talent let him address Sandy without dropping the tiny sack.

"I did warn you."

"When cats listen to humans, I'll listen to cats," Sandy
replied lightly. He flaunted his hindquarters at her contemptu-
ously and marched back into the underbrush.

"I see you've met Cesare," Amanda said.

"Oh yes. We had a lovely chat some time since. What's
he got in the sack? Chewing tobacco?"

"Poison." Amanda's voice was flat.

"Mm?" Sandy's brow lifted. "Lucky you. Hardly anyone can find a good mouser these days."

"Cass is right. You are used to wonders." Amanda
opened the door and stepped aside, motioning Sandy and the
rest in.

"Used to them?" Sandy laughed as she led the children
across the threshold. "My dear, I'm—"

The rainbow weavings of a thousand invisible hands
wafted from the bare beams of the ceiling. Each breeze that
chanced through the open door changed their living patterns.
Faces smiled and lips moved wordlessly within the embroidered borders, offering untold secrets. Willows set in alabaster
tubs spread their lacy fans of tender leaves. Their drooping
branches trailed through the burbling rill that meandered across
the floor. Everywhere in the half dark was the gleam and flash
of gold, the glow of ivory and the liquid fire of opal. Radiant
waterlilies opened at every footstep that the visitor took, cupping human feet with a soft, perfumed welcome.

Sandy's shoes and socks vanished. She felt the cool caress of the flowers against her bare skin. Her clothing too was
gone, transformed from the pragmatic textures of suburban chic
to a loose-floating robe of butterfly silk. At her side, Ellie too
now wore a smaller version of her mother's splendid attire. A
glance behind her revealed Davina in a more voluminous in-
terpretation of the same. Their heads were wreathed with infant
roses. Mrs. Taylor, sliding an iron bar across the front door,
turned to show the winged silver coronet on her hair.

Jeffy, in fiery silken tunic, ran across the flowering floor to
throw himself into his elder brother's arms. Cass sat on a chair
that was an arabesque of pearl-strewn silver, a shape of metal
that looked as if it had been grown, not formed by any hands.

"Welcome to our home, Mrs. Walters," he said, his
blue eyes sparkling with amusement. "Can I get you a Pepsi?"

An arm, wrapped all in white samite, thrust itself up out of the stream, a bottle in its hand. Cass accepted it, then studied the label.

"No caffeine."

Chapter Seven:

Family Matters

After Amanda put the wards back up, they had tea. Sandy kept shifting her weight nervously from thigh to thigh throughout the steeping, the pouring, and the highly Victorian cream-and-sugaring ceremonies of her hostess. It was hard to believe that the prosaic flowered blue Hide-a-Bed sofa on which she and Davina now sat was in reality a griffon-shaped settee carved from an impossibly huge chunk of amber, its cushions stuffed with jasmine. Though she sniffed and sniffed, she could not catch more than a hint of the crushed petals' perfume. She thought she sensed the faint crackle of static electricity when she rubbed her legs against the sofa, but that might have been imagination at work.

Davina was not so hampered by the limitations of ordinary senses. The Sighted girl rested one hand in midair, at just the height where the sofa-beast's point-eared head would be. When she balanced her teacup there, Sandy had to look away. Obviously physics was what you made of it.

"We haven't much time," Amanda said, passing around a plate of cookies. "Still, there must be a little grace. However fast his messengers reach him with the news, it will take him a while to decide on how he'll come for us."

"I'm sorry?" Sandy was suddenly aware that Amanda had been speaking to her for some time. Her mind had been elsewhere, still trying to pierce the mundane disguises of the warded room without benefit of magic. Was that the sound of trickling water she heard, or just the boiler in the basement? Did the Cape Cod curtains at the window hide a wise-eyed face? Ellie and Jeffy had run off to his room to play. He'd asked her if she wanted to play with his dragon's egg. Children always did accept marvels with more nonchalance than adults, Sandy reasoned. No one bothered to tell them there weren't dragons until much later.

Dragons . . . Sandy shruddered. She could still see Lionel holding that strange, ensorcelled sword in the middle of Fifth Avenue. It wasn't as if she herself hadn't experienced more than her share of dark enchantments.

But in Godwin's Corners, for God's sake?

". . . in Godwin's Corners that he first found me," Amanda Taylor was saying.

"Who did?"

"Kelerison." The woman raised her large, hazel eyes. "The King of Elfhame."

"Oh." Sandy knocked back a fast slug of tea. "Right. *That* Kelerison, the King of Elfhame; who else?"

"Elfhame Ultramar," Cass corrected. "Don't give my father more honors than he's due. He'll see to that for himself," he concluded bitterly.

"Of course it wasn't called Godwin's Corners then," Amanda went on. She put down her teacup and picked up a paperback book from the coffee table. Sandy squinted, trying to remember what really stood in that spot. A harp that played itself? A pot of gold? A caldron full of blood? More caffeine-free Pepsi?

The paperback was one of those Domino Romances. Sandy thought that Amanda had picked an odd time to catch up on her reading. The young woman was riffling through the pages of *Love Bade Me Follow* while she spoke. It was all very distracting.

" . . . a few farms, and not very good ones. The soil's too rocky. My mother died birthing my youngest brother soon after we came here from Sussex. I was barely sixteen, and looking after the house and the babies and helping Da with the cows aɪd our vegetable patch besides . . ."

The fluttering of pages of the book fuzzed into a blur. Sandy's eyelids drooped, sprang wide, lowered again. She did hear the sound of running water. She felt its cool kiss between her toes, and smelled the fresh green of watercress, the clean, hot scent of ripening corn. She pulled her calico skirt higher, kilting it up over her knees to keep it out of the brook, and waded in. The water rushed midway up her calves. Her straw bonnet, once her mother's, kept the sun from bringing out her freckles; highly unfashionable, and a trial to a girl who had once dreamed of having the milk-white skin of all the court beauties back in England.

Her sister Sarah could be trusted to mind the little ones
for a while longer. Sarah was twelve; it was time she learned
more responsibility. Amanda had claimed that she was only
going out to investigate the honey tree young Edward said he'd
found. Her little brother was bold, for six, but not bold enough
to brave a swarm of angry bees. Amanda promised she would
come home with the honeycomb, if his explorations proved
right.

Now here she lingered, by the brookside, a slab of honeycomb resting in her basket. She'd only been stung twice, to
her pride. She would have to go back to smoke the bees out to
get the rest—sweet golden liquid for her baking, wax to be
made into candles later on. One task led to another. She felt
she'd earned a little respite from the house. Between chore and
chore, she stole the time to dream.

Then there was a shadow on the water near her feet. It
fell over the rippling current in a cloud of gold, not darkness,
and she felt it as if it were a palpable thing when the edge of
it brushed her bare leg.

Her eyes were fear-wide when they startled up to see
him. He was clothed in the court fashion—or as Amanda recalled it from tumbled memories of England. White lace spilled
from his throat and sleeves, silver braiding edged his waistcoat
and the stiff cuffs of his creamy coat. Though he held a tricorne
loosely between his long, white, beringed fingers, the hair he
set it on was not the powdered wig she might have expected.
It was loose gold, and the sight of it alone made her yearn to
touch it and see whether anything on earth so lovely could
possibly be real.

She took the hand he silently outstretched to her. His
beauty had the power to banish fear. Her naked feet stepped
from the brook onto a silken carpet of woven dawn that suddenly overspread the grass. She could still hear the distant
sounds of the farm—the cows lowing as milking time came on,
the gabble of poultry in the yard, her father's hunting dog bark-
ing as the younger children romped and teased him. But then
she heard nothing more but words sweeter than any music,
words of wonder, words of promise, words that laid the impossible at her feet as easily as the carpet into which her bare
toes now dug deep.

The carpet separated into the petals of a briar rose. They
closed over the heads of girl and elfin. Light poured over the
closed flower, and it melted from the sight of the sun, seeping

into the ground. Only Amanda's basket remained, a curious wasp now treading over the abandoned honeycomb.

". . . and because I'd never seen the like of him, I believed him. He was always gentle, never fearsome—though in those first days together I did see many things that would have terrified me senseless if he hadn't been with me. It was only later that I learned he'd made a secret of the most fearsome thing of all."

Sandy's head was spinning. The book was back on the table, the vision was gone, but her fingers still tingled with the touch of inhumanly soft hair. She brought them to her lips, where a kiss taken from another woman's memory was burning.

"Time," said Cass. "I don't know why you make *that* my father's chiefest sin against you. Not when he had so many other faults more deserving of attention." He looked at Sandy meaningly. "Isn't that one of your dearest fantasies too, Sandy? To cheat time?"

"And be cheated in turn?" Amanda snapped before Sandy could object to Cass's uninvited use of her first name. "To go home, after what you think is only a few days' passing; to go back, because you don't want your family to worry about you, because you're so happy you can't bear to think of them being upset, and to find"—her voice caught—"to find that years have gone and they're all dead."

"He comforted her, of course." Cass took more tea. "My father's always been very big on making you see the good side of a bad situation. After all, time in Elfhame's always been different. Doesn't everyone know that? And Amanda wasn't alone. She still had him." He drained the cup. "He was all she had. A fine way to guarantee your lover's faithfulness, when you're her sole link to the changing world."

"Well, that son-of-a-bitch!" Sandy snorted.

"That son-of-a-bitch," Cass said, "is on his way here."

"Which is why we must be gone," Amanda said.

"No." The hardened way Cass uttered that simple word and Amanda's exasperated look told Sandy that this was not the first time they'd debated departure. "My mind is made up. We're staying."

Amanda turned to Sandy. "Can you make him see reason?"

"Who, me? I don't even know what's going on."

"Sandy . . . do you know that Cass loves you?"

Sandy gave the brooding elf a droll smile. "I've had an inkling."

"Then for God's sake, use your influence on him. Tell him we've got to leave now, before Kelerison gets here, while there's time!"

"I said no!" Cass's fist struck the arm of his chair, transforming it and him to shapes of silver. He was the storm wight springing from the lightning-blasted tree, the night terror given human form, the rage of an ancient world's first children against the insolent encroachments of men. Five star sapphires were beacons on his brow, girdled with a strand of silver, and his tunic was lifted from the foam of the sea.

Then he calmed, and the illusion of ordinary humanity came flowing back over him. "No," he repeated. "We're done running away, Amanda. This time I'll wait for my father, and I'll fight. If I can't defend you and the boy, how can I expect Sandy to believe me strong and worthy enough to stand true to her?"

"Just a minute here—" Sandy was about to object to Cass's multiple assumptions, but something caught in her mind as stubbornly as a fishbone in the throat. Suddenly it didn't seem so important to tell Cass what he could do with his tender passion. That would keep. This would not. "Amanda . . . why must you run away?"

"He'll take me back if I don't." Amanda's fingers interlaced around her teacup. "By force, if I won't come willingly, though he'll try persuasion first."

"My father fancies himself a great convincer." Cass's lips twisted in mockery. "Especially of women."

"I don't know what he'll do with Jeffy."

"Jeffy's not . . .?"

"The child is mortal," Davina said softly. "Full mortal, as I can read him. You've been deeper elven-touched than he, though his mother still consorts with lesser beings of the Fair Folk. Is that not so, Mrs. Taylor?"

Amanda nodded. "I was the first of Kelerison's mortal lovers to leave him before he tired of me. I met—I met a man of my own kind one summer when Kelerison was busy elsewhere in his realm. We fell in love. He didn't think I was crazy when I told him who and what I was, where I'd come from. We ran away together, he and I . . . and Cass."

The tomcat leaped from the darkness under the coffee table up into Sandy's lap, making her drop her cup and saucer. "And me," he said, with a splendid flourish of his banded tail.

"*I* was the one who tracked them down, afterward, and warned them. You'd think she'd remember that."

Amanda poured Cesare some cream in a saucer, which he deigned to accept on the cushion between Sandy and Davina. Sandy scratched the cat's neck as she asked, "What did he have to warn you about?"

"What do you think?" Cass spat. "My father doesn't like to lose what he considers to be his property. Oh, if he finishes with it himself first, then it's fine if he tosses it aside. But his pride gives him a damned tight grasp, and he doesn't look kindly on thieves."

Her voice barely rising above a murmur, Amanda recounted to Sandy how she had lost her mortal love. Throughout the narrative—told briefly, yet with deep pain—Sandy's eyes grew harder and harder behind her glasses, while two pairs of lines cut deep at the corners of her mouth and the inner edges of her eyebrows.

"His minions track like other hounds, by scent," Amanda said. "Blood lays the strongest trail of all, when it touches the earth or the water. That was why I kept such a close watch of Jeffy; for nothing, as it turned out. He's a child, and children will collect a hundred different scrapes and cuts, unless they're kept in a padded prison. I thought he deserved as much of a normal childhood as any other little boy. He was always so careful before this! But when he hurt himself like that today . . ."

"Like any other normal litle boy," Davina soothed.

"That was my mistake, thinking he and I could ever have a normal life." Amanda stood up. "I can't risk losing any more time. Cass, if you insist on staying here to face your father, farewell." She held his face between her hands and then kissed him tenderly on one cheek. "You've done more than enough for Jeffy and me. We must go on alone."

She started from the room, but a hard grasp on her wrist stopped her short. "Cass, please . . ."

"Cass nothing!" Sandy pulled Amanda back and made her sit down in her chair again. Waving a finger in the woman's face, she lectured, "Now you listen to me. You're not going anywhere. Not if it means you're running away. Do that, and you're admitting that you're this Kelewhozis's property. You're *no one's* property, got that? While you were being dragged all over Fairyland for a couple of hundred years, we got a constitution, Lincoln freed the slaves, women got the vote, and Gloria Steinem said it was okay to get old. I think. If you keep your figure. Anyway, this is the twentieth century, by God! A woman's got some rights. It's all a matter of defending them.''

"Didn't I say she had a fighter's heart?" Cass was on his feet and in full elfin battle regalia. The effect was dazzling, for besides his gemmed circlet he now wore a starry corselet, greaves, and a skirt of tasses. He brandished a dragon-tongue sword of smoky-gray steel and a willow-leaf shield. "You have nothing to fear now, Amanda! With Sandy by my side, I will defend you to the death!" He slipped his small shield high up his arm and tried to embrace his chosen lady.

"Oh, put that down before you stick yourself!" Sandy smacked his shield arm down and gave his sword hand a shove for good measure. Sword and shield winked away. *"I'll* do the defending here, and not to anyone's death. Unless you get scabbard-happy again." She scowled at Cass.

"No, 'm." Cass's armor dulled and vanished. He dwindled back into his seat and had more tea with much too much sugar.

"Mrs. Walters, how can you defend the lady?" Davina asked anxiously. "It's the Fair Folk, the King of Elfhame you'll be facing!"

"Elfhame Ultramar," Cass mumbled into his cup.

"How can you stand against magic?" the Welsh girl cried.

Sandy smiled. "You forget," she said. "I'm a lawyer."

"Law against the powers of Faery!"

"Why not? It worked for Daniel Webster against the powers of hell.''

The doorbell rang. Before anyone could react, Sandy blithely took it upon herself to answer it.

The family resemblance was astounding. If she wouldn't have known him from Amanda's vision, his face and form were similar enough to Cass's for there to be no mistake. They even shared the same overweening, superior smirk.

"The King of Elfhame, I presume?" Sandy tendered her hand.

"Kelerison, Lord King of Elfhame Ultramar," he replied, ignoring it.

"Sandra Horowitz, Crown Princess of Alimony till It Hurts," she snapped back, and slammed the door in his face.

Chapter Eight:

A Woman Has Rights, and Occasionally a Sharp Left

Sandy slumped against the door. "Good Lord, what did I just do?" she asked, eyes rolling.

"Do? You were wonderful! Magnificent!" Cass skidded onto bended knee before her, in the style of many a boondocks Little Theater Romeo. Sandy didn't care for the way he stared at her balcony from that angle, but her pulse was still running too fast for her to chide him.

"Cass is right, Sandy." Amanda's meek voice was full of unspoken admiration. "You stood up to him. I—I didn't think anyone unprotected could do that and live."

"But she is protected, Amanda!" Cass was on his feet. His hand darted for Sandy's chest. She smacked him.

"Young man—"

"The stone, my lady. Show her the stone you wear." Sandy's frown made him add, "If you please."

She wore Rimmon's token next to her skin, under the rough cloth of her shirt, though silk itself would have felt rough in comparison to the bloodstone's touch. She pulled it out of her collar by its chain and let Amanda come close enough to study the glowing heart of it, the intricately carved flowers of its milky setting.

Amanda was awed. "How did you get this?"

Sandy shrugged. She didn't want to speak of Rimmon now, not with Cass's eyes so heavy on her. *Rimmon is dead,* she told herself firmly. *Dead and done with, as he was before you loved his ghost. Free of you, as you must get free of his memory. For Lionel's sake.* She felt a pang of guilt when she thought of her husband.

Amanda did not press the question. She touched the stone with the ball of one finger. "Elfin, but not made by any of the tribes I knew. It doesn't even belong to the old-world gathers. Kelerison showed me examples of their work, and this is not—"

"Speaking of Kelerison, he's still prettying up your doorstep. What are we going to do about him?" Sandy jerked her thumb at the door. "Wait until he goes away?"

Cass chuckled. "You don't have that much time. My father is persistent. Also immortal."

"Not really. Is he? No one lives forever!"

"My lady, you've never heard how old some of his jokes are. Unless he meets a violent death, he will not die."

"You mean he's going to hang around out there forever?"

"Until he gets what he came for."

Sandy gave Cass a speculative look. The elven seemed to be getting a good measure of jollies from the whole situation. His every word and mannerism was brimming with an obnoxious air of passing amusement at the ways of mortals. She wondered what had possessed him to throw in his lot with Amanda if he looked down on humans so much.

All right, baby, I won't spoil the show. If you want something to tickle you, I'll provide. She opened the front door again.

Kelerison was leaning on the jamb. She'd seen wolves with smaller grins and duller teeth. The King of Elfhame Ultramar wore a charcoal-gray pinstripe suit, a pink shirt with matching handkerchief protruding from the suit's breast pocket, and what looked like a genuine gold collar stay. His socks had the sheen of silk, and his shoes were Italian leather.

There was a pink flamingo, a palm tree, and a hula girl hand-painted on his tie.

"You really are from another world, aren't you?" said Sandy.

"Well? Aren't you going to ask me in?" Kelerison's voice had the low, hypnotic rumble of surf in a coral cavern. Try as she would, Sandy could not assign a mortal color value to his ever-changing eyes.

"It's not my home," she replied, forcing herself to remember that behind all this beauty was one mean soul. She silently thanked Rimmon's spirit for his gift of the bloodstone. If it carried some measure of magical protection, she was glad of it now that she faced Kelerison. "It's not up to me to invite you."

"But it is your place to insult me, then slam the door on me." His eyes were cool, his smile momentary.

"Sorry. We were expecting the Roto-Rooter man. You can imagine our disappointment. My apologies."

"You can make them better if you'll have me inside and offer me a cup of . . . Is that Darjeeling I smell?" His finely drawn nostrils twitched. Sandy wondered whether the fragrance of tea was the only message he sifted from the air.

Her arm went up, barring the doorway. "You'll have to take my apologies right where you are. I don't think it's in my client's best interests to see you now."

"Your client?" This time the amusement was more pronounced. Kelerison's thin, mobile mouth was about to explode with laughter.

"Amanda Taylor."

"Ah! Amanda . . . For a moment I believed that my son had finally had the good sense to hire someone else to fight his battles. The Powers know, he never had the wherewithal to fight them himself. You haven't the look of a swordswoman. Still, there have been sports. Can you hold steel?"

Sandy felt hard hands on her shoulders dragging her back from the door. "I can hold my own blade!" Cass shouted.

Now Kelerison did laugh. "That's a fine greeting for your father after all these years, Cassiodoron. However, if there's truth in it, I'm glad. Step outside, boy, into the garden that Amanda has cultivated so well with the help of *my* subjects. Take off that gewgaw"—he indicated the twisted symbol at Cass's throat—"and summon any weapon you like. Let's prove the truth of your claims."

Sandy's eyes went from father to son, son to father. She could feel the air between them tighten to a metallic scream, like the links of a wringing chain. There was a barrier between them, hot and thick with many old insults, grudges, scornings. It pushed them apart and tugged them nearer at the same time.

Then she looked down and noted that father and son both took great care that their feet remained on opposite sides of the threshold stone. Even Kelerison's hand, resting so jauntily on the doorjamb, kept scupulously to his own side of the invisible dividing line.

". . . or shall I come in after you?"

All the tension of confrontation fell away as Sandy shoved Cass back into the house. "You're not coming in here for anyone, and you know it." She stood staunchly in the doorway, arms akimbo. "Not without an invitation. Was I supposed to say something like, 'Enter freely and of your own will,' or is that for vampires?"

Kelerison laid his right hand to his breast in an elegant salute. "No swordswoman, I see, but able to split hairs neatly without a blade. A fighter with hard words and sharp insights. My compliments, Amanda!" he called into the darker reaches

of the house. "You haven't entirely misspent our time apart."
To Sandy he resumed, "And what is your calling, my lady
Sandra Horowitz? A priestess? An herbwife? A wise woman?
A bard, perhaps, in these degenerate climes?"

"I'm a lawyer," Sandy said.

Kelerison blanched.

"Law . . ." The word shook on the air. "A woman of
law! Why not a mooncalf, too, and a cockatrice hatched from
the same shell! What can a woman know of any law but
whim?"

"I don't think I like your attitude. I *know* I don't like
the way you've been treating my client. I can't do anything
about the first, but I'm willing to make cultural allowances.
About the second . . . I'm hereby serving you formal notice
that Ms. Amanda Taylor, hereinafter to be called the plaintiff,
is entering a request for the formal termination of any and all
bonds, unions, and associations, civil, religious, and/or common law, heretofor contracted with you, Kelerison, hereinafter
to be called the defendant, otherwise known as King of
Elfhame. Ultramar!" She tacked it on before Cass could prompt
her.

Kelerison heard her out, his exquisitely arched brows
coming together and remaining so until she had finished. Then
very gradually his forehead smoothed. A charming smile played
over his lips.

"Is it any wonder we are so taken with you mortal
women? Spice! Pepper on the tongue, honey under it. You
please me, Sandra Horowitz. And I see that one of my kind
was once able to please you." His eyes danced lasciviously
over her bloodstone token.

Sandy clapped a hand over it, feeling unaccountably naked. "My pleasure is none of your business!"

"Ah, but my pleasure is yours. And it pleases me to let
you play your little game, for the time being. Chatter on. In
the end, I will have my way. I will have Amanda back, and
her brat, and you, if that's what I've a mind to."

"You'll have nothing!"

An icy wind rushed through Sandy's clothes. Kelerison
whirled, and Sandy leaned out of the doorway to see Cass,
once more armed and armoured, standing before the lilac arbor. "Come on!" he cried. "Come and fight me now, before
you do any harm to these innocent folk."

The King of Elfhame Ultramar chuckled and rubbed his
chin. "Why, Cass, I could almost think you meant it."

For answer, Cass craned his neck so that his father might see that he no longer wore the protective symbol or its chain.

Sandy felt a furry shape nudge her ankles. "Idiot," Cesare grumbled. "Hothead. *Contadino ignorante.* Jerk." The tomcat looked up at Sandy. "Well? Are you going to stop him before or after his father makes him into meatballs?"

From the garden, Cass was shouting, "I'm ready for you, Father! I won't run away again! For the breaking of Amanda's bond, for the blood of my mother Bantrobel, for the crown of Elfhame Ultramar, I challenge you!"

"Oh dear," sighed Kelerison, apparently much distressed. "And here I left my sword in my Sunday pants. Now what did I pack in this suit?" He made a great business of patting down his pockets until he slipped a hand inside the jacket. A mottled sphere of green and gold—a cat's eye marble an inch in diameter—twinkled beneath his fingers. "Ah! Not a sword, but it will have to serve." He flicked it into the garden.

The marble described a high, narrow arc in the sun, and dribbled to a halt at Cass's feet. It lay still a moment, then began to turn faster and faster, filaments of gold whirling out from it, a spiral galaxy in small. The threads of gold steamed up, caught one to the next, twined, wove themselves into a gyrating pillar tinged with green.

"Boo," said Kelerison, and the green and golden light flattened down into a cranky dragonet the size of a Labrador retriever. The reptile spat fire with no great accuracy and let loose a croaking roar that broke on the bass note.

It wasn't very impressive, as dragons went. Sandy had seen better—or worse—in her time. She was about to ask Kelerison whether that was the best he could do when she saw that the King of Elfhame Ultramar had done well enough to suit his purposes.

Cass was on his knees, sword tossed aside, cowering behind his flimsy shield. She could hear the sound of dry sobs and see his whole body shaking uncontrollably.

"But it's a *lousy* dragon!" she protested.

"A pitiful specimen," Kelerison agreed. He spared a scornful glance at his son. "I seem to collect pitiful specimens."

"Cass!" Amanda was at Sandy's back, trying to get the elfin prince to look up. "Cass, it's only a little one! It's more afraid of you than you are of—" She tried to push past Sandy. Kelerison smiled.

"Back!" Sandy dug in her heels and fended off Amanda.

"Can't you see that's what he *wants* to happen? For you to go out of the house so he can grab you?"

"Alas." The King of Elfhame Ultramar shrugged his perfectly tailored shoulders. "Discovered."

Sandy ignored him. "You stay right in there," she told Amanda, and yanked an umbrella from the porcelain stand beside the door. Kelerison made no attempt to impede her as she flounced past him, down the steps.

The dragonet had lost interest in Cass and was rooting up the tulip beds when Sandy whacked him in the sheave hole with the umbrella handle. The beast hissed steam and took off for the high country.

"There, that's taken—"

Sandy didn't even have time to dust off her hands when the screech of brakes from the street and a meaty thud made her flinch. A car door opened and slammed, and the voice of a harassed motorist came wafting over the hedge: "*What* the hell did I hit? A fucking porcupine?"

"You see, dear lady"—Kelerison's mellifluous voice oozed condescension—"it is unwise to defy me. That was but a sample of what I can do."

"Some sample. Your pet dragon gets taken out by the first car up the block. My client and I are not exactly trembling in our boots."

"But my son is. I have never cared for grand displays of power, though my lady Bentrobel has always been at odds with me there. I find them wasteful. Magic, like much else, should be conserved against true need. I prefer to use just *enough* power to get the job done. In this case, my goal is to recover strayed property. There's no need for me to do anything spectacular . . . yet."

"*Property!*" Sandy leveled the umbrella at Kelerison's nose. "Amanda Taylor is not your *property!*" She flung the bumbershoot down and linked her arm under Cass's, hoisting him up. The prince was still shaking badly when she dragged him past his father and shoved him back into the shelter of Amanda's house. From the threshold she thundered, "You may be the King of Elfhame Ultramar, but you're in Connecticut now, brother, and this is *America!*"

Kelerison twiddled his forefinger and Sandy's clothing was transformed into a Las Vegas overkill-couture version of the Statue of Liberty, complete with red-white-and-blue-spangled pasties and a torch full of sparklers. Sandy's mouth opened and closed indignantly several times before she kicked the door

viciously to shut out the sound of the King of Elfhame Ultramar having the best laugh he'd enjoyed in centuries.

Chapter Nine:

Grounds for Divorce

"There, there," Davina said gently, passing Cass a
cup of tea liberally dosed with brandy. She and
Amanda had been trying to cajole him into good humor for a
quarter of an hour. The elfin prince sat between them on the
sofa and refused comfort. "Anyone might've reacted so on
seeing a true dragon in broad daylight."

"No, no, not when it was such a puny thing." Cass
shook his head miserably. "There were always at least three
or four that size mucking about under my mother's throne;
common household pests. Her youngest flower maidens would
shoo them out before high court began, and nip their tails when
they didn't run away fast enough. A *mortal* was able to dis-
patch it!" His hand swept toward Sandy, who was ensconced
in an armchair, huddling under a sheet thoughtfully fetched by
Amanda. Though Kelerison had cleared off the property, his
departure had not restored her original clothing.

"Actually I think it was a Mercedes," Sandy said, "That
sounded like Fred Morris's voice, and if the dragon dented his
bumper enroute to its eternal rest, he's going to be pissed."
Her mouth twitched. "What I wouldn't give to be there when
he tries explaining it to his insurance company."

"It's no use." Cass's head drooped. "My father's right.
I'm a coward. I've always been one, and I'll be one until the
end of time."

"You're not." Amanda stroked Cass's silver-gilt hair,
"I won't let you say that. Who made it possible for Jeff and
me to escape Kelerison? You risked everything for us. A coward wouldn't do that. A coward cares only for himself. All the
happiness I ever knew with Jeff was thanks to you."

Cass looked away.

Sandy plucked burnt-out sparklers from her hair one by one.

"Cass, right now I don't care whether your father thinks you're the Queen of the May. We need your assessment of him more than his of you, and you're not going to give us accurate information if you're all curled up into a tight little ball of self-pity. So you fell to pieces over a midget Godzilla. Big deal! You should see me when I unearth a nest of worms in the garden. And God forbid anyone should see Lionel come face-to-face with a cockroach. Everyone's got his little squeamish point. Yours is dragons."

Davina rested her hand on his shoulder. "I still sleep with a wee light shining, against the bogles."

"What you've got is"— Sandy searched the air for the proper term—"*Dracophobia gravis*. Nothing therapy won't cure if you want to get rid of it. But in the meantime, don't let simple fear of dragons cripple your life."

There was a new hope in the elfin prince's face. "You mean . . . I'm not a coward after all?"

"Rest easy. You're just a neurotic like the rest of us."

"Praise the Powers!" He took the cup Davina offered and drank it off.

"Now, let's see where we stand." Sandy clasped the bloodstone as if for luck or inspiration, and not for the last time. "You've been saying that I'm 'protected' by this. Protected how? From what?"

"The same way that Cass and I—and Jeffy too—are protected by these." Amanda opened one button of her blouse to show Sandy the symbol she wore. A quick glance in Cass's direction showed that his was back around his neck. "It's a rune of ancient power to ward off the lesser mischiefs of the elvenkind and their kindred."

Davina leaned toward Cass for a closer look at his. Sandy caught herself wondering whether the Welsh girl didn't linger a bit longer than need be to study the silver tangle the elf-prince wore. "Ah, I think I've seen like marks on age-old stones near Caer Mab. Holy stones, we sometimes called them."

"Lesser mischiefs." Sandy frowned. "That doesn't sound like much protection."

"It covers every eventuality short of outright combat," Cass snapped. "Combat, and all the formalities it entails, isn't something my folk enter into lightly. We can do more harm than you'd care to imagine with our *lesser* mischiefs."

"You needn't sound so damned proud of it," Sandy retorted. "How about abduction? Does that come under the heading of lesser mischiefs? Can Kelerison just up and grab you, Amanda?"

"Not while I am in my own home, unless he's invited to cross the threshold."

"Aha! So I was right."

"And not if he ever wants to carry me over the border into the Elfhame Ultramar again."

"Which is exactly what he wants," Cass growled. "It won't be a triumph for Father until he can show his court the willing captive recaptured. Unless she gives her consent, by word or sign, she'd be worth no more to him than a changeling."

"The Fair Folk are famous for tricking mortals into consent," Davina put in. She averted her eyes from Cass's cool gaze and added, "Often a kiss was the sign."

"But he *could* whisk you off to somewhere like—oh—Poughkeepsie, for example?" Sandy asked.

"Poughkeepsie?" Amanda had to laugh. "What would possess Kelerison to journey there?"

"Maybe he'd got a Vassar girl on the side. Maybe he's visiting relatives. Maybe he wants to buy an IBM computer so the Tooth Fairy can run a spreadsheet, how should I know? It was just an example. My point is, if he can snatch you away by magic, he might pick some desolate spot as journey's end and use it to break your spirit, threaten to leave you there unless you agree to return to Elfhame Ultramar with him." Amanda was still smiling at the idea until Sandy added, "Or he might take your son."

Amanda's hand flew to her mouth. Cass put his arm around her protectively. "It's all right, Amanda," he reassured her. To Sandy he said, "You're right. Nothing could prevent my father from taking the boy; nothing in the realm of magic. He could even transport the child to Elfhame Ultramar, if he so chose. The symbol will not save Jeffy from that. He is young enough to be brought into the elfin halls without his agreement."

"Why does his age matter?"

"Have you heard of changelings? Mortal children spirited away and replaced by one of our own?"

"Good Lord, yes," Sandy said. "But I never believed it."

"And I never saw the sense of it," Davina added. "Why should the Fair Folk want to trade their own children for human ones?"

"The elvenkind seldom indulge the custom," Cass explained. "But we are only one of the Five Peoples of the Air.

Water sprites and the Winged Ones too prefer to raise their own babies, but the People of the Darkness—goblins, brownies, trolls, karkers, and that crowd—make the exchange often; for a good reason. Have you ever tried to housebreak a karker?''

"The pleasure's been denied me. Water sprites, Winged Ones, People of the Darkness, elves . . . That's four. You mentioned the *Five* Peoples of the Air, Cass.''

The elfin prince was grim. "The People of Blood make five. I wish they did not.''

"How old does a child have to be before he's safe?''

"When they reach puberty, the Fair Folk can't touch them,'' Amanda said.

"I don't like this.'' Cass frowned in concentration. "If Kelerison can steal your son—or my daughter, because I'm helping you—he's got too big a trump card in his hand.''

Cass came near and took Sandy's hands in his own. "He will never dare. If he does, he knows that I will kill him.''

Sandy did not like the way Cass's eyes glowed when he said that. She tried to withdraw her hands, but he wasn't letting go. *Like father, like son.* The tag kept running through her head. Her voice was hoarse when she said, "I'd better get home and start work on the case. I'll have to do some research. I—I'd appreciate it if you could lend me something to wear, Amanda.''

"Of course.'' Amanda brought her a raincoat while Davina went to get Ellie out of Jeffy's room. As Sandy slipped it on, Amanda said, "Thank you, Sandy. What you're doing for Jeffy and me—''

"Nothing's *done.* '' To herself, she thought, *Why is this woman thanking me? What in heaven's name good can I do her, really? Mortal law against a creature of magic? We're tilting at dreams.* She made herself smile. "I mean, nothing's done *yet.* But it won't take long. You're a free woman, and we're going to make Kelerison know it.''

Davina brought a very sulky Ellie back into the room. "Jeffy fibbed. Wasn't any dragon egg in his room, just an old turkey egg, and *that* was hollow.''

Cass gave the child his hand. "I'll tell you a story about a dragon on the way home. Will that make you happy?''

Ellie gave him a penetrating stare. "Tell it first.''

"Wait a minute, we don't need you to walk us—''

Cass cut off Sandy's protest. "I would feel better if I saw you safely home, and I'm sure my . . . mother agrees.''

Amanda squeezed Sandy's arm. "He's right. Let him take you home. You don't know Kelerison."

"What I know, I don't like. If you insist. . ." Sandy thought she caught the flicker of a sly smile on Cass's lips, but when she looked him full in the face, he was all sobriety. As the four of them walked down the streets of Godwin's Corners, he told Ellie the promised dragon story and seemed to be completely indifferent to both Sandy and Davina.

Then they were home.

So was Lionel. "Cass Taylor, I hope you're here with an excuse for missing class." Lionel flung open the front door while Sandy was still jiggling the key in the lock. His reading glasses had slid down his nose and his dark hair was as rumpled as his shirt. Sandy read all the earmarks of a rough day in the trenches of Academe.

"Yes, sir. Oh, yes, sir, I do. I mean, I am." Cass was seventeen again, and perhaps a shade younger. You could almost hear his knees knocking together as he confronted an angry teacher. Now that Sandy thought of it, she couldn't recall any boy of Cass's supposed years who acted half so skittish, awkward, and desperate to please adults.

He's so blaringly harmless. It's not natural. But it's damned good protective coloration. It caters to every adult's dearest fantasies about how they wish their teenagers would behave, so they don't question a good thing too closely. Nice move, Cass.

"Cass's little brother had an accident at school and his mother couldn't come for him," Sandy explained smoothly.

Lionel readjusted his spectacles. "What are you doing in that raincoat?"

"Avoiding arrest." Sandy dropped the coat. Ellie shrieked with delight at Mommy's spangled splendor.

"Good Lord!" Lionel yanked her into the house, the others coming after. He shut and bolted the door, then demanded, "Have you really lost your—get *away* from that open window!—mind?"

"Lionel, dear," Sandy said slowly, holding her husband's eyes with her own, "something new has been added to Godwin's Corners. Let me see, how can I put this? Darling, do you remember how you and I first met?"

The blood left Lionel's face. He tried to speak, but no words came.

"You see, Cass?" Sandy said, "You're not the only one who suffers from *Dracophobia gravis.*"

"Is that how you met?" Cass's eyebrows rose. "Against a dragon? You and . . . *him?*"

Sandy had heard the same scorn in Kelerison's voice when he'd learned she was a lawyer. She didn't like it any better when it came from his son and was aimed at her husband.

"I'll tell you all about it sometime." Every word was frigid. "For the moment, all you need to know is that Lionel—Professor Walters—and I have had some previous experience with the unearthly."

"You, yes." Cass stared at the bloodstone, and a good deal more. "But—"

Lionel whipped one of Sandy's own coats out of the hall closet and draped it over her, glaring at his student. "What business is it of yours, Taylor?" His hands remained on Sandy's shoulders and he pulled her back against his chest.

Cass returned Lionel's hard look. He was no longer playing at being the dream-perfect, impossibly docile seventeen-year-old. Though his features remained the same, something intangible about him seemed to take on the privileged mantle of years. "Since Sandy has seen fit to tell me that there is more to your past life than I thought, allow me to admit you to my confidence as well, *Professor* Walters. And the first thing you should know is that I prefer not to be called by a name that isn't mine."

"Now look, Cass—"

"Cassiodoron. *Prince* Cassiodoron, *Professor.*"

Cass let every human vestige fall away. He did not put on armor for his silent revelation, or even a tunic of nixie-woven watersilk. Nothing wrought by men or elvenkind hid his body from full view. Davina gave a little gasp, and even Sandy heard herself draw a long, deep breath of awe to see so much naked beauty.

Lionel's hands felt cold, even through the heavy wool of the coat. It took Sandy several moments before she realized that they were a dead weight on her shoulders. She touched them, and found them immobile. She dipped slightly and stepped out from under their empty grasp.

Lionel's eyes were fixed on the wall opposite. Davina and Ellie stood in similarly rigid attitudes, trapped in the chill hold of a spell. Their skins were hard and shone with the semigloss of mannequins, the minutes petrifying over them.

"Don't be afraid, Sandy." Cass's voice was in her ear.

"They're all right. I wouldn't harm any of your folk for the throne of Old Elfhame itself."

"Then what have you done to them? Why?" She rounded on him, fists up. He only smiled at her within a cocoon of opalescent light. She knew then that she would never touch him if he did not wish it. Her hands slowly came down. "Let them go."

"Soon." The rainbow aura faded from him. He was still unbearably fair to see, lovely as only the truly alien can be when it leaves all mortal things—the beautiful and the ugly alike—equally ordinary to the eye. He extended one beckoning hand to her almost languidly, as if his mind were on something else entirely. Her own arms rose with similar independent movement and she stepped into his embrace.

The garish costume his father had given her melted into a robe of translucent green silk, cool as the water of a mountain freshet. His mouth, when it covered hers, was honey sweet. When he permitted the kiss to end and she looked at his face, it was neither young nor old, as she and her race could reckon such things. No matter how many times he would put on his mortal appearance afterward, this was the face she would have before her eyes, his true seeming.

She drew back from him, breaking the enchanted hold of his eyes. "No . . . no, you had no right to do that."

"I know." There was no triumph in his expression. "It was base of me, but I had to do it. You would never have allowed it on your own, and that kiss . . . I could have commanded more. I know that I desire more. Will you thank me for that?"

"For what?"

"I knew you wouldn't understand."

"It wouldn't matter to you if I did," she said. "Would it?" He shook his head. "I thought not. I'm only . . . a mortal. You use your powers over us just because you can."

"If you had such powers, you would not use them?"

"Not for something like this." The name she thought she would never speak aloud again to another soul was on her lips. "Rimmon never did. He used the strength he had to fight what was evil, not to add to it."

"And you see my love as evil?"

"If you must compel me to love you, then—your love isn't love, and the evil is yourself. And Kelerison's, for never having taught you any differently."

Cass pulled back at the sound of his father's name as if

from a slap. His eyelids lowered. "A point. A sharp one. My
father doesn't know what he'll have to face with you, my lady.
With all your barbs, you can't convince me to stop loving you,
wanting you, but I will concede this: I swear by the sacred
stones of Old Elfhame never more to use my magic to gain the
smallest token of your affection. Oh, don't think I'm giving
up! I'll have you. But it will be love willingly given, on your
part. Are you content?"

"Yes. As soon as you add a promise not to use your
magic that way on any other mortals."

The Prince of Elfhame Ultramar made an incredulous
face. "Is that all? Well, to please you, I'll swear to that as
well. Will you tell me why I must?"

Sandy's teeth flashed. "Call it part of my retainer fee.
And heaven knows, *someone's* got to teach you some manners
or you'll never get a date for the senior prom. Now please
defrost my family and get me into some normal suburban
clothes. Lionel and I have a lot to talk about. He'll be a big
help to us, you'll see."

"I could almost think he was a serious rival." Cass
cocked his head at Sandy's unmoving husband.

"Hm," she returned, noncommittally.

The elfin prince gestured, and he became Cass Taylor in
the same breath that restored the three frozen mortals to life.
Sandy's instantaneous hair-crisping scream nearly refroze them
all.

"*This* is your idea of normal suburban clothing?" She
spread her arms so that all could see the ballooning muu-muu
she wore, flamingos and alligators in aerobic suits rioting across
the material.

"That's my idea of an improvement," said Cass.

Davina mumbled something in Welsh. "*What?*" Sandy
barked.

"The small revenges of Elfhame take strange form."

Chapter Ten:

You Won't Even Know I'm Here

Lionel was waiting for her when she pulled into the driveway. "Any trouble in New Haven?" he asked.

"Not a hitch." Sandy slammed the car door after getting a large, black book out of the backseat. "In the papers, I called him Thomas Keller—the name he's registered under at the Silver Swan Inn—but I tacked on his real name as an a.k.a. just to make sure: Kelerison, Rex Elfhame Ultramaris. Anything sounds legitimate in Latin. Let the court think he's a nut case. How about here?"

"No problems. Ellie got a little fractious about wearing her protective pendant, but Davina reasoned her into it; said Barbie and the Rockers all wear necklaces just like it. Ellie claims the iron wire's too itchy." He scratched his own chest through his rugby shirt. "I kind of agree with her. Is there such a thing as an allergy to magic?"

"Don't be silly."

"Hey, you're the woman who christened *Dracophobia gravis*. Maybe I've got . . . *eczema elficus?*"

"Lionel . . ."

"Okay, okay." He lowered his voice and added, "With or without a name, Cassiodoron makes me sick."

"My, my, do I hear the jolly green-eyed beast on the prowl?"

"You told me he's after you. How do you expect me to feel?" Lionel's brow furrowed. "I don't like the act he puts me through every day in class, Sandy. He's taunting me. Swear to God, the little creep's been behaving like even more of a klutz than before, especially when he knows I'm watching. I don't want to play 'Our Little Secret' with him. And when we run our regular game—"

"Don't tell me he's been playing an elf?"

Lionel touched a finger to the tip of his nose. "And winning by so damn much that he leaves the rest of us gasping. He makes a big deal out of it all being the luck of the roll, but then he looks right at me and . . ." Abruptly, Lionel hugged Sandy close. She could feel his arms shake with the intensity of his grip on her.

She tried to distract him. "Did Amanda call?"

"Every fifteen minutes since I've been home." He relaxed a little. "She really seems to think what you're doing—filing divorce proceedings and all—will exorcise this elf-king. She's probably haunting her phone. Are you going to call her now?"

"I suppose I should. Here, earn your keep." She shoved the book at him.

Lionel hefted it experimentally. "Doing a little light reading? What is this?"

"*Black's Law Dictionary.* I got an older edition cheap at the Yale Co-op. I figured that while I was in the neighborhood, I might as well see about adding to my law library, pitiful though it is."

"You can buy more books when you settle this case." Lionel chuckled. "What kind of alimony can you ask the King of Elfhame Ultramar to pay? Ten percent off the top of the pixie dust trade? A cut of toadstool rentals to leprechauns?"

Sandy wasn't laughing. "What am I doing this for, Lionel? How far is the joke going to go? Have you ever heard Cass talk about his father?"

"I'm too young to listen to gutter talk."

"I mean it. Cass has magic—you've seen it—but he really is just a boy by their system. His father is an adult, and a king, with a ruler's magical powers to command. What could he do if he felt like it? To Amanda? To Jeffy?"

"To us?" Lionel asked it for her. He put one arm around her, cradling the law book in the the crook of the other. They walked into the house. "He hasn't done anything yet."

"What does that prove? He could be toying with us. I feel like I'm acting in a farce. I go into New Haven; I file a divorce complaint for a woman who was born over two hundred years ago; I file it against a being to whom two hundred years is an afternoon; I call it divorce because I don't know what else to call it, but they were never married." She sat at the kitchen table and rested her head in her hand.

"No?" Lionel was genuinely surprised. He set the law book down in front of her and put the kettle on.

"You didn't know? Kelerison's wife is one of his own kind: Queen Bantrobel. She's Cassidoron's mother."

Lionel clattered around with the tea things. "I'm no lawyer, Sandy, but if Amanda never was Kelerison's wife—and forget about the problem of getting the elf-king to show up in court in the first place—how can a divorce do anything to help her?"

Sandy sighed. "Sometimes you build a case on a little evidence and a lot of wanting."

"What about when there's no evidence?"

"There is." A folded sheet of letter paper fanned from her hand to his. Beneath the logo of the Silver Swan Inn ("Godwin's Corners on the Green Since 1805") was a lengthy message in an ornate copperplate hand. Lionel read it carefully, and when he was done, he and the teakettle simultaneously released a long, slow whistle.

" '. . . endured your insults and threats for far too long, out of a misplaced tolerance for mortal foibles. I expected common sense to assert itself, that you would tire of your silly game. I have watched your comings and goings in ways you can never imagine, waiting. At first I told myself that it was only a woman's pastime, for lack of anything truly productive to occupy your—' Jesus, Sandy, don't kill him; he's got a rotten kid to bring up."

"Ha-ha. Read on."

" 'Now I see that you mean to see this charade through to the end, even to entering my name on the documents of your mortal courts of law. I warn you, if you remain bound to this foolish course of self-destruction, I will see to it that you regret it. Amanda is nothing to you. My son is less than nothing. Renounce them while you can. Share their folly and you shall share their punishment.' " Lionel refolded the paper. "And they say the art of letter writing is dead. What's this evidence of, besides terminal elvish snotitude?"

"It's what's kept me working for Amanda when every cell of my brain's screaming for me to stop, to think, to see that I'm wasting my time. Don't you see, Lionel?" She took the letter back and waved it under his nose. "Can't you *smell* it? All this blustering, all this posturing, all these dire warnings . . . He's *afraid!* Kelerison, King of Elfhame Ultramar, is afraid of me, of what I'm doing! If he weren't, would he be trying to frighten me off? No! He'd just sit back and laugh, then reach out and do whatever the hell he wanted with Amanda."

Lionel turned off the kettle and poured steaming water into the cups. "I think you're right. Maybe you aren't wasting your time with this case. But if Kelerison is that scared . . ." He looked troubled.

"Yes?"

"Shouldn't we be a little scared too?"

The phone rang before Sandy could answer. "That's got to be Amanda. Again. I'll get it," she said. She was gone from the room for half an hour. When she returned, her tea was cold and her face would have made Cassandra of Troy beg for Advanced Foreboding lessons.

"That was my mother."

"?"

"She's coming here tomorrow. She wants me to meet her for lunch. She's had a simply delightful letter from a perfectly charming gentleman who's heard *wonderful* things about her professional reputation."

"Your mother's little hobby? She's a Bright Choice Girl, God help us. She does everything but cure cancer by changing the way a person color-coordinates his wardrobe. Who'd call that a profession?"

"And so," Sandy forged on, "he insists that she and no other is going to handle his case, transportation paid and order guaranteed in advance. You can guess how thrilled he was to learn that she had relatives in Godwin's Corners. It's just exactly midway between New York and where he lives, and he was going to be meeting with a client there anyway, what an amazing coincidence, so why don't they get together at the Silver Swan Inn." Her teeth clenched. "I'll kill him."

"You mean the King of Elfhame Ultramar . . .?"

"—is going to get his colors done by my mom."

Kelerison smiled his most disarming smile as he raised Mrs. Horowitz's hand to his lips. Smartly turned out in a trim brown herringbone suit, his golden hair tastefully threaded with silver and the skin of his high-boned face lined just enough to be attractively craggy, the elf-king was every older woman's *beau ideal.* Sandy's mother giggled like a bubblegum-rock fan, though toward the end she tried to turn it into a throaty laugh. Sandy made a pained face, which went unnoticed.

"I can't express my gratitude sufficiently, Mrs. Horowitz, for your consenting to travel all this way just to accommodate me."

Mrs. Horowitz made deprecating noises. "I would have come all the way to your place of work, Mr. Keller, if you'd have preferred. Business is business. *I* take my career seriously." She shot a look at Sandy, but her daughter prudently had established eye contact with the life-sized wooden swan decoy sailing over the inn's public-room hearthstone. "And after that flattering letter you sent me, I couldn't do less."

"Madame is gracious. Shall we go in to lunch?" He offered her his arm, which Mrs. Horowitz latched on to like an anorexic lamprey.

"Catch you later, Mom," Sandy said. "I don't want to be the fifth wheel at a business meeting."

"But you must join us," Kelerison said suavely. "I insist. How often does a man of my years get to boast that he squired two such lovely young ladies at the same time?"

Mrs. Horowitz had mastered the whiskey laugh by this time, and she loosed it on an undeserving world. "Mr. Keller, if there were more gentlemen like you, we wouldn't need an Equal Rights Amendment."

"There aren't many like him," Sandy mumbled. "You can bet on that."

"Don't swallow your words, Sandra," Mrs. Horowitz rapped out briskly. "If you have something worth saying, say it so that we can all hear." To Kelerison she added, "You try and try with your children, but it never ends, does it?"

Sandy privately agreed that it went on forever. She trailed into the dining room in the frothy wake of her mother and the King of Elfhame Ultramar.

An iron-grip rapport was welded into place between Mrs. Horowitz and Kelerison before the second round of G&Ts had been cleared away. Sandy poked at a rose-colored abomination of shaved ice, tequila, and smooshed strawberries while her luncheon companions discussed children: King Lear Didn't Know the Half of It.

"At least your daughter can be said to be settled in life. Somewhat," Kelerison said. "Correct me if I am wrong. She has a nice house right here in Godwin's Corners—"

"It would be nicer if she kept it clean, but you know these young women today. Dusting isn't *relevant*, and waxing the kitchen floor isn't *fulfilling*. If the board of health ever checked up on them, then you'd see fulfillment."

"And she has a husband who's doing well—"

Mrs. Horowitz sniffed. "A teacher. He could do better. But I never say a word. It's not my business what he does with his life. Not one word. Such a *sweet* boy Lionel is, too. The things he puts up with . . ."

Sandy stabbed her swizzle stick into the pink slush in her glass and told herself it was Kelerison's heart.

"Then there's her child—"

"An angel. And I'm not just saying that because I'm Ellie's grandma."

Kelerison raised his glass. "I believe that, Mrs. Horowitz; though anything's easier to believe than the fact that a woman who looks like you is a grandmother already."

"Sandy was in a hurry," Mrs. Horowitz said, after the correct amount of oh-get-along-with-you-now tittering.

Sandy's chair scraped backward from the table. "I really have to be going. . . ."

"Sandra, *sit.*" Sandy sat. "Isn't that just like a child? Hasn't *touched* her drink, and completely forgot she ordered lunch, and yet whoops, tally-ho, off she goes. Where on earth do you have to be this very minute? Not that I'd be surprised to hear you'd scheduled something right on top of your own mother. God knows, Mr. Keller, I try not to intrude—young couples today love impromptu entertaining so long as it's *not* a blood relative; then it's *intruding*—but you'd think I was coming all the way up here from New York, through all that terribly exhausting traffic, every other day and twice on Sundays from the way my own daughter can't seem to wait to get our visits over with."

Sandy sank lower in her chair and took a long pull on her Montezuma's Lady. "I don't have any appointments, Mother. My mistake."

"Sandra, darling, didn't I give you a nice Gucci appointment book for your birthday? If you'd look at it, you wouldn't be flying off in all directions at once. Don't you have it with you?" Sandy's negative reply was met by a heave of the maternal bosom. "I'm not surprised. Not in the least. It was *only* bought at Bloomingdale's. Not on sale, either; full price. And what I would've heard if I'd have given you a nice blouse or some perfume instead. 'Mom, I'm a *career* woman! Mom, why don't you ever give me something I can use in my profession?' My Sandra's a lawyer, you know," she confided in Kelerison.

"Really." He sipped his drink, rainbow eyes fixed on Sandy over the glass's rim.

"Where *are* you keeping that appointment book, Sandra? No, never mind, don't tell me. You've either lost it in the hodgepodge you call a desk or it's still in its box on the hall table. The day you use it will probably be the day you write me a thank-you note for it."

Sandy stopped playing with her drink and disposed of it in one desperate gulp, then flagged the waitress for a refill.

Mrs. Horowitz made an offhand comment about too many drinks before five being bad for girls whose complexions are sallow to start with, then leaned across the table to implore, "Do *your* children give you any pleasure at all, Mr. Keller?"

"Not recently."

Sandy's lunch passed in a pink tequila fog while her mother and Kelerison commiserated on the shortcomings of their respective offspring. Through the pleasant buzzing in her ears, Sandy became marginally aware of the fact that Kelerison was speaking of having *two* sons; not just Cass, but Jeffy too was mentioned.

Mrs. Horowitz brought out the swatches at the same time that the mobcapped waitress wheeled around the dessert trolley. The King of Elfhame Ultramar ordered strawberries and *schlag* for the table while Mrs. Horowitz segued into her Bright Choice spiel. Sandy goggled at the plate of strawberries in front of her. A chorus line of Montezuma's Ladies did the *jarabe tapatío* across her line of sight while she valiantly tried to keep lunch from rising to the occasion. She came groggily to her feet.

"I really ought to be going. . . ."

"Nonsense, Sandra. Sit down and have some coffee. Black." Her mother's waspish tone and her own lack of intestinal fortitude made Sandy's legs fold obediently. "I'm sure Mr. Keller would like a younger woman's opinion on which Life Direction Spectrum looks best on him. We always get outside input, Mr. Keller, so our clients never have to have second thoughts about whether they were railroaded into a decision by a pushy consultant."

"Pushy, Mrs. Horowitz?" Kelerison adjusted the set of the mauve swatch currently draping his chest. "You?" His eyelashes were thick and black as the bristles on a mascara brush, and he could bat them without looking a whit less masculine.

"What do you think, Sandra? With that fair skin and hair I'd say he's a definite East, although those eyes . . ." She removed the mauve sample and tried a turquoise one on him for effect. "Now you look like the classic North type, except . . . Mr. Keller, you have the most perplexing eyes." She plucked at the swatch coquettishly. "They make me want to change your Life Direction from one minute to the next."

"Ah, Mrs. Horowitz, your daughter is already seeing to that."

"What?" Mrs. Horowitz's hands dropped into her lap.

"My Life Direction, as you say, has certainly been changed. My children may not be all I'd like, but I had hoped to see them occasionally. Thanks to your daughter's efforts, that won't be the case much longer."

Mrs. Horowitz's flinty stare slewed from Kelerison, noble and heavy-hearted, to her daughter, tiddlywinked to the gills. "Sandra. . ."

Kelerison's hand closed on Mrs. Horowitz's. "Please, Mrs. Horowitz; when I asked to see you today, I never knew that your daughter was *that* Sandra Horowitz. It is such a common name, n'est-ce pas?"

"Oui," Mrs. Horowitz replied in stony French. She had stopped shooting eye daggers at her child and escalated to tactical nukes.

"It was just a name on some . . . very painful papers."

Kelerison bowed his head and shaded his eyes with one hand. "She's only doing her job. I suppose you ought to be proud of her. If I were thinking clearly, I never would have mentioned the divorce at all, but when I saw her, when I learned she was a lawyer, when I put two and two together, when I think of never seeing dear little Jeffy again—" He choked nicely. "I shouldn't have brought up the subject."

Sandy was trying not to bring up anything else. She hadn't a prayer of mounting a decent self-defense when her mother went for the kill.

"You are handling this gentleman's divorce?"

"Oh, she's not interested in my side of it at all," Kelerison said meekly. "Don't trouble her."

"What's this about his never seeing his children again? Sandra, stop turning green this instant. I want an answer."

Sandy gave her peristaltic process a severe reprimand, swallowed hard, and was at last able to reply, "He can see them if they want to see him."

"Amanda convinced the older boy to run away with her when Jeffy was just a baby," Kelerison slipped in gracefully. "Cass is a teenager. It's a very difficult age, especially when you're dealing with a parent of the same sex."

Mrs. Horowitz's mouth grew small and hard as a nut as she stared at her daughter and thought back over the years to the truth of this.

"He's a very romantic boy, and he always was readier to believe Amanda's side of things. Freud was right. I hoped for a reconciliation, but by the time I traced them here, Amanda had already made your daughter's acquaintance and . . ." Kelerison shrugged, his eyes artfully moist.

The strawberries were rubbery, the *schlag* a puddle of curds, and the early diners just starting to be seated before Mrs. Horowitz finished with Sandy. She only paused long enough to assure "Mr. Keller" that he was one of the rare North-East blends and to take his order for a Bright Choice Life Direction Spectrum Wardrobe Compass Computer Kit. The King of Elfhame Ultramar discreetly paid the check and absented himself from the table while the harangue continued.

Only the thought of driving back to New York in the dark made Mrs. Horowitz call a temporary truce. "I'll be expecting your call when you've come to your senses and convinced Mr. Keller's wife to stop being silly." She rose grandly from the table. "Or I'll call you."

Sandy ordered a Coke to settle her various assaulted internal systems, and also to give her mother a good head start. She was feeling a little better when she stepped out into the crisp autumn air.

"Sandra . . ." Kelerison flowed from the shadows on the inn's long porch.

"That was dirty pool, Your Majesty. How would you like it if I called *your* mother in on this little mess?"

"My mother has passed into mythology. We don't see much of each other. I warned you. Will you be sensible?"

"Will you tell my mommy on me again if I say no?"

He gave a short laugh. "In all the years of my exile, in every conflict I have ever known, with every opponent I have ever faced, I have never once had to repeat a battle gambit. And why should I? A contest should be elegant as well as exciting. It should not merely crush the loser, but glorify the victor."

Sandy's hand closed on the bloodstone. "Don't tell me the story of your love life, 'Mr. Keller.' "

He made her a mocking bow. "My dear, for the duration of my stay here, you may call me Thomas. For Thomas the Rhymer. It's a pretty tale. He kissed our elfin queen and so became her thrall for three years, though that was by the time of Old Elfhame. Far more time had passed in the world above. When his service was done, he found nothing of his old life, nothing he had loved or known left. He thought he was doing a brash, bold deed, to take that kiss from the elfin queen. He learned that any mortal who tries to play the swaggering hero at our expense soon pays quite a different reckoning."

Sandy felt the bloodstone pulse like a small heart in her hand. A dear, lost voice whispered in her mind, *Do not fear him, my lady. You have faced greater evils than mere pride and ignorance.*

"Don't worry, my lord king," she replied. "I won't be kissing you."

Kelerison showed a wry smile. "Doubtless my son will be happy to hear that."

Sandy blushed a deep crimson that clashed with her red hair. "I won't be kissing him, either."

"A fighter, are you?" Kelerison's smile twisted even more. "Then you may win. Against him, I mean. Cassiodoron was always faster with his feet than with his sword when a fighter was about. He ran off shortly before Lord Syndovar was supposed to put him through the combat trial of manhood. It didn't take me long to wonder how much of his flight was for Amanda's sake and how much for his own."

An invisible hand seized Sandy's chin. Kelerison chuckled as she tried to slap away what she could not see and only flailed the air. His visible hands remained leaning on the porch rail while Sandy's chin was forced up.

"Yes, a fighter," Kelerison said, gazing into her eyes at his pleasure. "But why must you ally yourself with the losing side? Use your talents of persuasion for me, Sandra Horowitz. Surely you see that I will win in the end, and you would do very well to be with me when I do."

"If you're so sure of victory, why do you need me?"

Sandy tried to jerk her chin free, but the unseen grip on it was too strong.

"A whim. A wish to see whether this whole unpleasant affair can be terminated more quickly with your help. I don't want to keep Amanda in Elfhame Ultramar forever. There were simply some . . . loose ends left there that I thought she ought to resolve. Then she will be returned to this world, a free woman."

"And Jeffy?"

"Unlike some of my subjects, I have no interest in keeping mortal brats. Well, my lady? Will you aid me?"

Cold encircled Sandy's neck. The hand that clasped the bloodstone pendant felt heavy strands overlay it. The King of Elfhame's face rippled featureless and became a silver mirror that let Sandy see the wealth of precious gems set in gold now hanging in tiers of ruby, diamond, and sapphire from her neck.

Then Kelerison's eyes floated above the reflection of her own, and his thought was clear as if spoken aloud.

This is but a sample of how I reward those who serve me. Well, my lady? What is your reply?

Sandy spat into the mirror.

All the elf-king's magic vanished. The chains were gone, the grasp on her chin released, Kelerison was wearing his Thomas Keller mask again. It was a harsh, ominous mask.

"So my son has found his equal in folly."

Sandy put on a chipper look. "Tsk. I'm sorry if my turn-down was a little unpolished, Your Majesty. I'm new to the practice. For months I haven't had one client, and suddenly I'm deluged. But it wouldn't be ethical for me to change sides. You do understand?"

"I understand that whether you persist in this or not, I will have Amanda. If I can't convince you to abandon her cause out of plain self-interest, I'll find others of your kind to convince you for me."

This time Sandy's chin came up of her own volition. "If you mean anyone in my house, they're all on my side."

"I envy you their loyalty. However, you mortals are strangely interdependent beings, and there are more than just your household members living in this town."

A hostile glint came into Sandy's eyes. "What are you going to do?"

"Make a gift of Godwin's Corners to my subjects, sweet lady, and sign every card with your name. And Amanda's. How long do you think these simple people will be able to stand all the lesser mischiefs of Faery before they beg—no, before they *order* you to give up Amanda's case?"

"Nobody gives me orders." Sandy's hand tightened to a fist around the bloodstone. "And in case you've forgotten, this is America—don't you *dare* put me in that spangled outfit again, you bastard!—and the last king who tried bullying us into doing something we didn't want was George the Third. So you can take your lesser mischiefs and—"

Kelerison twirled his little finger.

A whirlwind corkscrewed down the chimney of the Silver Swan, tore shingles from the roof, leaped the porch railing, and swept Sandy up into the air. The wildly funneling wind dipped and soared across the dusky town green, the houses and streets below all a swirl, the early stars streaks of light to Sandy's eyes. She was frightened too breathless to scream, and by the time she had gathered enough breath for a hearty shriek, the mad ride came to an end with the twister grazing the steeple of the Congregational church and dropping her off on the roof.

The air beside her turned to tweed as Kelerison materialized, smugger than a spoiled cat, rump in the rain gutter and feet dangling over the edge. "Well, I see that that fascinating pendant of yours doesn't interfere with transportation spells. How useful to know. I beg your pardon, my lady, but what were you saying we could do with our lesser mischiefs?"

With a great effort to hold her hands steady, Sandy reached into the pocket of her skirt and extracted a large envelope folded into thirds. She passed this to Kelerison, who, with a speculative quirk of the lips, opened it. His expression passed from mild mirth to puzzlement to blackest anger as he read the contents.

"Now you can ship me all the way to Peoria, if you're too scared to face me here," Sandy said. "It won't make any difference where I am. The complaint's been filed, the process has been manually delivered, as per Connecticut state law, and you, sir"—she smiled stiffly to keep her teeth from chattering—"have been served."

Kelerison's shout of rage transformed him into a blazing fireball that shot from the steeple across the greater part of Godwin's Corners. Peg Seymour was among the first of the rubberneckers who came running to the scene, only to find themselves tapped for an impromptu rescue party. After they got Sandy safely down to earth, Peg used the considerable force of her personality to dismiss the other gawpers, categorically forbidding them to bother poor Mrs. Walters with any questions. She then insisted that Sandy come straight over to her house for a calming cup of tea.

It was always more convenient to grill a guest in your own home. The tea was no sooner out than Peg demanded what Sandy was doing shooting off flares from atop the Congregational church.

"I had to get someone's attention if I was ever going to get down, didn't I?" Sandy inquired innocently.

"But why did you go up there in the first place?"

"It's the best place in town for shooting off flares."

Peg grew suspicious. "Has your husband started you playing *that* game too?"

"Speaking of my husband"—Sandy finished her tea—"I should call home. May I use your phone?"

"It's in the kitchen, but so is my doggie. I'll just come along to hold little Kwai-Chang Caine while you talk."

Sandy wasn't too surprised when her hostess remained in the kitchen, conveniently close to the telephone, the entire time she was speaking to Lionel. As she did her best to calm her unnerved husband, using terms too vague for Peg to get anything juicy out of her eavesdropping, the inquisitive Miss Seymour gave up all pretense of loitering just to keep her Shih Tzu in check. Peg dropped the dog, who began to yap and run circles around Sandy's feet while she spoke.

The kitchen phone hung on the wall and the wall where it hung was lined with cabinets. Kwai-Chang Caine scrabbled in faster and faster circles, his barks and snarls rising as he drummed up courage for an attack on Sandy's ankles. Peg was playing the indulgent mother, ignoring the more obnoxious behavior of her darling while she rinsed out the cups. Sandy had plugged her ear with a finger trying to hear what Lionel was saying over the Shih Tzu's canine tantrum.

Neither she nor Peg heard the kitchen cabinet door creak open. Kwai-Chang Caine stopped yipping and concentrated on low growls. Something hollow thunked onto the floor. Sandy and Peg both glanced toward the sound at the same time.

It was Peg's new Preserv-a-Pak lettuce keeper, rolling across the linoleum under its own power. The large pink plastic bowl wobbled lazily along in a wide arc circumscribing the snarling Shih Tzu. There wasn't room enough for it to make a full circle, so when it came to the end of the arc, it simply backtracked as if this were the most natural motion in the world for an unabetted lettuce keeper. The second arc described less area than the first, and the third less than the second. The lettuce keeper was not just out for a jaunt; it was closing in on prey.

"Sandy? Sandy, are you still there? Sandy, what's happening?" Lionel got no answer. The rambling Preserv-a-Pak bowl had mesmeric power that a cobra might covet. Sweat slicked the handpiece of the telephone as Sandy watched the fur rise on Kwai-Chang Caine's scruffy back. His growls dwindled to whines. The bowl was rolling closer and closer to him with each arc it completed.

Suddenly, the lettuce keeper sprang. It clamped down over the tiny dog with a loud clop. Peg gasped and threw herself onto the bowl, but the moment she touched it, she gave a squeal of pain and clutched her hand. It was dotted with a horseshoe of bleeding pinpricks.

Seated cross-legged on top of the lettuce keeper was a wizened brown creature with a needle-toothed smile that slit its face from ear to pointed ear. "Ah, ah, ah!" It wiggled a stick finger at Peg. "Not nice to disturb. Ask Amanda Taylor. She will tell you what happens to naughty ladies who don't let brownies feed in peace."

"*Feed?*" Peg's face contorted with anguish.

The brownie folded down its ears and tucked in the tips to shut out the shrillness. "Oooh, so loud! Don't mind, lady, don't mind. Soon we'll be done." The Preserv-a-Pak bowl burped itself, which was a change from the usual. The brownie grinned. "See? All done!" It disappeared.

They waited until Lionel showed up to get Sandy, then made him be the one to lift the bowl. All that was left was Kwai-Chang Caine's collar and license and an oak leaf scrawled with the spidery words: GOOD DOG.

The war had begun.

Chapter Eleven:

The Siege of Godwin's Corners

Cee-Cee Godwin Haines stood at the top of the basement stairs and called down to her husband, "Dwight, dear, have you found the problem yet? The bake sale on the green's tomorrow and you know I can't do anything with no water in the house."

"Glub," said Dwight, thrashing his legs in the waist-high water.

"Oh, do be still, you graceless creature," the nixie pouted. "A little water never hurt anybody."

Dwight thrashed his legs, though not out of any desire to please. The supple water sprite had her legs wrapped around his chest and was presently using both webby hands to keep his head submerged.

"Dwight?" Cee-Cee caroled from above. "Dwight, I didn't hear what you said. Dwight, do you want me to call the plumber?" Her footsteps wandered to and from the basement door several times, paused on the threshold, then made sharp, determined echoes as she clomped down the steps.

Her scream echoed through the very dimly lit basement, frightening the nixie into a deep dive. She was no more than a flash of light and shadow to Cee-Cee's eyes, soon ignored and dismissed from mind in the presence of the great scream-inspiring disaster. Dwight came up spluttering.

"Cee-Cee, honey, it's all right, I'm fine, don't worry, she didn't drown m—"

Dwight's gasped reassurances did nothing to comfort his wife. She moaned like one in pain and exclaimed, "*Look* at all this water! I don't know why you wouldn't let me call the plumber. It's not as if we can't afford it. Oh, oh, ohhhh! I was storing some of the PTO tag sale things down here and now they're *ruuuuuuined!*"

Beneath the surface, the nixie swam between Dwight's splayed legs and tickled.

"They're antiques," Jennifer Franklin glibly told a browser. Of all the PTO mothers, she was the coolest under fire, mistress of turning the skeptical glance of potential customers into a helpless buying frenzy. A few words on the history, pedigree, and intrinsic value of some anonymous colonial housewife's piece of trash, and a shapeless chunk of wood and bad taste was transformed into a relic.

Had she lived in an earlier age, Jennifer would have done well as one of those merchants in True Cross splinter futures. But the age of great huckstering was gone and now she sat behind a table full of old stuff, contributed by young families, and convinced one browser after another that here was his chance to legitimize his own precarious toehold on the American Dream. One eighteenth-century tin pie plate in the house could do much to exorcise any dark-eyed ghost of Ellis Island.

"See those water spots?" Jennifer was pushing one of the items rescued from the Haines basement inundation. "This piece was in the Johnstown Flood."

"What about this one?" The buyer-to-be was a short man with a swarthy complexion and a Burberry overcoat, the very personification of the perfect mark for Jennifer's spiel. All around the PTO table were other stalls where more ethical vendors of antiques held court. They never bothered to say as much about their wares as Jennifer, but then, they also didn't sell half as many items.

Jennifer looked at the piece her victim was holding up. It was an alabaster egg, one of the Minimum Daily Adult souvenir requirements to be brought back by anyone who has ever visited Italy. The eggs usually retained their popularity after the trip for six months—twice as long as it took for their owners to misplace those charming tooled leather bookmarks from Florence. Then they hit the tag sale trail by the dozens.

"That is an Early American hand warmer," Jennifer rattled off without a blink or a thought to whether one could heat alabaster safely or not. "The eighteenth-century ladies would heat these up in a special basket hung over the fireplace and pop one into their muffs just before going off to church on those cold winter mornings. Have you ever seen George Washington's famous letter to Martha from Valley Forge in which he mentions how much he misses her hand warmers? No?" She dimpled modestly. "There I go again, expecting everyone to share my interest in the human side of our great country's history."

"But I am interessssted," the dark man said, rotating the egg slowly between his fingers. He held it up to the light of the sun as if candling the stone. "Tell me more, pray, Misssss . . . ?"

"Mrs. Franklin." Jennifer had a way of pronouncing her married name that left no doubt in the hearer's mind that yes, there was direct bloodline descent from *that* Franklin. Some of the unkinder townfolk said that she was the only twenty-seven-year-old they knew who affected bifocals and who couldn't wait for her long chestnut hair to go gray so that the Franklin heritage might be all the more pronounced. Still nastier souls asserted that Jennifer would shave the front of her head and develop a figure like a Franklin stove, if not stopped.

"Sssso? And did this Washington ever get his hands warm enough?"

"Well, there's no textual evidence, but I'm sure Martha was kind enough to send one or two along. Mind you, I'm not saying that this is the very hand warmer that George Washington used, but the stone itself is certainly old enough for that to be a—"

The dark man twirled the egg so that it spun around and around on the tip of his index finger. It twirled as swiftly and gaily as if it had been a child's pinwheel, and not an awkwardly shaped lump of stone. A robe of white shining spun with it, an illusion of light that made the alabaster egg seem to grow in size, to soften in outline. The creamy stone darkened to the buttery hue of spring crocus, deepened to rich orange, flushed with the radiance of blood.

"It warms well," said the dark man. "How much?"

"Buh—buh—buh—" Jennifer Franklin watched the spinning egg go through its transformations. For once she was speechless, and the only incident in Early American history she could hold on to in her mind was the witchcraft trials of Old Salem Village.

A crusty brown crack shivered down the length of the egg. The dark man flipped it into the air and caught it on the palm of his hand as it fell. The crack forked, spread, and the scarlet shell crumbled to powder as a moist, red, lizardlike thing emerged. It blinked dull black eyes at the light and curled in on itself.

"Ah. Thisss one is not good to me now, I fear." The dark man gave a rueful shrug of his shoulders. He took Jennifer's nerveless hand in his own and poured the creature into it. "I had wanted to hatch one myself, under more controlled circumsssstancesssss. But now, the beassssst is yours. They are faithful, you ssssee, to whoever owns the egg at the time of their hatching. Ssssssalamanders are sssso bourgeois. Property-consciousss even in the shell." He smiled at Jennifer with hooded eyes. "At leasssst your hands will be warm thissss winter." He hurried off toward the cotton candy stand.

"Salamanders?" Jennifer peeped. She stared at the creature in her hand. It did look like the common amphibian her brothers used to tease her with in years past.

No it didn't.

Hairs of gray smoke were rising from the tiny animal's paws, each minuscule claw emitting its own contrail. It moved its flat head sluggishly from side to side, pinpoint nostrils flaring whenever it snuffed up the scent of smoke from its own paws. White sparks winked on its snout, then turned to seeds of dancing fire. A crackling ridge of flame raced up the beast's spine.

Jennifer screamed and dropped the salamander into the grass. Immediately a ring of fire poofed into being around it. Passersby saw it and started to shout for help, gesticulating and milling about. A pair of boys from the high school took action by grabbing opposite ends of the PTO tag sale table and running it away from the small conflagration. Dimestore crockery, promoted to the status of vintage Fiesta Ware by the Franklin fiat, went crashing. "Depression glass" that hadn't been more than a handful of silica until 1959 met a similar fate. Painted tin was trampled and battered past the point where even Jennifer could explain it away as being the scars of slave-versus-free toleware involvement in the Civil War.

Not that Jennifer was worrying about the merchandise just then. She was running for her life. And scurrying after, like an earthbound comet, the faithful fire-elemental blazed a smoking trail through the Godwin's Corners antique show on the green.

"Wasn't that Jenny Franklin?"

Pat Brownmiller looked up from the plates of baked goods she was setting out on the PTO bake sale table and wrinkled her nose. "Yes, and look at the time. She's not supposed to leave her place at the tag sale stand until half past. She came on the same shift as I did, but you know Jenny. Thinks she's something special because of that last name of hers. If you ask me, Chad Franklin would've done us all a favor if he'd have let her keep everything *except* his last name when the divorce went through."

Betsy Rogers giggled, then sniffed the air. "Do you smell something burning?"

"If it's anything salvageable, Jenny will sell it next week, claiming it was scorched in the War of 1812 when the British burned Washington."

"Washington burned?" The dark little man sidled up to the bake sale table, his blunt face full of sympathy. "Ssssuch a shame. Martha should not have sssent him more than one hand warmer. If they hatch ssssimultaneoussssly, they fight."

In a voice meant for Betsy's ears alone, Pat Brownmiller remarked, "Who is this loon?"

At a similarly low pitch, Betsy replied, "I don't know. He's no one from this town. Maybe New Haven?"

"I think to get them this creepy, he'd have to commute up from New York." Pat cleared her throat and in her most affable manner asked, "Can I help you, sir?"

The man pointed at the masterpiece of the bake sale, a triple-layer strawberry cake. Fresh berries ringed the top, all of them plump and temptingly juicy in spite of the fact that autumn was not high season for such fruits. The berry in the very center of the cake was a four-bite gem.

"Who did thisss?" the dark man demanded.

"Why, I did," Betsy Rogers admitted, slightly confused by the fellow's somber mien. "Would you like a slice?"

"Cut it up?" His eyes flashed, and right then the two woman saw that they were pure black, unrelieved by even the smallest encirclement of sclera. Deep in the heart of those lightless eyes, a six-pointed slash of red twinkled, an asterisk of bloodlight. "Haven't you done enough?"

Pat was a woman of the best old Yankee breed. Though her legs begged her to put them to best use, she would die before deserting her post in the face of an itinerant madman with inhuman eyes. One of her ancestresses had once scared off a catamount in the wilderness by shouting selections from *Pilgrim's Progress* at it.

Pat could not do less. She contained her fear and leaned across the table, trying to stare the dark man down. "If you don't like strawberries, fine. Other people do. Now do you want the whole cake, a slice of the cake, a different cake, or maybe a bag of Toll House cookies?"

"Murderers." The dark man's lips curled back. Pat was close enough to see that he hadn't a tooth in his head. Gum ridges the color of swamp water served that purpose. "Shamelessssss killers. Their deathssss are on your heads. May their spiritsssss haunt you forever!" He whipped his Burberry closer to his squat body and stalked away.

"Didn't want the cookies either." Pat brushed it all away. "New Haven nut case. My God, I can understand saving the whales, but what did a strawberry cake ever do . . . ?"

Oh woe! Oh woe!

"Paaaat . . ." Betsy's voice squirmed with terror. "Pat, the strawberries . . ."

They rocked back and forth on the icing, digging little cavities in the white sugar. The central berry rose two inches into the air, by honest measure, and stayed there. Its surrounding sisters wailed a treble dirge and prostrated themselves in the snowy icing.

Oh most precious life, child of sun and rain and just a little spray to keep off the aphids! Oh gift of slow ripening into full beauty! Tender white petals of my blossoming youth, was it for this you seduced the wandering bee? That in the end, full of time and sun and sweetness, I might be torn from the leafy bosom of my mother, crammed into the harsh prison of a plastic box, have the last green reminder of my origins wrenched from my very guts by the grim huller, and end thus, a mere ornament?

A green-skinned girl no taller than a toothpick materialized beneath the levitating strawberry. Her cheeks and eyes alone were rosy, and there was a seed sprinkling of black dots across her face. She balanced the huge berry on her head and

swayed back and forth as she gave vent to further dolorous
lamentations. One by one the other berries atop the cake rose
up to join their sorrows to hers, each of them likewise borne
high by its own genius spirit. They echoed the cry of *Woe! Oh
woe!*

It was a circumstantial impossibility to have a Greek chorus strawberry layer cake carrying on at the big antique show
on the green and not attract some notice. The crowd that gathered, gathered quickly and stayed forever. They were most
affected by the central berry's bewailings. Vaughn Collins, a
man of steely stomach who wrote scripts for used car TV com-
mercials, was actually seen to weep. His wife Corinne angrily
demanded Betsy Rogers's immediate resignation from the local
chapter of Greenpeace.

Alas, alas, they tell us that to this end were we born! the
main spokesberry groaned on. *To sate the fearsome appetites
of our betters, so they claim! Go, go thou all and study whither
appetite may lead! Ask of Sandra Horowitz the price of uncar-
ing ambition! Seek out Amanda Taylor and learn the wages of
vanity! Oh, we might have been spared this, but for them! Oh
seedlings, my seedlings, now we shall never meet! The runners
propagate, and to what purpose? It is better that we die. . . .*

The spirit sank down beneath the weight of her berry and
was gone from sight. The ring of her sisters too returned to
lifelessness. A little red juice dribbled down the side of the
cake.

Pat Brownmiller looked around the ring of faces staring
at her, some tear-streaked, some hostile.

"We also have some nice brownies," she said lamely.

"Never mind that," Vaughn Collins growled, swiping
the last of his tears away. "Where's this Sandra Horowitz?"

Cee-Cee leaned on the jamb of the cellar door. "Dwight,
darling, I'm leaving for the sale now. Are you sure you'll be
all right?"

"Perfectly fine, angel," her husband called from below.
"You go ahead and have a good time."

There was a short pause. Cee-Cee frowned as she considered whether or not to tell her husband what she had done.
Sometimes it was difficult to know whether to tell the whole
truth, carefully selected portions of the truth, or chuck the
whole mess and lie like a trooper. Near as she could remember,
the latest issue of *Time* had made much of "The New Domestic

Diplomacy: Whiter Lies, Longer Marriages." She acted accordingly, as the media directed.

"Precious, I gave an eentsy-beensy phone call to Mr. Andropoulos—you know, that nice old handy man Priscilla absolutely swears by?—and I asked him if he'd pop by to give you just a smidgen of advice. Do you mind?"

"Tell her you don't mind," the nixie whispered, massaging the back of Dwight's neck. "Otherwise she'll be down here trying to make you do it her way." The water sprite draped a crisscross of duckweed on Dwight's bare chest.

Dwight gasped as sharp, fishy teeth grazed lasciviously over his skin. "Whatever you say, sweetheart!" he yelled upstairs. "Anything at all!"

Soon—barely soon enough for Dwight—the sound of Cee-Cee's departing car voomed past the basement window. He turned to embrace his own personal siren.

She wiggled away and submerged in the water that still welled up through the very pores of the house foundation. Dwight waded after, splashing like a grounded tuna and calling her name, which came out as an inarticulate gargle. She surfaced behind him, laughing, and snared him with the golden net of her hair.

"So much hurry! Even sailors offer me a drink first."

Dwight was surprised. "I thought you only drank water."

The nixie laughed again. "Never! Who better than I should know what fish do in it?"

They had cracked their second bottle of the '79 Pouilly-Fumé when Mr. Andropoulos let himself in.

"I quit!" In her office overlooking the green, Laura Young slammed her appointment book closed. All around her was the shrapnel of yet another meeting with the Godwin's Corners Historical Society bigwigs. This year's major project was the restoration of the Elspeth Morgan House, the oldest structure in town, dating back to the seventeenth century, before Godwin's Corners was even officially founded.

To be tapped to design the interior decoration of the historic house was an honor. The publicity value alone would be the making of the consultant lucky enough to be chosen, but to top it, the remuneration for the job was generous.

No one had told Laura that she would be spending most of her pay on antacids and headache remedies.

She paged through a catalog of paint chips, all in colors

certified an authentically colonial. There was more than one
such tome lying around the office, as well as books of stencil
designs, floor-cloth patterns, and furniture and accessory
guides. It only wanted a consensus of opinion from the restoration committee before the actual work could commence.

It might as well have wanted the moon.

Laura tilted her chair back and closed her eyes. She could
still see the Lees, mother and daughter, arguing vehemently
with Dennis Tuttle over whether to hang seven cooking imple-
ments beside the Morgan House kitchen fireplace or fewer. He
kept slapping the piles of photocopied documents in his lap—
"Original, contemporary sources which I have collected at
great personal inconvenience and expense"—and shouting that
Elspeth Morgan could not possibly have kept house with merely
one ladle and a toasting fork.

Viola Harper jumped into it then, declaring that she spoke
for all Godwin's Corners when she said that the purpose of the
Morgan House restoration project was to recreate a typical sev-
enteenth-century home and not to build a shrine to Elspeth
Morgan, never mind what Mr. Tuttle's mother's maiden name
had been.

"Well, if authenticity means nothing to you, perhaps you
shouldn't be on this committee," Mr. Tuttle had sniped.

"If sensible expense means nothing to you, maybe we
ought to resign together," Viola shot back. "If you're that
interested in authenticity, let's not forget to include a para-
graph in the descriptive booklet that mentions the fact that Elspeth Morgan was nearly tried for witchcraft!"

"She never was!"

"Only because the witchfinder they sent from New Haven died under mysterious circumstances at Lee's Tavern!"

The meeting shattered into a three-way fight over witchcraft, authentic colonial salmonella, and the probable sanitary
standards of the Lee ancestors in the Good Old Days.

"Same time next week?" Dennis Tuttle had asked Laura
archly as the committee filed out in angry silence.

"I'm going to be doing this forever." Laura smacked
the desk. "They're never going to agree on one damned thing.
You can't make reasonable human beings out of committee
members. It would be easier to turn a pig's ear into a pocket-
book."

"Or spin straw into gold," said the dwarf in the corner.
He hobbled forward on bandy legs, his red beard sweeping the
floor. An incredible leap lifted him onto Laura's desk, where

he sat tailor-style on her appointment book and twitched his icicle-shaped nose. "Can we talk deal?"

Her recent ordeal with the restoration project committee had left Laura's psyche bruised and tender. She hadn't the strength to question the dwarf's reality or her own sanity. It was easier to accept what she saw at face value and ask the manikin what he meant by "deal."

"I use my magic to make that batch of doodlebrains agree to the very next set of interior design ideas you lay before them. In exchange for this—"

"Uh-uh. If you want my firstborn son, you're out of luck. I had four daughters before I got my tubes tied."

"What would I want with one of your human brats? That changeling trip is old hat. I'm into self-actualization, not acting out my ambitions through my kids. Or yours."

"So in that case"—Laura looked askance at the little man—"what's the catch?"

A fan of full-color pamphlets whipped open in the dwarf's hands. "Have you heard the good news about being a Forest-fresh Seven Steps to Home Beauty System distributor?"

Twenty minutes later, Laura Young was putting her signature on a document that bound her to become a Forestfresh products distributor for twenty years in return for specified spells of compulsion to be worked as desired by the Connecticut area general manager.

"Which means me. I hope you make your quarterly sales quotas, milady," the dwarf remarked. "The boys in the head office, they don't take excuses."

"They're the ones who'll take my firstborn son?"

"They're the ones who'll slap a fattening spell on you if you screw up. Ten pounds permanent gain for every time you come up short. Kids grow up and leave home, but thunder thighs are forever. Those head office boys know it. Seven of the toughest little workaholics in the dwarf game, and I'm not just whistling Dixie."

Laura's pen paused in midsignature. "Um . . . shouldn't there be an escape clause in here somewhere? A way I can get out of the payment conditions?"

"You bet. It's traditional. I got Sandra Horowitz to draw up this baby, and she is one lawyer who knows her way around with the Little People. Hey, I wouldn't be in this town at all if not for her and Amanda Taylor."

"Horowitz . . ." The name sounded familiar. The amount of small print in the contract was daunting, but if she couldn't trust a fellow human being to look out for her own, Laura figured it was a sorry world. Still, no harm in playing it safe.

"What kind of escape clause?"

The dwarf winked. "Old stuff. Piece of cake. Remember that peasant girl I made a queen? She couldn't even sign her own name, and *she* managed to wiggle out. It's a sweetheart clause, believe me. Happy-ever-after city."

Laura looked suspicious. "You're making this contract I sign sound *too* easy to get out of. Why?"

His leer stripped her to her skivvies and blushes without removing one actual item of clothing. "Let's just say I think we've got enough Forestfresh distributors totzing around, but not enough bods like yours, sweetmeat. Be a shame to hide that stuff under a bushel of lipids. Can I buy you a drink after we tie up our business?" The gleam in his eye implied that business was not the only thing the little man wanted to tie up.

"First tell me about the out clause. What do I have to do? Guess your name or what?"

"Something like that. You guess, you got it. Simple, *neh?*"

Promises were empty air, but lechery was honest. If he claimed to desire her unfettered by flab, he must mean it. Laura's head still hurt from the recent meeting and she felt at least as smart as any jumped-up peasant girl. It was a matter of believing in her own abilities. Besides, after reading umpty-nine thousand fairy tales to four kids, she knew how the story went. The dwarf began to whistle "I Am Woman" sotto voce while she pondered her options. Laura signed. "Okay, I'm in. Do your stuff."

A golden spindle appeared in the dwarf's gnarled hands. Thread fine as spiderweb spun itself out between his fingers. He rocked back and forth on Laura's desktop as he worked humming "Unter den Linden." The thread snaked down from the desk, across the floor, and hootchie-kootchied up to the windowsill.

The dwarf stopped spinning and cut the product free. "Sic 'em," he told the thread. It looped one end of itself to the stock of an old Brown Bess musket Laura had hung on her wall for colonial clout and leaped out the window. The musket moved only slightly when the thread went taut, but was not jerked from the wall. Instead, the thread stretched itself thinner and thinner before Laura's eyes, until all that told her it was

still there was the minuscule tremblings of the anchoring Brown
Bess.

"Twang on it if you want," the dwarf said. "It'll hold."
He slipped his thumbs under the embroidered suspenders of his
lederhosen. "Fact is, that's how you activate the spell. Right
now that thread's frayed itself into as many strands as there are
committee members. Each strand's tied itself into an invisible
hangman's noose—one size fits all—and dropped over their
necks. Now all you've got to do is get your designs set so you
like them, call a meeting, show them to those bozos, and ask
for the go-ahead."

"And if they don't give it to me? If they start fighting
each other again? I twang that string and . . . ?"

"They choke. Oh, not to death, but they won't be blow-
ing any birthday candles out too easily after. And they don't
get their breath back until they come around to your way of
seeing things. You'd be surprised the effect a good garroting
has on the spirit of cooperation. So, how about that drink,
honey?"

Laura found the dwarf's upfront lust a refreshing change
from the usual cut of swains a divorced mother of four had to
pick from. Either they acted like they were doing you a favor
or they tried snowing you with the Sensitive Man pose by
bursting into tears over dinner and blabbing about how they
wouldn't feel degraded if a woman supported them until they
finished that novel. Not so her diminutive admirer. He kept
playing with his spindle while he waited for her to lock up the
office, and the intimate feminine garments his magical spinning
made would have reduced every Bawdy Boutique in the country to Chapter XI had he marketed them.

"Care to try one on for size?" He rolled his banjo eyes
at Laura as he held up a shimmery scantling. "Be nice and I'll
see about maybe knocking a C-note off your quarterly sales
quotas."

Laura laughed at him. "You're cute, but you're getting
a little ahead of yourself. Thanks to that escape clause, I'm not
going to have to meet any quotas. Rumpelstiltskin is your
name."

"Of course it is," the dwarf snorted. "Always was, always will be. What's that got to do with the price of Forestfresh catbox deodorizer?"

"But—but I guessed it! I guessed your name! That means
I get out of my part of the bargain."

"Are you for real?" The dwarf pinched Laura's rump.

"Yeah, I guess you are. Babyboo, you think a slick lawyer like Sandra Horowitz'd put a dipstick escape clause like that in a contract? Guess my *name*, f'Pete's sake? Kidstuff!"

"You said . . . !" Laura yanked her copy of the contract from her portfolio and skimmed it desperately, lips moving.

"Right there." Rumpelstiltskin kindly pointed out the clause she sought.

She read it. She paled. She looked at her creditor with just the same expression of hopelessness the peasant-girl-turned-queen had once worn. Her lower lip trembled.

"I've got to guess your Social Security number?"

"Without benefit of bureaucracy or computer." The dwarf twirled the scantling around one finger and gave Laura a sideways ogle. "A C-note off the quarterly. Think about it."

Later, in a hastily booked room at the Silver Swan Inn, Laura Young shimmied into the magic-woven scantling. Her mind was not on the business at hand, though. She was seriously thinking of how well her daughters would cope after their mother was arraigned for the murder of Sandra Horowitz.

From the bed, Rumpelstiltskin whistled Dixie.

Cee-Cee Godwin Haines came home to a strangely quiet house. She was dying to tell Dwight all about the weird happenings in town. Sandra Horowitz's name was on everyone's lips, generally followed by a snarled threat. Likewise the name of Amanda Taylor was being bandied about, but mostly with confusion attending it. The reclusive woman was an unknown quantity, a mousy presence to whom no one who *mattered* in Godwin's Corners society had to pay a second thought, or even a first. Now, however . . .

"Dwight! Dwight, sweetie!" Cee-Cee sought him here and sought him there, but her husband remained damned elusive. At last she wandered into the kitchen, where she almost tripped over an open toolbox and a set of sopping wet denim overalls. The basement door was ajar and the sounds of gentle sloshing rose up damply from belowstairs.

"Why, of course!" Cee-Cee had to smile at her own absentmindedness. In the aftershock of an animistic bake sale, she had all but forgotten Mr. Andropoulos's promised visit to dehumidify the Haines basement. "Yoo-hoo, Dwight! Mr. Andropoulos!" Her voice carried well, but no one responded from down under.

And yet they were there. Who else was laughing like

that? And . . . moaning for mercy? And—could it be?—imploring someone for one more go at "playing Flipper"?

Cee-Cee came from *those* Godwins, and *those* Godwins had not gotten a town named after them by dithering about at the top of the basement steps. Cee-Cee plunged into the damp darkness, looking formidable and determined.

Mr. Andropoulos didn't hear her coming, though the wooden stair echoed her every step and he was standing right on the first tread above water. An empty wine bottle was in his hand and a pair of boxer shorts was on his grizzled head. Beyond that, he wore basic duckweed and a smile.

"Mr. Andropoulos!" Cee-Cee shouted his name several times before she realized he wasn't hearing a thing. When she tapped him on the shoulder, he did turn and take notice.

"Ah, Mrs. Haines!" He kissed her resoundingly on both cheeks. His breath reeked of vintage Nuits-St.-George. "God bless you, dear lady! You have made an old man very, very happy!"

"Mr. Andropoulos, I never intended to make you—"

"Cht! Just a minute." He probed his right ear with thumb and forefinger and extracted a pellet of wax, then did the same to the left. "That's better. So long as you do not listen to their song, you are safe from falling under their spell. This does not mean"—he winked roguishly at her—"that you cannot enjoy whatever else they may offer you. They are better sports about it than the old tales tell."

"*Who* are?"

Mr. Andropoulos bent over and dredged up a submersible flashlight. He aimed it out over the waters and flipped on the switch. A beacon illuminated the darkness.

Dwight and the nixie were caught in the spotlight and in very imaginative *flagrante delicto*. Cee-Cee's shock was tempered by intellectual curiosity. In ten years of marriage she had never imagined how flexible her husband could be, in the proper circumstances.

"Uh . . . hi, honey." Dwight wiggled his fingers in greeting.

The nixie wiggled everything else.

"I'll say 'hi' to you in court," Cee-Cee spat.

A small white slip of pasteboard materialized in the air before her eyes. It was a business card with Sandra Horowitz's name and profession tastefully embossed on it, and a line beneath saying "Divorces Our Specialty."

"Tell her I sent you!" the nixie called merrily as Cee-Cee stormed up the stairs.

Sandy was having a tuna fish sandwich when the stone came smashing through the kitchen window. The anonymous note on it read, *What could we expect from New Money?*

The first phone call was Kelerison, laughing, but those that soon followed were all too human.

Chapter Twelve:

Meeting of Minds

Lionel looked at the mess in the yard. "I didn't think things like this happened anymore," he said. "Not in this century." He knelt and poked at the still-smoldering mound with a stick. The stench was unbelievable. Sandy held her nose.

"It's better than lynching, I guess," she said through pinched nostrils.

"By how much?" Lionel scraped a glob of melted pastel plastic from the edge of the burn site. "What the hell is this?"

"Looks like Preserv-a-Pak lettuce keeper. Or one of their freezer containers. Kind of hard to tell in its present condition." Sandy gestured at several small bits of metal in the ashes. "What are those?"

Lionel used his stick to get one out. It was not so badly melted as its brothers. You could still see the wings, though they had drooped into the body, and some of the facial features remained.

"It's a gaming piece."

Sandy sighed. "Leave it to Peg to react rationally."

The bushes rustled. Lionel grabbed his stick like a club. "If that's those damned pixies again . . ." His jaw clenched.

Sandy laid a restraining hand on the stick. "Come on, honey. Out of all the rest of the refugees from Grimm, the pixies have been the least harmful."

"After what they did at the track meet?"

"Those were the *fairies,*" Sandy explained patiently. "They're smaller, but they're much more obnoxious."

"Not too small to grab the whole Godwin Academy hurdling team and airlift them all the way to Guilford! You try explaining to one of those shoreline towns why you're harvesting track runners out of their elms."

"Oaks," Sandy corrected. "They put the Booster Squad up the elms."

"Five boys have been withdrawn from the academy already." Lionel clutched his stick all the more grimly. "They had plenty to say to their parents on the phone."

"About me?"

"And me, as your husband. And Cass Taylor's family. The fairies made plenty sure that those kids knew just whom to thank for that nonscheduled flight." The bushes rustled more, and there was the hint of mocking laughter. "Come out of there, you litle vermin!" Lionel shouted.

The rhododendron leaves parted around a pointed, feline face. Cesare's whiskers twitched, and he set down the small white drawstring bag he held in his teeth. "Vermin, am I? *Mondo putana!* These are the thanks I get. I demand an apology," the cat said coldly.

Lionel was in no mood to placate anybody but himself. "What do we have to thank you for, Cesare? Eating us out of every scrap of lox in the house just because Sandy's a soft touch for a whiskered face?"

The cat spat with remarkable accuracy, right past Lionel's left eye. "For one, since we speak of vermin, you might thank me for keeping your miserable home vermin-free."

"That's any cat's job."

"Job?" Cesare's antennalike eyebrows quivered in disdain. "You confound me with a common mouser? I am an artist! In my small way," he added modestly.

Lionel picked up the little white bag and dangled it between his fingers. Sandy recalled having seen it in the cat's possession more times than this, and she admitted to a hog's load of curiosity about it. "What're you schlepping around in this, cat? Your 'art' supplies? Or a dead mouse?"

"Put that down," the cat said calmly. "Or at least hold it farther from your gaping mouth. It is poison."

"No fooling." Lionel chuckled.

Just then the underbrush shook with a host of minor tremors, and five moles staggered out into the sunlight. With piteous convulsions they died, one by one. A look of great perplexity gathered itself on Lionel's gauntly handsome face.

There was something damned familiar about the disposition of the burrowers' tiny corpses.

"The final curtain of *Hamlet, Prince of Denmark,*" Cesare supplied, without so much as a blink. "See, that skinny one in black is the prince—it took me some time to cast that role properly, believe me—the other male with the slightly debauched appearance is the usurping uncle, the young gray sprat is Laertes, and the plump female—ah, *permiso . . .*" Cesare patted the mole in question a little closer to the Claudius counterpart. "Better. The female is Gertrude, as I was saying. A fine presentation, although I did better with *Othello.* Fewer bodies, a lesser challenge. I really must learn to adjust the dosage for body weight. Just because it worked with mice . . ."

Lionel put down the white sack quickly. "You couldn't—you didn't—you *poison* your prey?"

The cat was incredulous. "How else did you expect me to kill them?" He flexed his paws. "I have frequently mourned the lack of an opposable thumb. *Jesu!* What a fencer I might have been! But then, who would have trained the moles to the blade? No honorable duel, but a slaughter. I am a cat, not a butcher."

"You poisoned them and could control where they'd fall?" Lionel surveyed the tableau. All that was missing was a pair of rapiers, some empty wine cups, and a surviving mole to announce that Rosenkrantz and Guildenstern were dead. Otherwise it was pure Old Vic.

Cesare touched the fallen sack with one respectful claw. "It is *La Cantarella,* preferred by my first masters two-to-one over any other leading remedy for dispatching one's expendable associates. With this one may control the time of death, and thus where the body will be when it dies."

Lionel was well versed in some of the less salient points of Renaissance history. The name *La Cantarella* struck an immediate bell. "You knew the *Borgias?*"

The cat proved himself an even more astounding beast in that he managed to shrug. "In passing. But my first true and heartfelt allegiance has always been to Prince Cassiodoron. That is why I am here. Or do you think your moles are more worthy of my attention than those of your neighbors? Which brings me to the second reason for my presence."

He turned his eyes to Sandy. "We have lost the game. My lord prince Cassiodoron will give in to his father. He will secretly surrender to King Kelerison, submitting himself to whatever punishment and humiliation the Lord of Elfhame Ul-

tramar may devise. Mark me, my lady, I know the king well.
He will not disappoint Cassiodoron's worst-imagined nightmares in his choice of punishments. The prince believes he can
slip off secretly, but Amanda will know. Kelerison shall see to
that. And once he makes sure that she finds out where Cass
has gone . . . she will surrender too.''

"No! She can't!'' Sandy felt Lionel's comforting hand
close over her own tightly balled fist as something distant, un-
real. "You must be wrong. Has Cass *told* you he's going to
do this?''

"He has told me so in greater than words. The most
carefully closed mind is not strong enough to keep out the
family cat.'' The big tom's eyes were fixed in moon stare.
Sandy felt the truth of what he said in her marrow.

"I have to stop him,'' she said quietly.

The cat's words came inside her head. "It is for your
sake he means to do this. He fears for your safety should his
father continue to goad these townsfolk. He has lived long, my
young master, and seen many things that your people do when
fear binds them into a mob. He also knows that for those of
your faith . . . it is often much harder.''

"My faith . . .?''

The cat nodded at the remnants of the fire. "He saw
more than one of these in the times when we still dwelled in
the Old Land. More than one, in more than one country. I
sometimes think he has been drawn to you because your folk
share something of the outsiders' blood he feels in his own.
You are different. So is he.''

"I think your young master could do with a trip to Tel
Aviv. Outsiders!'' This time Sandy did feel Lionel squeeze her
hand. She drew strength from his presence without knowing it,
as she had so many times before. "Enough so-called civilized
people have been trying to foist that role off on me and mine
over the centuries. We don't need the elves getting in on it too.
No one's going to make an outsider out of me!''

The cat was unmoved. "There is a romantic air that
clings to being otherly.''

"You can catch your death of cold from that romantic
air. If your master finds something mysteriously attractive about
being an outsider, he can keep it. I like it inside, thank you,
where it's maybe dull, sometimes, but it's always nice and
warm. I'm just as much an insider as any other human being,
and I'll fight to stay that way. Go back to Cass, Cesare. Tell
him not to do anything rash until he hears from me. Thank him

for his sympathy, if you think that will please him, but make him see that I can take care of myself.''

''Sympathy?'' The cat's slitted pupils dilated inexplicably in the full sunlight. ''Is that what you call love?''

Sandy's own hand uncurled. Her fingers twined with her husband's. ''I know what love is, and I know better than to panic over a few fringe incidents.'' She gave the smoking heap of trash a look of disgust. ''With certain exceptions, this is still America. Before you can stage a pogrom here, you'd damned well better make sure you've got a license for it. I've got faith that we'll be protected by the one institution that made this country great, without regard for race, creed, color, or shape of ears!''

The cat looked skeptical. ''Democracy?''

''Bureaucracy.'' She turned to Lionel. ''Call Harv Thornton, babe. Time to get tough. Godwin's Corners is going to have us a town meeting.'

Sandy and Davina hurried to the Congregational church on the green through a topaz autumn dusk of crunching leaves and woodsmoke. ''Mrs. Taylor said she'd meet us there,'' the Welsh *au pair* said, though her doubt was clear to hear.

Sandy shared Davina's misgivings. ''Cass is staying home to keep watch over Jeffy, and Lionel brought Ellie over to their house for extra protection. He even dug up that old sword of his.''

''Steel has not the banning power over this breed of elven that it had in the old country,'' Davina murmered.

''A sword's still a wonderful comfort. Trust me on that. And you only *mentioned* steel to Cass that time. I wonder how brave he'd be staring down a blade's edge?'' She sighed. ''I hope Amanda shows up. She really doesn't have any excuse not to be there. We need her testimony.''

''I'm coming.'' Amanda emerged from the shadow of a great tree. Her face was partially concealed in the drape of a gold-shot woolen shawl cast over her head and shoulders. ''When I found out what Cass meant to do, I had enough. This time, I don't run; I fight Kelerison.''

Sandy gave her a quick hug. ''That's the spirit!''

Amanda smiled shyly. ''It's a spirit I've forgotten. My pa always used to say that I was the scrappiest of all his children. He said he wasn't afraid to leave me alone with the little ones back in the cabin. If any danger came along, he knew I'd stand up to it.'' She turned her face to the moon and Sandy saw tears tracking her cheeks. "I never even did get to say good-bye to him."

Inside the church, all heads turned to stare when Sandy, Amanda, and Davina made their entrance. Sandy held her head high as she swept down the center aisle and up the platform steps at the front where a table and podium for the town council members and speakers had been set up. Without waiting for an invitation, she commandeered the microphone.

The hell with it, she thought. *I'm a newcomer, I'm New Blood, I'm New Money, and I'm—yes, by God, I am a lawyer! And a female one at that. If I didn't act pushy for any one of those reasons, they'd be disappointed.*

She took a deep breath and grasped the podium for support. "Friends . . ." It was an unfitting beginning, to judge from the looks knifing up at her from the floor. "Fellow citizens, let's get right down to it. I'd like just one of you to stand up right now and tell me what's been going on in this town for the past couple of days."

"Us tell *you?"* Hoots of laughter followed the anonymously shouted question.

"Yes, *you* tell *me!"* Sandy shouted back. "Just because my name's been bandied about—and Amanda Taylor's too—doesn't make us the masterminds of these shenanigans. Tell me here, now, out loud, in your own words! Say it straight, make a joke of it, do it off the cuff or rehearse it until you're tired of hearing yourself talk, but say it so we can all hear how it sounds when it's put into words instead of scribbled down, tied to a rock, and smashed through my window! *What's been happening here?"*

There was a very brief silence. Very brief indeed, for Peg was in the audience and now she rose up like an indignant blowfish to huff, "Something nasty's going on in Godwin's Corners and it's all your fault!"

Sandy leaned across the podium. "Specify."

"My dog was killed. My poor"—a sob caught in Peg's throat—"precious puppy was—was—*devoured alive* by—"

"I've called the media, you know."

Peg choked.

"They said they'd be happy to send someone out here to investigate."

Peg stammered something incomprehensible.

"I've taken the liberty of giving them your name, among others."

Peg's face turned the color of a good New England clam chowder.

"Now what were you saying devoured your dog?" Sandy's lips curled up lazily. "Speak up. When they get here, they'll want some really interesting interviews."

A low mutter rippled through the massed townsfolk of Godwin's Corners. Still on her feet, Peg blushed a maidenly rose. She tried to continue testifying to the fate of Kwai-Chang Caine, but a series of glottal blocks kept her silent. She sat down.

"Nothing more to say, Peg?" Sandy's palms were sweating, but only the podium knew it. She glanced sidelong at the town councilors seated in a row at the long table a little behind her. Those of them who were not taking furious notes were engaged in intense conferral. Heads were shaken in wisdom and despair. Harv Thornton nibbled his Mark Cross automatic pencil, desecrating it with toothmarks as if it were the lowest of board of ed. yellow wooden handouts.

"How about you, Cee-Cee?" Sandy's index finger made a flamboyant stab at the lady in question, a gesture of which Perry Mason might be proud. "Would you like to tell everyone here what you told me over the telephone when you accused me of breaking up your marriage?"

Cee-Cee clutched her Nantucket purse with both hands and compressed her lips tightly. Her backbone bored into the pew behind her. She was too well bred to blush, but she could steam very nicely.

"Not"—Sandy's finger now lifted on high to illustrate a point—"that Cee-Cee ever claimed *I* was the one who seduced her husband. Just my employee. She made that clear. She's honest. I'm sure she'll be just as honest with Mike Wallace or Dan Rather or whoever *People* magazine sends along here to cover the story." She folded her arms. "That's going to be some story, Cee-Cee, if you tell them what you told me. Do you think Dwight's going to back you up? Or Mr. Andropoulos? Bugs in your home computer are one thing, nixies in your basement are another."

From the far left rear of the room, old Mrs. Talbot raised a white-gloved hand and was recognized by the chair. Aided by her niece Emma, she rose to her feet and leaned on the pew ahead.

"Young lady," she said in her firm voice. "Young lady, I believe that you may stop this performance of yours without calling upon any more specific cases. You have made your point.

Were we to tell anyone outside of this town about our current predicament, we should all be adjudged insane—victims of mass delusion, at best, as were those unhappy folk in old Salem village. I, for one, should prefer not to have my mental health debated, particularly as I am of advanced years and do not wish to have my last will and testament brought under question by Emma's brother Brian once I am gone.'' She lowered her voice and added, ''We don't talk about Brian.''

The indistinct sounds of agreement filled the Congregational church. Sandy tried not to smile quite so much, but the grimace had gelled into place at the height of her anxiety and now refused to be disenfranchised. *After this, addressing a hanging jury should be cupcakes,* she thought.

She pushed herself off the podium with an effort and said, ''Thank you, Mrs. Talbot. I'm on your side. I think we all are. I haven't actually called in the media. I simply wanted to illustrate our situation—*ours,* not just *yours.* This is my home too. I haven't lived in Godwin's Corners long—some of you here tonight represent families who've got one century of residence for every year of mine—but even so, I love this town. I don't want it reduced to a headline on the front page of the *National Enquirer* or an entry in some *Weird New England* guidebook. I don't want to see the green overrun with tourists, or the street signs changed to 'Pixie Place' and 'Queen-of-Air-and-Darkness Lane.' I don't want my Ellie to grow up and get a job hawking cute little plastic unicorns with thermometers growing out of their foreheads.''

Peg led a chorus of gagging sounds in which the ladies of the Godwin's Corners Garden Club were loudest.

''I wish we could close our eyes and have all of these—incidents vanish,'' Sandy went on. ''We all know that *something* strange is happening, just as we know how the rest of the world would react if they ever found out. We don't want that. But we—or you—do want to know why these things are happening. You're entitled.''

The town meeting hushed expectantly as Sandy motioned for Amanda Taylor to join her at the podium. The young woman's shoulders shook under her sparkling shawl, but she laid her hands on the smooth old wood and controlled the urge to flee. Amanda Taylor began to speak, and although her tale was first greeted by incredulous whispers and a few fingers tapping temples to indicate doubts about her sanity, in the end the people of Godwin's Corners understood the source of their own mischances with the world of Faery.

"He wants me back," Amanda concluded. "He's only waiting for me to consent, and then he'll leave you and your town alone." She turned to Sandy, who had discreetly taken her seat while Amanda spoke. "Mrs.—*Ms*. Horowitz has been trying to make me see this through. She seems to think we have a hope of severing all my ties with Kelerison if we persist with our lawsuit. I don't know why mortal law should bind an elven. The threat of it certainly has angered him." She dropped her eyes. The microphone scarcely picked up her voice. "You are all suffering from that anger. It isn't fair. While I've been up here talking, I've also been thinking about it. Why should anyone have to fight my battles for me? What am I to any of you? I am nothing, no one, a stranger among you. This is your town. For your sakes, I will give in to the lord of Elfhame Ultramar and leave you in peace."

Amanda tried to descend from the platform, but found her passage blocked by none other than Cee-Cee Godwin Haines. "Don't you *dare!*" She stamped her foot for emphasis, though the thick sole of her topsider absorbed most of the sound. "My people—I'm one of *those* Godwins, you know— knew your people. Not the Taylors, of course, but your original family. As soon as I heard you give your maiden name I thought it sounded familiar."

"One of the first families of Godwin's Corners," Dennis Tuttle chimed in, waving his omnipresent sheaf of original source material. "Elspeth Morgan mentioned them in her journal. She borrowed a toasting fork from your sister."

Mrs. Lee nudged her daughter. "I thought Elspeth Morgan was a trifle before that lady's time?"

Miss Lee shrugged. "I don't think Elspeth Morgan had much respect for time, or much else. Anyway, she's got the only gravestone in the old burying ground with question marks all over it and no guarantee of a body under it."

The Lee family's comments were lost in the common clamor of welcome and acceptance now being tendered to Amanda Taylor. Sandy let the tension trickle out of her bones as the most prominent and powerful in the small sphere of Godwin's Corners society came forward to put themselves into Amanda's service.

Harv Thornton, Chairman, summed it up for all present when he said, "If I hadn't've seen what this Kelerison person's capable of, I'd've marked you down for touched, Mrs. Taylor. But he's cut his own throat—if he's got a throat—by dragging in this whole town to be your witnesses. Okay, so we can't tell anyone else about him and his minions. So what? He's still got us to deal with, and you've got us to count on. You're not giving up. This is your home, we're your friends, your neighbors, maybe even your blood, and we know how to stand up for one of our own. You too, Sandy.''

"Sue his tights off!" someone shouted from the floor.

Peg sidled up the platform and whispered, "I'm sorry about what I did in your yard, Sandra dear. It was just that poor Kwai-Chang—oh, I'm *so* embarrassed!"

Old Mrs. Talbot had Emma help her all the way up the aisle and onto the platform where she grasped the podium and declared, "We the people of Godwin's Corners have weathered the blizzard of seventy-eight, the hurricane of eighty-six, and Lord save us, the Summer People. We can weather elves."

As the hall exploded into cheers and applause, Sandy could almost feel sorry for the King of Elfhame Ultramar.

Chapter Thirteen:

The Revenge of Godwin's Corners

Emma followed her aunt's advice and used more follow-through on the downswing. The umbrella struck the unicorn a slight blow on the muzzle, making the beast snort in confusion without deterring him from his purpose. Emma uttered a tiny squeal of distress and ran around the corner of the house. The unicorn followed.

From her place in the window seat, old Mrs. Talbot clicked her tongue and remarked to herself, "Dropped the umbrella too. Such a fuss. When will that child learn?" Continuing to mumble over the shortcomings of the new generation, she took up her blackthorn walking stick and went to see about settling matters properly.

In spite of advanced arthritis, Mrs. Talbot carried herself with stiff dignity and self-possession. No one looking at her could begin to guess the agonies she suffered with each step. She walked out the front door and intercepted her niece on the third circuit of the family homestead. Emma cowered behind her aunt's tastefully flowered challis dress as the relentless unicorn came charging down upon them both.

"Begone, sir!" The blackthorn stick struck the horned creature sharply dead center between the nostrils. Mrs. Talbot followed up this blow with another, broader smack to the right flank, trying to turn him. The unicorn reared in pain, lashing the air with his cloven hooves not three inches from the old lady's face.

He got the blackthorn across the pasterns of both forelegs for that. "Down, sir! Down, I say!" Mrs. Talbot menaced him with her stick. The unicorn's glass-green eyes rolled in his head. Here was a breed of dragon he had never before encountered. His nostrils flared, and he tossed the tangle of his mane in confusion. Head lowered, he backed a few paces away.

Mrs. Talbot bore in upon him, making threatening gestures with her blackthorn despite the nastily shining silver horn that might have converted her to the world's first DAR shish kebab. Emma clung to her aunt's skirt and came tippy-toeing after. "Oh please, Aunt Viv, don't hurt him!" she begged.

Mrs. Talbot's small, cold eyes pierced all the more deeply when seen from the other side of her bifocals. "Not hurt him? Emma, while I find this palpable evidence of your good morals a comfort, I will not have my schedule of obligations interfered with by mere beasts."

"My . . . good morals?"

"Your virginity." The old woman snapped out the words as if they were somewhat distasteful. "Good gracious, don't you know anything about unicorns? It's only the virgins they bother. Our Emergency Action Committee has already set up a hotline for those poor put-upon souls who are being harassed by the creatures. Peggy Seymour has been chased up a tree three times already since the unicorns showed themselves. Not the same tree, mind. And it has been quite, quite unbearable for those poor young men at the academy. Another seven members of the senior class have asked their parents to withdraw them from school after unicorns singled them out for attention." Her tone grew icy as she added, "There was no need for anyone to tell the classmates of those young men what made them so attractive to the beasts. The ragging has been inexcusable. In my day, virginity was not regarded as an affliction or a shame."

Emma wrung her fingers abjectly. The unicorn took this chance to try circumnavigating Mrs. Taylor in order to attain his goal, and got another whack from her walking stick.

"Stay, sir! Stay!" Mrs. Talbot addressed the unicorn with the no-nonsense steadfastness of voice recommended for cowing the larger breeds of dog. Something regal went out of the animal, though Mrs. Talbot was just as unmoved by his large, mournful eyes as by his formerly warlike stance.

"Emma, come. We are in danger of tardiness. Had I considered the possibility of your maiden state making us late for a social appointment"—she glared alternately at her niece and the unicorn—"I might almost have wished you otherwise."

"Me too," muttered Emma. She gave the unicorn a wistful look as her aunt shooed her along.

The Godwin's Corners Emergency Action Committee met in the dining room of Sandra Horowitz's home. There was some small delay getting people in the front door.

"It's no use, Mrs. Walters!" Davina called to Sandy from the foyer. "There are five unicorns waiting out here already, and they're every one of them blocking the door."

Mrs. Talbot twitched her nose and slewed her eyes from face to face of those committee members already present. She was clearly calculating the unicorn-to-virgin probabilities. Dennis Tuttle squirmed uncomfortably. Miss Lee crossed her legs and tried to look happy. There was Emma's unicorn, of course, and one of the creatures might have picked up the scent of the girl-child living in this house, but as for the fifth . . .

Davina passed through the dining room with a wicker rug beater in her hand and a determined expression on her face. They heard the kitchen door open and shut, and not long after there came from the front the sound of dull thuds on cervequine hide and the high-pitched belling of persecuted unicorns who were just trying to do their jobs.

Davina reentered by the front door, looking draggled and tired. The rug beater was broken. "It's no use," she said. "Miss Seymour arrived with another one just as I was driving off the rest."

To give credit to Davina's words, Peg Seymour breezed in and nabbed herself coffee and a bagel before sitting down. She wiggled her hindquarters into a chair and said, "Stupid beasts. They are doing their best to get their horns stuck in your Ellie's swing set now."

"Good. That'll keep them out of our hair." Sandy opened a looseleaf binder. "We're almost all here. Doris from the library sent her regrets. She can't get out of her house."

"If she says she's scared of the unicorns chasing her"—
Mrs. Lee smirked—"she lies."

"Doris has a limoniads in her kudzu, if you must know."

Miss Lee's snicker was a lot like her mother's, only more
nasal. Doris Perkins, absolute monarch of the Godwin's Corners town library, had once accused the eternally kittenish Miss
Lee of returning *Love's Devouring Passion* with peanut butter
gluing up the chapter where the Elvis impersonator seduces
Brandi Donner. Mrs. Lee protested in vain that her daughter
would not be caught dead reading such guff. At thirty-nine, a
girl of her Kathryn's breeding had higher tastes. Still Doris
slapped them with the cost of replacing the book.

"Limoniads? People who pay lip service to housework
deserve to be overrun with the six-legged horrors," Mrs. Lee
said.

"For God's sake, limoniads haven't any more legs than
you do. They're flower nymphs, the way dryads are tree
nymphs and oreads—oh, the hell with it. They got into Doris's
patch of kudzu and made it grow like nobody's business until
she'll need a machete to get out of her own house. We've
dispatched a pack of Cub Scouts to handle it." Sandy turned
a page in the binder. "Fortunately, the stuff doesn't keep her
from making phone calls, and in the meantime she gave us
plenty of good suggestions over the wire. I've taken the liberty
of divvying them up into assignments."

Sheets were passed out to the committee. Dennis Tuttle's
pepper-and-salt eyebrows rose as he read until they were lost
in the thatch of his grizzled bangs. He lowered the paper to his
lap. "Why me?" he whined.

"It's a dirty job," Sandy replied.

"This doesn't look so bad." Peg squinted at her own
assignment sheet. "Public awareness coordinator. I like it."

"Couldn't you spell 'gossipmonger,' dear?" Mrs. Lee
whispered to Sandy.

"I don't know about this." Kathryn Lee frowned over
her orders. "I'll have to get the parents' consent."

"That's where you and Peg team up," Sandy told her.
"This is one action that calls for full, townwide cooperation,
and I mean *full*. Adults, children, men, women, old and young,
everyone."

Miss Lee thrust out her underlip. "None of this is going
to work. What can we really do against the Lord of Faery? He
and all his creatures are *magic!* How can we fight that?"

"Are you kidding?" Sandy grinned and picked up a copy

of the Brothers Grimm from the table. "We wrote the book. Several." She pointed in turn to a volume of old ballads, a scattering of paperback fantasies, a dog-eared pile of gaming manuals and graphic novels borrowed from Lionel's students, and assorted books of folklore.

Then her smile faded. "We're modern, educated, serious people. We're adults. We've been fighting magic for longer than you know. And I'm afraid we're winning."

Peg Seymour saw the unicorn loitering near the jewelry store and let him get her scent. She walked quickly but never seemed to flee, allowing him to follow her without breaking into a trot. People on the main street saw them coming and stood aside. It was no use crossing the street to avoid encountering the fabulous steed, for the opposite sidewalk was already the turf of Emma Talbot, who had picked up her own unicorn entourage.

As the two maiden ladies strolled on, additional unicorns joined them. Either the tracking was poor elsewhere or the animals had a sort of telepathy, informing their brethren that here were two likely subjects who didn't hit or make you work up a lather to catch them. By the time Emma and Peg had gone the length of the town, they each had four unicorns apiece in their wakes.

At the corner of Maple Street, toward the end of town where the wetlands commenced, Dennis Tuttle fell into step beside Emma. He had a dozen unicorns sniffing at his heels and he didn't look at all pleased with his success.

"Where's Kathryn?" Emma asked. She spoke as one conspirator to another, without making eye contact. Emma, Dennis, and the rest had learned that unicorns were proprietary, and tended to guard their own selected virgin jealously from other unicorns and even from other virgins.

"At the rendezvous," Dennis replied out of the corner of his mouth. "She got them. They're waiting."

"I've never been so nervous in my life." Emma's words were barely audible. She pressed dripping palms together and wiped them surreptitiously on her skirt. "I'm petrified to think of what will happen if this doesn't work. 'Always keep moving,' Davina told us. What happens if you stand still?"

"I think they wait for you to sit down," Dennis said. "Then the unicorn lays its head in your lap."

"Then what?"

Dennis thought about it. "Then . . . ." He cast a furtive

look over one shoulder. Three more unicorns had fallen in behind him. He felt ice in his bowels. "Keep moving," he said hoarsely.

For all practical purposes, the town of Godwin's Corners ended where the sidewalk did, boundary signs notwithstanding. The last street before this was itself a roughly paved road without concrete walkways, and it was here that Emma, Dennis, Peg, and their horned followings all converged. The three separate herds of unicorns did not care for the merger, but the narrowness of the street left them no choice. They shouldered each other roughly, trying to keep their eyes fixed on the sole virgin of their fancy. It was not easy, and more than once Emma shuddered when she heard the sharp clack of huge teeth and the shrill scream of the bitten animal.

Up the slight hill they went, under the limbs of old sycamore trees, past the American Legion hall, and into a stretch of open ground that, miraculously, had not yet been blacktopped or condominiumed over. Grass still grew there, autumnal golden blades brightened by a few late-shining purple stars of aster fenced only by a distant stand of pine trees. The humans could hear soft whickerings of wonder and delight from a number of throats behind them. They did not look back, but marched on, until they were in the very center of the field.

And then Peg Seymour cupped her hands to her lips and shouted, "Come and get them, girls!"

The pine woods exploded. Laughter wilder and sweeter than any other sound on earth rushed from the fragrant evergreen shadows as a horde of little girls, all between the ages of eight and twelve, came running into the meadow, arms outstretched to the unicorns.

It was over in a few minutes. The beasts never knew what hit them. Kathryn Lee had had to conscript every willing and qualified Girl Scout and Brownie in town, with a few Campfire Girls thrown in for safety in numbers, but it was necessary. Sandy had suggested a minimum of three girls per unicorn to guarantee success. It worked.

Elflock-tangled manes were unraveled and combed silky by small, eager hands, then braided up with bright ribbons. Lumps of sugar, carrots, even granola bars were thrust under the beasts' noses, and an endless stream of cloying pet names were trilled into their ears. The unicorns found themselves kissed, caressed, hugged, coddled, and spoiled from all sides. It was an assault of very human enchantments, no less compelling than Elfhame magic. Huge, age-wise eyes lifted to link glances above the sea of adoring young faces. A calm, mutual agreement was exchanged. Whatever their original orders had been, the unicorns had reached a decision of their own. They liked this just fine.

They let the little girls lead them all away and left the adult virgins to their own devices.

"It worked." Kathryn Lee sounded as if she still had trouble believing it.

"Did we get all of them?" Emma wondered.

"I covered the academy campus." Dennis still sounded miffed. "You ladies covered the town proper. I'd say we got them all."

"But will the ruse hold them?" Peg asked. "What's to stop them from breaking free of the little girls and coming back after us, or the academy boys, or any transient virgins in the neighborhood?"

A shy, knowing smile touched Emma's lips. "You never were horse-mad, were you, Miss Seymour?"

Peg shuddered in just the way a brood mare might twitch flies off her coat. "They do smell so."

"Then you can't know a thing about the bond that forms between a young girl and her horse. Some people will tell you it's all in the girl's imagination, but—"

"They're wrong," Kathryn said hotly. "They don't know anything!" Tears leaked from her eyes.

"Did you have a horse, Miss Lee?" Dennis put the question gently and dared to let his arm rest on the woman's plump shoulders. He was gratified when she did not jerk away, but snuggled more deeply into his bird-boned chest.

"Lord Rheingold Silver the Bruce Wyremad's Pride, the most spirited gelding there ever was in the world! I called him Brucie. He died when my mother told me we couldn't afford lessons anymore." A sob tore her throat. "He died because he pined for me, I know he did!"

Peg Seymour made a disgusted sound. "Beasts are beasts. Pining for you, no less! Really, Kathryn, you're a little old to be weeping over a horse."

Dennis found his reedy arms closing protectively about Miss Lee's daunting dimensions in just the way so many Brads, Winthrops, Dirks, and Stewarts behaved in the Mistglow Romances he read on the q.t. ("It's for my mother, Miss Perkins.") It was an alien action, reeking of testosterone, and he found he rather enjoyed it. Just for grins, he tried thrusting his chin out and tightening his jaw muscles.

"If you're incapable of comprehending the finer emotions, Miss Seymour, at least have the courtesy not to mock what you don't understand!''

"Hmph! I understand that there's more work to be done." Peg turned on her heel and stalked back to town, Emma Talbot hurrying after.

"Oh, Dennis, you were *wonderful!''* Kathryn burrowed into him more fiercely. Dennis felt a rising heat in his loins. Usually the sensation panicked him into drinking three pots of chamomile tea and doing some research on the Morgan family tree. He was always afraid that if he did anything more direct about answering his glandular imperatives, he would do the wrong thing, do it poorly, do it far too hastily, and be laughed at. Better to drink tea. But this time he was far from home, in the middle of a meadow, and for once he didn't feel as terrified of his own fleshly impulses as formerly. The shadow of a rampant unicorn hung against the sky with a double-dog-dare-you leer on its face.

"No, Kathryn," he breathed. "I am not wonderful. You are.'' Their lips met and fused together on contact. They sank down into the windswept grasses, and though passion swiftly overcame their every scruple, blood and breeding indicated the old Yankee gentleman. Dennis still took that extra moment to check their flowery bed for unicorn chips.

The dark man in the Burberry raincoat leaned across the rail fence and cursed the prancing unicorns in an unknown tongue. "Is thissss how you obey your king? Worthlesssss beastssss! The girls have gone. Come! Leave thisssss place! There is work for you!''

He rose into the air and floated over the fence, coming down beside the largest of the fabulous creatures. It was a stallion, with a silver-tipped white coat and a horn so translucent that the blood pulsing within the shaft gave it the illusion of a captive rainbow. The big steed's mane was braided into a series of loops, each decked with a blue ribbon rosette, and his breath was still sweet with sugar.

The dark man glowered into the unicorn's liquid eyes. "Did you not hear me? Lord Kelerisssson demands that you lead the herd back to the academy grounds! Ssstrike there, and we may yet cause the mortal woman's mate to lose his job. That will sssstab her deep! Come, I sssay! Sssserve your king as he bids you!''

"That won't do you a stitch of good, young man.'' Old

Mrs. Talbot had a clear voice that carried well, even across the breadth of an open paddock. She came toward the dark man, leaning on Emma's arm. "You might tell your employer that he'll get no further use out of these unicorns. They are entirely attached to the girls. Believe me, I have tried to shoo them off, as an experiment, and have had no luck whatsoever, though the girls are all in class now." Her eyes narrowed as she drew nearer. "I hope I shall have better fortune shooing *you* away."

The dark man's all-black eyes returned Mrs. Talbot's gimlet glare. "Old fool! If it wantsss the children to fetch the unicorns, do you think the lord King Kelerison will balk at that?"

He flung back his Burberry, and the raincoat transformed itself into a cape of reptilian scales, blue and green, wildfire smoldering around the hem. Beneath it, the dark man was naked, and Emma gasped to see any near-human form so misshapen, any being so repulsive to the eye. A reed flute showed itself in the dark man's twisted fingers, and he moistened his lipless mouth with a pebbled gray tongue before he began to play.

"That will do," Mrs. Talbot said, and her walking stick put bite behind her words as she smashed the flute from the dark man's hands. "We'll have none of your Pied Piper nonsense in Godwin's Corners. This happens to be a school day, and truancy is sufficiently widespread without your encouragement."

A hawk's hunting cry split the dark man's face. He leaped for Mrs. Talbot, hands clenched into claws, his cloak of scales streaming fire. The old woman gave an involuntary shout for help, arms crossed before her face, and stepped backward without looking. She trod on a small tussock of grass and her ankle turned under her, then snapped with the brittleness of her years. She fell, and the scream of pain she uttered left no doubt in Emma's mind that her aunt had at the very least broken her hip as well.

"You . . . you *coward!*" Emma grabbed up her aunt's walking stick and drove it down hard on the dark man's skull. Not even Mrs. Talbot could criticize her follow-through this time. It made a rubbery noise on impact, but it stopped him before he could reach the old woman. He staggered, eyes blinking. Emma raised the blackthorn for a second blow.

The unicorn spared her the trouble. He was between her and the dark man, flailing his razored hooves at the creature, jabbing in with his horn, slashing huge rents in the fiery scale cloak with his teeth. Threads of flame wriggled and went out wherever the unicorn's horn touched. The magical cape lost its fire, then its light. The scales turned ashy gray, charred black, and the dark man curled into a ball of cringing terror beneath. The unicorn blew scornfully through his nostrils and showed his fallen foe his hindquarters before prancing away to where Mrs. Talbot lay.

The unicorn bent his neck and touched her with his horn. A wave of something more than light emanated from the pearly tip and spread over the woman's body in a tide of healing. Mrs. Talbot stared into the unicorn's impassive face as her body responded to the grace of magic. The unicorn lifted his head and trotted off in the direction of the stables to wait until his three special girls should come from school to spoil him further. He was unconcerned with human awe or gratitude. He had only been doing his job.

Emma breathed a prayer of thanks when she saw her aunt healed of more than those broken bones. Mrs. Talbot got to her feet as easily as a schoolgirl and announced, "My arthritis! Emma, it's gone!" She came over to where her niece still stood above the trembling dark man and stared at him with just the same cold disdain as the unicorn had used. "Let that be a lesson to you." She turned her back on him. "Come, Emma. This is only a start."

But it was not in Emma's nature to pretend that an enemy's pain was less real than an ally's. Her heart ached with pity. She was softer than her aunt Vivian would have liked, but that was her nature. Leaning on the blackthorn stick, she knelt beside the dark man and rested a hand on his back. "I'm sorry," she said.

"What do you know of sorrow?" Every word was a groan. Emma winced in sympathy when the dark man moved, revealing the bleeding gashes that the unicorn had dealt him.

"You—you attacked Aunt Vivian, and she's an old woman. I had to protect her. What you did—"

"You think I did it freely? That it was my pleasure to act thus?" Pain throbbed in the night eyes, shone in the bloody star-shaped pupils, yet the dark man managed a bitter laugh. "But of course you do! I am a monster to your earthbound eyes, and what is ugly without must be damned within. The shell betrays the substance. If I would tell you the truth of my seeming, your eyes would say I lied. What is ugly, is evil, always."

"No." Emma shook her head. She slipped her arm beneath the dark man's head and cradled it. She thought of her own plain face, and her innate shyness. Better than any fence of witch-called thorns, better than any ring of enchanted fire, they had kept Emma isolated from all the mundane princes of her world for what seemed like over a hundred years. She knew much of unattractive shells and the secrets they could hide. The blackthorn fell to the ground. She took her own handkerchief and dabbed at his wounds. "No."

"Liar! You mouth what makes your soul feel justified, but your heart knows the truth! You find me hideous, body and soul!"

The words and the gesture were simple. "Not hideous; sad." And a kiss on the lipless mouth, given with a compassion more rare than pity or love.

"Emma!" Mrs. Talbot was scandalized. "Emma, what are you—oh! Oh heavens! Oh dear!"

The beautiful young man broke through the dark man's shell in a hatching more dramatic than any salamander's birth. The old skin flaked away and rode a passing wind into oblivion. The man remaining was tall and golden, his eyes the color of hyacinths. His cape, tunic, and hose were all the shades of blue in a changing summer sky, and he drew a joyfully surprised Emma into an embrace that lasted far too long for her aunt's sense of propriety.

"Young man." Mrs. Talbot tapped him smartly on the back. "Young man, as Emma's nearest living relative—with the exception of her brother Brian, and we don't talk about *him*—I think we should discuss your intentions before this unseemly display of affection goes any further."

The extraordinary eyes reluctantly turned from Emma's ecstatic face. He spoke in a voice half honey and half music. "Madam, I am Prince Fergus MacNuada of Eire and Faery, with vast domains in both your world and my fay sire's. A curse was placed upon me by a disgruntled Englishman when I refused to sell him certain portions of my Connemara estates during the Great Potato Famine."

"Forgive me if I question your word," Mrs. Talbot replied.

"Because of the long lapse of years between the famine and the present? But I am of the blood of Elfhame."

"I don't question your pedigree. It is simply that I cannot picture a proper Englishman cursing in public."

Prince Fergus had a smile to charm mercy from a stone. "He had been stationed in India and picked up some of the

more unfortunate native customs, including powerful magic.
The curse worked, and I became such an embarrassment to my
old-world relatives—mortal and elfin both—that I left the estates in trust and emigrated. King Kelerison gave me a post in
his court, but now"—he returned his fondest look to Emma—
"now that this blessed girl has broken the spell's power with
a kiss, I am free to return."

Mrs. Talbot frowned.

"With her, of course," Prince Fergus added.

Mrs. Talbot glowered.

"—as my lawfully wedded wife—"

Mrs. Talbot's eyes shot sparks.

"—after an Episcopalian ceremony."

Mrs. Talbot smiled. "Bless you, my children."

Kelerison was in his room at the Silver Swan Inn, deep
in a dream of mortal women, when there came a knock at the
door. He grumbled and opened it without getting out of bed,
putting a minor itching spell on whoever was unlucky enough
to have disturbed his rest.

Scratching furiously in a host of embarrassing spots,
Rumpelstiltskin entered.

"Well?" Kelerison stretched his long bones until his back
arched. "How soon before these townsfolk tear the brazen
wench apart for me?"

"Bad news, Your Majesty." The dwarf used his golden
spindle as a backscratcher.

Kelerison sat up straight, eyes afire. *"Bad* news? I don't
care for bad new. How bad?"

"Well . . . they neutralized the unicorns, for one."

"Unicorns—" The King of Elfhame Ultramar snapped
his fingers. "I only threw them in for nuisance value and dec-
orative effect. One brownie is worth a dozen unicorns in plaguing mortals into submission."

Rumpelstiltskin became so upset that he forgot to scratch.
"Got the brownies too," he muttered.

"What?"

"It's not my fault, Your Majesty, I swear!" He made
the Old Sign over his heart and kissed his pinkie for emphasis.
"You didn't give me but a handful of the People of the Darkness to deploy, and second stringers, most of them."

Kelerison's brow darkened. "I don't need Bantrobel inquiring into my present business here on the surface. If I di-

verted too many of our subjects, she might suspect something and come after me.''

The dwarf sighed noisily. ''Queen Bantrobel hasn't come after you in more than a century. What makes you think she'd care enough to start nosying in now?''

''My lady wife might act indifferent to my comings and goings, but it's no more than a ploy on her part. She does care!'' Kelerison's expression challenged contradiction.

''As you like it, Your Majesty.'' Rumpelstiltskin's shoulders rose and fell.

''What I would like is to hear is what's become of our effectives.''

The dwarf decided that the inevitable could not be softened by delay. ''They got 'em with the shoes.''

''?''

''Shoes, Your Majesty. You know us People of the Darkness. Too damned close to the land, that's our problem, never really able to cut the ties to the old country like you elven. You're assimilated, but us—we're still too ethnic. Customs, customs, customs . . .'' He shook his head and scratched under his arms.

A charge of raw, irritated power from Kelerison blasted every itch on the dwarf's body into kingdom come. ''Stop your gibber and tell me what happened!''

''They put out their old shoes, that's what!'' Rumpelstiltskin shouted back. ''Reeboks and Nikes, Maine trotters and topsiders, even a gaggle of Thom McAns. There wasn't one doorstep in all Godwin's Corners that didn't have a bowl of milk and a set of cruddy treads on it last night. Even up at the Godwin Academy there were paper cups full of Grade A outside every dorm room and sneakers shot to hell.''

The dwarf sighed. ''You know how it was in the old country? There never was a brownie, gnome, or karker could resist a free drink, only after it's down the hatch, we're honor bound to pay back the treat with a service, and that's always been free cobbling. There are only so many of us here with you now, Your Majesty, and there are only so many hours a night, and cobbling—really fine cobbling—takes time. We're old-world craftsmen who take pride in our work. By the time it was sunup, we'd finished the shoes but there wasn't any time to do any mischief.''

''That accounts for one night,'' Kelerison said testily.

''One night, sure; and the next; and the next. Never saw

so many shoes in my life! If I ever meet this Maude Frizon chick, I'm gonna—''

"The Winged Ones! Surely *they* have been accomplishing something more concrete?"

The dwarf doffed his cap. A tiny winged sprite sat crosslegged on his bald spot, but at the sight of Kelerison it took to the air, buzzing nastily. The King of Elfhame Ultramar plucked it by the wings and forced it to calm down long enough to make a report. He heard it out, then tilted his head toward Rumpelstiltskin.

"I am astounded. I didn't know you could jury-rig a Japanese beetle trap."

"The Horowitz broad sent Prince Fergus around with a letter offering to trade you seventeen bags full of pixies, fairies, and assorted limoniads for an interview at her place this evening at six."

"She dares to set times and conditions?" Kelerison roared. "Summon Prince Fergus to me! I will have him take care of her."

The dwarf tied knots in his cap. "Prince Fergus is off the payroll."

Kelerison slapped one hand over his eyes. "Who broke the spell? A mortal?"

Rumpelstiltskin made a small sound of assent. "He said to tell you thanks for the memories and the bride's registering her patterns at Tiffany's."

Kelerison's body lost much of its stiff-boned pride. "Is there more?"

"I—uh—I—"

"*Et tu,* Rumpelstiltskin?"

A tear or two of bleak defeat took the scenic route down the dwarf's long nose before splashing to the floorboards. "No sense putting it off, sire. He'll wait forever, if he has to, but he said he's gonna see you and he means it. Take my advice: don't fight him." More tears followed. "I tried; I lost."

The King of Elfhame Ultramar was off his bed of luxury and on his feet. Shining layers of air were already molding themselves into armor on his body, and a sword spiked out of his hand. "A warrior! The Powers be praised, at last they send me an honorable challenge, in the time-honored style of trial by combat. Ah, it shall be sweet—"

Rumpelstiltskin dared to lay a restraining hand on his master's sword arm. "Uh-uh," he said.

Kelerison watched, bemused, as the dwarf went back to

the door and opened it. On the other side waited an apparition so startling that the King of Elfhame Ultramar forgot to drop his armored guise but stood there, in full battle splendor, staring like an upcountry pumpkinhead.

Well might he stare. His caller was a hybrid more fearsome than any chimera or griffon. From neck to feet he was the picture of impeccable haberdashery. His Italian wingtips matched exactly the color of his Crouch and Fitzgerald attaché case, both in mellow burgundy leather. His sober navy suit hung well and was smartly, though not ostentatiously, creased at the legs. Even his tie—that most treacherous of sartorial shoals, that scrap of fabric upon which many an otherwise sane man lavishes the worst lunacies of misguided self-expression and is thereby wrecked, fashionably speaking—even that was a demure navy-and-burgundy silk rep, with a faint stripe of yellow as discreet as the finest assassin.

From the neck up, the man was a punk. Though his silver-lensed sunglasses were Dior, though his Mohawk was thoughtfully dyed in the Princeton colors, though the crucifix dangling from one pierced ear was probably Cartier, he was a punk.

"Mr. Thomas Keller?" He walked in without an invitation and sat in the ladderback chair beside the room's small secretary. His attaché sprang open on his knees and a series of manila folders spread their contents over the desk.

Kelerison nodded. "Yes?"

His caller thrust out his hand. "Brian Talbot." He waited for his host to sheath his elf-forged blade before they shook, then he glanced back at the documents in front of him. "Also known as William Kell, also known as 'Mad Jack' Kelly, also known as Billy-Bob Kelso, also known as Tom Kelsey of the sixties band Little Tommy and the Underhill Revolution?"

Kelerison nodded again, stiffly. Rumpelstiltskin gaped at his lord. "A band? When the hell did you pull that one off? Your Majesty," he added.

Brian Talbot stepped in before Kelerison could respond. "Mr. Rumpelstiltskin, I'm not into pulling rank, but I'm a busy man, okay? You can catch up on the past later. Anyhow, the best Little Tommy and the Underhill Revolution ever did was a warm-up act for Jimi Hendrix and a *real* short gig at Woodstock. Had a song that made it about halfway up the charts. What was it, devil-something?"

" 'Demon Lover.' " Kelerison sat heavily on the bed. "Number thirty-seven for two weeks."

"With a fishing sinker. Good while it lasted, though, huh?" Brian grinned. Two of his upper incisors were capped with silver, two of the lowers with copper, and all of his canines had been stained lapis blue. He rapped a sheaf of papers straight. "So okay, all the a.k.a.'s as above, plus also known as Kelerison, King of Elfhame Ultramar, right?" Kelerison's mouth slipped wider by a sizable notch. "Right. And not one damn penny paid to the IRS—that's me"—he laid a hand to his bosom and bowed modestly—"in, oh, let's say since there *was* an IRS? Here.''

A familiar-looking bundle of boilerplate was shoved into Kelerison's hand. The King of Elfhame regarded the subpoena with the loathing due an exceptionally slimy garden pest. Rumpelstiltskin whimpered beneath his lord's glower.

"It wasn't my fault, Your Majesty. It was that mortal woman I tried roping into the Forestfresh biz. She—''

"I warned you. Forestfresh!" The elf-king's lip curled. "I can't understand the blind greed of you People of the Darkness. You can spin straw to gold, yet you insist on dickering about with petty-cash schemes like that!''

"Hey, what do you have against free enterprise?" the dwarf protested. Indignation made him overly bold. "How about you elven? I never saw a mortal female yet who came close to your own kind in the looks department, yet there you go, chasing one earthbound skirt after another and sending *me* home with excuse notes to your wife! And it's not just you, Your Majesty, it's just about any elfin male worth his sword. Me and mine going after mortals, I can dig it. You ever see what one of our women looks like?''

Kelerison shuddered. Rumpelstiltskin nodded with satisfaction and continued: "So you're greedy one way, we're greedy another. Anyhow, spinning straw to gold—that's against the law here, isn't it?" He looked to Brian Talbot for confirmation.

The hound of Internal Revenue gave it. "I'm pretty sure it is. Could be called counterfeiting, could come under the heading of an individual citizen holding too much gold." He slid his shades down the bridge of his nose. "You *are* a citizen? Our records say so, and you've got a Social Security number, but—''

The dwarf looked proud. "Every soul down Elfhame Ultramar way's as much a citizen of these here United States of America as any mortal whose ancestors came over on the *Mayflower*. That's how long we've been here. Longer.''

"No shit?" Brian shuffled his papers back into the attaché and snapped it closed. "I've got half a mind to drop in on
Aunt Viv and tell her that. It always torks the hell out of her
to hear somebody else has deeper bloodlines than her family.
Too bad she's not speaking to me."

"I can see why." Kelerison's thin skin of mortal seeming peeled away. He let Brian have the full effect of his exotic
features, the searing rage that could only kindle properly in
elfin eyes.

Brian chuckled, safe behind his mirrored lenses. "You
think it's my look? Shows what you know. I'm good at my
job; damn good. So damn good that they don't mind if I keep
the look—potential undercover work opportunity, they call it.
Nah, the look's nothing to the department and nothing to Aunt
Viv either. But the minute I got this job and zinged *her* with a
delinquency rap, she cut me off dead. Said she'd expected me
to maybe turn to dealing drugs, and was all set to forgive *that*,
but this was one over the line." He had a snicker the Marquis
de Sade might have cherished. "By the time the department
got through auditing her, she had to dip into her *capital!* Never
forgave me. Never."

He was almost out the door when Kelerison called,
"Stop! Tell me, how did you learn this much about me?"

Brian leaned against the jamb. "Well, man, directly
speaking, your little friend there ratted some so's we'd go easier on him." Rumpelstiltskin cringed. "But we got onto *him*
through a Ms. Young—"

"She sicced 'em on me in trade for *them* calling up my
Social Security number, Your Majesty!" The dwarf was on his
knees, wringing his hands. "Have mercy! Now *I've* got to
make her Forestfresh sales quotas!"

"—and she got the idea for calling us in from another
woman—a real sharp legal type named—"

"Don't tell me." Kelerison's mouth was a brittle line.
"Sandra Horowitz."

Brian snapped his fingers. "You got it. And a Ms.
Amanda Taylor helped us out a lot too, giving us some of those
a.k.a.'s you've been using over the years. Nice ladies."

The power of great magic coupled with the immeasurable
strength of great anger gathered around Kelerison like a thun-
derhead. His silver armor tarnished black from the force of his
wrath. "You moth, are you blind to who and what I am? I am
Kelerison, Lord King of Elfhame Ultramar! Are you arrogant

enough to believe that *this* has any meaning for me?'' He crumpled the subpoena in his hands.

Brian calmly brushed the top of his black-and-orange Mohawk. ''Got me. That's not my department. Like Ms. Horowitz said, no harm in trying, okay? If it doesn't work, we tried; if it does . . . Hey, I really like that heavy metal stuff you're wearing, y'know? Outtahere.''

The subpoena slowly came down at Kelerison's side. He closed the door after Brian without moving from the bed. Rumpelstiltskin crept closer to his lord. ''Your Majesty, I'm real sorry, I swear that I—''

''Six o'clock,'' Kelerison said grimly. ''She herself has summoned me. Let her doom come to her out of her own foolishness. Six o'clock tonight. I will be there.''

Chapter Fourteen:

The Case of the Angry Elven

''**P**ass me *Black's*, Cass,'' Sandy said, not looking up from the shuffle of yellow legal pads and Davina's crisply typed research notes. The room so long consecrated to be Sandy's in-home office, and so long unused, now looked as jumbled and lived-in as the most ambitious proto-lawyer could desire. It was crowded with books and papers and people—only three people, but what with the books and papers taking up so much space, those three had to hustle if they didn't want to do their assigned tasks sitting on the floor.

''What's *Black's*?'' the elfin prince asked. He had laid aside his mortal looks from the day his father's vengeance had begun. Now he sat at Sandy's feet, long legs folded elegantly under him as he occupied a cricket stool. There was something magical, or at least gravity defying, about the way he managed to keep his balance on so precarious a perch.

''You know what *Black's* is.'' Sandy sounded irritated. She did not look away from her scribblings. ''You've passed it to me enough times.'' She would not look at him.

"That was Davina."

First playing dumb, now outright lies. She knew it for a lie, and she knew why he was lying too. He wanted her to look at him. Just as strongly, she did not want to do that; perhaps even more strongly.

"I think he's right, Mrs. Wal—Sandy." Davina still didn't sound comfortable addressing her employer so familiarly. She was cozily tucked into the room's one armchair, a law book on her lap. "I'm sure it was I always fetched it for you, and not Cass."

The close air stank with conspiracy. No matter what Cass said you could depend on Davina to back him up to the death. There was little need to ponder why. It just wanted one look at the elfin prince, and Sandy's head seized on the excuse, turning to do so without a by-your-leave from her brain.

It was distracting and disconcerting to tear her eyes from the paperwork and meet Cass's gaze, for all that it was sensually rewarding. In the most brightly lit room, his beauty added an extra glow to the air. In a snug place like this, the only light coming from a green-shaded cashier's lamp over the desk, an upright lamp beside the armchair, and a pair of electric wall scones, the prince was a cool flame meant to draw the fascinated attention of those mortals his father so aptly called "moths."

Cass had also been watching MTV and had practiced a come-hither pout that Mick Jagger and Billy Idol should have protected by patent. He was using everything he had on her, and Sandy didn't like it. She didn't like it at all, for three distinct reasons:

For one, now that she had real work to occupy her time, she had ceased to dream of Rimmon. She still thought of him, she would always remember him with the tenderness and rose-tinged regret proper to the most memorable love affair of one's life, but he was out of her dreams. She only saw his face when she summoned it. She didn't need or want to be reminded of him by another of his kind.

For another, she was a respectable married lady, and a mother. It sounded stodgy, but prudes led very safe lives, and Sandy felt she had all the perils she could handle just then. And prosaic as it sounded, she did love Lionel: a cozy, placid, domestic love that she might have wished were a shade more

. . . piquant? No, no, that was the way back to impossible dreams of alien pleasures, and all the lost passion she had felt in Rimmon's arms.

No more! Sandy gave herself a sharp reprimand. *It was safe for me to fantasize an elfin lover when there wasn't a chipmunk's chance I'd see another elf this side of those Christmastime abominations. Now . . .*

She studdied Cass's upturned face. There was nothing on earth to touch him. His father was handsome, tempting, with the added appeal of his uncounted years of life to whisper in a mortal woman's ear, *Oh, the ancient delights I might share with you, my love!* But Cass was young, for what he was, and in youth there was a sweeter seduction, even when the youth in question had last had his diapers changed when the Great Pyramid of Giza was a pup.

Reason number three why Sandy hated Cass's unrelenting courtship: it was starting to work.

"*Black's Law Dictionary!*" Sandy barked at the elfin prince. "There! On the table behind you! Oh, never mind, I'll get it myself." She pushed away from the desk and stomped past him, brows beetling, growling this and that about lazy kids. Peevishness might help her cool the little fires that ran up her limbs and settled uncomfortably in her belly whenever the light struck Cass's marvelous eyes in that certain way.

She dropped back into her chair like a sack of salt and ravaged the pages of *Black's* at random. She had totally forgotten the term she wanted to look up in the first place, but damned if she was going to let on. The columns of legal phrases in English, French, and especially Latin had a soporific effect when read aloud. Sandy didn't want to go to sleep, just to put her fractious blood on hold.

"*Res caduca; res communes; res controversa; res coronae; res corporales,*" she intoned in a pleasant singsong. "*Res derelicta—*"

"Don't." Cass seized her wrist so abruptly that she came near to falling out of her chair. "If you want me to go, if I'm bothering you by being here, just say so. I'll leave you. It would be cruel of you to banish me, but my lady"—the allure was gone from his eyes, no longer luminous with offered desire, but flat and dull with fear—"that would be less cruel than this."

"Cruel? Less cruel than what?" Sandy was bewildered. "How am I being . . . ?"

The window shattered. A ball of marshfire flew past Sandy's head and hit the opposite wall with a sizzling thud. Davina jumped out of her chair and beat the flames out with a cushion. Cass too was on his feet, hot words in his own language pouring from his lips.

Kelerison leaned on the windowsill, smirking. "Happy Father's Day to you too, Cassiodoron. Though I doubt you've any substance within your body more potent than maidenly tears. You'll sire nothing with those but poetry." He shifted his glance to Sandy. "I believe you said six o'clock?"

"You might have knocked."

"I remember the last time we stood on opposite sides of a door. So does my nose. Ask me in and I'll fix the window."

Cass placed himself between Sandy and his father. "Keep him out, my lady. I know that look of his. He'll give you his word of honor that he'll parley peaceably, then turn on you if you trust him. He'll betray you too."

Kelerison laughed. "What a weaver my son is! How old do your mortal brats grow before they start fabricating such falsehoods against their own parents?"

Davina came up on Cass's right side. Her dark eyes flashed almost as brightly as if she too had some smattering of elfin blood in her veins. "Maybe it's you that's the liar, Elvenlord!" The music of her voice was as mighty as a tempest-stirred sea. "Why should we believe you against your son? We've heard more than enough of your doings, and you have shown your hand in this town."

"This one burns, Cassiodoron." Kelerison put both elbows on the sill to cup his chin. He regarded Davina steadily from beneath his birdwing brows. "You are championed by women again—your fate, it seems. Well? Will you prove to your fair shieldmaid that I am the traitor you call me? A fine accusation"—his tone shifted from light banter to a more somber note—"from one who has betrayed his own kind, his own race, his own family to go haring off as a mortal woman's lapdog! Do they know why you fled with Amanda, my dear son? Did you paint yourself as the perfect knight, rescuing the fair lady from my filthy clutches?"

"Damn you, Father . . ."

"Or did the truth slip out somehow? How you yourself lusted for her—and so you did, if my eyes didn't betray me as much as my own son! I was there, when you thought you and she were alone in her bower. I heard your words of love— pitiful, faltering things so vague that she assumed you offered her *filial* love! But I knew. I read your lecherous little soul in your eyes. Ah! Say nothing, Cassiodoron! Lechery is no shame for us. Cowardice, though . . . cowardice in love as in all other facets of your life.''

"Call me coward again!" Cass lunged forward, but Sandy grabbed him and held tight.

"Don't, Cass! He'll pull another dirty trick out of a hat; or another dragon. Take your own advice, for God's sake, and don't trust him one inch in a fair fight!''

"Brava, pretty lady.'' Kelerison clapped his hands languidly. "I see you mean to pass judgment before you hear the evidence. Or do you just want to preserve my heir's handsome face for your later enjoyment?''

Sandy pushed Cass back with all her strength. He touched Davina by chance, and Kelerison was the only one who saw how the Welsh *au pair* colored a violet rose when the elfin prince's skin brushed her own.

"I asked you here, so come in. I'm not afraid.''

"If I give my word that I come in peace, will you take it?" the elfin king asked.

"I don't need it." Sandy gave a crooked smile. It only faltered a fraction when Kelerison accepted her invitation by walking right through the wall. The smashed window melted itself whole behind him.

He took the one comfortable armchair in the room, where Davina had been curled. "Cassiodoron tells you not to expect me to keep my word, yet you seem to trust me even without it. How strange. Why?''

Sandy went back to her chair at the desk, leaving Cass and Davina to stand uneasily between herself and Kelerison. "If it's no good, why bother getting it?''

"So you've sided with my son.''

"I've sided against you in the matter of Amanda's freedom. Other than that . . .'' She looked at Cass and was surprised to see that his eyes were fixed nowhere near her. They stared with searing hatred at Kelerison, who appeared to be unaware of his son's peculiar devotion. Cassiodoron was himself just as unaware as his father of the soft, imploring gaze in which Davina's dark eyes bathed him.

Oh, Davina, Sandy thought. She sighed. One problem at a time and first come, first served.

"Your Majesty, let's waste no time.'' She spoke with a briskness she didn't feel. Inside, she was a mass of squealing nerves. Her fingers strayed to the open copy of *Black's* on her desk and rifled the pages. If she had two steel balls, she would have outclicked Captain Queeg. "I've got a few bags full of your smaller subjects in our toolshed. I'm willing to trade you their release for your agreement to get them and their kind the hell out of Godwin's Corners."

Kelerison lifted one eyebrow and the corresponding corner of his mouth. "I adore negotiating with terrorists."

Sandy's face grew warm. "Call it guerrilla tactics. This is open war, and you declared it. If you want to end it, call off your troops and let Amanda go."

The King of Elfhame Ultramar slouched back in his chair. "Why should I?" he asked. "We're at stalemate, you and I. I can send my subjects against you and your people from now until Lastday. Granted, you can counteract some small measure of our doings. But you can't stop us. We are immortal, my dear. We don't tire as readily as you when it's a case of siege."

"Oh, I can hang on longer than most, Your Majesty," Sandy replied without even the ghost of a smile.

"So stupid?"

"So persistent. As your son himself noted, I belong to a human subgroup noted for our tenacity. A stiff-necked people. We're very good at keeping faith where common sense says forget the whole thing."

"True. You are a woman." Before Sandy could say that she had meant something else, Kelerison spoke on: "I see I have a worthy foe in you, and I respect that. Very well. Let's talk terms of surrender. I will release Amanda unconditionally. I will not interfere in any way with your petty mortal playtoyings in the courts of law. She and the brat will go their own way, and I shall allow this."

"So far, so good." Sandy shifted her weight, uneasy before so much apparent good sportsmanship on the elf-king's part. *Black's Law Dictionary* shifted with her, the big book lying open in her lap, her fingers still turning the pages at random. "But I sense a conjunction coming."

"Dear woman . . ." Sandy felt the words take the form of a lingering caress down her cheek. "How right you are. Terms, I said, and terms affect both sides. For all I promise you, I ask one thing only in exchange: let my son come home again with me to the halls of Elfhame Ultramar, there to be bound by a sacred vow nevermore to seek the surface, nevermore to wander in the realms of mortal men."

"No!" Davina cried out before she knew it. Her shout of refusal was swallowed by Cass's own, yet Sandy and Kel-

erison both looked at the Welsh girl first, at the elfin prince as
an afterthought.

"You haven't the power to make me obey those terms,"
Cass declared, his pale skin darkening.

"Do you mean me?" Kelerison asked. "Or your lady?"
His lazy eyes taunted Sandy. "What a coup for you, my dear:
rid of me *and* my son in one swoop. Your tiny world will be
the better for it, I'm sure you'll agree."

"Mrs.—Sandy, you're not thinking of accepting his
terms?" Davina dropped to her knees and clasped the edge of
the desk to steady herself. Her eyes begged mutely for an answer. Kelerison chuckled indulgently to see her so.

The elfin king could not have known that the one thing
above all others that drove Sandra Horowitz wild was a pater-
nalistic chuckle. She'd heard it more than once too often on
the lips of male relatives, professors, and colleagues from her
law school days, all of whom treated her career aspirations as
the punch line to a three-years-running knock-knock joke. If
the chuckle were backed up by a pat on the head or a chuck
under the chin, homicide was possible. Even without these
added affronts, the sound of "there-there, you cute little girl-
child" laughter made her see blood red.

She bolted to her feet. *Black's* hit the floor. "I don't
make deals with anyone's life but my own, and I won't impose
your terms on Cass, no matter what we'd gain!"

Again Kelerison chuckled, knocking a new nail into his
coffin with every jocund syllable. "You hear that, Cassiodoron?
My felicitations. It seems you may have a chance of seducing
this one, if you persist. She cannot bear the thought of being
parted from you. Why, she might even follow you into our
own realm, by the twisted paths guarded by the People of
Blood. As for the fat one"—he nodded scornfully at Davina—
"she is yours already. No challenge there."

Davina's gasp was harsh, its rough edge cut sharply by
the sound of Sandy's flat hand smacking Kelerison across the
face. "Get out of my house!" she shouted. "You haven't come
to talk. You've come to prove you're an obnoxious bastard.
Well, we all know that, so your job's done. Get out of here.
Take your brainless insults with—"

The hand that had dared to strike the elfin king clenched
of its own will. Each finger lost its stiff articulation, turned
fluid, writhed itself green and scaled, lidless eyed, flicker
tongued. Five small serpents coiled from a knot of reptilian
skin that had been Sandy's hand. Their mouths spread scarlet,

showing fangs, and they had no qualms about sinking these into their nearest brethren.

Sandy's silent shock broke with the first stab of fangs into flesh. Her still-human hand groped for the wound automatically, and the serpents bit it deeply. The room whirled with the pain of it, the lamps blazing into sunrise bands across her sight. Stunned, she stretched out her hands to the others.

Davina screamed and toppled backward from her knees. Her fingers clawed for something to hold on to, closed on the first thing they touched, tore pages from the law book. Cass jumped away from the fluttering sheets as if they were the serpents. In a daze of terror and agony, Sandy noted this with the peculiar slow-motion clarity that often sharpens the eyes in a disaster.

"My book . . ." Her words were jumbled, slurred. "Don't hurt my book, Davina. It cost Lionel a lot of money. Please give it to me before . . ."

The study was full of elfin laughter.

"What in Heaven's name is going on in here?"

Sandy blinked mildly as the shout echoed in her skull. She felt herself drifting in a place of soft, warm shadows, like the ghosts of cats. It was a very pleasant sensation, really, so restful after all her sharp-honed plans and orders. She was weary of taking charge, so weary! She would let someone else see to Kelerison now. Yes, let Amanda step into what was her own fight. Surely the woman couldn't be that much of a pudding?

I've done enough, Amanda. Now let me rest . . .

"Sandy! Sandy, what's the matter with you?"

There it was again, that too-loud voice. It disturbed her guests. It had frightened Amanda away. It wasn't Cass's, or Kelerison's, and it certainly wasn't Davina's, though the girl had a deep enough voice for a woman. Whose was it? Sandy's eyelids closed. Whoever it was, she ought to tell him he was being very rude. Some people wanted to sleep.

"Professor Walters, grab that book!"

Ah! Now *that* was Cass's voice. She would know it anywhere. "Thank you, Cass," she murmured drowsily. "It is a very expensive book. Lionel would be upset . . . upset if I told him . . . What? No, I can't tell him. It would hurt his feelings if he knew that I wish I could have you and . . ."

Someone had her mutated hand in his. It was a very cool hand, cool even in contrast to the snakes, and they were cold-blooded creatures. In the rushing noise that poured into her

ears, Sandy heard another voice, colder still: Kelerison's. Only
Kelerison's voice could be so cold.

"Get away from her, Cassiodoron! She knew what she
risked, standing against me. Let her learn! I forbid you to use
your healings!"

The slim hand tightened on hers. Cass's reply was senseless, only a tune whose words were inhuman.

"Be careful, Cass." Sandy's lips were drunken as she
spoke. "I don't want the snakes to bite you too."

"The book, for the sake of all you love!" (How nice,
now Cass was speaking more clearly. She could understand his
words again although they were coming from farther and farther away.) "Read! Read! I can bear it!"

"Read?" That male voice again. It sounded confused,
frightened.

The room was growing chill. Sandy forced her eyes open
and saw a wide, black shape, like the wings of a devilfish,
extending from the chair where Kelerison sat. But where was
the elfin king? She could not see him for the darkness. A damp
wind rose, and the black shape rose with it to block the lamplight.

"Read!"

A scuffle. The hand no longer held hers. She felt the
dusty tufts of a rug against her face. She turned herself over
onto her back and saw three figures looming above her like
standing stones; three figures, and a wave of darkness.

And one of them held a book. He was white, white, fiery
white behind the open volume in his hands, and he read aloud
words that were strange, yet not so strange or musical as the
unknown language of elven.

*"Haeres est aut jure proprieta—proprietatis aut jure
representation—tionis. . . ."*

The chill was fading from her flesh. She was warming.
The heat came in gusts that ceased to blow whenever the reader
stumbled, or hesitated over a word. The weights left her eyes.
It was easy to see now. The whiteness became Cass, and Li-
onel and Davina were with him, staring into the open copy of
Black's.

"Haereditas damnosa . . ."

Cass took a long, quavering breath. There was sweat on
his upper lip, beads of it trickling down his brow. Sandy in-
stinctively raised her hand to wipe it away and saw the snakes
stiffening, dying, bleaching back into five familiar fingers as
he read on.

"Haec est—est final—finalis con . . ."

Cass staggered. He fell to one knee and steadied himself on her. *What am I doing on the floor?* A crackling went through her skin. She sat up suddenly and snatched the book from his hands. Her eyes whipped to where the dark wave loomed, and in its heart she saw Kelerison's taut face. He bit his lip. Sweat streaked his face too.

Cass tore a final word from the open page: *"Nocent."* The boundaries of his father's darkness shivered. Before they closed, his eyes implored Sandy to understand.

She did, though she could hardly believe the evidence that lodged in her belly instead of her brain. The book was in her hands, and she knew. *That would be less cruel than this.* She knew why Cass had said that, she knew why Kelerison had not just laughed and ignored her "playtoyings in the courts of law," she knew that there was a power to do more than stalemate the King of Elfhame Ultramar. A word of law, a word of power, and words of power in grammarye were Latin for more than a whim.

"Nomina sunt notae rerum," she read. Cass writhed on the floor near her. The words exercised their awful spell on him as well as on his father. It was a potent, painful thing to see, but she could not stop. *"Nomina sunt symbola rerum."*

"For the love of heaven, carry him from here!" Davina shook Lionel roughly. Sandy's husband was a man waking from a dream, but he woke quickly. He slid his arms under Cass's knees and back, lifting the long body and bearing him out of the room as fast as possible. Davina hovered on the doorsill, her eyes dancing nervously from Sandy to Kelerison to the way Lionel had taken Cass.

"Operis novi nuntiati . . . It's all right, Davina, you can go help Lionel with Cass—*nuntiatio!"* Sandy hit Kelerison with an adlibbed habeas corpus while Davina made her escape.

All the blackness cloaking the elfin king was gone. It had soaked off into the air and disappeared. Still firing off one Latin law term after another, Sandy climbed back into her chair without taking her eyes off Kelerison. Each phrase struck him harder than the one before. Their separate meanings were unimportant. A *Vadium ponere* was worth as much as a *Vagabundum nuncupamus eum qui nulibi domicilium contraxit habitationis.* She only stopped when her opponent slipped senseless from his seat and lay in a heap on the rug.

Sandy wasted no time waiting for him to recover. She tore strips of paper from her legal pads, fastened them into long yellow loops, inscribed each one with *Collatio bonorum* and *Dementia praecox,* and tied them loosely around Kelerison's wrists and ankles. As a happy second guess, she stapled two strips into a collar emblazoned with *Errores scribentis nocere non debent* and noosed it around his neck.

Kelerison moaned as he regained consciousness. He tried to move his hands and gave Sandy immediate proof that her paper manacles were just that; they tore with no trouble.

"Watch it! I've still got the book." She held it out at him like Van Helsing stabbing a cross at Dracula.

Kelerison removed the paper collar and rubbed his head. "So you do. Well. You have found your weapon. Now you see why I have such a distaste for those legal documents you insist on forcing into my hands."

Sandy thought of the word *subpeona.* "Because of the Latin legalese in them," she said.

"Latin! I remember saying to my sire, King Oberon, just before the Great Emigration, 'At least we shan't have to fear the cursed tongue of wizardry in the new land.' " He winced as he chanced on a still tender ache. "Simple folk settled this land—uneducated, or suspicious of Latin as too Romish for their minds, or both. I imagined Elysium."

He sighed heavily. "I forgot the lawyers."

"Never a good idea," Sandy said.

"No, it never is a good idea to forget the proper measure of your foe." The elfin king's eyes narrowed. "Where is my son?"

"Safe from you."

"Safe from . . . ? Then he *is* safe? The words did not hurt him too much?" Kelerison smiled with satisfaction. "I never yet saw him braver or more worthy of his blood than when he turned that book against me. Can I see him?"

"What for? If you want to torment him more, you'll have to find another opportunity. He saved my life from you, and I don't feel like letting you near him."

"Your life. Would you believe that sleep was the worst venom those serpents' fangs contained? That I would not take your life for such a little thing as a slap across the face? No? I thought not. Your mind is set. You will believe of me what you have already decided to believe."

"Enough about me." Sandy's finger held a place beneath a choice Latin phrase in *Black's.* "Let's talk about you, Your Majesty, and what you're going to do now."

"No doubt you'll tell me." His mouth quirked.

"First, you get all of your subjects out of town, like I said before. Second, you sit back and let Amanda's action against you go through. No interference! And that includes plaguing the New Haven judiciary with any and all of your so-called minor mischiefs. Third, you get off your son's case too."

"And if I don't, you come at me with that book. Is that so?" His face was expressionless as he observed her victorious grin. The King of Elfhame Ultramar stood. "So be it. I will give you my word—although my son has taught you to doubt its worth—and concede on all points. It is a tradition among my folk for a battle's loser to make his conqueror a gift. What can I give that you would accept?"

"The news that you're leaving will be plenty, thanks."

"No more than that?" Kelerison raised his hand. A white flower with a silver heart blossomed in the palm. "Yet hear me, Sandra Horowitz: that elfin talisman you wear is a love gift to shield you from my folk's small evils, the book you hold will keep us at a distance from you with its cold, hard words of judgment while we walk in your world. Do not be fool enough to think that either one can keep the deeper powers of magic from invading your life. Do not grow overconfident. Do not expect this to be your last battle. The sword is the only finality for my kind as well as yours. Let this counsel be my victory gift to you."

The lamplight held, but the King of Elfhame Ultramar was gone. The white flower lay on the open pages of *Black's*. Tentatively, Sandy lifted it to her nostrils and inhaled a fragrance of spice and sea.

She found Davina and Lionel fussing over Cass on the living-room sofa. The Welsh girl was stroking his face with a damp cloth and Lionel had broken out the cognac.

"Is he all right?" Sandy asked her husband.

Lionel was having a shot of the cognac himself. He looked shaken. "I think so. Sandy—babe—I didn't—in there, when Cass told me to read from that book, I didn't know what he was talking about. I didn't know it would do any good. I'm sorry."

"The Powers spare me from having any warriors like you under my command in the Lastday battle," Cass snarled. "While you'd nitter around and question orders, the bloodtide would sweep us all into the sea!" In quite a different tone, he softly questioned Sandy. "My lady . . . my dearest, fairest lady, are you well?"

Lionel and Davina made brittle excuses and left the room

before Sandy could object. She might have sought one or both of them, but Cass groaned weakly from the sofa and sank into the pillow, looking pathetic. At a loss, Sandy assumed Davina's vacant post with the damp cloth. She laid the silver flower on Cass's chest, the law book on her knees.

"Now that's over, you're going to have to explain to me why *Black's* came near to totaling you and your father."

Cass's huge eyes twinkled. "Nothing in this world exists without something to bound it. We elven have a saying—" Here he rattled off something in his lilting native tongue. " 'Only the Infinite is infinite' is a very inadequate translation."

"I'll say. The world's not ready for Zen elves."

"Let me try again: 'No power is so powerful that the Powers have not made another power to overpower it.' "

"That's worse," Sandy said, "but I get the idea."

"In the old country, the old beliefs bound my ancestors. They could be conjured away by mention of iron edges and standing stones and a host of other charms."

Sandy remembered Davina trying to use such things on Cass at the Preserv-a-Pak party. "Why don't they work on you?"

"Why?" Velvety lashes veiled his eyes. "Our scholars are still pondering the question. We only know what happened, not why. When we crossed the wide sea to come here, it was as if a great sword descended and cut the ties of old beliefs. We felt it. I still remember how joyfully my parents reacted when the revelation touched them. They were free!" He grew dreamy, thinking of it. "I think that was the last kindness I saw pass between them," he added ruefully.

"I still don't see why—"

"No heart, human or elfin, can remain empty of some belief. The People of the Darkness believe in the endless sheltering warmth of earth's womb, the water spirits in the eternal song of the father-sea, the Winged Ones in the immortal instant of a flower's greatest beauty. Only the People of Blood have none, they claim. If your folk came to this new land and left the old beliefs and their protected power behind, you soon forged new ones: belief in the perfection of a dream; belief in the holy nature of the new; belief in trial by income; but over and above and encompassing all these, belief in the constraining power of the law."

Cass took Sandy's hands and pressed them to his heart. The white flower's petals were crushed, the scent dizzying in her nostrils. She was falling forward, into the elfin prince's eyes. His lips were drawing hers closer, his words passing unnoticed from English to Elfin, hypnotic in their rhythm. *Black's* was a hard wedge between their bodies, but their lips would still touch.

And at the first brush of mouth to mouth, Sandy sat bolt upright and cried, ''No!''

''No because you will not have me? Because your flesh wants none of mine?'' Cass asked. ''Or no because adultery is against your laws?'' He touched the crushed flower to her lips. ''I wish I could take you back to the halls of Elfhame Ultramar, Sandra, elf-lover, lady mine. You would be different there. You would pour the fire of the sun into me with your passion. It was in a world far from your laws that you took your pleasure with the one who gave you this, wasn't it?'' He gently tapped the bloodstone pendant and read the answer in her face. ''I thought so. In our realm, there is only the law of combat and the law of loving. But because we have dedicated our magic to the service of your lands, we must be bound by the same laws that bind you while we walk the surface.''

Sandy tried to stand up. Cass's grasp held her seated. ''I have to go.'' She sounded hoarse. ''Lionel may need me.''

''I need you.''

''You? You're fine. You don't need—and Davina looked upset. I'd better talk to her about what your father said. She can't help—''

''My father isn't still here, is he?''

''He's gone. He surrendered. He—'' Sandy's forehead creased. ''I think he threatened me before he left.'' She repeated Kelerison's departing words as well as she could remember them.

Cass's frown mirrored her own. ''The tradition of the loser's gift is one of our oldest. To violate it . . . But why would my father balk at that? He already betrayed our laws of loving when he betrayed my mother.''

''But you said that adultery—''

''He struck her!'' The elfin prince's face was aflame. ''What greater betrayal is there than to give pain where you owe love? She complained against his philanderings with mortal women, as she had every right to do if it pleased her, and he struck her. He knocked her down!'' Cass lowered his voice. ''They began the quarrel over my refusal to accept a battle challenge and my father called me a coward. The quarrel grew, changed course, shifted from me to my father's mortal lovers,

and ended when he hit my mother, Bantrobel. He claimed to
be sorry, afterward. He swore never to do it again.''

"Did he?''

"I wouldn't know. It was soon after that that I helped
Amanda escape.''

"Then he might have kept his word, Cass.''

"Trust him, then!'' The elfin prince shouted in her face.
"I won't make that mistake!''

"If it is a mistake,'' Sandy responded softly.

Chapter Fifteen:

Lost! Lost!

"**L**ionel, aren't you supposed to be in school at this
hour?'' Sandy peered into the kitchen as if she
were a stranger in her own house. Her husband sat at the table,
moodily scrying the future in the swirls of melting Cremora in
his coffee mug.

"Yeah,'' he answered, all his enthusiasm in the grip of
rigor mortis. "I am.''

"So, get going! Your job wasn't exactly a model of security these past few weeks. I *know* it wasn't your fault, but
you ought to put in your classroom appearances on schedule,
to show everyone things are back to normal.''

Lionel rested his arm on the back of the chair and gave
his wife a belligerent look. "*Are* things back to normal?''

Sandy tried to see what he was getting at. "Well, Cee-
Cee Godwin Haines just paid Daisy Septic System Cleaners a
small fortune to pump sewage out of her basement—which
wouldn't be so odd except she paid them another small fortune
last week to pump the sewage *into* the basement. And Dwight
Haines has suddenly taken a great interest in water sports, going halfsies with Mr. Andropoulos on a boat down at the ma-
rina. It's not even a big statusy sailboat, which you might
expect; it's a by-god fishing trawler. But hey, that family was
teeing off with a bent nine-iron for years.''

"Do you call it normal to have *him* hanging around this

house at all hours?'' Lionel gestured out the open kitchen window just above the sink. A point-eared silhouette perched on the sill, lazily rubbing his jowls on the potted mums.

"Cesare?" Sandy looked at the tomcat. "I feed him, so he hangs around. You don't like that?"

"I don't mean the cat. I mean—he's out in the garden with Davina and you *know* who I mean! How come you don't ask why *he* isn't in class? He's still enrolled at the academy. He's got midterms coming up. Is he going to hocus-pocus his way through them?"

"Well, for . . . Lionel, you object to *Cass?*"

Lionel's mouth grew sullen and small. "Cass. I love that. As if he were the boy next door. What is he, anyway? If he wants to play human, let him look like one again! Let him go to his classes, do his homework, go to his *own home* sometimes! And if he's an elf, let him be one someplace else than our house. We don't need him."

"Darling, listen to reason. This whole town knows Cass for what he is. No one minds—not after what we've all gone through. Even Peg Seymour's asked him to explain gaming to her. She wants to try running a troll, she told me. It would be silly for him to go back to that old mortal disguise."

"And not half so pretty." Lionel sneered.

"He's only hangs around our house until it's time to pick up Ellie and Jeffy from school. He saves Amanda and me the trouble of going to get them, and guards them all the way home."

"What's he guarding them from?" Lionel didn't bother hiding a sliver of his skepticism. "The bogey man?"

"The bogey man might be his uncle. It's his father he's worried about."

"Ha! Present a case like that in court and the jury will stay nice and cool when the wind blows through the holes. Item!" Lionel held up one finger. "Kelerison's gone. He gave up. He packed up all his little goblins and left town, word of honor. Item!" A second finger sprang up. "What use would Cass be if his father did decide to come back? You told me how the brave warrior reacted to that pint-sized dragon. One of those in his path, and all we'd see of Cass would be heels. Item!" Three fingers bristled. "Davina's more than capable of picking up the kids from school. That's her *job!* So why is Cass really hanging around our house, as if I couldn't guess?"

A flowerpot crashed into the sink. Cesare made tongue-clicking sounds as he delicately crossed the sill. *"Permiso, signor, signora.* Allow me to answer this most burning problem.'' He twitched his whiskers at Lionel. "Obviously my young lord, Prince Cassiodoron, is lingering in your home with the intention of seducing your wife. He has not chosen to confide in me; therefore I can not say whether his desires will end with a single bedding, several, or if he intends to persuade her to flee with him for good. Where? To the halls of Elfhame Ultramar, perhaps. It is the traditional choice, the elvenkind's poor answer to your Pocono Mountains. *Ecco!* Your questions are answered, signor. There now remains one of mine for you to answer in turn: in the name of all your cherish, if an elf-lord in full possession of magic covets your wife, what do you think you can do about it?''

Lionel's whole face stiffened. "I know where that copy of *Black's* is," he said meaningfully.

"So you will read law over him until the pain of binding is so great that he will have to go?" The cat's golden gaze turned to Sandy. "You know this man of yours? Is he capable of that?''

Sandy shook her head.

"Don't you think I have the courage to fight for you?" Lionel shouted.

"Lionel . . .'' She tried to explain, but a siren's whine blared through the sunlit air. Lionel was still carrying on, threatening to levy all sorts of ghastly challenges on the elfin prince if he laid one wandering eye on Sandy. Most of these were obscured by the siren's wail, and the rest were obliterated by the sharp, shrill ringing of the telephone. Sandy ran to answer it as if racing to a lifeboat, but Davina rounded the doorway and had the receiver first.

Cass came after her, his arms full of iris and anemones that now bloomed seasonless in Sandy's garden by the same enchantment covering Amanda's. The captured limoniads had chosen to remain behind and show their helpful side. It was their own version of the Fair Folk's loser's gift. The Prince of Elfhame Ultramar cocked an inquisitive ear to the siren's howling.

"Dear God . . .'' White-faced, Davina hung up the phone. Tears flowed from her eyes. A nameless foreboding slithered around Sandy's heart and squeezed. "Oh, Mrs. Walters . . .''

Her voice would not respond. Lionel had to be the one to ask, "What is it, Davina?''

"The school . . . the school . . . the children . . .''

* * *

It was a crater dug by an invisible meteor, a smoking pit gouged out of the ground where a house once had stood. The playground equipment was twisted to slag and tangle behind it, the building foundations black with burning.

The children stood clustered around their teacher. Miss Foster was trying hard to keep her voice level as she assured them that it was all over, everything was all right. As their parents arrived on the scene by ones and twos, sometimes they would not go to them. There was more security in the herd. They clung to what they could. Their young lives had never been meant to hold such an experience. The lucky ones would be convinced that it had been just a dream.

"Oh, thank God, thank God . . ." Each parent spoke the same words as he or she picked out a boy, a girl, a face that had suddenly become more precious than the eyes searching for it in the huddle of other children. There were tears, but they were joyous. There were embraces that might never end.

Sandy, Lionel, Amanda, Cass, and Davina stood at the edge of the pit, looking down into hell. Two small faces were missing from the crowd.

"What happened?" Lionel's tongue was thick, but he had to ask it.

Miss Foster gave the last of the children into parental arms and came forward. "Professor Walters, I'm so very, very sorry."

"What happened?"

She recoiled sharply, with a hissing intake of breath. She inhaled and exhaled deeply, twice, before she could begin. "We were about to go out for recess when I thought I smelled smoke. Jeffy—" She glanced timidly at Amanda, but the woman was too numb to react to mention of her son's name. "Jeffy said he smelled it too. It seemed to be coming from the basement. I told the children to take partners and get ready to leave. We were all out the door when—when—it was as if the whole building caught fire everywhere at once. It was like standing in front of an open furnace. The force of it was enough to knock you off your feet. Four sheets of fire went up in an instant, then vanished, just like that! You'd think the whole place sank into the—"

"You said you were all outside. You said the children were all out." Lionel's face and voice were dead things.

Miss Foster quailed. "We—we were. I made the children go out first. I came last, to make sure they were all out. The fire went up so suddenly that the back of my coat's scorched. Look!" She turned a sooty shoulder to prove it.

"But they weren't all out, were they." There was no question asked, only a dull despair.

"Professor Walters, I *saw* Jeffy and Ellie leave this building! They chose each other for line partners and they were the second pair in line. I *saw* them leave!"

Lionel was haggard, his eyes lost in the dark circles that had come as suddenly as the freak fire. "Then where are they, Miss Foster?" he asked. "Where are they?"

Cass leaped into the pit. There were no fallen timbers, scarcely any debris beyond a thick layer of ash. He brushed this away and picked up two small chains. Runesigns twirled merrily in the air, their bright metal traceries only a little smudged by the fire's passage.

A wall of black ice crashed down over Sandy.

Chapter Sixteen:

Getting Down

The sedative wore off with the sudden shock of summer lightning. Sandy's eyes blinked open into the darkness. She was aware of pain in her throat, as if she'd been screaming or shouting for a long time. For an instant, she couldn't remember why she would have wanted to scream so much.

Then she remembered. Her eyes opened and closed on the grit of long sleep. She had no more tears. "Lionel?" Her hand groped for his across the coverlet and found his side of the bed smooth and empty. With the remarkable eccentricity of the mind trapped in nightmare, she noted that whoever had put her to bed had not even bothered to remove the spread or cover her with anything. She was still fully dressed. Only her light autumn overcoat had been taken off. It made her irrationally angry, thinking of how mussed and stained the bedspread would be thanks to someone's thoughtlessness. She hung on to the anger as a drowning woman might hold on to a branch too small to hold her up in the middle of a flood-gorged river.

"Lionel!" This was all his fault. He never cared enough about the house, never appreciated all the small attentions that went into keeping up its appearance. And if he ignored a hundred minor exhortations to keep his feet off the furniture, to put a coaster under a wet glass, to unball his socks before dropping them in the hamper and hang his shirts up as soon as they came out of the dryer, who got the blame for the end results? Not Lionel. It wasn't fair.

It wasn't fair. . . . Tears did come, answering to self-pity when they would not come for grief. Sandy turned her face into the pillow and cried. She saw her daughter's face, laughing, scowling, refusing to obey the simplest household rule, just like her father. *You pick up this room, young lady, or no TV! Don't you talk back to me. You won't get to go to Maddie's party if you get that dress filthy. Go wash your face. Brush your teeth. No, you may not have another story, you've had three already and it's time you were in bed.*

So many more tears.

"Sandy . . ."

"Oh Lionel!" She flung herself onto her back and threw her arms around him, dragging him down onto the bed with her. "Lionel, what are we going to do?"

Icy blue eyes lit by their own fires glowed in the dark above her face. "I'm not Lionel." Sandy's arms dropped back quickly. "Too bad," the elfin prince added wryly.

"Cass, what are you doing in my bedroom? Where's Lionel? Why aren't you with Amanda? If she ever needed you—"

"They sent me to bring you. You are the one we all need now." His hand was smooth and warm in hers. "Come."

Amanda sat beside Lionel on the living-room sofa. Davina stood behind them, like the omnipresent British butler from a drawing-room comedy of manners. She even carried a tray of tea things to complete the effect, but the cups in front of Lionel and Amanda were empty. Sandy too met her offer of tea with a curt, negative shake of the head. She took her place in an armchair and waited for them to speak. She hadn't the strength for more.

Cass took an embroidered footstool and placed himself at Sandy's right hand. No one present objected. Sandy thought she saw a passing look of longing cross Davina's face when the Welsh girl looked at the Prince of Elfhame Ultramar, but she had no sympathy to spare.

Oh, stop your stupid dreaming, Davina! See where dreams have gotten me!

"Are you better, Sandy?" Oddly enough, it was Amanda who broke the silence—Amanda who always went about on velvety mousefeet, between one whisper and another. She wasn't whispering. Her voice was hard and crisp, making it clear that she wasn't making small talk; she wanted a factual report on Sandy's current physical condition.

"I'm on my feet," Sandy replied. "I feel like I want to die, but I bet I could walk to the grave without any assistance."

"You'll be doing enough walking, soon." Amanda's face was stone, black stone chips where human-colored eyes should have been. "The children may be alive." There was no preamble to soften the statement. "I believe they are."

"You believe." Sandy checked herself from saying anything more. This was no time for sarcasm.

"Yes, I believe!" Amanda's shout made the electric lights seem to flicker like candle flames. "I'd like to say I *know,* but I thought it would sound too arrogant. But if it means convincing you, all right, then: I *know* they aren't dead!"

Sandy darted a look at her husband. Lionel's deep sigh trembled in the shadowy air between them. He sat like an old man. Amanda would need to do more than offer those few flimsy words of hope if she would reach him. Sandy's eyes fell to Cass for confirmation or denial.

"Amanda is—most likely right, Sandy," he said. His fingers were worrying something. When they unclenched, she saw the charred runesign necklaces that had hung around Jeffy's and Ellie's neck. She touched the elven-gifted bloodstone pendant at her own throat without being aware that she did so. "I can't believe that my father would feel such deep hatred, such a hunger for vengeance, that he'd kill children to punish their parents."

"Wouldn't he?" To Sandy's surprise, it was Amanda who spoke so bitterly. "Is that why we've been running away from him for so long, keeping Jeffy safe from him—at *your* urging!—when all the time there was never any danger to my son?" She slashed the air with her hand, cutting the past away. "If it had been just my life at stake, I could have faced Kelerison ages ago! I am afraid of him, but I could have dealt with that fear and covered it. I'm no coward. But when it was fear for Jeffy's safety . . . You were the one who kept at me, kept telling me we had to flee for the child's sake. *For which child's sake, Cassiodoron?*''

The Prince of Elfhame Ultramar stood up, tall and beautiful by lamplight. He acted as if Amanda had not spoken at all. ''I'll be in the garden, getting our equipment together. Join me there when you've persuaded them—as you must. Sandy, for your daughter, believe Amanda.'' He went out into the night. Davina put down the tea things and followed him, gliding unnoticed form the room.

Amanda leaned back on the sofa and released a long breath. ''He can't help being as he is. I shouldn't have said that. We need his goodwill more than before, and there's no guaranteeing he won't turn as petty and malicious as his father if I push him too far.''

Sandy protested. ''I don't think Cass would ever—''

''He's an elf.'' Amanda rapped out the word like an insult. ''They're immortal. You'd expect them to be noble and serene and utterly steeped in the wisdom of the ages. They're not. I know. I lived in the halls of Elfhame Ultramar, and I know. They're children: children too powerful for punishment, children with nothing to do all day and all the days of the earth to do it. Do you come from a big family, Sandy?''

''I'm an only child.''

''You, Lionel?''

''I had a brother.'' Lionel did not recall Richard warmly, though thinking about the way his brother had died always made him ill.

''Then you will know. Even when there are just two of you, the squabbling starts. When there's nothing to do, you fight. It takes a parent to stop you, and sometimes that doesn't work. Well, imagine a whole world of children who are immune to punishment, who can gratify their every whim, who don't even have the possibility of natural death to make them do something constructive or creative or special with their lives so that they'll be favorably remembered after they're dead. Then imagine how one of these children might react the first time he doesn't get his own way.''

''But they can be killed.'' Lionel's hands grasped one another so tightly that the tendons stuck out and the knuckles whitened. ''With any weapon?''

''Iron works fastest.'' Amanda gave him a look of approval. ''That much hasn't changed, though they don't run and hide at just the mention of the word. Oh yes, iron kills them.

They are strong and sly. You don't want them dying slowly, or they'll find a way to take you with them.''

"I have an old sword. I used to collect those sorts of things—''

"Lionel!'' Sandy exclaimed. "What are you planning to do? Go to Elfhame Ultramar and hunt them all down? Strap Kelerison to your fender after a sword fight, which of course he'll have *no way* of winning? Even if it weren't impossible to confront Kelerison on his home ground—''

"It's not impossible,'' Lionel burst in. "That's where we're going now. That's what Cass and Amanda came over here to tell us. We're going to Elfhame Ultramar to find the children. They say they're still alive down there.'' His lips moved as his gaze wandered vaguely. "Ellie is still alive. I have to believe she's still alive.''

"And Jeffy. Think, Sandy!'' Amanda was in command. "If they were dead, wouldn't we have found some evidence of that in the ruins?''

Sandy's heart wanted to believe Amanda, but reason made her say, "There was nothing left after the fire but ashes. The necklaces with their signs—they were made by Cass's magic. They'd be proof against the flames, but everything else was—''

"Why didn't we find *just* the runesigns? The chains were there too! The chains were never elven-touched, the way the runesigns were. They should have melted away in the fire. It's as you said it might be: Kelerison has stolen our children to make us follow. He's lost on our battleground, so he wants us to fight on his. All that we must do is find the gateway into Elfhame Ultramar. It may be plain to see, it may be concealed. He's capable of toying with us as much as he likes, as an appetizer to his revenge, but he'll let us find it eventually. He won't make the mistake of being *too* clever when he wants us down there.'' A wolfish smile changed Amanda's face. "His mistake is that he expects us to run headlong into his trap, unprepared, two hysterical women.''

She rose from the sofa. She was wearing the same coat that had shielded Sandy when Kelerison decked her in showgirl splendor. She shrugged it off. A loose-fitting shirt of light chainmail glittered down to her knees. A small sword, a stiletto, a rawhide sling, and a pouch that must contain stones or lead shot, all hung from her belt.

"I have tried to fight him fairly. This ends it. He killed my husband and he stole my child.'' She patted the sling.

"What is there for a mortal woman to do in the halls of Elfhame Ultramar all day, awaiting her master's pleasure?" Amanda's laugh sent chills down Sandy's spine. "Children will fight, to pass the time. The elves place great value on the martial arts. Their greatest master of arms is Lord Syndovar. He found it amusing to teach me the use of weapons during the hours that the two of us were unoccupied, the way a man might teach a dog to walk on her hind legs. Well? Will you come? Gateways shine brightest by night. Have you more arms than just that sword to bring?"

Sandy stole a glance at Lionel before she answered Amanda's challenge. Life and hope were back in his eyes. "I could bring *Black's*."

"No use. In Elfhame Ultramar, it is their laws that bind."

"Okay, then I'll take the fireplace poker." To Amanda's quizzical look she replied, "It's iron, it's sharp, and it's not more than I know I can handle."

"I'll get the sword," Lionel said. He bounded up from the sofa with reborn energy. When he returned, he had changed from his rumpled clothes into jeans, a lumberjack shirt, a denim jacket, and Timberline boots. The sword hung scabbarded from his belt by a pair of makeshift loops. He also carried two wicked Sheffield carving knives in lieu of daggers, and a red ripstop backpack.

"I got our highway emergency kits in here," he said proudly. "Astronaut blankets, flares, matches, first aid, you name it. And a bottle of brandy."

"Well, if this is turning into an expedition, maybe I should pack some granola bars," Sandy suggested.

"Granola? Oh, for God's sake, who needs that? Just change into something better for roughing it and let's get going!"

When Sandy came down from switching into her own version of Lionel's gear, she found the other four already outside. Cass and Amanda both wore shin-length cloaks. She was pretty sure that the elfin prince had a set of mail on under his, though she wondered whether an elf could stand having so much iron so near his skin. As if in answer, Cass scratched himself vigorously all over for the first of many, many times.

Davina was the only one not tricked out for wilderness living. The Welsh girl wore sensible Oxfords, woolly stockings, a twill skirt, a heavy sweater, and a navy pea-coat, but that outfit was more appropriate for going to do the marketing

than for plunging into the elfin realm. She also carried a backpack. "Provisions," she explained when Lionel asked. "I only
hope I've tucked up enough granola bars." A small shadow
rubbed at her ankles and meowed until she added. "And tinned
fish, yes."

"Davina, you shouldn't come," Sandy said.

"Why not?" The girl stiffened haughtily. "I'm an extra
pair of hands. I was a Girl Guide not long since. What's more
to the point of it, I have the Sight, and where we're bound, we
may have grave need of that."

"Let her come," Cass said. The darkness was not enough
to cover the grateful look Davina gave him.

They marched through the deserted streets of the town
until they came to the place where the kindergarten had stood.
Yellow police barricades surrounded the crater. There were no
lights on in the windows of either of the neighboring houses.
It was very still.

"This is the best place to begin our search for the gateway," Cass said. "I think he must have spirited the children
away at the fire's height. He would need a gateway on the
spot."

"There," Davina whispered. She pointed into the hole.
"The northwest corner."

Sandy saw nothing different about that part of the ravaged foundations and said so. Cass reached for her neck and
raised the bloodstone pendant to her eye.

"Some of the Sighted have the power to recognize the
gateways into the elfin realms." He looked at Davina with
great respect. "I did not know that she had the gift to such a
degree. If you will look through this, you will see what she
sees, my lady, and perhaps more."

The milky setting of the bloodstone was hollow in the
middle. It was like the frame around a lens, though until now,
Sandy had never thought of Rimmon's gift as anything so practical. She did as Cass told her, holding it to her right eye like
a monocle.

Deep in the heart of the vanished building, a heptagon
of purple light glowed. Thinner threads crossed and recrossed
it, a twinkling cobweb pattern. The filaments seemed frail, but
Sandy suspected that they would be rigid as steel if she put her
hand to them.

"I thought so," Cass was saying. "A gateway, the very
way by which my father stole the children out of the heart of

the fire. Look again, my lady, and you will see the road into Elfhame Ultramar through the bars.''

"I'll see it when I'm on it." Sandy sat on the edge of the foundation and started lowering herself into the pit. The others followed her lead. Cesare bounded down with scornful ease and a grace that left even Cass looking clumsy by comparison. Lionel tried to ape the elf-prince's leap and landed off-kilter, twisting his ankle. He bit back any cry of pain, and when Sandy noticed him wincing as he walked, he claimed it was nothing at all, or something else. Amanda and Davina let themselves down with more circumspection and caution than the menfolk. They all ranged up into a line in front of the gateway.

"No, no. Back up a bit there." Cass made Lionel take three painful steps to the rear. "If you are standing in the same space as the gateway when it opens, it will tear you apart."

"I can't even see where it is!" Lionel protested. "How can I be sure I'm standing okay now?"

Cass had a fox's smile. "You'll just have to trust me."

Sandy peered through the bloodstone again. "You're fine, Lionel." To Cass she said, "Open it."

The elfin prince bowed. "My lady desires and it is so." She had the odd feeling that he was making fun of her. In the back of her mind was the galling notion that elves would always look down on mortals as only the very beautiful and the very privileged feel entitled to do with their inferiors. Cass might protest an undying passion—and who better than he should know the meaning of the word *undying?*—but she would still be a mortal when the passion did die, and so to be readily dismissed. She remembered all the times her mother had told their pampered family spaniel, Pantagruel, that they were all going for a nice drive in the country, only to stop at the vet's.

It didn't matter if you lied to a dog.

She touched the bloodstone. *If things had turned out differently, would you have loved me forever, Rimmon? You weren't of the same tribe as Cass—an elf of a lost world called Khwarema—but you were still elvin. And though what I loved of you was your ghost, it was more than capable of every act of love. Your forever was death's—more endless even than Cass's romantic notion of the word. But would that have made any difference? Death's wisdom over the heart's whim? I would have always been what I am: Sandy Horowitz, a mortal girl, a mortal woman now. Could you have loved that to the end of eternity?*

She used the bloodstone as a lens again. Cass was at the gateway, hands starred as wide as they could reach. He laid them on two of the cobweb's points and let the purple glow seep up through his fingers until his whole body was sheathed in light. He spoke a word that might have been a birdsong, and touched his forehead to the gateway. It fell into a sparkling powder at his feet. Lionel and Amanda, unsighted as they were, took a step back and breathed hard. Sandy lowered the bloodstone. Even without its aid, she could see the border of the gateway shining in the dark, and beyond it, a white road. The way into Elfhame Ultramar was clear.

Cesare was the first one over. *"Eh, bene!* Are you coming?"* He switched his tail impatiently.

The last one through was Davina. Though Cass urged her to hurry, before the gateway closed itself, she lingered to kneel in the dirt and scoop up a handful of the purple dust, mingled with the ashes from the kindergarten fire. She tied it up neatly in her handkerchief.

"You never know what will come in handy," she said. "Nor when it will be needful."

"Or if," Sandy said irritably. "Hurry up!"

Davina came along, still wiping her sooty hands on her skirt. The gateway closed, cutting off the light of the upper lands. There was a dirty rose glow in the sky, and the sky was all around them. Only the slant of the white road under their feet gave any indication that there were such directions as up and down. Sandy had the uncanny sensation of being in free-fall, fixed by magnetic boots to the one tongue of metal in all the universe.

"Heavens!" Davina exclaimed. "Is it like this throughout your father's realm, Your Royal Highness?"

Cass's laughter came back in a sharp echo from an unseen barricade. "There's no call to use fancy titles with me, Davina. I'm still Cass to you. To all of you. No, this is just the fashion of gateways, to open on a void. You could call it an antechamber into Elfhame Ultramar. It will change soon enough further down the road, I promise you."

His promise held true. They had gone less than six yards along the downward sloping white road when the shapes of pine and fir trees pricked up their crowns on both sides of the way. The sky turned from rose to the deep teal blue of evening, though this shift was quickly lost from sight as the evergreens met overhead and closed off all sight of it from the travelers.

They went by ones and twos until the white path between

the pines narrowed to single file. Cass led, with Cesare trotting just a few paces ahead, Amanda coming after them, sword drawn, Sandy and Davina came next, with Lionel playing rearguard, his eyes lurching from one thicket to another, his old sword in his hand. He looked extremely nervous, but still willing enough to confront anything the dark wood might disgorge.

Davina made little noises of pique as they walked. She kept rubbing and scrubbing her hands on her skirt until Sandy halted, exasperated, and turned on the girl. *"What* is your problem?"

Davina stopped short, and Lionel almost rear-ended her. "Hey!" he shouted. It was too loud for the forest, the dim trees commanding stillness from all who walked in their shadows. Cass and Amanda stopped and glared back at their companions.

"Don't you know anything?" Amanda hissed. "Hush! You'll have Kelerison on us."

"And what's so unusual about that happening?" Sandy shot back in a stage whisper. "There's only *one* road that I can see. We aren't straying from it. He might as well have left a breadcrumb trail, and a few THIS WAY, PLEASE signs. We're already walking the way he expects us to go, so don't tell me we're going to surprise the old bastard!"

"My father isn't near," Cass said. "I would know."

"More wishful thinking," Sandy muttered.

Cass stroked the sharp outline of his ears. "These are not just for show, my lady. I am a keener tracker than most of my kind too. My mother always said it came from her tribe—great hunters all. My father said it was a skill I acquired so that I might hear my enemies coming and hide sooner." He showed his teeth. "This time, he was right."

"And I have even better hearing than my lord," Cesare added. "Couple that with my fine sense of smell—"

"Well, I wish you might smell me out a handkerchief, *cariad,*" Davina said softly. "For I fear it's all my fussing over this soot that's made Sandy lose patience with me. I can't abide untidiness." She held up her dirty fingers. *"Has* anyone a handkerchief?"

An ash shaft flèched with kingfisher feathers whizzed through the air, passing between Davina's splayed fingers before burying its flint head in the thick trunk of a fir tree. The white cloth tied to the shaft came off in the Welsh girl's hand, leaving her staring dumbly at it.

Her comrades were staring just as dumbly at the elfin
archer who melted out of the woodland.

"Be my guest," he said. His bow went up again, another
arrow nocked and ready.

A second archer, bow similarly ready, emerged from the
other side of the path. One golden eye sighted down the length
of this arrow to Sandy's heart. "Any other requests?"

Chapter Seventeen:

In the Lands of the Fair Folk

"Lionel." Her husband's name escaped in a strained
whisper from the corner of her mouth. "Lionel, I
really wish you'd put that sword down." At the very edge of
vision she saw the iron blade drop to the white path.

"We surrender," Lionel said, palms raised. "Please
don't hurt her."

"Hurt her?" The first elf was honestly surprised. He
looked at Cass. "Have we any reason to hurt her, my lord
prince?"

Cass ran a thumb down his jawline. "Oh, not really,
Fazhim. She's been a little reluctant . . ."

"With you, my lord?" The second elf—the one who had
drawn a bead on Sandy—lowered his weapon. "Why?"

"That one, my friend Tiv"— Cass indicated Lionel—
"is her husband."

"You mean her wedded lord?" Tiv gave Lionel a severe
once-over.

"They don't use that term anymore, up there." Bright
blue eyes danced with mockery. "Although from what I have
observed of their behavior, there are still many women who treat
their husbands as lord and master, no matter what the verbiage."

"That's a damned lie!" Sandy shouted. Her voice came
rifling straight back at her. The echoes of Elfhame Ultramar
were strange, hard things. Sometimes they set off echoes of
their own. She clapped her hands over her ears to shut out the
reverberations. Oddly, no one else seemed to be affected.

"Sandy's right," Lionel said. He looked a little sheepish as he added, "I'm not her lord and master. Sometimes I can barely get her to match up my socks when the laundry's done."

"Laundry?" Fazhim inquired.

"Clothes washing," Cass translated. "She also used to do the cooking, until this lady came to live with them. Another female, note that. And she performed the cleaning of their house, all the rooms."

"His place too?" Tiv looked scandalized. "And washed his clothes? And cooked his food?"

"I help with the housework." Lionel's objections were lodged in a weak voice. "And I cook pretty well."

"*All* the rooms." Tiv still couldn't believe it.

"*Helps* with the housework. Largess. Condescension in the flesh, or I'm a brownie." Fazhim shook his head. He stowed his bow and arrow before taking Sandy's hand in both his own. His face was dark as walnut-juice stain, his clustered ringlets jet black until a random change of light showed them to be the depthless purple of a midnight summer sky. "Dear lady, and you are declining the attentions of my lord prince? Let us not even consider the delights and refinements of the flesh he might show you! Let us neglect to mention the perfect health you would enjoy in his company, whether or not you chose to dwell there above or here below. Let us forget entirely the fact that you would be pampered and cosseted beyond the wildest dreams your poor, crippled imagination could spew forth. My lady: *he would always pick up after himself!*"

"And do his own laundry," Tiv tacked on, with a smug look in Lionel's direction. "We all take care of ourselves in Elfhame Ultramar."

"How jolly," Sandy stated. "I hope that includes taking care of your own business and letting us take care of ours." She cocked her head at Cass. "Who are these bo—people?"

The elf-prince laughed long and loud. The bristly branches of the fir trees trembled. He strode forward to sweep Tiv and Fazhim into a hearty hug. "These are my milk brothers, lady mine! They are of good blood, which they disgrace continually. Or have you two given that up and become respectable since I left?"

Tiv's hair and eyes were both the color of new-minted gold, and gleamed with equally metallic sheen as he shook his head, grinning. "We've been doing our best, in your absence, to make Lord Syndovar despair."

"We're nowhere as good at it as you were," Fazhim

said. "But we do try. He says he hopes to be dead long before Lastday, rather than have to watch us keep up our end of things on the field of battle."

"Once he said he'd rather mate with a karker and live in the burrows than have someone mistake him for an elf, the way we were disgracing our people." Tiv spoke with rich satisfaction. He patted the bow on his back. "Of course, so long as we hold our own on the archery field, he can't turn his back on us completely. So to speak."

Amanda came to stand with Sandy and the other mortals. The elf-prince's reunion with his milk brothers cast them all into the tenuous place of outsiders looking in.

"All that's lacking is a cave," Davina whispered. "We poor souls inside it, huddled by a wretched fire, and the flint-scraped skins of animals barely covering our bodies, while out in the storm we see our first glimpses of the Fair Folk dancing with the lightnings."

Sandy shivered. "Well," she managed to say. "Well, at least we had enough sense to come in out of the rain."

Cass was lecturing his friends on the peculiar ways of mortals—the female of the species in particular. Tiv and Fazhim shook their heads in wonder so many times that they gave the impression of watching an invisible tennis match. Cass capped his descriptions of mortal absurdity with a short disquisition on the necktie, and tales of how humans wives dutifully trotted off whole skeins of these absurdities to the dry cleaners.

"Enough!" Sandy cried. She picked up the sword Lionel had dropped and pointed it at Cass's dainty nose. "Instead of showing off for your friends, try remembering why we're here. Believe it or not, there's one thing even more boring than wiping out ring around the collar, and that's listening to an elf make fun of neckties." Her eyes darted to Tiv and Fazhim. "Ask him how many neckties he has in his own closet up there, why don't you? Besides the necktie he had to wear as part of his school uniform."

This time Tiv's expression went beyond shock. He backed away from Cass in purest horror. "Neckties? You, my lord?"

"It must be true, what Lord Syndovar preaches." Fazhim clearly deplored the truth of it. "The upper world is a poisonous place, its seductions permeating the very soil of the world until at last they seep down into our own sweet lands. He would close off all the gateways, if he could, and still the influences would trickle into Elfhame Ultramar by the tracks of worm and beetle, through the very stones.''

Tiv snorted. ''Oh, don't exaggerate! Lord Syndovar's always been one to rule by fear first, respect second. You're talking just the way he'd love to hear it. As if *we* could be influenced in any way by something so transitory as human culture. I myself have made more than one visit to the surface just to see what all the fuss was for, and I was almost disappointed. Mortal contamination! What a myth! Get *real*, Fazhim! And as for you, sweet lady, we know all about your quest and are here to help you, so put down that sword.''

Slowly, with many a suspicious look at the two elfin archers, Sandy passed the sword back to Lionel. Her empty hand closed on the handle of the fireplace poker for reassurance.

''Good. Now come with us.'' Fazhim took command and plunged into the forest on the left-hand side of the path.

If it had been difficult keeping up a single-file line of march on the white road, it was that much worse when there was no clear path to take. Fleetingly Sandy wished that Tiv had gone first—his gold hair would have been easier to keep in sight among the trees—but Fazhim's dark coloring, his moss-green tunic, his russet hose, all served as excellent camouflage. Camouflage was not one of the qualities Sandy would have preferred in a leader.

No, it wasn't easy going at all, and it grew harder. Without a path, the party spread out, each one picking his or her own way through the wood. No one seemed to have the patience to go one after the other when there was no clearly indicated road. So long as they kept at least one of their fellows in sight, they felt they were doing all right.

Which is fine in theory, Sandy thought. *Unless the person in front of you is following a third person who's decided that you're the one he'll follow.*

She was in a nasty mood. The fireplace poker kept banging into her leg when it wasn't catching on things by its hook—scraping the bark off trees, tangling in bushes, and more often than both of these, snagging where there was nothing visible to snag on. Every time the poker got caught, Sandy got jerked back by the belt. Her jeans were too damned tight to begin with, and her solar plexus didn't appreciate the intermittent jolts it was getting.

''Sandy, what are you doing?'' Cass materialized from a thicket at her right hand as she struggled with yet another of those unseen poker grabbers. He was silvery cool, and he deftly twitched the poker free for her. "The others are in camp already. We were worried about you. Here, take my arm. I'll guide you."

They entered the little clearing arm in arm. Sandy didn't think anything of it until she saw Lionel staring at them. She unlooped her arm from Cass's at once and rushed to sit by her husband's side. She felt his arm shake when he put it around her.

"All right." Cass squatted by the small campfire, if a name reminiscent of burnt s'mores and sticky-fingered scouts could be applied to a willow-green flame burning in a silver bowl that rested on the winged back of a slumbering topaz lion. "Now we can—the wards are up, Fazhim?"

"They're up. The minute you crossed that ring of stones, your images continued bumbling on through the forest. They'll keep going until they hit the westbound track, if anyone's watching for you."

"Kelerison won't bother with watching," Amanda said. "If he does, he'll know better than to believe we'd get so lost, with Cass leading us. He'll just sit in the high court and wait, but we won't fool him with wardstone-made images."

"Still, it's not as important that he knows where you are, as that he doesn't know where you are." Tiv looked proud of himself for that one. "Our lord king may not believe the images, but he will never know the exact point at which your true bodies stopped and your shadow forms went on. A little privacy, that's what the wards provide. No eavesdroppers allowed; or possible." He gestured off into the shadows beyond the fire. "I thought I was going to ruin myself moving those stones, but it was worth it. No matter what the ladies claim, when it comes to setting up wards, size counts."

Sandy peered into the darkness. All she saw were trees. "What stones?" she asked.

"There, the great gray ones." Davina tried directing her attention. Sandy still saw nothing and said so. Lionel seconded it. The Welsh girl understood. "There are times I forget the gift of the Sight is not everyone's. Mrs. Taylor, can you see them?"

Amanda shook her head. "It's been years since my last annointing."

Cass slapped his forehead. "Idiot!"

"No argument, my lord." Fazhim's teeth were bright.

"No wonder my poor lady kept getting tripped and tangled in snares that a half-blind troll would see! Tiv, Fazhim, tell me you've brought a jar of the stuff.''

Tiv uncurled his fingers. Four small, round, cork-stoppered clay bottles balanced on his palms. "Just so, my lord. One apiece. Haven't you found mortals to be rather finicky about germs?'' He passed the little pots around.

Lionel unplugged his jar and gave the contents a mistrustful sniff. Sandy offered her opinion that it looked like blue Crisco and smelled like a French cathouse. "Nothing personal, Cesare,'' she told the tomcat.

Cesare was too busy rubbing up to Davina, who in turn was preoccupied with opening several cans of sardines. Paper plates came out of her knapsack as the fish was divided into eight small portions. Tiv gave his share to the cat, after a cursory glance, and Fazhim did likewise.

"You wouldn't have any granola bars on you?'' the dark-haired elf asked hopefully.

"It's fairy ointment,'' Amanda told them as she dipped her fingers into the scented goo. "It lets you see your whereabouts just the way the Five Peoples see things down here.'' She smeared the stuff over her eyelid, going up to and past the brow. "Cover the entire eye, the whole compass of the socket. It won't hurt to go a little past the borders, just to make sure.''

"Must I?'' Davina was no more enchanted by the too-sweet smell of the ointment than Lionel. "I have the Sight.''

"And no idea of where your Sight ends,'' Amanda countered. "Not everyone with your gift could've seen the gateway, remember? Do you want to learn the limits of your Sight at a crucial moment?''

"Needs must.'' Davina sighed and imitated Amanda's expert application technique. Lionel did the same.

Sandy balked until she caught Tiv watching her, a poorly controlled smirk twisting his lips into all kinds of bizarre grimaces. She rested her eyeglasses on her knee and used the fairy ointment. It was cool at first touch, a coolness that rapidly warmed until it reminded her of the steaming washcloths her mother laid over her eyes to combat sinus headaches. Then the heat faded away.

"That wasn't so bad.'' She put her glasses back on and looked around her. "I still don't see any stones, though.''

"You will. Now that you have prepared the eye, you make the second application.'' Amanda took a dollop of ointment onto her right index finger, and with a gesture familiar to contact lens wearers everywhere, she held one eye wide open

with two fingers of her left hand while she plopped the blue
unguent smack onto the eyeball.

"No way." Sandy crossed her arms.

"If you leave it half done, you go blind," Amanda
pointed out in an irritatingly reasonable tone. "Soon."

Sandy sucked in her breath through clenched teeth, said
a raw word, and slopped a healthy blob into her own eye. Then
she howled.

"You get used to it," Amanda said. "It's only the first
time that hurts. Do the other eye—all of you, don't just sit
there. I meant what I said about going blind."

The clearing resounded with agonized caterwaulings in
three distinct timbres. The elves covered their ears and looked
like a grouping of Martyrs of the Early Church.

"Thank the Powers, the wardstones hold sound in so
well," Tiv commented. "The fat one, there, sounds like a bog
gnome in the mating season."

Cass flicked his fingers at the golden-haired elf and Tiv
yelped in pain. "You—you *stung* me, you—you—you *wienie!*"

"Just to let you hear how melodious your own voice
sounds when you're hurting, little brother. And her name is
Davina Goronwy, and her size is little business of yours."

Lionel blinked azure tears away and wiped the overflow
from his cheeks with his shirtcuff. "Sandy? Sandy, how do
you feel?"

Sandy had her eyes squinched shut as tight as they would
go. "This had better be worth it," she growled.

Cass touched her arm. "My lady, to know that you must
open your eyes."

She did, and her long-drawn exclamation of wonder
braided itself into and over and around Lionel's and Davina's.

They were still in the forest, but the trees had grown
translucent, their interiors made visible. Lithe spirits pent
within the bark slithered up and down the length of the trunks,
swimming through the grain or floating in the heart of the wood,
as the mortals watched.

Some were young females, hair and skin the same deep
scarlet as the sap rising into the bud. These lived in saplings
of oak and ash, elm and willow, beech and the frondy mimosa
that had sprung up among the evergreens, unseen until the application of the fairy ointment. The pines and firs were home
to green-bearded sires and dreaming matrons with hair the sweet
yellow of new-split softwood, ripe breasts full and round and
brown as pine cones.

The tree spirits were not the only beings living in the forest. With the ointment's aid, the mortals saw grass where no grass had been, and a beetle-busy multitude of tiny sprites scurrying through the blades, a few of which themselves housed slim green creatures shaped rather like tadpoles—all head and eyes, the body trailing away into a filament tail.

At last Sandy understood why she had kept snagging the poker when supposedly nothing was there. The underbrush was at least twice as thick in reality as it had been to unannointed eyes. Parrot-colored shrubs grew chest high, tossing their trefoil-leaved branches in the air without the aid of any breeze. The air itself was thick with winged beings, bright and elusive, whose jeweled hues would leave earthly butterflies dead of envy. Each shrub was trying to lure at least one of the innumerable flying creatures to land amidst its temptingly perfumed foliage. When lures did not work, the shrubs tried grabbing at anything within range.

"Why do they do that?" Davina asked.

"Sssh." Cass took her by the hand to very edge of the warded campsite. "Watch."

One airborne creature succumbed to the lure of an especially virulent fuchsia-and-teal shrub. In a flutter of wings, it landed on a beckoning branch and buried its face in a cluster of scented leaves. Almost at once, the leaves flew off in different directions, unveiling three sprites exactly like the newcomer, only wingless. They set upon the visitor with piping cries of glee and carried their pinioned victim deep into the heart of the bush.

"Dear lord! Will they eat her?" Davina was aghast.

"Him," Cass corrected. "He's safe as may be from immediate consumption, for a male newly mated. Powers that be, my lady, would you devour your own husband, as if you were no better than a she-spider?"

"Yes, but . . . three of them to one male?"

"And one triad to every mature leaf cluster on that shrub. It's usual for all three to breed too. If it weren't for the inherent cunning of the males at avoiding capture, I don't know where we'd be. My father's courtiers sit around complaining and wondering why they can't take a deep breath in summertime without getting their teeth full of pixies!" Cass rested his hands on his hips. "Why do we waste so much time on the battlefield and spend so little on worthwhile things, like getting these damned pixies to *stop it?*"

"Now I've seen everything," Sandy said.

"Then it's working for you too?" Cass was at her side again. He behaved as if the earth had mistaken Lionel for a canape. "Can you truly see as I see?"

"I can see the stones now," Sandy cried. "Oh, and so much else!"

The stones were marvelous to see, each one taller than two elves, a deep blue gray striped with tracks of red lichen and furry moss, here and there the star of a minuscule yellow flower that had no name in the lands above. Garlands of blue gentian crowned the monoliths, wreaths of flowers and striped bronze ribbons fit for any bride to wear.

The sky of Elfhame Ultramar had shown itself too. The tops of trees were ghosts that faded in and out of sight, but never assumed enough solidity to obscure the bright dome above. "It's . . . blue." Sandy sounded cheated.

"We have made it so," Cass told her. "Blue and bright, without a sun to account for the color. Were you expecting dark caverns, or the underside of a grave mound? The blue fades with the waning of our day, which runs just opposite to your own. But"—here he sighed—"there can be no sunset; no sunrise; and if we want a light to guide our steps in the dark, we must kindle our own. There is no moonlight, there are no stars."

Fazhim's shoulders twitched. "There are nights I'd be more than glad to have a friendly moon at my back. Pray the Powers we don't cross paths with any of *them* on our way to the high court."

"*Them* who?" Lionel demanded.

The elf regarded him with sad, pansy-heart eyes. "Jungies. Heads. What does it matter? You couldn't do anything to stop them."

"Junkies?" Lionel repeated, getting it slightly wrong. "Heads?" To Sandy he said, "Sounds like Central Park all over again."

Fazhim began drawing a map in the dirt. "Here is the white road, and here is the great stream, and here is the high court, with outlying regions, and here are we."

Sandy and the others leaned in to watch his sketch take shape. Fazhim gave no scale, but the distances still looked daunting. "It's a good thing for you that Tiv and I came out to meet you," he said. "Your fastest route to the high court is by boat on the great stream, in spite of the dangers, and we sailed up in one of our swiftest."

"I never came down by this gateway before, so I didn't

know we'd need a boat," Amanda said. "But if we come by the great stream, won't Kelerison be able to intercept us when it emerges from the forest, into the parklands *here?*" She stabbed at the high court with her dagger point. Fazhim flinched.

"My lord Prince Cassiodoron is not without other friends," Tiv said. He dared to pat Amanda's hand, even though it held an iron dagger. "Nor are you unkindly remembered, my lady. Of all King Kelerison's fancies, you were the only one who never treated us as if we were magic fetch-and-carries, as in the old-country tales. Fazhim and I are but two of a comradeship of seven, all of us my lord prince's friends. We've left two others well placed along the water route, to watch for any of Kelerison's patrols and either warn us off or throw additional wards around us."

"Throw? Something that big?" Lionel jerked a thumb at the standing stones.

"Wards set over you on earth must be of earth; wards cast over water are of water."

"We left the remaining three in the high court proper," Fazhim continued. "Their job is to create an internal disturbance, if a distraction is needed when we arrive, and to watch over the children."

"The children!" Lionel's hand reached for Sandy's and squeezed it.

"Well, of course." Tiv lifted his moth-light brows. "We said we knew all about your quest. It's hard enough keeping two mortal babies under wraps in a normal court, where there's some elbow-room available, but in our High Court? When we're not dealing with babies, but good-sized children? Mean ones," he concluded sourly. He rolled back the sleeve of his sepia tunic to show a set of small tooth marks.

"Ellie's?" Sandy whispered.

"I never bet on a sure thing," Lionel whispered back. For the first time in too long, Sandy saw him smile.

"She would *not* curtsey to Queen Bantrobel." Tiv pulled the sleeve back down. "I was there. I saw it. I tried to make the child comply for her own sake, in case Queen Bantrobel should get sticklish about etiquette—she does, from time to time, then gives it all up within a fortnight. This was the thanks I got."

"Tiv is right," Fazhim spoke up. "I was there too, when the children entered the court. I was surprised that my lord King Kelerison was not there as well, but it's always been his

way to drop his latest bundle of surface-world gleanings right
on the High Court doorstep and zip off again as the fit takes
him. No consideration for where we're to find room to stow
his latest mania, no thought to leaving care and feeding instructions—''

"In this case, let us hope that feeding instructions were
not included," Cass said.

"You want him to starve our children?" Sandy's indignation was seconded by whole generations of Horowitz women
who had died with the words *One more bite, darling, there are
poor children in some other country* on their lips.

Cesare purred and butted at her legs until she took notice
of him. *"Madonna,* if you would have your children back
again, pray that they have been starved. One taste of the food
or drink of Elfhame Ultramar and they are bound to this realm
forever.''

"Like the myth of Persephone," Lionel suggested.

"That's why we posted Simyna, Gathel, and Loris at
court. One of them will always keep an eye on your children
until you can reach the palace. Oh, don't worry!'' Tiv made
calming motions with his hands. "They won't really *starve.*
It's a simple thing for us to slip up to your world and bring
down some mortal fare for the little ones.'' He rubbed his
injured arm. "Give them something else to chew on than elf-
flesh. Nasty little buggers.''

"No mortal contamination's possible, huh?'' Lionel
murmured for Sandy's ears alone.

Cass stood and stretched. "The sooner we relieve Simyna, Gathel, Loris, and the rest of their duty, the happier
these ladies will be. Take us to the boat now, my brothers. We
can speak of our plan of attack once we're aboard.''

Fazhim went from one standing stone to the next. His
fingers sliced off a sliver of rock from each monolith as if they
were made of soft cheese. "With these we can have a modified
ward around us on the way to the great stream," he explained
for the mortals' benefit. "But it's a very weak spell. You must
be completely silent and always walk within the triangle whose
points will be Tiv, my lord Prince Cassiodoron, and myself.''

It was a substantial march to the great stream, one passed
in absolute silence, with total attention focused on the positions
of the three elves. Since the fairy ointment had revealed all the
hidden obstacles of Elfhame Ultramar, Sandy found the way
from the campsite to the boat much faster and less frustrating

than the way from the white road to the campsite, even though it was three times as long. What she could see, she could avoid.

The boat itself was a large, flat-bottomed craft that resembled a mahogany sardine can. The wood of it gleamed, but there was no ornamentation, no place to shelter from the light of the sky, no oarlocks, and no sail. As Cass helped her into the boat Sandy saw that there were also no cushions, no life-jackets, and no seats.

Amanda took her place cross-legged on the boat's smooth bottom, facing what might have been called prow or stern with equal accuracy. The others took their cue from her. Cesare chose Davina's lap to honor with his presence and went to sleep while Tiv and Fazhim pushed the boat into the water, then took their own tailor-fashion seats among the mortals.

Only Cass remained standing. The boat was taken up by the current of the great stream and floated with it. Amanda had indeed chosen the prow rightly. Cass was stationed in the stern. He spoke a few words, and the vessel took on speed and a firmer direction.

"Now there's something new in outboard motors: Elven-rude." Lionel chuckled. Sandy slapped his hand.

She glanced back at Cass over her shoulder and saw him stretch out his arms to the waters.

The boat began to sink.

"Illusion." Cesare's sleepy cat voice forestalled any cry of distress from Sandy. "See, it is only a bubble of water that my master has drawn up around us to be our ward."

"Elegantly done, my lord." Fazhim grinned his approbation. "If all our battlefields were magical alone, no one could find fault with you."

"You too, my brother?" Cass's voice throbbed with hurt. "This from you?" His arms fell to his sides and the watery dome over them burst. He sat down in the boat, which slowed back down to the lazy, bobbing flow of the great stream's current.

"My lord Fazhim meant it as a pleasantry." Tiv squatted beside Cass. "It was a compliment. Will you not take it as it was intended, for the love we all share?"

In the cramped quarters of the boat, it was impossible not to eavesdrop, not to see every facial expression of your mates unless backs were turned or eyes averted deliberately. Cass's eyes flashed so fiercely that Sandy would have turned away if there had been room to do so.

"He *knows* my shame! You and he are the only ones

who do, besides my parents and Lord Syndovar. I risked much to tell you of it. Fazhim should have had a measure of common sense. He should have known better than to speak of it at all, pleasantries and compliments be damned!''

"Oh, for—'' Tiv slapped his knees and straightened up, all thoughts of peacemaking tossed aside. "So you sulk over it, while this boat goes drifting wardless, just to teach us a lesson!'' He took over the helmsman's place Cass had abandoned and got the boat going strongly downstream again.

"I'll speak a few truths for you, my regal milk brother,'' Tiv remarked from his station in the stern. "No one outside the royal family would *care* about your so-called shame, even if they all knew about it. But you like the idea of having a deep, dark, hairy secret. Does it ennoble you? Does it make you into the tragic hero you'd love to be? I'll bet it does!''

"Tiv, Tiv, hush, please.'' Fazhim made frantic motions with his hands. "We have no wards up. Shall I?''

"This far upstream?'' Tiv laughed. "No one in his right mind comes along the banks here, so close to where the Heads wander. Why waste the power?'' He returned to Cass.

"Secrets! You're just like your sire. He's been tighter than a filbert for centuries with all the precious secrets of Lord Oberon's last gifting, and you've picked up that secret-snug-away obsession from him. It must give you both a feeling of importance to think you know something we don't know. Well, after all these years, no one in all the high court believes there *was* a last gifting, and if there was, that it was more than a pair of waterproof cobweb boots of your lady grandmother's weaving!''

"There is more to it than that.'' Cass spoke dully. His eyes gazed into the past. "My father took me into the chamber of the casket, once, soon after our arrival in this new land. The times were hazardous, though few of the Fair Folk knew it. He came home from one inland expedition with Lord Syndovar looking filthy and haggard. He told me that I must look into the casket with him, to hear Lord King Oberon's charge to his regent, in case something should happen to him. So I looked, and I saw the last gifting.'' He bowed his head into his hands. "May that be the last of it.''

"More melodramatics! You always were like that. You always yowled loudest of the three of us, carrying on like you were going to die if you didn't get center tit every single time!'' Tiv's shining hair caught the dying light and held it like a halo as he laughed at his friend. "Come on, my lord, lighten u—''

The hiss was thin as thread, the sound of impact covered by Tiv's last words. For the second time, Sandy found herself looking into the elf's golden eyes with an arrow between them, only this time the hawk-flèched shaft protruded from Tiv's heart.

Chapter Eighteen:

Homecoming

Tiv's body toppled from the boat, but no splash came from the great stream. A forest of mottled pale blue and green hands sprouted from the waters to catch the corpse as it fell. Water spirits—fishtailed, finned, web-fingered, and some fully human in shape—carried the elf's body to the shore, never letting so much as a finger trail in the current of their home. They laid him out on the bank and dove back into the stream.

The bank itself was suddenly crowded. Nine elfin men had appeared from among the tall stands of frosty white and tawny gold reeds that rattled empty stalks in the wind. They all carried bows and arrows, six of them aimed and ready to fire on the people in the little boat. Two more played guard, holding between them an elf-woman dressed in the males' preferred garb of loose-necked tunic and tight fitting hose, in the earthy colors of stone and moss, soil and tree. She did not struggle in their grasp, but stood with crop-haired head bent, submissive and waiting for however they would dispose of her.

The ninth elf-man came down to the water's edge. He stood above Tiv's body without sparing it a glance. The elves were a beautiful breed, and he was no exception, yet as Sandy looked at him, her stomach soured. His long, wild, gray hair was a storm from the soul of the sea, his huge almond-shaped eyes as blue and burning as Cass's, but with no depth to the flame. He was in the peak of form, his muscles moving beneath the silk of his tunic with a tried warrior's assurance. He would look absurd if caught up in the figures of a dance, but when swords did the dancing, then he would move and stalk and meet and kill his foe, all beautifully.

It was only then that Sandy realized that their boat had not moved from the moment of Tiv's death. It sat where it was as if anchored in the water, without even the slightest bob or drift.

"Don't match strengths, my lord Prince Cassiodoron," the elf-man called over the water. "Not even you can break the hold all nine of us have on your craft. Bring it to shore. If you refuse, my men will loose their arrows and your friends will die."

Cesare arched and hissed. "Lord Syndovar speaks with all the diplomacy of his sword."

Amanda stood up very slowly, holding her hands well away from her body so that the elves ashore might see she had no weapon to hand. "Will you kill me too, my lord?" She lifted her chin so that he could have a clear view of her face.

"My lady." The tall elfin lord made a curt reverence. "A pleasure to see you again. Do we have you to thank for bringing our wandering prince home?"

"You might say that."

"Then I suggest you use the same good influence that has brought him this far to make him obey." Lord Syndovar never smiled. "Otherwise I fear that yes, I will have you killed too, and then where would that leave your son?"

The boat lurched so hard as it shot in to shore that all of those seated in the bottom piled into one another. Cesare growled and spat as spray sprinkled his fur, and Amanda, standing when the lurch came, was nearly pitched into the great stream. There was another jolt when the craft hit the bank and beached itself.

Cass jumped lightly ashore and gave Lord Syndovar a bow that was barely more than a quick inclination of the head. "You request"—the word was bitterly ironic—"and I obey. You would think that you were the royal prince of this realm and I the underling. By what right did you kill my brother?"

"You honor him too much, or else your speech is sloppy. He was your milk brother, nothing more. I have spilled no royal blood." Lord Syndovar's face was carved of icebound rock. "He was a traitor to Elfhame Ultramar, and by that, a traitor to our truly royal overlord, King Oberon of Elfhame. Choose your friends more discreetly in future."

"Traitor! Where's your evidence that Tiv was any more a traitor to this land than you?"

A tiny quirk at the corner of Lord Syndovar's tight mouth

suggested very fleeting amusement. "For that, I suggest you speak to the lady there."

The elf-woman began to babble before Cass could turn toward her, let alone ask a single question. "My lord, forgive me! We were discovered in the high court. They have us all—had us. I am the only one left alive. Gathel, Druvin, Simyna, are all dead, and now Tiv . . ." Sobs bubbled out of her chest. "They surprised Druvin and me farther downstream, killed him outright, questioned me. They said they would give me to the Jungies if I didn't talk. My lord, my dearest lord, you have been gone so long! You can't know the fear we live with, the souls the Heads devour, the captives the Jungies take and enslave. Lord Syndovar's own son—seven of them before we found his hair, bloody, nailed to the palace doors!"

Lord Syndovar stepped in front of her and dealt her four short, sharp slaps. He turned to Cass again, smiling as if he had done no more than arrange the set of a flower in a vase. Eyes sharpened by the fairy ointment, Sandy saw the elf-woman's lower lip had been split.

"Now you know why I may use the word *traitor* so freely, Your Highness. I will trouble young Lord Fazhim to join Lady Yaritel. His name as well as Lord Tiv's came up in the conversation when she told us of your juvenile plot to defy the lord of Elfhame Ultramar."

Still in the boat, Fazhim stifled a moan of fear. Sandy had never seen a mortal man so possessed by terror before. *Who better than the immortal would have leisure to learn how sweet living can be? The longer you stay in one place, the harder it is to leave it. Who would be less eager to greet death, knowing only life for so long?*

"Are you calling me a traitor too, my lord?" Sandy could almost swear that a faint aura was forming hair-thin around the elfin prince, the visible essence of the rage he held in check.

"You, Your Highness?" Again the twitch of Lord Syndovar's thin lips. "For you, we could not call it treachery. It's a family matter, between yourself and your father; one I hope to see settled soon." Having said this, he was no longer interested in the prince. "Lord Fazhim, we are waiting."

The archers on the bank readjusted their aims. Now all arrows fixed on Fazhim. He did as Lord Syndovar's curt words and brief gestures directed, avoiding Cass's eyes as he took his place beside the elf-woman. Her guards backed off, drawing small daggers from their belts. It was a formality. The prisoners had lost any desire to try escaping. Fazhim pinched thumb and forefinger together and a petal of green silk appeared. He tenderly blotted the blood from Lady Yaritel's chin.

"We will waste no more time here." Lord Syndovar motioned to his men. "The boats." It wanted only one man to lower his bow and strip back the magical wards concealing three silvery gray boats among the rushes. Their prows were all adorned with the rampant forequarters of a winged horse, lashing hooves painted gold, upswept wings bright as the aurora.

"Your boat shall remain here. The Jungies may have it, for all I care." Hearing that voice, Sandy could not imagine Lord Syndovar caring about anything. "Your group will ride two in a boat, with the exception of yourself, Your Majesty. You shall sail in the lead boat, with me. Two of your party to three of mine . . . Yes, I think that should assure everyone's good behavior."

Sandy did some fast toting up on her fingers and reached her own horrified conclusion a heartbeat before Cass. "You're going to kill them!" she exclaimed, pointing at the two prisoners. "Just like that!"

"Dear lady, please . . . ." Fazhim's velvet eyes implored her silence. He put his arm around Yaritel, who was weeping without a sound.

"Murderer!"

"Sandy . . . ." Lionel's atempt at quelling his wife was no more effective than Fazhim's. She was out of the flat-bottomed boat, on the bank, and bristling at Lord Syndovar. The elf's superior height made it a comic sight, an Irish wolf hound beset by Peg's late, unlamented Shih Tzu, yet Lord Syndovar did not look amused.

"You are outspoken, for a mortal female." His lips pursed. "Old too. To my experience, it is only the very young of your sex who chatter so. They have their youth as an excuse for all manner of foolish excess, but they are trained down, eventually. Why has no one done something about you?"

"I was a hard case, so they sent me to law school to get properly humiliated. That didn't work, so they let me be a lawyer. Ask your precious king how good I am with a copy of *Black's* sometime. Oh, and you might try visiting the surface world more often than once every two centuries. Decalcification is good for the brain."

The eyes of every elf widened in astonishment as Lord Syndovar lifted Sandy high in the air, laughing. He swung her around once before setting her down, and steadied her, still chuckling. "Fire and flame! And is there a glow as well, or all crackle and spark? You are right, little one. I have neglected my studies. You shall ride in my boat with Prince Cassiodoron. No; alone. Your Highness will forgive me, but I have never seen a creature like this before. It might almost explain . . ." He glanced at Amanda. "Be kind enough to ride with your father's chosen, Lord Prince. Once we reach the high court, I shall have to conceal her from Queen Bantrobel's sight; an unfortunate necessity."

Sandy brushed off her sleeves as if Lord Syndovar's grip had left a residual slime clinging to them. "I prefer not to associate with murderers unless it's a professional obligation."

"But you do wish to see your child again." Lord Syndovar held out his hand with feigned courtesy as every drop of fight drained from Sandy's face. "Our boat?"

The cat Cesare jumped from his boat to Lord Syndovar's without bothering to touch the bank. The others walked more circumspectly to the boats they were assigned. Lord Syndovar himself saw to the confiscation of their weapons, stowing the collected armory in a green wooden box. He also directed his men to take their places in the gray boats, leaving only the prisoners, himself, and Tiv's corpse on the shore.

With a look of passing distaste, the storm-haired elf ran his hand through the air above Tiv. A wrinkle in the grass humped itself high as a wave to cover the body. That chore done, he regarded Fazhim and Yaritel.

"My fair travelling companion seems to think I will kill you," he said in a carrying voice. "Perhaps in her world they treat traitors otherwise. Well, for the sake of her sweet company, let there be no blood spilled between us." He raised both hands to his lips and seemed to blow a kiss into the cupped fingers, then seized the prisoners' own hands before they could react. "You are free."

Yaritel fell to her knees, doubled over. Fazhim's mouth was foul with harsh sounds that could only be the vilest curses of his people's tongue. He bent to cover the shaking elf-woman with his body as Lord Syndovar, indifferent to the abuse trailing after him, stepped into the lead boat and by the power of his will launched it.

The three gray boats sailed into the middle of the great stream. Sobs and wailing from the bank followed them. Sandy clung to the gunwales, straining to see, until Lord Syndovar commanded one of his retainers to take his place at the helm

to propel the craft forward. "You let them go free." Sandy
wanted to believe it, yet didn't dare.

"You find that odd?"

"You were going to kill them."

"I was going to have them die. There is a difference."

"But abandoning them there—"

"That will suffice. We shall never see them alive again."

Sandy knit her brows. "Fazhim—Maybe he's disarmed,
but it's not difficult to obtain new weapons, make them, maybe
get help from those little creatures. And the woman was re-
sourceful enough to make it all that way upstream—"

The cries of despair were dwindling with distance. A
mellow dusky light was falling on the great stream where the
three gray boats rode low in the water. Lord Syndovar dipped
his hands into the stream.

"Fazhim and Yaritel are both able woodcrafters. I trained
them myself, and I was bred in both Sherwood and Teutober-
gerwald. They might also beg help of the People of Earth and
the Winged Ones. Then too, they have the magic they were
born with. It won't save them." He lifted his hand from the
water. A goblet of limpid ice had formed. "Some wine? Or
something lighter?"

Sandy ignored the offer. "Why not? If they have magic,
what can't they do?"

Lord Syndovar gazed at her speculatively. "An odd
question, coming from one who, I believe, proved the answer
of it to my lord King Kelerison. They have every power but
the one they need to survive. I have removed their ability to
set up wardings. All wardings. Only for a little while, so you
might compliment me on my sportmansh—"

A fearsome crash overwhelmed his words. Sandy whirled
around in her seat to see a series of seven huge pine trees go
toppling into the great stream, one after another. Clouds of the
Winged Ones swarmed up over the water, filling the air with
their high-pitched cries of panic. One scream, deeper than the
rest, tore through the multicolored curtain of their flight, and
a second, deeper still, dying to a piteous bubbling.

"Well," said Lord Syndovar, cocking an eyebrow. "A
Stone Giant. I had thought them extinct in these parts. I shall
have to make a report to Her Majesty." He tried offering Sandy
the goblet again, and was again refused. "Ah yes, the *geas* of
our food and drink. I had forgotten. It has been so many years
since I indulged in a mortal fancy. Oh, not that you have anything to fear from me on that score, my lady. I merely asked

you to travel with me so that we might entertain each other on a higher level. You are the one who stood up to my king, the rumors say. I'd like to hear all about it.''

Sandy wasn't listening. Her eyes still looked aft, from where the chilling sounds had come. ''They're dead.'' Her fingers tightened on the rail.

''I'd hope so. What a Stone Giant would do to one of our folk alive, well, I'd rather not imagine.'' That made her stare at him, which in turn coaxed another of those small, cold smiles to his lips. ''So much you would know, isn't there? And not the slightest idea of how to begin asking. Here, my lady.'' He pressed the cup into her hands and would not accept refusal. ''Do not drink, but see.''

There was nothing in the goblet one minute, and the next it brimmed with a turquoise liquid topped with silver ripples. The ripples chased each other around and around the goblet's rim, forming outwinding spirals that cleared the central whirlpool to a mirror of the past. Lord Syndovar's words brushed her ear. ''I give you a gift I can well afford, sweet lady: A vision of the past that I know by heart. For once a vision is called up from what has been, the same seeker may never call it back again. This, I can spare.''

''Shh!'' Sandy did not take her eyes from the goblet. With an impatient jerk of the shoulder, she bid the elven lord keep quiet. He only laughed.

''You will need my voice, my lady. A vision is but that: sight without sound. I must explain what you see. Aha! There. It comes.''

The vision came, and when it did, Sandy fell headlong into the magic of that seeing. Her cupped hands held nothing, for she had entered the world Lord Syndovar had summoned. She stood beneath an arch of rock crystal, carved into the likeness of Assyrian winged lions, their paws closed around crossed golden spears. Trailing vines rich with small purple flowers draped the warring beasts, buzzed with the chatter of Winged Ones in miniature court dress.

Sandy looked out from the shelter of the lion arch. She was in a great hall whose walls were likewise crystalline, excepting only where fair silk tapestries, woven in the hues of a Persian garden, overhung the luminous walls. There were flowers everywhere, their perfumes singing through the air. Only a little sweeter, only a shade more lovely to see than the flowers were the folk of Elfhame.

''Welcome to the high court of King Oberon.'' Lord

Syndovar's voice insinuated itself into the vision. "Come and stand beside me, lady."

Sandy looked about the gathering of elves and saw a younger Syndovar, his hair long, black, bound back into a series of plaits whose ends were caught up with small bronze ornaments. He wore court armor over his short, plain white wool tunic—a bronze breastplate and greaves of Homeric antiquity—and carried a sword and ash-hafted spear of like design. Beside him stood two elves whom Sandy recognized at once—Kelerison and Cassiodoron, with the cat Cesare wound around the prince's ankle, drowsing.

As she approached the group she passed a length of bare wall where the crystal was smooth and polished to a high degree. In that mirror she caught sight of herself, and it made her come up short. Her brief cap of red curls had been transformed to waves of shining hair that fell the length of her green velvet dress, itself trailing out behind her. Her freckled skin was clear now, paler than human, finer, and her hands, her feet, her face were all the long, slim, attenuated features of the elfin race. Huge eyes that held their own inner light stared back at her out of the crystal, and the delicate sweep of faun-shaped ears lent her face a peculiarly tempting look.

"And you are among the least lovely of our women," Lord Syndovar said. "If one of your mortal males pursues one of our ladies, can you blame him? Yet when one of us seeks out one of your females, how can it be other than a madness? A foolish, reasonless madness?"

"Thanks for the compliment." Sandy spoke, but the elfin woman she was never moved her lips.

Now a bustle and a murmur ran through the assembled elves. Someone of importance was coming. A tall elf whose face resembled Kelerison's and whose coloring was Cassiodoron's to the life entered the hall and all made way, bowing before him. He took no throne, but instead mounted a low drum-platform of carved crystal set in the center of the hall and raised a green onyx staff. He spoke, and Kelerison came forward to kneel.

"King Oberon. He has summoned his folk to tell them of the changes in the upper world. New thoughts fly. Ships sail into the sunset, seeking new lands even beyond Tir n'an Og, finding them. Soon men of the Old Lands will sail there and not return. They go blindly, as mortals always do, not knowing what awaits them. Worse: they do not know what they leave behind."

Sandy lifted questioning eyes to the young Lord Syndovar at her side. He smiled at her, a smile so much warmer and more feeling than any she had seen on the living Syndovar's lips that she wondered how and why the change had come over him. Then the present elf-lord spoke, answering her unvoiced question.

"Magic. The very force that underlies all lands in the old world. The force that bears life, true life, the life where dreams may come and hope to be made real. No country can breed men who are better than animals if it lacks the underpinning of magic. It was kindled long and long ago—not even we know how—and formed the marrow of our race. All the Peoples of the Air were born of it. Where we dwelled, in that time of all beginnings, there the first men became aware of what they really were. By our presence."

"This is going to come as one hell of a shock to the American Museum of Natural History," Sandy responded. "Will we have to re-name it Darwin's Theory of Elfolution?"

Though the younger Lord Syndovar continued to smile at her, she sensed his present form frowning. "I don't get it."

"You wouldn't. Speak on."

"But see, it is King Oberon who speaks! That scroll he places in his son's hands commands Kelerison to take a party of the younger elves and steal aboard the westbound ships of men. We shall go with them, for the love that has always been between our peoples." Syndovar's voice grew rough and bitter. "The great love between elves and men. Yes, for that we are to go into the west and establish the realm of Elfhame Ultramar, so that the mortal clods who have always needed our magic presence to lift them from the mud may not fall back into it. We are the guardians of the imagination, the warriors who battle to keep the path of dreams clear, the givers of genius and heartfire. What would the new lands be if they were only of the natural world?"

The vision chopped back into silver ripples. The ripples twinkled in the cup and spun themselves into a second seeing. Sandy was still the red-haired elf-woman, only now she wore a fog-soft cloak and stood at the rail of a ship heaving to along a strangely familiar shore. At her side was a man in a steeple-crowned hat, his white neckband much the worse for wear. His dark clothing was stained with recent sickness, but his fever-brightened eyes rejoiced to see the land. He was unaware of her presence.

She looked behind her. A body of people in garb familiar

to every schoolchild who ever stapled paper feathers onto an oaktag turkey knelt on the deck while the sailors scrambled back and forth, around and through and on top of them. A few standard maritime curses salted the hymns.

Running with the sailors to hold a knot or discreetly undo a tangle were the ever-helpful gnomes and brownies, dwarves and karkers. Soaring and swooping through the rigging the Winged Ones starred the plain canvas sails with their bright bodies, minding the set of every line. And standing among the kneeling mass of mortals, the elves turned their eyes to the western shore and sent the first arcs of magic to fasten their souls to the new land.

"Son of a bitch, you came over on the Mayflower!" Sandy exclaimed.

"Some of us did. Some of us packed more expediently and arrived at Jamestown. My lord Kelerison anticipated us. He landed on Hispaniola, making his way north by degrees, gathering up the scattered Peoples of the Air to dwell first and foremost in the High Court; for good cause. We thought to spread our colonies throughout the land, but we never did. Instead, the realm of Elfhame Ultramar clings to the eastern seaboard like a thin coat of seaweed. Would you see our reunion, my lady? King Kelerison's return to his people? It will tell you a great deal."

The question was rhetorical. Already the vision was changing. A delegation of elves stood in a darksome cavern. Sandy was there, and as the seeing gained reality she became aware of small hands fumbling at the front of her dress. The infant in her arms whimpered for his mother's breast. She suckled him, in spite of the disdainful looks she saw some of the other nobly-born elf-women give her.

"They think it unfitting to nurse their own. You might have hired a karker for the job. But that was never your way, was it, my love? The easy way, the acceptable way, the safer path, none of these ever suited you." An arm fell around Sandy's shoulders. She looked up from the suckling infant to the adoring eyes of young Lord Syndovar. "It was you who convinced me that our duty lay in the west, though an arms master of my skill could have retained an honored place in King Oberon's court. You spoke of how our magic was more needed there, in the new lands. You persuaded me of the rightness of the journey. If a land of men lacked magic, it would fall. The lesson of Atlantia was one you never forgot. See, my lady, the lesson that comes now!"

The darkness parted. Kelerison came stumbling into the gathered glow of his waiting people. In his arms he carried a stripling elf with gashed and bleeding skull. The right side of his face had been caved in, and the whole spectacle was made more horrible by the tenacity of the life yet in him. He was still just barely alive. He only died when Kelerison laid him on the earth.

"My lord king's youngest brother, Hylanteron. They traveled together on that first voyage to Hispaniola, and nearly all the way up the mainland coast before *this*. Look at our proud king's face! Not even Kelerison himself is sure of what has happened. They were scouting the new land, bringing the smaller landing parties north to join us, and a blow was struck out of the alien darkness. We did not know how to explain it, either. See how we gasp and chatter? If you could only hear us! Like squirrels. By coincidence, King Kelerison tells how his brother had just loosed an arrow at a squirrel instants before his death. Some argue that Prince Hylanteron must have stumbled in the course of his hunt. There are strange chasms here, terrain we have yet to adapt by our magic. We will change the native landscape, of course. That is our prerogative. After much discussion, we agree that it is all a terrible accident. We will build our realm beneath the lands of men as planned. Nothing more will happen."

The liquid churned, then burst into a nine-pronged star. Sandy gazed down at the face she had last seen in the rock crystal wall. Was this another mirror? The eyes were closed. How could the elf-woman see her reflection that way?

"The spirit leaves the skin. You were only a visitor." Lord Syndovar's thin forefinger touched the surface of the seeing and the scope of vision irised out. Cast in a huddle of anguish across the elf-woman's body, the young Lord Syndovar's hand closed on the arrow-shaft between his lady's breasts and wept. Small faces, unelfin, unreadable, ringed those two in the clearing where they lay. Then they and the vision were gone.

A cool river breeze soothed Sandy's burning face. The ice goblet melted between her hands and trickled away. Lord Syndovar was watching her with a cat's steady stare. "So you see, we had not come to a magicless land after all. We might have left, then. We should have. There were more deaths. There were deaths on both sides."

Lord Syndovar drew up a leather pouch from his belt and spilled the contents into his hand. Sandy thought they were carved acorns, a pile of the burnished brown nuts that over-flowed the elf-lord's cupped palm. Several tumbled into the bottom of the boat. She picked them up to return to their owner.

Then she saw the eye-sockets, no larger than pepper-corns, and the infinitely fine delineation of the skulls. Lord Syndovar accepted his trophies from her. One by one he let them drop back into the leather pouch, hearing each hollow, chalky *tik* with deepening satisfaction.

"Whose are they?" Sandy whispered.

"They are the skulls of the Jun-ge-oh." His eyelids low-ered to a slit. "Do not think less of me for their size. I have killed all breeds of the vermin that inhabit this land. The Stone Giants crush and kill and devour their prey. They are slow and stupid, easier to trick than trolls, no challenge, poor hunting. The Flying Heads can stave in an elf's ribs or lay his stomach open with a single blow of their bearpaws, but they too are all appetite. A noose, well cast while they feed at a baited trap, snares them by the hair and a knife blade, spear thrust, or arrow does the rest. It is the Jungies who are the worst of all: the Jun-ge-oh, the little people. They are intelligent, you see."

"I—never heard of—"

"Have you heard that there were men in this land before your own people arrived from the east? Where there are men, magic. Magic, and the children of magic."

"I think I see." Sandy wraped her arms around herself, feeling an inexplicable chill in the balmy air of Elfhame Ultra-mar. "The squirrel Kelerison's brother shot—"

"One of them."

"A mistake." The chill bored into her bones. "And your people and theirs have been fighting ever since."

"My *people,* as you put it, know nothing. To most of them, the Jungies and their like are tales to liven up a banquet table. Other explanations are found when one of our number dies. Only those who are chosen to train for fighters ever learn the truth about why Elfhame Ultramar is so small a kingdom. It is a slow process, building up an army of the elect, but we elves can wait."

"Wait for what?"

"Lastday." Lord Syndovar blinked slowly, like a croc-odile. "When my army has grown great enough in force of arms and force of magic to destroy the Jungies and all their kind utterly, completely, beyond even a dream of memory."

Sandy was silent, and Lord Syndovar chose to talk no more. The gray boats sailed on down the great stream. The forests and stands of reeds to either side thinned to wetlands and water meadows. For a time in the great stream's meandering course the grassland turned to sheets of solid rock. Distant lights flashed green and red, yellow and blue and all the colors of a peacock's tail. A thick, cloying smell of incense and burning perfume came in the mist that blew across the water. Fish-tailed women with large, bare breasts perched on the more jagged rocks at the water's edge hailing the vessels with musical words. The two retainers in the lead boat returned their calls good-naturedly. Sandy didn't understand the words, but she knew the tune.

"Things are a little lax in this section," she commented.

Lord Syndovar made a moue. "Influence. It is a sorry thing. The land derives its character from the magic underlying it, but there appears to be some traffic in the other direction as well. We are below New York and Atlantic City hereabouts. The great stream wanders, and does not follow the contours of the world above. We shall be away from this region soon."

The elf-lord was right. The water meadows returned, and with them came the sounds of youthful voices. Among the pale primrose grasses with their nodding green seedheads, a throng of elfin lads and lasses dabbled their feet in the water and raised sparkling cups of violet wine in salutation to the passing vessels. Sandy thought she heard Cassiodoron's name called, among the unfamiliar syllables. She craned her head and saw him sitting with Amanda in the boat following hers. He was all hunched up, unresponsive to the jolly greetings from the bank.

One of the elf-lads tried to get a reaction by more direct means. He threw something at the boats. It missed Cass's vessel and landed in Sandy's lap. She held the yellow sphere up as if it were a phoenix egg.

"A tennis ball?"

"I care less for this region than for the last," Lord Syndovar said. "They are all New Magic here."

The sky of Elfhame Ultramar grew dark and light and dark again. Sandy felt no need for sleep, and certainly no desire. "Our times are yours," Lord Syndovar explained. "But while you dwell among us, you share a part of our indifference to any time."

At last the great stream began to pass buildings of brick and dressed stone. Piers jutted into the water, nixies and tritons darting in and out among the pilings. Roofs flashed gilded tiles, and where the great stream poured its waters into a smoking gulf that smelled of the sea, a series of barred barrel arches linked the banks. Atop them was a wide bridge of speckled blue agate, waterstairs winding down from either side. On the bridge's platform a brilliant assemblage of elves jostled and hummed and threw the occasional rose.

The gray boats tied up at the left-hand waterstairs, just below the facade of a castle of cornflower spires and stone walls the subtle shade of old ivory. A multicolored grandeur of elves descended, led by a female whose beauty, bearing, and sumptuousness of dress identified her well before she whisked Cassiodoron from his craft and pressed him to her heart.

"My son! My darling! Welcome home!"

Chapter Nineteen:

The Politics of Surprise

There were no cheers.

These elves are a self-contained lot, Sandy thought as she and the other mortals stepped onto the waterstairs. *Or maybe they're all just as snotty as Lord Syndovar even to one of their own.*

No one offered the ladies a hand up. No one bothered to keep a weapon on them either. Perhaps it was bad manners to do so in the presence of the queen, or else it didn't seem worth the bother. With so many sources of magic power surrounding them, what could a paltry gaggle of mortals do?

Cassiodoron broke his mother's embrace and stepped back to kneel before her. Every motion had the stiffness of tradition extraordinarily mated to the fluidity of an exotic dance.

"My lady mother." He kissed her hands. "Am I truly welcome here?" He spoke so that the mortals might understand his words. It might have been a declaration of courtesy or a challenge.

"Can you doubt it, my dear one?" Queen Bantrobel replied in the same coin. She was a dark beauty, with a look of ancient Egypt. Her voice fluted exquisitely.

"It's easy to doubt many things"—Cass glowered at Lord Syndovar—"when your friends are cut down in front of you and called traitors."

"Oh," said Queen Bantrobel. "That."

And the queen of Elfhame Ultramar stretched out her hand to Lord Syndovar, drew him to her side, and slipped an arm around his hips. They were both tall—she a hairsbreadth more than he—yet she managed to contrive to rest her head on his shoulder. The picture they presented was unmistakable in its intended message. Cass's mouth dropped open an inch, then snapped to as he tried to hide his reaction.

"Darling boy." The queen closed her eyes dreamily, snuggling closer to Lord Syndovar. "I was told it was necessary. A wise ruler heeds her wisest counselors, if she has half a brain, and acts as they suggest. You'll understand someday, when you're all grown up. I *am* sorry about your friends. They should never have gotten involved with that silly conspiracy."

"Conspiracy!" The elf-prince stared at his mother and her paramour. "There was no conspiracy. All we desired was to recover two mortal children, wrongfully taken into our realm. That was my father's doing, as you must know."

"Word does travel fast down here."

"You also know how uncooperative he can be when it comes to giving up the things he's taken."

"So I do." Queen Bantrobel's eyes drifted to rest on Amanda. "What a surprise, my lady. I thought we'd seen the last of you."

"I haven't come back because I wanted—"

"Silence!" The word cracked like a whip. Amanda murmured something in the elfin tongue and retreated. In a more sedate tone, Bantrobel addressed her son once more:

"So you thought your friends would help you to rescue the children—darlings, both of them, even if the female is a sight quick-tempered—and then you would all return to the surface?" She planted a kiss on his brow. "You adorable idiot. As if they'd have let you go!"

Cass would have risen from his knees, but a hard look from Lord Syndovar reminded him of the proprieties. Sandy could see his teeth clench, a muscle along the jawline twitch.

"The Queen of Air and Darkness would appear to be a dip," Lionel whispered in her ear. "And her royal son is royally pissed. No doubt about it: we're going to have to tighten up the zoning laws in Godwin's Corners."

"Shut up." She clasped hands with him. A single

squeeze communicated their mutual relief to hear that Ellie was all right—if a sight quick-tempered.

"Why wouldn't they let me go?" Cass demanded. He pitched his voice low so that the crowd of elves on the bridge above could not hear. For all they knew, the queen and her son were catching up on old times.

"Well . . ." Queen Bantrobel shrugged her shoulders, soft, brown, and bare above the froth of her carnelian gown. "They'd need *someone* to fill the throne once they'd deposed your father. Don't goggle at me, Cassiodoron! Your face will freeze like that and everyone will think you're a pond-grim. It's not your fault, dear; not at all. You've always been someone's pawn, always naive, always the romantic. And gullible?" Her pretty laughter cascaded over her son's bowed head in a shower of ice water.

"But why would they want to do such a thing? The most Tiv ever cared about was the color of his newest court robes. Fazhim was happiest if left alone with his poetry, and the rest—"

"You ascribe your own political apathy to all your contemporaries, my lord prince," Lord Syndovar purred. "It is easier to hide one's faults in a crowd, isn't it?"

"I do wish you'd have stayed where you were needed, Cassiodoron." Queen Bantrobel sighed. "Bad enough your father goes rabbiting off to the surface every second moment, but when you run away too! No one really likes a female regent. Such a great many of our subjects *will* mutter in corners about what use is an absent king, and why doesn't he lead his warriors in one final assault against those nasty, primitive, savage Jungies and the rest. Just one good battle, massacre them, and be done with it. We'd appreciate the security of being able to go where we like in this new land, and we certainly could use the extra room. I *know* the pixies need more breeding space."

Cass nodded his head. "Therefore, since the king is absent so much of the time anyway, why not be rid of him altogether? I see. So they were traitors, my poor friends. You executed them for wishing to depose the king."

"No, dear. Their crime was not that they thought to depose your father." A sphere of transparent rose quartz appeared in Queen Bantrobel's hand. She positioned herself in such a way that no one on the bridge could glimpse the vision she called up into the shining ball. A gilded silver star of light spidered over the surface. In the heart of the rock, for all on the waterstairs to see, King Kelerison lay bound with iron chains, hand and foot. The signs of a recent struggle marked his face with bruises and dried blood. "But that they didn't think of it first."

Bantrobel had a charming giggle. "Lord Syndovar has your father pent in the maze. Can you see the hedge of everbright behind him? You know the one: it's where you made such a spectacle of yourself during your trial of passage, and over that teeny little dragonet the gardener keeps in there to scare off the crows. Now this is to be our little secret, Cassiodoron. You mortals *can* keep secrets too, can't you? Do try, if you want to see those sweet little ones of yours again."

The rosy sphere popped between her fingers like a soap bubble. She looped her arm under Cass's elbow and raised her son from the stones. "Politics always gives me such a headache. And you must all be famished. Shall we go into the feasting hall?" She tilted back her head so that the mortals on the waterstairs and the elves on the bridge were equally able to hear. "You are all invited!"

"When will we see the children?" Sandy whispered urgently to Amanda.

"At the queen's pleasure." Amanda sipped her wine without apparent concern. The mortals had been relegated to a separate table, well below the salt, there to be served with food and drink of undeniable surface origin. Whatever else she was, Queen Bantrobel was a considerate hostess.

They were the only ones being waited on. Around them, the feasting hall was a milling confusion of scores of elves, all looking after their own interests. True to what Tiv and Fazhim had said, elves picked up after themselves. It was a little less than a virtue when it meant whole tables full of them were forever getting up and down to fetch some tidbit from the sideboards during the great royal feast.

"This reminds me of my cousin Max's bar mitzvah," Sandy said. "They had a buffet."

The sloe-eyed young elf-lass who was their table's impromptu servant overheard and repeated, "Mack-sez 'bar mitzvah'?" in dulcet trills.

Sandy smiled wistfully. "You wouldn't understand."

The elf shrugged. *"Vuh den? Ahz a yur uf zier!"* She flounced off muttering of *goyisher kopfs*.

Lionel stroked his chin in speculation. "Symbiosis," he said. "That's the operative word. I'm willing to believe we get some benefit from their magic running under our land, but they don't come away empty-handed either.''

"Professor Walters . . ." Davina's mellifluous voice was raised timidly. "In the Old Land we knew we needed the elfin magic to sustain us, to lift us that much closer to the stars, but what earthly good could such fair creatures derive from our poor sorry doings?''

Lionel winked at her. "You'd fit right in here, Davina, with an attitude like that. What can the deathless learn from the doomed? What can the most gorgeous beings on earth learn from a race whose number-one ticket to Nirvana is getting a face-lift and lipo-suction? Look up there.'' He pointed to the dais where Queen Bantrobel had installed Cass on his father's throne. To her right sat Lord Syndovar, and though his was an ordinary chair, no one seeing those three together could doubt where the true power of the realm sat.

"I've never seen anything so beautiful in my life before,'' Lionel went on. "Bright and immortal and glittering as a diamond. Hard as one too. Look at Lord Syndovar in particular. Now there is an elf who has kept his contacts with our world to a minimum. His contempt for us is perfect as his posture.''

"He looks as if someone shoved a steel rod up his—''

"Sandy, please.''

"Well, it's true!" Sandy exclaimed. "Lionel's right, Davina. Just look at Lord Syndovar, and the Queen of Airheads and Darkness next to him. Even Kelerison was better than they are. You could reason with him . . . a little.''

"So you could,'' Amanda interjected. "He was—he *is* selfish, but not completely so. He knows that there's more to the world than his desires, whether or not he likes it.''

"And look at Cass!" Sandy noted that Davina did this most willingly. "Imagine how he'd be if he hadn't spent so many years in such close contact with mortals. He's learned from us. There's something in him now to temper the arrogance of immortality, to bring out the soul.''

"The Fair Folk have no souls.'' Davina's every intonation seemed to mourn that lack among the elvenkind.

"Bull,'' Sandy said succinctly. "They've got at least as much soul as a mortage banker. Whether they act as if they ever use it or not . . . but that doesn't mean they don't have any.'' Her hand closed around Rimmon's bloodstone pendant, and her gaze wandered back to the high table. She saw a fading face out of memory where Cass's own should be. "Our envy mustn't let us deny the truth. Look at him, and tell me he has no soul.''

Davina hadn't the artifice to conceal the yearning in her own eyes. "Oh, he has. He has."

Queen Bantrobel stood, clearing her throat for attention, and all her court rushed back to their seats under Lord Syndovar's cold eye. "I have the *nicest* announcement to make!" She clapped her hands together. "In view of our lord King Kelerison's unfortunately extended absence, our very beloved son Prince Cassiodoron has agreed to assume the throne of Elfhame Ultramar from now until, oh, whenever.''

Restrained applause greeted this announcement, underscored by the sound of utensils scraping leftovers into the silver bins at the end of each table. Cass stood up beside his mother and bowed to the assemblage.

"Of course if our dear, *dear* lord ever should come back, Prince Cassiodoron will step right down from the throne that very instant. But in the meantime, he has appointed Lord Syndovar as his chief adviser, a choice I endorse most heartily.''

A number of murmurs weaseled through the crowd. These passed mostly from one inscrutably lovely face to the next, with hardly a tremor of the features to betray the flight of gossip. There were exceptions. Those elves who had had contact with the surface made themselves obvious by tongue clickings, knowing nudges, and certain unfortunate finger gestures.

At a nearby table, a hard-faced elf rose and signed that he wished to speak. Sandy recognized him as one of the archers who had backed Lord Syndovar. "Your Majesty, we have let too many years go by already, waiting for our lord king to lead us into a battle that never comes. The Powers be my witness, I would like to believe things will be different under Prince Cassiodoron's rule, but he too has spent years among mortals. Some say he has his father's tastes.'' The elf looked right at Amanda. "What sort of influence is that for a potential war leader?''

This time the commotion in the hall was general.

Bantrobel was livid. "He is *my* son too, and—''

"Mother, please." Cass gestured for silence. "My people, you do deserve an explanation. I have been away from you for too long. Let us say that I needed to spend time enough among mortals to appreciate my own kind all the better. Those of you who have dwelled on the surface will know what I mean. Those of you who have never had to suffer the experience, be advised by me: remain in the halls of Elfhame Ultramar. If you searched and searched, you couldn't find a sillier earthspawn than the human race. In their ignorance, they fill buildings full of books with what they call wisdom. They believe in the quark and the virella and the diatom, because some people in white coats decreed that such things exist. You can't see them with the unassisted eye, but that doesn't matter. The White Coats have spoken! But just let another human claim belief in the merfolk, or the Winged Ones, or even in us . . . Well, then they send for some other people in white coats to take care of them.''

The tables buzzed with scandalized reactions.

Queen Bantrobel's expression softened. ''Cassiodoron, I never suspected that when you ran away, it was for educational purposes.''

Cass laughed. ''And the things mortals have taught me! They hate in the name of a god of love! They make war in the name of peace! They fancy themselves the lords of creation because they are able to destroy it all! Oh, my people, avoid them. If my words will not be enough to teach you, see what I have brought back.''

He waved his hands and the four mortals floated up from the table. Sandy grabbed for Lionel, but the elf-prince's spell had sent them tumbling in freefall without a second's notice. They drifted apart. Cesare took the opportunity to jump onto the table and browse among the abandoned plates. A gust of Winged Ones swept down from the carved rafters of the feasting hall to guide them as they flopped awkwardly in midair. The elves looked up, some with scholarly interest, some for pure amusement value, some with unconcealed disgust.

''I think you'll recognize this one.'' Cass pulled an invisible string, bringing Amanda down to earth just before the high table. ''She was my father's chosen. He gave her many gifts, not the least of which was long life. Rightfully, she should be a pile of yellow bones by now. Instead she took it into her head to run off with one of her own flimsy breed. You may have heard how I fled with them. My people, what use are our lives if we can't fill the years with satisfied curiosities?''

A phantom hand materialized to stroke Amanda's cheek. Cass tugged the magic guy wire and she flew back up to float with the others. His fingers tweaked another portion of the air and Davina alit.

''I must admit, they fascinate me, these mortals. See the grotesque variety of shapes they come in! Yet this one is a

phoenix in the body of a river horse. She has the Sight, and a
voice to rival any one of yours, and she has the ability to put
herself into another person's skin: an actress, they call her.''
His tiny smile was the twin of Lord Syndovar's. ''It had better
be a big skin if it's to hold all of you, my lady.'' Davina too
was whisked back among the rafters, to be replaced by Lionel.

''Behold one who thought he was my teacher! And
this''—he plucked Sandy from the air—''is an even rarer beast:
a woman of law. Don't laugh at this one, my people! She is
formidable. I watched as she held my father at bay with words
alone. She is the cleverest of the lot, and in spite of that, I was
able to lure her into our realm with the rest. And here I mean
to keep her.''

He seized Sandy's hand in an unbreakable grip. Liquid
golden light flowed from his heart, down the length of his arm,
and laved her body with transforming magic that gowned and
jeweled her in more splendid style than Lord Syndovar's lost
lady. Her robes were sky-blue satin, foaming with white lace,
and the sparkling red slippers on her feet matched the parure
of rubies at her neck, wrist, and throat.

''Now, just a minute—'' Lionel stepped right into a wall
of mist that sprang up from the floor and wrapped itself into a
tube around him. His objections could still be heard, but from
very far away. The cylinder tilted onto its side and wafted high
into the air, then flicked open like a throw rug being shaken
out. Lionel slid across the void and hit the minstrels' gallery
heels first. He clung to the balusters like a monkey. There was
scattered applause from below.

''Sir Devron is correct.'' Cass inclined his head toward
the archer as he pulled Sandy closer. She was too torn between
anxiety for her husband and her still-absent child to put up a
fight. ''I do have my father's tastes.'' His arm was about her
waist, and he forced her head up to meet his kiss. Its rough
fire left her breathless.

Someone from the lower end of the hall shouted, ''Way
to go!'' At a sharp hand signal from Lord Syndovar, the sur-
face-tainted enthusiast was escorted from the premises by a
pair of his men-at-arms.

''My father's tastes''—Cass favored his subjects with a
wicked smile—''but more than my father's wisdom. Sir Devron, have no fears. The wisest ruler knows himself, and dele-
gates accordingly. Let my lord Syndovar come to me!''

The cold elf-lord rose slowly from his place. He looked
somewhat bemused by this summons, and his expression stated

clearly that he did not like unexpected puzzles. He liked even
less the ceremonial necessity of kneeling to his prince, for that
meant kneeling also to Sandy.

"My prince?"

"My lord. As my chief adviser, what would you say if
I told you that it is my pleasure to press the war against the
Jun-ge-oh—"

"Your Highness already knows my opinion of—"

"—tomorrow?"

Lord Syndovar remained unmoved, but his voice lost a
little of its frosty self-possession. "You—surprise me pleas-
antly, my prince. I did not think you would be the one to urge
us into battle so early in your reign. But then"—he stole a
glance at the helplessly floating mortals—"I seem to have given
you less credit than you deserve in many instances. So, we ride
tomorrow?"

"Ah, no, my lord, not 'we.' You do, for I name you
warlord. The wisest ruler, as I said, knows himself, and I know
that my skills lie elsewhere than in battle."

One-handed, he swept Sandy from her feet and over his
shoulder in a fireman's carry. This time she did kick up a
ruckus, and Cass was a shade too slow in bearing her off to
avoid having her catch Lord Syndovar in the nose with one
lashing scarlet heel.

The Prince of Elfhame Ultramar smiled a lame apology
and whacked Sandy's backside lustily. "Calm down, wench!
Lie still and enjoy it! You'll thank me for this someday!" Victorious, he bore her from the feasting hall.

This time there were cheers.

Chapter Twenty:

Amazing Grace

C ass lay back on the bed. "Was I good?"
   Sandy gave him the Bronx cheer. It carried all the
way across the vast bedroom. "Don't start building a glass
case to hold any Oscars just yet."

The elf-prince looked hurt. "Well, I had to do something to get you out of there."

" 'Wench'?" She took a blue apple from the bowl at her elbow and absentmindedly began paring it with a jade knife. " 'You'll thank me for this someday'?"

"It was the best I could think of." Cass punched the pillow. "The court bought it, didn't they?"

"I'll never understand elves. And this get-up." She raised her azure skirts to gawk at her red footgear. "Who does your wardrobe? George M. Cohan?"

"This *is* America, as you kept reminding my poor father. I thought you'd appreciate the red, white, and blue."

"Three and a half cheers. Was this abduction necessary?"

"Yes," Cass said, sitting up. "It was. I had to make sure at least one of you was free to help me, to make my mother and Lord Syndovar think I'm otherwise occupied while the war preparations go on. You were the most credible choice."

"It *might* have looked odd if you'd tapped Lionel." She admired the job she'd done on the fully peeled apple.

"But I will. I will need you all before I'm done."

"What for?" The apple was an inch from her mouth.

"To help me rescue my father." The Prince of Elfhame Ultramar snatched a stiletto from beneath his pillow and threw it with unmatched speed and accuracy. It *tzinged* through the air and struck the apple from Sandy's lips, impaling it on the wall behind her armchair. She gaped at her empty fingers, then at him. "Don't eat that," he said mildly. "Not unless you've got the next century free to visit. It's one of ours."

Now Sandy's mouth hung open in earnest. "Oops."

"As much as I would like this little byplay of ours to happen in reality," Cass went on, "I would not have you remain in my land against your will. And I won't ever have you willingly, will I, Sandy?" She shook her head and he sighed. "That is the real paradox you mortals pose: the faith in love you sometimes keep for no reason anyone can see. Divorce at an all-time high, and I pick the one woman who refuses to keep up with the times!"

"In my family, we don't believe in divorce," Sandy said lightly. "Just homicide." As soon as she said it, she wondered whether Cass knew she was joking.

His face betrayed nothing. "Is he rich, your Lionel? Is he so handsome that time will pass him by? Will he give you

all you ever desire? Is he . . . ?'' The elf-prince's fingers described a shape of exaggerated proportions.

"None of your damned business!" Sandy retorted. In a
more subdued tone she added, "Anyway, no. No more than
usual."

Cass flopped back among the pillows. "Then I just don't
see it!"

"Love, elves, and quarks. Now you see them . . . Wait
a minute. Rescue your father, you say?"

"You saw what they've done to him, my *lady* mother
and Lord Syndovar. How could she!"

"I'd say your mother finally got fed up with your father's
carryings-on and decided to give him a taste of his own med-
icine. Kelerison hasn't been the model of married fidelity.
Maybe Lord Syndovar has his charms"—Sandy screwed up her
mouth—"if you're fond of Popsicles."

"But that is no reason to put him from his throne! To
imprison him in the battle maze!" Cassiodoron's shoulders
shook. "You don't know what an awful place that is. The
everbright that forms its walls is an enchanted plant that first
grew in the gardens of Hecate. It drinks all the magic out of
us and uses our own powers to conjure perils we must face
with only ordinary weapons. To go through the battle maze is
our oldest, most difficult rite of passage."

Sandy crossed the room to sit beside Cass on the bed.
She rested her hands on his back and stroked him in just the
way she used to comfort Ellie when the child woke from a
nightmare. "Was that the test you failed, Cass?" She put no
shame into her words. "Was that why Kelerison called you a
coward?"

A deep sigh moved beneath her calming hands. "Whatever he's said or done to me, I can't leave him like that. Praise
the Powers that inspired me to give Lord Syndovar the toy he's
always wanted: carte blanche for all-out war on the Jungies.
He'll be mustering his men right now, ready to march with the
dawn. That should keep him out of our way."

"When we go to rescue your father?"

"And your child. And your husband. And Jeffy, Amanda,
Davina . . . maybe Cesare too, if he's taken to clawing my
mother's throne again. They're all in the dungeons, Sandy.
They were sent there as soon as the feast ended."

"How do you . . . ?"

Tapestries hung to either side of Cass's bed. At Sandy's
startled question, the left-hand one was pulled aside from be-

hind. The same sloe-eyed elf-lass who had waited on the mortals at the feast greeted her with a cheerful, *"Wie geht's?"*

"Sandy, may I present Loris? My ears and my eyes."
Cass raised the maiden's hand to his lips. "Lord Syndovar did
not discover all of my so-called traitor friends."

The right-hand tapestry flipped back just as suddenly and
a small whirlwind bolted from the dancing dust motes into Sandy's lap. "Mommy! Mommy! Mommy!" Ellie's satin dress
slipped and slid against Sandy's as the two of them tried to
hug and kiss and talk, all at once. Jeffy watched this undigni-
fied display with the solemn gravity befitting a lad wearing the
livery of Queen Bantrobel's household pages.

Ellie babbled about the big fire, about how she and Jeffy
had been almost out the door when he thought he heard his
mother calling him. Who could say it was impossible? The past
week, Godwin's Corners had teemed with impossibilities. Jeffy
stole back, evading the lines of escaping children. He had to
be sure. No one was looking for a child to run *into* a burning
building. Every panic-stricken eye was on the way out, the
teacher's too.

"I had to go back with him," Ellie explained quite rea-
sonably. "He was my line buddy. You never get separated
from your line buddy. I thought maybe I heard Mrs. Taylor's
voice too. Only it wasn't her, it was this man. He was all
wrapped up in a cape and he had this funny lizard on a leash,
and wherever that lizard ran, it all came up fire."

"A salamander," Cass commented.

"So it ran all around us, and it was on fire, and Jeffy got
scared 'cause we couldn't get out and his Mommy wasn't there
after all and he started to cry—"

"Did not! *You* did!!"

"I didn't! You're a liar, Jeffy. It was me told the man to
help us get out."

"Did not!"

"Did too! Liar, liar, pants on fire!"

"Ellie, please . . ." Sandy tried to get her daughter back
on the track.

The child took a much-needed deep breath before continuing. "So *I did too* tell the man. Only he said we had to take
off our necklaces first because of something—a door we
couldn't go through—I couldn't understand, but I did it.
Mommy, I know I'm not supposed to talk to strangers, or do
what they say, but it was all on *fire* in there!"

"You did just fine, Ellie." Sandy gathered her child

closer to her and twined the long hair through her fingers as if
it were the most precious gold.

"Anyway, the man brought us down through this purple
door, and there were these unicorns waiting—*real* unicorns,
Mommy, honest! I'm not telling stories! So we rode on them,
and mine was silver with a lemon mane, just like My Pretty
Pony, only it kind of smelled, and we came to this castle and
the queen came out—Mommy she is *so* beautiful. She's even
prettier than Barbie and the Rockers. And the man started talking to her, about us, and she looked mad at him, but *right then*
these other men jumped out of *nowhere*, honest! And there was
an awful big fight, and lights flashing, and smoke, and they
killed the s'mander dead, and there were *real swords*, and then
they put chains on the man who brought us, and they took him
away." She paused and seemed to be thinking something over.
"The queen looked kind of unhappy when they did that. But
then she took us inside, and we got new clothes, and the guys
who beat up the other man came back and one of them told
Loris to watch us—"

The elf-maid curtsied. " 'Keep them out of my sight'
were Lord Syndovar's exact orders. That was my pleasure."

"—and Jeffy was supposed to be the queen's *slave* or
something—"

"I'm a page, not a slave." Jeffy snorted. "Boy, you
don't know anything, Ellie." Full of self-righteousness, he in-
formed Sandy, "She didn't even *curtsy* to Queen Bantrobel.
And she *bit* someone."

Tears were trickling down Sandy's face as she smiled.
"Don't bite elves, Eleanora; you never know where they've
been. Just wait till I get you home." She laughed deep in her
throat and rocked her daughter like a baby. "Oh, just you wait
until I get you home again!"

"*I've* been in a dungeon," Ellie countered, wriggling out
of Sandy's arms. She sounded proud of the fact.

"When our plot was discovered and word of your approach came, Lord Syndovar had them imprisoned, yes," Loris said. "My lady, don't look so pale. It is not the sort of
dungeon you imagine, with spiders and rats. Really, it was no
worse than a one-star Miami motel."

"But to lock children away!" Sandy was aghast.

Loris agreed. "Lord Syndovar should only grow like an
onion, with his head in the ground. I fear that the dungeon
where he has placed your friends is not as wholesome. Prince
Cassiodoron no sooner carried you out of the feasting hall than

he had his men reel them down from the rafters and march them away. Queen Bantrobel made some small objection, but he ignored her.''

"I named him warlord and gave him his war," Cass said grimly. "My mother is no longer worth his while. I expect he thinks that once he's won the battle, he can take care of me too, as he and his minions turned on my father."

"Let him have a *miesse meshina,*" Loris said.

Sandy caught at the elf-maid's sleeve. *"Where* did you learn to talk like that? On the surface?"

Loris turned bashful. "Some. But mostly from Leo."

"A nice Jewish boy, huh? My mother would love you."

"Well . . . no. He's a dybbuk. But he's a *very nice* dybbuk, and he knows right where to go for the best kosher pastrami in Flatbush." She batted her eyelashes coyly. "That's why I joined the prince's supporters at court; the moderates. We know we're not the only ones living in the magic web of this land, and we don't think the answer is war. You should only know how many wars it would take! If Lord Syndovar found out there's more than Jungies and Heads and Stone Giants out there, and that I was keeping company with one of them—"

"He'd *plotz,*" Sandy finished for her.

"Let him *plotz.*" Loris waved her hand. "Only first, he'd kill me, and I'd rather skip that."

"So would we all." Cass sprang from the bed. "And so we will once we're together again. Did you have any trouble bringing the little ones here from their cell?"

"It was unguarded, with a simple spell on the lock. When I had them out, I took the hidden route to your room. Lord Syndovar wouldn't waste men on watching the children's cell, but where the lady Amanda and the other two are . . ."

"If we're lucky, the guards there are also Lord Syndovar's men, and he'll have rallied them to make preparations for tomorrow." Cass glanced out at the starless dark, framed in the arches of his bedroom windows. "We have half the hours of the night. That should be enough to reunite our party and—" He paused. A look of apprehension, bright and short as summer lightning, flashed across his face.

"And save your father from the maze." Sandy linked her fingers with his, holding Ellie with her other hand. "We're with you, Cass. This time you won't have to enter it alone."

He tried to look confident, but the effort was not enough.

"Mortals may stand together in the walls of everbright," he said, "but every elf who enters the battle maze, goes alone."

Cass's prediction as to the disposition of dungeon guards proved right. The more picturesque cells were on the second-from-lowest level of the palace, reached by tower stairs that corkscrewed down into the foundations via a route ill-traveled. Torches burned beside those cell doors where there were prisoners—in this case, only two. A single guard minded these, none too attentively. The rest of the corridor lay in darkness.

"The guards bring their own lanterns to reach their posts," Loris explained to Sandy as they hung far back in the stairwell shadows and peered down the hall. "That, or they conjure up palm glows. We don't need as much as you mortals do to see by."

"I can't see *anything!*" Ellie whined, trying to squirm past her mother.

The guard heard her, and pricked up his ears exactly like a fox. Loris clicked her tongue.

"A shayne oytser. Now we'll have to act quickly." She spoke some words into her hand and a puff of dandelion light formed there. Holding it well in front of her, she sashayed down the corridor, hips swinging.

The ruse was straight out of the annals of Grade-B swashbuckler movies. Sandy could almost taste the popcorn as Loris distracted the guard while Cass neutralized him. The only difference was that instead of sneaking up with a sock full of sand, the elf-prince turned invisible, strolled up to his mark, and laid a sleep-spell on him. A second conjuring opened the cell doors before the guard hit the floor.

"Daddy! Daddy!"

"Mama! Mama!" This time Ellie wasn't the only one running into a parent's embrace. Jeffy forgot all about the dignity of his page's livery as he rushed to his mother's arms. Cesare ambled out of Lionel's cell and washed.

"Well," Sandy said to Cass. "That was easy. I'm almost disappointed."

"She doesn't like easy?" Loris regarded her prince and cocked her head at the mortal. "She wants harder?" She turned to Sandy. "Lady, have I got a maze for you!"

"I don't like this," Sandy said, holding the sword up awkwardly in front of her as she took the measure of the towering walls of everbright.

"Now she doesn't like it." Loris sighed. "There's no pleasing some people, my lord prince."

The battle maze grew on a hilltop within sight of the palace, yet far from the main land and water routes linking the elfin high court with the rest of Elfhame Ultramar. It was a sensible arrangement, if what Cass said of the strange plant's magic-draining properties was correct. Though an elf had to be flanked by the crimson hedges before he lost his powers temporarily, most of the Fair Folk preferred knowing that the battle maze was a good, safe distance away from their daily doings.

"No one comes here who doesn't have to," Cass said. His voice cracked slightly every time he looked at the waiting maze. "Everbright does its own guard work."

"I'll bet they couldn't post a guard here if they wanted to," Sandy said. "They're all busy elsewhere. The palace forecourt was teeming with troops."

"Like fleas on a bitch," Cesare remarked.

"I didn't think we were going to get past them," Lionel said. He too held a sword, carrying it well away from the heavy folds of his hooded cloak. "Some of them looked like they could peer right inside my hood and know I wasn't elfin."

"We can thank Davina for getting us through," Amanda said. Jeffy hung close against her side, but he managed to smile shyly at the Welsh *au pair*.

"It was no great thing I did." Davina's modest disclaimer was overturned immediately by the Prince of Elfhame Ultramar himself.

"No great thing! I never saw anything like it. With your hood *down*, no less, you marched right up to the men at the gate and convinced them that we were all of us in Lord Syndovar's secret service!"

"Well, he looks the part of one who'd have his spies." Davina cast a nervous glance back toward the palace. "And if tomorrow he wars against the native spirits of this place, what's to stop him from someday wishing for all the surface territory too? He has no respect for mortals. He'd seize the sun from our eyes and think it no less than his due. I only claimed we were bound for the surface, and that was the truth. That we were Lord Syndovar's agents . . . the Bard himself took liberties with the truth at times."

"But with your hood *down!*" Cass seemed unable to get over it. "Looking every bit as mortal as you are!"

"If we're spying on the surface dwellers, we must look

like them.'' Davina dimpled under the elfin prince's admiration. She touched the children's hair fondly. "The guards even complimented us on how well we'd disguised our dwarven assistants.''

Ellie became indignant. "I am *not* a dwarf!''

"You're a *gonif*, is what you are,'' Loris said. "And I want your word of honor that you'll stay close to me when we go into the maze.''

Sandy dropped her sword. "We're not taking the children in there?''

"We must.'' Cass was staring at the clusters of shining leaves, each shaped like a star, and the gleaming black twigs from which they grew. "We can't leave them out here, in case someone should happen to pass this way. Loris and Davina can mind them—''

"And I,'' Cesare volunteered. "That is, if they can show some respect for a *cavaliere*'s tail. It is *not* a pull-toy, eh?'' Ellie looked innocent.

"I'll mind Ellie.'' Sandy took hold of her daughter's hand decisively. "I don't know why you gave me that sword anyhow, Cass. I've got maybe half an idea of how to use it.''

"To be frank''—Lionel looked at his own sword askance—"the same goes for me. If I had to fight with it, maybe I could do it right, but I don't know. It's been years.''

Cass picked up the fallen blade and put it back in Sandy's hand with a determined look to match her own. "This sword is iron; iron from the Old Land, from the time of the first forgings. It's even older than Hecate's cursed hedging. Age holds magic. Whatever you meet inside there, this will be the one substance that may save you.''

She tried pushing it back at him. "Then you carry it as a spare. We'll all stick close to you. That's the only logical way: you know the maze.''

Cass looked as if he wanted to say something, but changed his mind before the words could come. Firmly he closed Sandy's fingers around the leather-wrapped hilt of the sword. "Then carry this to humor me, and let us go in.''

The space between the walls of everbright was wide enough for two people to go abreast. Cass led, with Lionel beside him. Amanda followed, holding Jeffy by the hand, with Sandy and Ellie coming after them, but the children soon paired themselves off, leaving their mothers to go ahead. Loris and Davina came last, keeping a watchful eye on the little ones.

The cat trotted from one end of the line to the other as it suited his whim.

No one spoke. The children whispered together at first, until the pervasive stillness made their smallest sound come loud enough to frighten them into silence. The growing walls went straight for a long while, then jagged left, taking the party into a section of the maze where the night of Elfhame Ultramar above seemed even darker, and the heart hungered for even a memory of the stars.

There was a squared-off barricade of everbright at the next clearing, dividing the path in two. "This way." Cass signed for them to follow him by the right-hand branch. They all did, though the barrier hedge made it narrower going and they had to fall into single file. Sandy slung her long skirts over one arm as Amanda took a sharp left on the path in front of her.

Sandy did the same, and stared at a solid wall of leaves. "Children, I think we took a wrong—"

She turned. No one was behind her. No one and nothing but another solid wall of everbright. The way to left and right lay open, but a moment ago it had been thick hedge. She bent her head back, calling everyone by name, stretching her neck as she tried ineffectively to look over the top of the labyrinth's walls. All she could see was dusky sky.

"Damn." She sat down with her back to one wall. Grass grew between the everbright hedges, grass so ordinary that it taunted her, magic-stranded. She plucked a blade and chewed the end.

The starry red leaves rustled just around the corner. At once she was on her feet, racing toward the sound, calling out, "Lionel! Ellie! Cass! Lionel, it's me, wait! Lionel!"

She ran headlong, unseeing, into strong, open arms. "My lady, and have you forgotten my name at last?"

"Rimmon . . ." Her knees gave way as she met his eyes. His hold on her tightened, keeping her on her feet until she was able to stand unassisted. His fingers brushed the bloodstone pendant on her neck.

"Not forgotten. As I have never forgotten you." His breath was warm, bearing memories that woke into fire under her skin. It flowed between her parted lips, and the bloodstone token kindled its own blaze when their bodies pressed close.

Abruptly, she pushed him away, arms stiff, every nerve in her body raw. "You aren't—you can't be here. Rimmon, this isn't real!"

"How real was I when we were lovers in lost Khwarema, my lady? A ghostly lover, a world of phantoms. My land lay on another plane than this, yet by the power of the everbright I can come to you here, be as real as you could want me, be bound to you by flesh and spirit as long as you desire."

"No." Sandy put as much space between them as the walls allowed.

"No?" His look implied that he thought she must be playing games with him. He tried to embrace her a second time. The iron sword thrust between them. He shied away from the old, cold metal.

"I did love you, Rimmon." She tried to keep the tears from choking her words. "If you really are Rimmon, if you're not just an illusion."

"I will understand?" He was an elf of another world, another dimension of existence, a more delicately formed example of the breed. His brows were finer, and they could express such nuances of feeling that Cassiodoron looked like a barbarian beside him. "I do." He folded his hands across his chest. "Tell him I remember his valor, and that I envy him his love." He did not need to name the name.

Sandy clutched one hand over the other on the sword's hilt until her knuckles hurt. "You are Rimmon. You really are. But I don't know how it can be."

He pointed at the bloodstone in its milky setting, being careful not to move too suddenly, or gesture too near the sword. "You have always had the power to call my spirit back to you, my lady. This place drinks the magic of the living, but it pours that power into the hands of the dead, and death crosses all dimensions. Through that gift I gave you years ago, it called to me. Because it is not of this plane, these plants have no power over it. You hold all the magic I ever commanded in my life in that little token."

"Rimmon, I don't want it. I don't need—"

The elf smiled. "You don't. You have magic of your own. But keep mine anyway. You never know." He bowed, and became a twirling spiral of mist that encircled Sandy's neck as it fed into the glow of the bloodstone.

"Be careful here," Cass whispered. "Warn the children."

"Why?" Lionel whispered back. "Do you see something?"

The elf-prince gestured with his sword, but all Lionel

could see was an unexpected widening in the maze. In the center of a grassy square grew a dainty little pear tree, its branches heavy with blushing fruit.

"Remind them not to touch it. One bite consigns them to Elfhame Ultramar forever."

Lionel nodded and looked over his shoulder to pass the word. Spindly black twigs scraped his nose and a handful of red leaves fell to the grass.

"Cass!"

"So it changes already." The elfin prince was not surprised. "Yes, it must, with Loris and me inside there's double magic to feed it, and Davina has the Sight."

"You knew this was going to happen?" Lionel grabbed Cass's arm. "That we'd all be separated in here?"

Cass gave him a flinty stare until he removed his hand, then replied: "We had to come inside; all of us. There was no choice, so why should I have worried you any sooner? I do admit, I expected to be cut off from everyone. If I have to be lost in here with a companion, I'd pick someone else."

Lionel could meet flint with flint. "I know. You made it plain enough. And Sandy's made her answer plain too, hasn't she?"

"Perhaps I've been asking the wrong person." Cass looked at the pear tree. "If you would take a bite of that fruit, Lionel, I would make you the equal of any of my companions. You would have every gift my favor could bestow, never growing old. Death would come as a dream, long deferred, and until you chose the final sleep you would live a life that few mortal men can imagine. Have you ever looked closely at Loris, Lionel? At my mother? Where have you seen such beauty in the upper lands? That could be yours too, without games or bargainings. You would find our women more generous than yours in matters of love."

He picked a pear and offered it. "One bite."

Lionel tossed it over the everbright wall. "No thanks."

"You too? As stubborn as she is, after all I would give you? You could both stay on here below, you know, and your child."

"So you could give Sandy back to me when you finished with her?" Lionel patted Cass on the back. "We're out of the classroom now, Taylor, but here's some extracurricular advice: never equate a woman with a library book."

"What is the *problem* with you people?" Cass stamped

his foot. It came down hard on a brindled cat's tail sticking
out from under one of the hedges.

"*Mrrrrow!*" Cesare shot straight up in the air, shrieking,
tail fluffed out like an electrified squirrel's. He narrowly
avoided having Lionel slice him in two with a wild sword
swing. He landed cursing all lead-footed elves and adminis-
tered a tender licking to his injured appendage.

"Problem!" he spat between licks. "It is you who have
the problem, my lord, not being able to see the solution when
it is right before your eyes. You want this man's wife? You
won't get her with pears and promises. You have a blade in
your hand—as does he, so it will seem a fair fight. Use it!"

"Uhhhh . . ." Cass eyed his sword, then Lionel. "If
Sandy ever found out I killed him—"

"Blame his death on the maze, fool! It is more than well
supplied with horrors enough to kill a man. Have you forgotten
about the pit near the labyrinth's heart? I'll dare wager that
Lord Syndovar has not stocked it with bunnies. *Dio!* Am I the
only pragmatist here?" Cesare tucked down one last wayward
wisp of fur, then told Lionel: "I do not bear you any grudge,
signior. This is merely an intellectual exercise. For all I care,
you may try your skill at tossing my master into that pit, tit
for tat. It will discourage him from courting your lady, I guarantee."

"I'll pass. Sandy does her own discouraging."

The cat's skeptical glance treated elf and man with equal
scorn. "Then swear brotherhood and be damned." He showed
them his hindquarters and stalked into the bushes.

Cass and Lionel stared after him, then at each other, then
they burst into injudicious laughter that shook the scarlet leaves
around them. They were still laughing when they clasped hands
and took Cesare's last recommendation.

"Maybe you should find someone your own age," Lionel suggested.

"Know any nice seven-hundred-thirty-nine-year-olds?"

"Of course they're lost," Loris said, trying to calm Davina. "They're children. They're supposed to do whatever will
upset the nearest grown-up the most. Don't worry, we'll find
them. I've heard it said that all paths in the battle maze lead
to its center at last."

"Heard? You don't know?"

"This is my first time inside. Elfin women don't have to

pass the maze unless we insist we want to be fighters. There aren't too many of us who choose that way."

"Why not?"

"Because, *faygeleh,* while the men are *potchking* around with swords, we ladies are perfecting our magic. One good spell can do the work of a hundred spears, and with less schlepping too."

"Dear God! We can't just hope you heard correctly. We have to find them!" She bolted down a side passage without waiting to see if Loris was coming.

Loris was not. The black branches interwove across the gap in the hedge almost the instant Davina went through. The elf-maid shrugged and took a newly opened alternate route.

Davina ran down the alleyways of everbright. "Jeffy! Ellie! Children, where are you?" She passed the open square where the pear tree grew and prayed that the little ones would not be tempted by any similar snares that might lie in their paths. Her dramatic training got good use in the battle maze's many twinings. She could shout their names and run at the same time without getting short of breath.

Eventually, though, she stopped. She was back in the small court of the pear tree. The fruit could not lure her, but the trunk could. She rested her back against it and closed her eyes for just a moment.

Loud cawing woke her. Two fat crows sat in the branches, pecking at the fruit. She laughed at them as they hopped from limb to limb, their harsh cries playing counterpoint to her delight.

Laughter and cawing died in a sharp hiss louder than any serpent's. The crows flew away, leaving the Welsh girl to face the gardener's dragon.

Eye to eye with the beast, Davina realized the truth of the old elfin saying: *there is no such thing as a little dragon.* Like every adult in the party, she had been issued a sword. It lay beside her on the grass, but as she groped for it, the dragon slammed its paw down atop her hand.

She screamed for the balcony standees.

"Not with the flat, not with the flat, not with the—oh, shit." Cass's shouted instructions had about as much effect as his disgusted curse. Lionel's sword was already on the downswing, and he wasn't trained enough to turn it in midarc against the force of momentum.

Hitting a dragonling on the head with the flat of a blade only puts it in a foul mood. A seasoned swordsman might have had time to get in a second blow, using the blade's edge as radical reptilian mood therapy, but Lionel was strictly amateur.

On the other hand, the dragonling was professional right to the core. All business, coldly efficient, it smacked the sword out of Lionel's hands with its tail. The everbright hedge parted to let the blade whirl past, then closed over with a Venus flytrap's curt snap.

Noxious smoke and a few wafers of flame rose from the dragonling's nostrils. It lost interest in Davina. Lionel had earned its undivided attention.

"Cass . . ." He knew he was too old for his voice to squeak like that. He edged to one side, and the beast tracked him; to the other, the same. He knew what would happen if he started to run, but he knew he was going to do it anyway. "Cass, please help . . ."

Cass stared and stared at the dragonling. The nightmare was on him again. He was a million miles away from the ugly creature and the man it meant to kill. This was only a puppet play. It was all happening inside his head—it couldn't be real, such a blood-touched terror. He was the Prince of Elfhame Ultramar, trained from childhood by the finest warrior in the shadow realms, Lord Syndovar. He had no magic here, but nothing could take his blade skill from him. Could it? It had to be a bad dream. He was only a coward in his dreams; only in his dreams where he couldn't move, couldn't raise his sword, couldn't even speak.

"Cass . . ." When the dragonling's attention shifted from her, Davina crawled away as furtively as she could, not daring to take her blade with her. Still on her knees, she reached up and touched Cass's sword arm. "Cass, you have to help him."

"*Perche fa?*" Cesare nudged his shoulder against the elf-prince's leg. "Elegant, my master. Play this out well, and you'll have her—the one you desire—after a suitable period of mourning for her husband, naturally."

"*Cass!*" It was Lionel's last call before he broke and ran. The dragonling snorted happily. It hunkered down, dug in at the blocks, and went for him with a roar.

That roar was the starter's gun that snapped Cass out of it. "Lionel! I'm coming!" He ran right into the everbright that sprang up to bar the way behind the dragonling. Davina crashed into him from the back.

He whirled on her, grabbing her wrist. "Quick! You have

the Sight! Which path will take us to them?'' He held Davina
so tightly that she cried out in pain.

"Not in here! I haven't the Sight in here!"

The lower vocabulary of a Godwin Academy day boy got
a full workout. "He can't run forever. I have no way of knowing which is the shortest way. If we take the wrong turning
and the dragon catches him first—Davina, what can we do?''

"You'd want to help him? I thought that Mrs. Walters—''

He saw himself in her eyes, himself as he must have
looked to all the mortals he had come to care about: fair to see
on the surface, but empty inside. Empty of everything but
greed, desire, self.

"I don't want Mrs. Walters anymore. And she never
wanted me." He only wanted that vision of himself wiped
away. "But I do love her, Davina. I love her as I love Amanda
and Jeffy and—because I love her that way, I can't let Lionel
die.''

The Welsh girl fetched her sword from under the pear
tree, held it like a cricket bat, and said simply, "Stand back,
Your Highness.'' Up went the iron blade.

Black twigs and red leaves flew every which way. She
put everything she had behind each stroke, and she had plenty.

"Grazie a Dio, someone practical at last!'' Cesare ex-
tolled her efforts.

"Woodchopping was the one exercise would ever help
me slim,'' she remarked as the hedge collapsed under her
blows. "Of course I couldn't find anywhere to do this in London, which was why I did put on a bit more flesh than was
flattering.''

She and Cass stepped through the gap. The leafy wall on
the other side leaned in toward them for a second, exhibited
the first vegetable double-take tropism in history, and tore its
interwoven branches apart getting out of their way. So did every
other everybright hedge they approached until there was a clear
line of sight broken open for them that did not stop until it
intercepted Lionel and the dragonling.

"My lady, you are *magnificent!*'' Cass kissed her lustily
before plunging past. He raced through the frightened maze
and came to Lionel's aid just in time.

Just in time indeed. The hunt had ended in another clearing. No pear tree bloomed there, but a pit whose lip was blasted
and bare. An awful roaring echoed up from its depths, and a
stink of stale blood hung over it. On the brink, Lionel was

doing his edge-away-edge-back dance while the dragonling watched him with the canny calculation of a prime sheepdog. It made a few false lunges, to test him. When he didn't tumble backward into the pit under a feigned attack, the beast began to build up a head of internal steam for the real thing.

Whether it meant to barbecue Lionel where he stood or coax him over the edge with a fiery blast, the dragonling never got to demonstrate. Light and deadly, Cassiodoron struck with the proper edge of the blade and split the creature's skull. Something like lava gushed out. Lionel took a step backward to avoid it, and it was only Cass's reflexes that saved him from going into the pit *ex post facto*.

Man and elf staggered a safe distance away, leaning on each other. Lionel was pouring out his undying thanks all over Cass's modest denials when a look at Davina shut him up. He had often seen her mooning over the elfin prince in Godwin's Corners, but this was something different. It wasn't the adulation normally aimed at someone up on a pedestal—that just-sit-there-pretty-and-let-me-look-at-you-with-my-tongue-hanging-out gaze. What was it?

Whatever it was, the elf-prince was giving her just the same sort of look in exchange.

"He could be ugly," Cesare said.

"What?" Lionel was the only one who seemed to hear the cat. Cass and Davina had wandered back toward the pit. The roars and stench from down below weren't there for them.

"I said, he could be ugly, and still she would see him as she sees him now. That is how he sees her as well. They have learned to use their eyes at last, those two." His whiskers twitched. "Have a care, signior! You are smiling as if you had just escaped a Frank Capra movie festival."

"I am n—hey! Where are they?" The pit and the dead dragonling were still there, but Cass and Davina had vanished.

"Who knows?" Cesare was unconcerned. "All paths lead to the heart of the maze. We shall meet again. Come with me, my friend, it is not far now. Ah! Mind the pit. We must pass very close to the edge, and Lord Syndovar has outdone himself this time. A gorgogriff."

"A what?"

"Part gorgon, part griffin. If you fall into the pit, it rends you and eats you, but if you only peep over the rim, its eyes turn you to stone. Then it eats you."

"That's horrible!"

"On the contrary. The griffin is part bird, and what better

way for it to get gravel for its craw than to manufacture it itself?''

Lionel looked narrowly at the cat. ''How would you know what's in the pit unless you looked? And if you looked, why haven't you turned to stone?''

''I could say, cats are the exceptions to all rules. I could say, I overheard it in the palace. I could say''—Cesare showed his pearly fangs—''that I am lying in my teeth. Why don't you see for yourself what's down there?''

Lionel didn't move. The cat yawned. ''Trust is a wonderful thing, signior. So is wisdom. Elfhame Ultramar is not paradise, but it does have a balanced ecology. Fools are always at the bottom of the food chain.''

Lionel concentrated on keeping his own balance as the tomcat led him around the edge of the gorgogriff's pit and through the opening in the hedge.

''Kelerison?'' Amanda touched the elf-king's battered cheek. His eyes remained closed. She knelt beside him in the heart of the battle maze and pulled a tuft of grass to hold near his nostrils. It stirred with his breath and a knot untied itself from around her heart. She touched his face again, gently. ''Kelerison?''

His eyes opened slowly. She could see the doubt he must feel on seeing her. ''I'm here,'' she said. ''Yes, I am.''

''The boy.'' His voice was husky. He tried to reach for her, but the iron fetters were short. His wrists were bound together, and his ankles, with a length of chain that linked upper manacles to lower, and to a thick collar.

''He's with us. I could forgive you for many things, Kelerison—for killing Jeff, for persecuting me—but not for that; not for stealing my son.''

He closed his eyes. She noted how cracked and dry his lips were, and she fought away the pang she felt for him. Her past was full of too many days and nights of loving him. That was over—things had changed in the present—but the past never could be changed.

''I didn't want to. For the sake of peace . . . They will deal only with the pledge that my heirs will not stir up the war again after I am dead. They demanded to meet with father and son together.''

''Jeffy isn't your son!''

''But Cassiodoron is. If I took your son, you would follow me, and then he would follow you. He always did. You

stole him from me first, Amanda.'' Tears tracked through the
grime of the elfin king's face. "You stole him . . . after I drove
him out. Every time we meet, I drive him further away, and
further.'' He tried to wet his lips with a dry tongue. "I should
have told them that I have no son at all. How can I lie to them?
They see through lies. But is it a lie? Do I still have a son?
There should be love between a son and a father. The Powers
witness, I still love my own father, over miles, over centuries!'' His voice broke. It was very small when he said, "And
I still love my son.''

She dried his tears with a corner of her sleeve. "He loves
you too, Kelerison.''

The King of Elfhame Ultramar only shook his head.

"He does," said a second voice, and Sandy was at his
side, across from Amanda. Together they helped him to sit up.
"He brought us here to rescue you.''

Kelerison's sight was blurred, yet one by one he made
out the figures of a mortal man and woman standing nearby,
also two mortal children in the care of an elf-woman. Though
her hood was up, covering her face entirely, he marked her by
the special grace with which she bore herself. Only one face
was missing, the one he most needed to see.

"If I could believe . . . Not just for me, for all our folk.
They want peace as much as we do, but—''

"Who wants peace, Father?'' And Cassiodoron was
there, cupping his father's face in his hands with the greatest
care. More tears slipped between his fingers as Kelerison recognized his son. "No, please, don't cry, talk to me. Who wants
peace?''

"Cassiodoron, then you are—you did—'' The elf-king
could barely speak, between tears and joy. He won back self-
control and said, "The Jun-ge-oh. The—we were wrong to call
them *Jungies,* savages. A mistake, it was all a mistake. My
brother thought he shot a squirrel. He killed one of their people. They are so small! What would we have done if some
stranger invaded our homeland, killed our folk without prov-
ocation? They fought back. We countered. All the killing . . .
mistakes, mistakes. Finally I learned. All the time I was away
from the high court, Cassiodoron, did you think I was pursuing
pleasures in the mortal world?''

Cass nodded, and the elf-king gave a sad laugh. "I'll
wager your mother thought the same. If she only knew! I looked
forward to the day that I could share the truth with both of you.
I was trying to approach the Jun-ge-oh. It took a long time. I

neglected many things: you, my son; my beloved Bantrobel; you too, isn't that so, Amanda?''

"You were gone . . . so much." Amanda smoothed back the hair from his brow. "I could understand how your queen must have felt when you brought me to Elfhame Ultramar.''

"So you grew lonely, and you found one of your own to ease the loneliness, just as she did. I was a fine peacemaker. Trying on one front to work things out with the Jung-ge-oh, on the other hunting you across the surface world as if you were a beast. Pride is the undoing of the elvenkind." He slumped with weariness as he added, "And through it all, trying to keep my dealings with the Jun-ge-oh a secret from Lord Syndovar. He hated them too much to ever consider peace. I couldn't blame him, but I couldn't let him ruin our chance to set things right in this land. Well . . . he found out, and this is what he makes of a peacemaker.''

They were all still when he finished speaking. Lionel took a place beside Sandy and, with a muttered excuse to Kelerison, began to examine the elfin lord's bonds. "Will these open if I touch them with my sword?" he asked Cass.

"They are all iron of the same forging. Neither has the greater magic.''

Lionel held up one finger. "Magic's not the question in this maze. There's a time for spells"—he fumbled in the pocket of his jeans and brought out a familiar object—"and there's a time for calling out the Swiss army. What do you think, Sandy? Corkscrew, hole punch, or nail file be the best for picking a lock?''

The rock that struck the jackknife from his hand was small, but the one that stretched him out full length in the grass was a little bigger.

"Remain where you are," said Lord Syndovar.

Chapter Twenty-one:

Trial

"He's alone," Sandy whispered. Her fingers stole around the hilt of her sword. She did not dare to look at Lionel. This was no time for blind rage.

"He is," Cass confirmed. "I sense no others nearby, but—" He tilted his head to one side, listening. "No; too far off. I must be mistaken. Only Lord Syndovar, and his pride. That is his miscalculation."

"My prince, you are not the only one with a hunter's ears." Lord Syndovar snapped a twig of everbright and let the thick red sap drip into his palm. "I am alone. My men need their rest for tomorrow, and in this maze, I need no help to take care of you. Do you think you can rush me, Cassiodoron, overwhelm me with your numbers? With *these?* Children! Females! You are the only warrior in the lot."

"Care to prove your point?" Sandy tucked her skirts back, ready to move.

Lord Snydovar stepped away from the hedges. He left his sling and a sack of throwing stones discarded among the roots. In one hand he carried a sword, with the other he drew an iron dart from his belt. He held the latter high so all of them might see it.

"A venomed tip. My prince, you have seen my speed on the training field. Tell your friends whether or not I can sink this barb deep in your father's eye before they can reach me." He smiled as Amanda hesitantly moved to shield Kelerison. "He killed your mate, as I overheard you claim, and still you would protect him?"

"Even a murderer is given a fair trial where I come from," she replied.

"And your noble sentiments are not at all colored by the fact that our king was once your bedmate too. Is that so?"

Kelerison tried to push Amanda away from between himself and Lord Syndovar. "Don't provoke him, Amanda. Don't endanger yourself for me. If there's payment due for your lover's death—"

"I will thank you to tend your own debts and keep out of mine, my liege. I can pay them or not, as I like." Lord Syndovar plucked a small, flat, gaudily wrapped packet from his belt and presented it to Amanda with a courtly flourish.

Kelerison watched impotently as she undid the paper, discovering the man's wallet inside. Dried seaweed crackled when she opened the billfold and saw her own photo in one plastic sleeve, Jeff Taylor's driver's license in another.

"I wouldn't have you die in the dark, my lady," Lord Syndovar said, above her muted weeping.

"No!" Cass protested. "When we ran away from the

easo *

clinic where Jeffy was born, I summoned a vision. I *saw* my father and Jeff Taylor meet. I *saw* the sword—''

"And did you have the stomach to witness the actual slaying? No?" Lord Syndovar was enjoying himself. "How delicate of you. Almost as delicate as your royal father, when at the last moment he suffered the mortal to live."

Amanda blinked her tears away. "Kelerison . . . you didn't kill him?"

"I thought I would," the elf-king said. "I came intending to do it. But when we met, and when I saw that he loved you enough to defy his own death for your sake, I couldn't. Not in the face of that love."

"Better a horned brow than bloody hands, eh?" Lord Syndovar chuckled. "No idea at all of what real honor means. Fortunately, I was there to look after the prestige of the throne— your father's most trusted lieutenant, I followed all his comings and goings. Well, nearly all. I wasn't so chary over one mortal's death as he. It took but a moment." He ran his thumb up and down the iron dart.

Amanda hugged Kelerison close as she sobbed out old grief and young joy at his innocence.

Lord Syndovar grew irritable at this display. "My lady, if you don't move out of my way . . . Hm, never mind. Failing that target, there are others." He looked meaningfully at the children. Their hooded caretaker took them under the folds of her cape, but the dart had a tip long and sharp enough to make that a useless gesture.

"Put your weapons down."

They looked to Cass for a sign. Attack? Obey? Reluctantly, he motioned for them to do as Lord Syndovar ordered. There was no other way. One by one they placed the iron swords at the elf-lord's feet. When it was Cass's turn, Lord Syndovar stopped him.

"Not yours, my prince. You will need it. I do not intend to leave this maze full of unfinished business."

"A challenge, my lord?" Cass faced up to him boldly.

"Tomorrow, when we ride against your father's precious new *allies*, the legions of Elfhame Ultramar will be led by both warlord and king."

The meaning of his words left Cass livid. "And you called my friends traitors!"

"If I did not rid our realm of you and your sire's rule when I might, then I would be a traitor indeed. You and he are of the same feeble stock. Cowardice does not come into the blood from nowhere. Peace! You would abase all elvenkind before those buckskinned vermin, Kelerison? As you abased yourself before that mortal man? You would have us treat them as equals? Next you'd have us pacting for coexistence with rats! You have forfeited the right to rule. Elfhame Ultramar needs a strong lord over it, one who knows how to deal with any race that defies us.''

"You have no vision, Syndovar," Kelerison said weakly. "You never did have any imagination. Try to destroy the Junge-oh, and you will destroy our own race with them.''

"If we die, we die as warriors." His eyes flashed at Cass. "Let us see if your son can do the same." He intoned the formal words of challenge: "By moondark and starcrown, by blood dance and deathsong, I call you to combat, Cassiodoron, Prince of Elfhame Ultramar. If life must be taken, let it be so. Let no man of the elfin blood come between us in this battle.''

"Let no man of the elfin blood come between us in this battle." Cass repeated the ritual words of acceptance. "Name the ground.''

"Within this maze—I would match swords with you, not magic—beside the pit." Lord Syndovar cast a scornful look at the others. "Now there only remains for you to name the weapons—which should be obvious—and the judge. A fine lot you have to choose from.''

"I choose empty hands," Cass replied. "And Sandy "

"Empty hands?" Lord Syndovar frowned as Cass threw down his sword. Grudgingly, he did the same.

"Judge? Me?" Lord Syndovar's astonishment was nothing compared to Sandy's. "I don't know anything about this! I have to see how Lionel—"

"He lives." Lord Syndovar's lip curled. "I did not choose his death, for the moment. There will be time to arrange that afterward.''

Davina turned Lionel over carefully, examined the lump already forming on the side of his head, and lifted his eyelid. "He is alive, Sandy, and he'll be coming around soon. Go with them. I'll tend to him. Go, for all of us.''

"Empty hands . . ." Lord Syndovar mused. "And a mortal female to judge us. A woman of law, though; why not? You have acquired curious ways on the surface, my prince. When I take the rule of this land, I shall put an end to all contact with mortals. It sets too many things on ear.''

"And of course my mother will second your every decision. What justification do you plan to give her for having killed her husband and her son—if you can?''

The elfin lord had a wry smile. ''She will need to hear few justifications in a prison cell. I have not found Bantrobel to be quite tractable enough to suit me, lately. From the time my men and I subdued her mate, she has been strangely hard to discipline. I tire of being opposed.''

''You, imprison Bantrobel?'' Kelerison managed to laugh. ''She's the one you should fear to match magics with, not my son.''

''You too had greater powers than I, Your Majesty.'' Lord Syndovar made an ironic reverence to the manacled king. ''I will manage Bantrobel.''

In accordance with the traditions of elfin combat, only the opponents and their judge would go to the battleground. Cass adjured each one of his party by name, even the children, even the still-unconscious Lionel, making an oath of nonintervention on their behalf.

''Do you think mortals can be honor-bound?'' Lord Syndovar sneered at the proceedings. ''I place greater faith in their weakness than in their word. What can females and children do? Only the male might have been some danger to me, and I have seen to him. As for your sole elfin ally—another female.'' He hardly glanced at the caped elf-woman.

''Loris will not interfere. I've already put her name to the oath.''

''Then why do we wait?'' He was impatient to leave the maze heart, eager to lead the way back to the gorgogriff's pit. ''My sword is down, and this''—he shoved the iron dart back into his belt—''comes with me only as surety of your friends honoring the battle's verdict.''

Cass paused, looked at Davina. She came to him and embraced the elfin prince with all the warmth of recent love. ''I will say God be with you, my dearest,'' she said, ''but not good-bye.'' She pressed her cheek to his. ''I wish I had some token of mine for you to wear.''

''I carry all the proof I need of your love in my heart, sweet lady. But here.'' He took a plain silver ring from his finger. ''Wear this for me.''

Sandy thought she heard Lord Syndovar growl the elfin version of ''Ugh, mush.'' He spoke sharply to Cass in their own language, and the lovers broke from one another.

The everbright seemed to be in a cooperative mood. One turn and a short straightaway brought them to the clearing where

the pit lay. Sandy's stomach lurched at the sight of the dead
dragonling beside it. She gave Cass a nervous look, wondering
whether his dracophobia carried over to fear of dead ones too.
She was mildly surprised to see him look right at it without a
qualm.

"Well, what do I do?" she asked.

"As judge, you must give the signal to begin," Lord
Syndovar told her. He flexed his hands. She saw how much
larger they were than Cass's, how battle hardened. Even empty,
they were a formidable weapon.

*What the hell was Cass doing, calling for bare-hand
combat? Sword against sword, he'd have had a fighting chance!*

She motioned for Cass to come to her. Lord Syndovar
raised an eyebrow inquisitively. "To say good luck to him
before I start being the impartial judge, do you mind?" Sandy
snarled.

"Be my guest, lady."

Sandy jerked Cass aside and hissed in his ear, "Are you
out of your mind, fighting him this way? What are the odds
against him ripping you in two?"

Cass gave her a know-it-all stare. "Better than if I'd
matched blades with the one who taught me every trick I know
with the sword. But fighting him empty-handed, I have the
advantage of the unexpected and—"

"And?"

"I saw *Rocky Three* and every Bruce Lee movie ever
made three times each, that's all!"

"Yi." Sandy slapped her forehead and Lord Syndovar
decided that it was as good a starting signal as any. He leaped
for Cassiodoron.

Sandy jumped out of the way as the two elves went down
in a dust-raising tussle. It looked like the worst of every sixth-
grade recess playground fight. The Marquis of Queensberry
was an unknown entity in Elfhame Ultramar, but from the general moral tone of the struggle, the Fair Folk received World
Wrestling Federation broadcasts just fine.

"No biting! No biting!" she shouted at the knot of arms
and legs as it rolled by. "Bare hands only!"

Cass was the smaller and sprier of the two. He slithered
out of Lord Syndovar's grasp and scrambled back onto his feet.
Then, while his foe was getting up, he hollered, "Heeeeee-
yah!" and tried a flying kick.

Lord Syndovar took one small pace back and intercepted
Cass's ankle *en passant*. He dangled the elf-prince upside-down

a moment, then primly said, "Empty-hand combat also means no feet, my lord." He dropped Cass on his head to make the point stick.

Cass was only slightly stunned, but that sufficed. Lord Syndovar threw himself on top of the younger elf, flipped him onto his belly, and yanked his head back by the hair. One arm hooked around Cass's throat and squeezed. The elf-prince thrashed and gurgled, then pushed up with his hands on the grass for all he was worth. Without a clear weight advantage, Lord Syndovar lost his seat on Cass's back when his victim bucked that way. As soon as he was free, Cass nimbly countered with an elbow jab to Lord Syndovar's temple. The elder elf reeled.

Again! Hit him like that again right n—oh, no, Cass! Why won't you learn?

"Yah!" The number-one member of the Bruce Lee Fan Club (Elfhame Ultramar chapter) tried a karate chop. They always worked so well in the movies.

They worked less efficiently when there was a dead dragonling cluttering up the battleground. Cass hit a smear of still-smoking brain matter and skidded, the chop going wild. Lord Syndovar ducked in under Cass's flailing arm and executed a perfect hip throw without ever having seen *Deadly Apprentices of the Venomous Fists*. Cass slammed down on his back with his feet hanging over the lip of the gorgogriff's lair.

A scream crawled to the top of Sandy's throat. She held it back, afraid that if Cass still had a chance to escape, she might distract him. It was a thin hope. Lord Syndovar did move as quickly as he claimed. Between one thought and another he tugged Cass up, had both the prince's arms pinioned behind him, and by wrists and hair forced him to lean far over the edge of the pit.

"Your time as judge is almost done, my lady," he called to Sandy. "I can give you one last matter to decide in this battle, though. Shall I fling him to the beast as he is, or shall I compel him to gaze into the monster's eyes first? Shall he die as torn flesh or broken stone?"

Something cold touched Sandy right above the heart. She screamed as an alien hand snapped the bloodstone pendant from her neck. All Lord Syndovar's attention was on his captive, taunting the elf-prince with the choice of deaths awaiting him below. He heard the scream and laughed, not knowing its true cause.

"Give its magic to me!" the hooded elf-woman whispered, thrusting the bloodstone into Sandy's face. "Now! At once! Release its power into my hands, or else it will do as little to save him as an ordinary stone."

Sandy peered into the darkness of the updrawn hood and saw Egyptian eyes. She seized the elf-woman's hands, pressed the bloodstone to her lips, and said, "Serve her, Rimmon, and be free."

Without more delay, the elf-woman dropped the bloodstone into the pocket of Lord Syndovar's discarded sling and loosed it swift and true. Sandy's spirit flew with it in the several small eternities it took for the stone to reach its mark. In midflight, it opened bright wings that cut the lines bounding time and space, severed the limits between worlds. Kneeling on a ray of light, the elfin archer Rimmon launched one final arrow from his bow. Then he was archer and arrow and stone, and the force of all three stuck Lord Syndovar.

He spun with the impact, throwing Cass safely away from the pit, onto the grass. The bloodstone was a scarlet stain at his throat as he and it fell into the depths. There was a glad, anticipatory roaring from below, an oddly dull crash, and silence.

Cesare snaked through the everbright roots and contemplated the prospect in the abyss. *"Porca Madonna!* He must have caught the monster's eye while he was still falling."

"What do you see down there?" Sandy asked, keeping her distance.

"A gorgogriff with a smashed head and a statue of Lord Syndovar." Cesare flicked his tail. "An excellent likeness. You would think these stupid beasts would turn their victims to talc, but no, it must be marble! No wonder they're an endangered species. I say: survival first, artistic integrity second."

"I couldn't have said it better myself," said Queen Bantrobel, drawing back her hood.

"Mother!" That was the last fully coherent sentence Cass addressed to her for several minutes. He followed it with disjointed accusations of ruined family honor, flagrant oath breaking, shameless disregard for the rules of elfin combat, and thanks for having saved his life.

His mother pointed out quite rightly that the formal call to battle only forbade *men* of the elfin blood from butting in, that it wasn't her fault if they all thought she was Loris, and that therefore since her right name hadn't been mentioned in the oath-taking ceremony, she'd been free to meddle all she liked.

"I saw Lord Syndovar heading for the maze and I knew what *he* was up to. Hmph! One eentsy fling and he thinks he owns me *and* the throne *and* the right to try murdering my husband! I wanted a word with him"—her eyes glittered nastily—"but the first person I found in the maze was Loris. I sent her *right straight out* and back to the palace to muster my personal troops. They should be taking care of Lord Syndovar's war-happy bunch about now. Of course I did borrow her cloak, and I will give it back, and I'm so pleased to know your father isn't completely mortal-mad, Cassiodoron, and—did I forget anything?"

"Not a thing," Sandy said. "Your Majesty, you have the makings of an excellent lawyer."

"I hope that's a compliment," the Queen of Elfhame Ultramar replied.

Lord Syndovar's statue was hauled out of the pit and given prominent display in the palace forecourt. It was marble, as Cesare observed, with the exception of a small bloodstone in a flower-carved setting that had melded itself into the elflord's breastbone.

"We could chisel it out," Cass offered. He and Sandy were alone. The others were busy helping convert part of the dismantled army's baggage train into wagons to take them all to the nearest gateway to the surface.

"Let him be." She sighed. "It's only a bit of stone now."

"But it was a gift of love from—"

"When will we come out into our world?" She changed the topic brusquely. "I mean, I know time is different down here. Will it be months since we entered Elfhame Ultramar? Years?"

"Days. Two weeks, at the most. That's why we're sending you up by a different gate than the one you came down. Time is just as warped as space down here. Pick the right gateway to go up by, and you travel in any direction you like through time *and* space, with respect to surface reality. It's all relative," he concluded sententiously.

"What pointy ears you've got, Dr. Einstein."

Cass beamed at her and gave her a hug that was pure friendship. "I shall miss you, dear lady! I wish I were going back to the surface world with you, and to Godwin's Corners, and to my place at the academy. You know, I was hoping to make it into Yale in a couple of years, maybe get an MBA. . .''

"No one's stopping you. Your father's throne is secure, there won't be any war with the Jun-ge-oh—why not come back with us?" Slyly she added, "Davina would be pleased."

Something large and friable hit a wall inside the palace. The sound of voices raised in unfriendly debate came from an upper window. Sandy couldn't understand a word they were saying, but the uproar turned several elfin heads in the courtyard. Cass blushed.

"Mother has *almost* forgiven Father for his mortal dallyings," he said. "And he has *almost* forgiven her for Lord Syndovar. Someone has to referee, or they'll turn to hurling spells at each other next, and that would be disastrous. Oh Sandy, you have no idea how much I wish I could go back with you and Davina and Jeffy and Amanda!" He looked at the window, very much the philosophical young man, just as three books and an eavesdropping karker came flying out. "I guess it's impossible to have everything you want, even when you do know magic."

"But not," Sandy said, "when you know me."

Epilogue

" "Mommy, we're going to be *late!*" Ellie jumped up and down in the doorway and nearly upset the monstrous philodendron that Peggy Seymour had sent over as an office-warming present. She had already done in the strawberry begonia from Cee-Cee Godwin, and Sandy sometimes asked herself how long it would be before Dwight Haines's gift aquarium would also succumb to Hurricane Eleanora.

"All right, all right, I just want to read this letter from Davina. It's been months since we heard from—"

"*Now,* Mommy! Jeffy said they were leaving right at noon, and I bet it's almost that now!"

Sandy pointed at the clock on the mantelpiece above her office's false fireplace. "It's not even eleven," she said, "and you know they'll wait for us." But she knew Ellie would give her no peace until they were out of the office and on the way over to the Taylor house.

Not the Taylor house for long, she thought as she tucked Davina's letter into her pocket and switched on the answering machine. Her law practice was picking up, and soon she would have to interview secretaries, but in the meantime the machine let her postpone that responsibility. *Not after today.*

It was glorious May weather. Daffodils stood in their trumpeting rows before the house where Sandy had rented office space, and the freshly lipsticked heads of tulips. All of Godwin's Corners was splashed with flowers. The lilac arbor in Amanda's yard didn't need any magical help to bloom on a day like this. A few supernumerary Winged Ones sat in the shade of the blossoms, bored and sulking.

Amanda was lashing the last suitcase to the roof of her car when Sandy and Ellie strolled up. Jeffy let out a squeal and dragged Ellie off to some hidden corner of the garden while their mothers made their farewells.

"Write, okay?" Sandy said. "Or call. California isn't the end of the universe."

"You know I will."

"The check clear?"

Amanda's nose crinkled. "The world would be in pretty bad shape if the King of Elfhame Ultramar were a poor credit risk. Anyway, if his checks bounce, I know where he lives." She smiled back at the old house.

"I still can't picture you out in the Silicon Valley."

"We need a change of scene, and it was a good offer. I'm only a secretary, but there's on-the-job training for advancement."

"At least the weather's better. And California isn't supposed to be *too* freaky."

"Yes, the San Andreas trolls speak of it highly."

Jeffy and Ellie had to be called seven times before they appeared, swearing that they hadn't heard a thing. It took Amanda repeated tries to get her son settled and seat-belted into the car. He and Ellie both wore the hard, tight faces of children who were dying to be very grown up about this. When the car drove away, Ellie collapsed into Sandy's bosom.

It was only after an emergency visit to the local ice cream vendor that she recovered enough to tell her mother about her engagement. "Jeffy said he's going to come back from California to marry me when he's big, and I can't get married until then, and he gave me this so I could remember all that." A dented iron locket shaped like a round snuff box dangled from the gold chain around Ellie's neck.

"That's nice, dear," Sandy said, not really looking at it. Now that her daughter was somewhat consoled, she took the time to read Davina's letter.

> . . . *and about time! I never thought I was as thick as that, Sandy, but for so many months to go by and me without the slightest idea! I have been on a slimming program, true, and that sometimes will upset the natural cycle of things, so perhaps I oughtn't tax myself too strictly for stupidity. Too, I have always tended to carry extra ballast, if I may say so myself.*
>
> *Will you believe what made me realize my situation at the last? It was that mix of purple dust and ashes I scooped up from the gateway we passed. It never served me any use but as a souvenir, yet one fine night I found myself sipping tea and pouring one teaspoonful after another of the stuff into my cup and drinking it down. What do you suppose my mother and da will say when I tell them? "How did you know, Davina?" "Oh, by*

*the craving I had for a taste of Elfhame Ultramar!" Did you
ever think a girl would find that out from a handful of pixie dust
in her tea? At least this way is kinder to the rabbits.*

*Otherwise I am in fine fettle, and hope you are the same.
I have just obtained a role on the BBC—some low-budget sci-fi
effort of theirs, but it is paid work. My "condition" won't be
noticeable to others for some time yet. I appear to be coming
along at a quarter the rate of a normal pregnancy—the father's
longevity at work even now, I suppose. My physician says he's
not seen another case like it. Wait until he sees the birth!*

Sandy paid the check in a daze. She didn't know whether
to be more shocked by Davina's news or by the Welsh girl's
bumptious Girl Guide optimism in the face of her condition, as
she put it. Something had to be done. With Ellie in tow, Sandy
marched down the main street of Godwin's Corners, eyes
sweeping to right and left, searching for the folk who would
have to do it.

They were just going up the steps of another of the house-
to-offices conversions when she found them. Queen Bantrobel
looked charming in her madras skirt and Peter Pan–collared
white blouse. She waved happily at Sandy, standing on tiptoe
in her Maine trotters.

"I do hope there hasn't been any trouble seeing dear
Amanda off?" she inquired when Sandy and Ellie joined them
on the old Victorian mansion's porch. Sandy could only shake
her head.

"With the closing, then?" Kelerison's hand darted inside
his seersucker jacket. "Any additional costs? I'll write you a
check."

Cass kept his mouth shut and smiling, the epitome of the
well-bred Godwin Academy student, waiting for a direct question before speaking when in the presence of his elders.

"It's nothing about the house. You can move in tomorrow, Your Maj—Mr. and Mrs. Keller." Old habits held on.

"Now you *know* we're Tom and Banty to you, Sandra
dear," the elf-queen chided. "Well then, if you'll excuse us,
we do have a group appointment with Dr. Proudfoot now, and
then we have to get Cass back to the academy at"—Bantrobel
checked her Rolex—"two sharp. Must run. *Ciao.*" She and her
husband breezed through the door.

Cass lingered a bit longer. "Cesare said to thank you for
the lox you sent him, and—is there something you wanted to
see me about?"

"Oh, nothing that won't keep." She waved for him to
follow his parents. It wouldn't do to keep Godwin's Corners'

foremost family therapist waiting. She would figure out the most tactful way to tell Prince Cassiodoron about the facts of transatlantic child support later. At a quarter the normal rate of fetal development, there was time enough.

The elf-prince paused in the doorway. "They're assimilating nicely, aren't they? Mother's even talking about joining the DAR."

"They're a credit to the community," Sandy deadpanned.

"What was that all about, Mommy?" Ellie asked as they walked back toward Sandy's office. It was the same question she'd been asking at intervals for the past three blocks, getting no answer.

Sandy stopped, held her daughter by the shoulders, and dropped to her eye level. "Ellie, I want you to promise me something right now. I'm your mommy, and I love you. I want what's best for you, and the best life you can have is the simplest, believe me. So never, never, never more have anything in your whole life to do with magic, okay?"

"Okay." Ellie looked dubious, but she laid her hand on the iron locket and squeezed it. "I promise," she said. "No magic for me. Never, never, never."

From inside the iron cell came a muffled flutter of wings, the scrape of tiny hooves, and a soft, small neigh that sounded like laughter.